Praise for the Novels of Whitney Gaskell

Good Luck

"Mon
alon

"Gask
high
hear
arro

"Froth

"Ther
scho
all it

"An e
it wa

"[Thi
with

"Poig
Trac

includes *Waiting to Exhale*, *The Circle of Five*, and *The Dirty Girls Social Club*." —*Booklist*

"It's like reading a really juicy grown-up Judy Blume book."
—Wacky Mommy

"Filled with humor, charm, and richly developed characters."
—Fresh Fiction

"A laugh-out-loud, witty view of motherhood." —*Romantic Times*

Testing Kate

"Whitney Gaskell delivers a vibrant story and memorable characters that will appeal to chick-lit and women's fiction readers.... This storyline about the first year of law school remains fresh yet familiar in the capable hands of Gaskell.... *Testing Kate* is a testament to the remarkable skill of its author to turn a stressful situation like law school into a delightful novel."
—Fresh Fiction

"Gaskell...relieves the high school–like atmosphere with sharp dialogue and various forays into New Orleans culture."
—*Publishers Weekly*

"A very readable, enjoyable story, and readers will root for Kate all the way through and cheer her decisions at the end."
—Romance Reviews Today

She, Myself & I

"Smart, funny, sexy, and refreshingly real . . . unputdownable."
—Melissa Senate, author of *See Jane Date*

"Engagingly written."
—*The Boston Globe*

"A warm, funny, charming, and engrossing story that will hook anyone who has a sister—and any lover of quality fiction who doesn't."
—Valerie Frankel, author of *Fringe Benefits*

"A gossipy, funny book about women you'll think you've met."
—*The Facts* (TX)

"Engaging . . . rapid page-flipping reading . . . Funny, intelligent, and rational, this book is a joy to read."
—Curled Up with a Good Book

"A fresh, clever story about cold feet, morning sickness, and the one who got away."
—Beth Kendrick, author of *Second Time Around*

"Will appeal to readers of both chick lit and women's fiction. . . . You'll find yourself laughing up a storm. . . . This reviewer is not only searching for the author's backlist, but is also anxiously awaiting her future releases."
—A Romance Review

"A witty, fast-paced, and intensely entertaining journey through the lives of three unforgettable sisters. Whitney Gaskell finds the humor and the heart in each and every one of her characters, a talent that makes the pages come to life and literally turn themselves."
—Lindsay Faith Rech, author of *Losing It*

Also by Whitney Gaskell

Pushing 30

True Love (And Other Lies)

She, Myself & I

Testing Kate

Mommy Tracked

Good Luck

When You Least EXPECT It

When You Least

Least

EXPECT

It

A Novel

Whitney Gaskell

Bantam Books Trade Paperbacks New York

A Bantam Books Trade Paperback Original

Published in the United States by Bantam Books,
an imprint of The Random House Publishing Group,
a division of Random House, Inc., New York.

BANTAM BOOKS and the rooster colophon
are registered trademarks of Random House, Inc.

Library of Congress Cataloging-in-Publication Data
Gaskell, Whitney.
When you least expect it : a novel / Whitney Gaskell.
p. cm.
ISBN 978-0-553-38627-1
eBook ISBN 978-0-553-90762-9
1. Adoption—Fiction. 2. Triangles (Interpersonal relations)—Fiction. I. Title.
PS3607.A7854W47 2010
813'.6—dc22
2010001862

Printed in the United States of America

www.bantamdell.com

1 2 3 4 5 6 7 8 9

Book design by Elizabeth A. D. Eno

For George

When You Least EXPECT It

One
INDIA

I've always loved the light by the ocean at the end of the day. Those magical moments, just as the sun is sinking low in the sky, when everything on the beach is cast in a rosy, golden glow. I raised my ever-present camera and snapped a few shots of Miles, Rose, and Luke as they played at the water's edge. The three of them had found a stick and were taking it in turn to throw into the water for Otis, our black and white border collie mix. He barked happily and plunged into the foamy white surf after it.

"Otis is going to smell like a fish after this," I said, lowering the camera.

Jeremy was in the middle of attempting to get the charcoals on the hibachi to catch fire. He looked up in Otis's direction and grinned. Jeremy had an appealing, open face with a high fore-head, long chin, and oversized, Jimmy Durante nose.

"Maybe he's part fish. He's always loved to swim," he said, running a hand through his short red-brown hair until it stood up on end.

"It's good to see him active. His arthritis has been so bad lately," I said.

"Otis and I are both getting to be old men," Jeremy agreed. He sat back on his heels, admiring the charcoal, which was now smoking nicely. It had been a warm day—typical weather for West Palm Beach in the late spring—but there was a breeze blowing off the water.

"Not so old," I said, dropping a kiss on the top of his head. I settled down on the plaid blanket we'd spread out over the sand, and began to rummage through the cooler.

"What gourmet delicacies are we cooking up tonight? Breast of duck in a sour cherry reduction sauce? Beef tenderloin with roasted shallots?" Jeremy asked, settling down next to me on the blanket. He lay on his back, his hands folded behind his head, and closed his eyes.

"Hot dogs," I said, holding up the plastic-wrapped package. "Followed by marshmallows."

Jeremy opened one eye and squinted at me. "God, I love you," he said reverently.

"Because I brought hot dogs?" I asked, smiling down at him.

"Partly because of the hot dogs. But mostly because of the marshmallows," he said.

"Not just marshmallows," I said. I rummaged in an oversized tote bag and pulled out a box of graham crackers and a six-pack of chocolate bars. "We're going to make s'mores. Your favorite."

"Will you marry me?"

"I'm already married to you."

"Good thing. A woman who serves me processed meat products and s'mores. What more could any man want?" Jeremy said. He sat up, propping himself on bent arms. "Should I call the wild bunch up here?"

"Give them a few minutes. The hot dogs still have to cook," I said, pulling a bunch of bamboo skewers out of the bag. I looked at them doubtfully. "Do you think these are long enough to roast the marshmallows on? I don't want one of the kids to catch fire."

"Yeah, we'd have a hard time explaining that to Mimi and Leo," Jeremy said.

"They'd never let us babysit again," I agreed.

The children belonged to my best friend, Mimi, and her husband, Leo. They were on a romantic overnight getaway to South Beach, so Miles, Rose, and Luke were spending the night with Jeremy and me.

"Are the coals hot enough?" I asked.

"They should be," Jeremy said, reaching for the shrink-wrapped package of hot dogs. He pulled the dogs out and, one by one, dropped them on the grill.

While the hot dogs sizzled, I got out paper plates, napkins, mustard, and a bag of potato chips. The children, sensing food was imminent, abandoned the stick-tossing game and ran up the beach toward us. Otis, soggy but triumphant, followed them at a trot, proudly holding the stick in his mouth.

"I'm starving," Miles announced, tripping just as he reached us. He tried to cover his embarrassment over this clumsiness by flopping down on the blanket, but his cheeks flushed red. Miles, ten, had recently gone through a growth spurt and was still getting used to his new longer legs and arms.

"You're always hungry," Rose said, daintily brushing the sand off her bare legs before sitting down cross-legged next to me. Rose, age eight, was our goddaughter. She was her mother in miniature—the same slanting dark eyes and full lips, an identical cloud of dark hair. The only traces of Leo were evident in her long nose and slightly squared chin.

"Look who's talking," Miles retorted. "Mom says that you eat more than you weigh on a daily basis."

"Liar," Rose said, but without much rancor.

Six-year-old Luke, who'd been unsuccessfully attempting to convince Otis to part with his stick, sat down next to his sister. He had a sturdier build than his lanky big brother and still had baby-rounded cheeks. His small, square feet were caked with sand. I considered brushing them off, but then decided it was a lost cause.

"What are you making for us?" Luke asked. He regarded me with large, suspicious brown eyes.

"Hot dogs," I said as I handed out plates with rolls and chips on them. "There's mustard here. Does anyone want ketchup? Or relish? I have chopped onions, too."

"Dinner is served," Jeremy said, setting a paper plate full of hot dogs down on the blanket. Miles and Rose fell on their dinners as though they hadn't eaten in days, but Luke frowned and poked his hot dog suspiciously.

"I don't like hot dogs," he said.

Otis perked up at this. He sat down at the edge of the blanket and stared meaningfully at Luke's hot dog.

"Yes you do," Rose, Miles, and I said in unison.

Luke was going through a stage where he claimed not to like anything served to him, including foods he'd happily eaten since he was a baby.

"I don't," he insisted.

"Just try a bite," Jeremy suggested.

Luke looked doubtful. Otis licked his chops.

"Hot dogs are really unhealthy," I said.

"They are?" Luke asked.

I nodded solemnly. "In fact, your mom probably wouldn't approve that I made them for you. I bet she'll be really mad at me when she finds out."

"That's okay, we won't tell," Miles assured me. I winked at him, and he grinned.

Luke was intrigued. He picked up the hot dog and took a microscopic bite. Deciding that it was acceptable, he took another, larger bite. Otis drooped with disappointment.

"Do you know what hot dogs are made of?" Rose said conversationally. "They make them out of—"

I cut her off before she could complete her thought. "It's probably better not to talk about it while we're eating."

Rose giggled. "But it's really gross," she said temptingly.

Luke looked up, his mouth full of hot dog. "What's gross?"

"I can touch my eyeball," Jeremy said quickly.

"Ewww!" Rose said, safely distracted.

"Let me see!" Luke said.

Jeremy—who'd worn contacts for twenty years—obliged, touching his right index finger to his eyeball.

"Don't you think you should wash your hands before you do that?" I asked.

"I want to try!" Luke said, stuffing the last of his hot dog into his mouth.

"I don't think that's such a good idea," I said, with a sudden vision of calling Mimi with the news that we were in the emergency room having Luke's scratched cornea tended to.

"Don't worry," Jeremy said, lowering his voice so Luke wouldn't hear. "When I first started wearing contacts, it took me forever before I could put the lens in without blinking."

Jeremy was right; there was nothing to worry about. As soon as Luke's finger was an inch away from his eye, his eyelid snapped shut.

"I bet you a billion dollars you can't do it," Rose said.

"You don't have a billion dollars, half-head," Luke retorted, trying—and failing again—to touch his eyeball.

Half-head? Jeremy mouthed at me. We both swallowed back laughter.

"I won't need it," Rose said smugly. "But you will."

Miles, the pacifist in the family, was rarely drawn into arguments with his bickering siblings. Ignoring Rose's taunts and Luke's attempts to touch his eyeball, he stood, pulled a Hacky Sack out of his pocket, and began kicking it.

"Are Hacky Sacks back in? I haven't seen one since high school," Jeremy said.

"My soccer coach says it's a good way to improve your ball

control," Miles said, shaking back his long hair. He'd talked his mother into letting him grow it out and was immensely proud of its shagginess.

"I used to be pretty good with a Hacky Sack," Jeremy said. He stood, and Miles passed him the ball. Jeremy kicked it once off his heel and sent the small beanbag flying. Miles chased after it.

"*Used to* being the operative words," Jeremy said sheepishly.

"Let me try," Rose said, springing to her feet, always eager to join in a game.

Miles kicked the Hacky Sack to her, and Rose juggled it expertly before kicking it back to her brother.

"Good job, Rose," I said.

"She's better than me," Jeremy said.

"Rose is the star of her soccer team," I reminded him. "She gets more practice than you."

"Girls rule and boys drool," Rose crowed.

Miles passed the ball to Jeremy again, but Jeremy wasn't able to catch it and it fell to the sand.

"Whoops," Jeremy said.

"You just need some practice," Miles said supportively.

"Why don't you have kids, India?" Luke asked.

The question caught me off guard. It wasn't that I hadn't heard it before. Jeremy and I were in our mid-thirties and had been married for seven years, so I'd gotten used to being asked about our baby plans. Acquaintances at cocktail parties, clients of my photography studio, even cashiers at the grocery store. I suppose asking someone if they have kids is pretty harmless. Unless, of course, you happen to be infertile.

Normally, I give an abbreviated version of the truth: that we very much wanted a baby, and were hoping to get pregnant, but it hadn't happened for us yet. I never mention the grittier details—the extensive medical exams, the hormone injections, the failed IVF cycles. Repetition had made this little routine nearly painless.

But I hadn't been expecting to hear the question from Luke, in these idyllic surroundings, while relaxing with the kids. Instead of my usual, measured response, I found myself stuttering, "W-why do you ask?"

"It's just that if you had a kid, Jeremy would have someone to practice Hacky Sack with," Luke explained, as though it were the most logical thing in the world. Which, to a six-year-old, it probably was. "And I'd have someone to play with when we visit you," he added.

Jeremy looked sharply at me, his face etched with concern. I smiled at him, and shook my head slightly to let him know it was okay.

"If we did have a baby, it would be a long time before he was old enough to play with you. And by then, you probably wouldn't want to play with him, because you'd be so much older," I explained to Luke.

Luke considered the wisdom of this argument. "But I wouldn't be the youngest anymore. And I'd have someone to boss around."

"That's true," I said.

"If you had a girl, it would almost be like I had a sister," Rose said.

"Yeah, and if it was a boy, it would be like I had a brother," Luke continued.

"You already have a brother," Rose informed him, her voice dripping with sarcasm.

"Yeah, thanks, Luke," Miles said mildly, still juggling his Hacky Sack.

"Besides," Rose continued, "India and Jeremy are *my* godparents, not yours. So if they had a baby, it would be my sister or brother, but it wouldn't be yours."

Rose liked to lord her superior claim to Jeremy and me over her two brothers whenever possible. It had the desired effect now. Luke swelled with outrage.

"That's not true! Take it back!" he demanded.

"It is too true. Right, India?" Rose said.

Both kids looked at me, as though I were the referee. I tried to remember what Mimi did at moments like this, and had a vague recollection of her saying that if there wasn't actual bloodshed, she stayed out of sibling warfare.

"Okay, everyone simmer down. I promise that if Jeremy and I ever do have a baby, you can all be official big brothers and sisters. Yes, Rose, that includes Luke," I said. "Now, who wants to toast a marshmallow?"

"Me, me, me," Miles, Leo, and Rose chorused.

"Me, me, me!" Jeremy chimed in.

Otis had drifted away to sniff at a dried patch of seaweed. But at the word *marshmallow*, he scampered back over. I handed bamboo skewers around, and after warning the kids to be careful around the hot coals—and then nervously repeating the warning over and over, until even laid-back Miles was rolling his eyes— the toasting of the marshmallows commenced. Once everyone's marshmallow was properly browned and gooey—or in Rose's case, charred black, which she insisted was how she preferred them— Jeremy passed around graham crackers and chocolate bars.

"The s'more," he announced, holding one up for us to admire. "The world's most perfect food."

"I don't like s'mores," Luke said, looking at his suspiciously.

"Good! More for me," Jeremy said, making a pretend grab for it. Luke backed away, screeching with laughter.

"No! I changed my mind!" Luke said, giggling. "I do like s'mores!"

"So why don't you have kids, India? Don't you want them?" Rose asked as she munched on her s'more.

I should have known that Rose wouldn't be so easily thrown off topic. When in pursuit of a goal, Rose displayed terrifying single-mindedness. Someday she would make an excellent CIA interrogator.

"Who wants another marshmallow?" Jeremy asked quickly.

"Because I think you'd be a good mom," Rose continued.

"Thanks, sweetie," I said. I put an arm around Rose, and she snuggled in toward me. Her hair smelled of baby shampoo and smoke. Suddenly, without warning, tears burned at my eyes.

"What about me?" Jeremy asked, threading another marshmallow onto his skewer.

"What about you?" Rose asked. She grinned impishly. "You'd be an okay dad, I guess."

"Thanks for the vote of confidence," Jeremy said.

"Maybe India doesn't want kids," Miles suggested.

"Why wouldn't she want kids? She likes us," Rose said.

I laughed at her indignation. "Jeremy and I would love to have a baby. But sometimes adults who want to have children aren't able to," I explained, wiping away my tears before the kids noticed them.

"Why not?" Luke asked.

How do you explain premature ovarian failure to kids? I wondered, before quickly realizing that you don't. It was much better to stick to generalities. Still, I couldn't talk down to them. All three of them hated that.

"You know what it means when a woman is pregnant, right? That she's going to have a baby?" I asked, suddenly having an unpleasant vision of the kids demanding that I go into a detailed explanation of reproductive biology. But luckily, Rose and Luke both nodded. Miles had gone back to his Hacky Sack and didn't seem to be paying attention. "My body doesn't work the right way. No one knows why, really. But I can't get pregnant."

Luke began feeding Otis marshmallows straight from the bag. Rose, however, was keen to hear more.

"How do you get pregnant?" she asked.

Jeremy and I exchanged a panicked look. But before either of us could speak, Miles chimed in.

"You don't know?" he said. "I thought everyone knew that. The woman makes an egg. And then the man—"

"Miles, not a good idea," I said quickly.

"Yeah, buddy, I think that information might be above their pay grade," Jeremy said.

Miles blinked at us, clearly confused as to why we were interrupting his biology lecture.

"Your brother and sister are a little young to hear the details," I explained.

"I am not too young!" Rose said indignantly.

"Eggs? Like, bird eggs? In nests?" Luke asked.

"Mimi is going to kill us," Jeremy murmured to me.

"Maybe we should talk about something else," I suggested. "And give me those marshmallows, Luke. Otis will get sick if he eats any more."

"Really?" Luke said, perking up. "Do you mean he'll puke?"

But Rose wasn't ready to change subjects. "Why don't you adopt a baby?" she asked. "One of the girls in my class, Jenny Mathers, was adopted from China when she was a year old."

Another look passed between Jeremy and me. We'd reached the point in our marriage—and our infertility struggles—where we could have whole conversations without saying a word.

"That's something we might consider," I said cautiously.

Jeremy and I had talked about adoption, although only in the most abstract, general terms. Early on, we'd made a decision to pursue in vitro fertilization first. On three separate occasions, Jeremy's sperm was used to fertilize donor eggs in a glass dish, and then, three days later, the embryos were placed in my uterus via catheter. Each time, the IVF had failed.

"You should," Rose said confidently. "Jenny Mathers can do a handstand and a full split."

I nodded. "Very impressive."

"I can do a cartwheel. Do you want to see?" Rose asked, jumping to her feet.

"Absolutely," I said.

Rose attempted a cartwheel, but wasn't able to get her legs all the way around. She tumbled onto the sand with a shriek.

"The sand is too soft here," Miles said. "Watch me."

He ran down to the firmer sand by the water's edge and demonstrated a cartwheel, timed perfectly so that he landed on his feet just as the water lapped back in. Rose ran after him, followed by Luke and a joyful, barking Otis. Jeremy sat down next to me on the blanket.

"S'more?" he asked, offering me his plate.

I shook my head, and wiped away the lingering tears. "No, thanks. I'm all s'mored out."

Jeremy looked worriedly at me. "You know it's all going to work out, right?"

"I know," I said, although I knew no such thing.

Jeremy put his arm around me, and I leaned toward him, resting my head on his shoulder.

"We'll figure it out," he said.

I nodded and tried to swallow back the emotions welling hotly in my throat. I'd tried to stay upbeat through the first IVF cycles. But with each additional failure, it became harder to stay optimistic.

Not now, I thought. *I'm not going to worry about it now. Not on such a beautiful night.*

The soft early-evening light was dancing on the waves, shimmering as the tide rolled in. A pelican flew by, his wings just barely skimming the water. Rose was attempting a handstand, assisted by Miles holding her ankles. Luke tore off large hunks from a hot dog roll and was throwing them at an excitable flock of seagulls.

"Come on, let's go join them," I said, standing and brushing the sand off my bare legs.

Jeremy got to his feet a bit more slowly. "Okay, but I'm not doing a cartwheel," he said. "I'd probably throw out my back."

I laughed and brushed my wind-blown hair out of my face.

"Come on, old man," I said, and held my hand out to him. "I'll show you how it's done."

But later that evening, as I cleaned up the kitchen, putting away the picnic supplies, I found it harder to escape the whirlwind of my thoughts.

It had been two weeks since we'd learned that the last round of in vitro fertilization had failed. Jeremy and I had discussed whether we should try again, but hadn't yet come to a final decision. No small part of our indecision was the cost. At twenty thousand dollars per cycle, IVF wasn't cheap.

When Jeremy and I first married, we'd bought a cozy bungalow that we'd fallen in love with at first sight. It needed a ton of work, but had the benefit of being located in West Palm Beach's historic Flamingo Park neighborhood. It also came with a tiny guesthouse in the back that Jeremy, a science fiction writer, immediately claimed as his office. Between our sweat equity and an unexpected upswing in the housing market, our little house had doubled in value in the seven years since we bought it, which had allowed us to take out a home equity loan to finance three rounds of IVF.

But I wasn't sure if the bank would approve another, larger loan. And even if they did approve it, what were the odds that another round of IVF would be successful? Or another after that? I could spend years letting them shoot foreign fertilized eggs up into my uterus, only to have my body spit them back out two weeks later.

Rose's words suddenly came back to me. *Why don't you adopt?*

She made it sound so simple, so obvious. Taking someone else's unwanted baby into our desperate-for-a-baby home. The theory had a nice ballast to it. Of course, it meant that the child wouldn't look like either of us—even with the borrowed-eggs scenario, any successful pregnancy would have resulted in a baby that inherited half of its DNA from Jeremy. Did this matter to me? Would it matter to Jeremy?

I thought about it, trying to imagine a baby as unlike Jeremy and me as possible. A baby with a fluff of dark hair and serious eyes. A little girl who danced with the natural grace I'd never known. A boy who loved to run until his legs tired and his breath came in gasps. A child who would be mine, even if he or she didn't come from me. A child who would call me Mama. I would hold him in my arms, and he'd wrap his chubby arms around my neck. I'd blow kisses on a soft, round stomach. I'd inhale that sweet baby smell, until it swamped all of my senses. . . .

A longing washed over me that was so intense I had to put a hand on the countertop to steady myself.

The back door opened, and Jeremy came into the kitchen, Otis panting at his heels. I was right—he *did* smell like a fish.

"Are the troops all tucked in?" I asked.

"They're in their sleeping bags, but no one's gone to sleep yet. They're asking for cocoa. Which they apparently want served in a thermos," Jeremy said.

At the children's insistence, Jeremy had pitched a borrowed tent in our backyard, and the three of them were sleeping out there.

"Isn't it a little hot out for cocoa?" I asked.

"You would think. I already had to talk them down from building a campfire, which I'm pretty sure is against the city code," Jeremy said.

I poured some milk in a pan and turned the burner on

underneath. "I don't think I have a thermos. Will they accept their cocoa served in regular old mugs?"

"I'm sure. Are there any marshmallows left?" Jeremy asked. "Or did Otis eat all of them?"

I reached into the cupboard and pulled out a new bag of marshmallows. "Ta-da."

"Excellent. What else are you hiding in there?"

"Two bags of Hershey's Kisses," I admitted.

"You've been holding out on me!"

"They're not for us. They're for you to bring to the sci-fi convention tomorrow," I explained. Jeremy would be manning a table at the annual South Florida Science Fiction Convention, or Sci-Con for short.

"Okay, I'll bite. Why am I bringing two bags of Hershey's Kisses to SciCon?" Jeremy asked.

"I thought it would be a good marketing trick. You put the Kisses out in a bowl on your table. And then when people stop for the candy, you can sell them a book," I said brightly.

"No," Jeremy said.

"Why not?"

"Because bowls of Hershey's Kisses are not very manly."

"Do you want to be manly, or do you want to sell books?"

"I want to sell books in a manly fashion," Jeremy said.

I rolled my eyes, but put the Kisses back in the cupboard. "I'm worried about them sleeping outside. Do you think it's safe?"

"It'll be okay. I'm going to stay with them."

"Is there room in the tent for you?"

"No. I'll sleep on one of the chaise lounges," Jeremy said. We had a pair of chaise lounges next to our tiny pool, another feature that had sold us on the house.

"It's supposed to rain tonight," I protested.

"So? I don't melt," Jeremy said, smiling.

"But you've got SciCon tomorrow. You need to be well rested."

"I'll be fine." Jeremy pulled me into his arms and nuzzled his chin against the top of my head. "You okay?"

I nodded. "I'm fine. The kids didn't notice anything, did they?"

"Those three? They notice everything. But what exactly are you referring to?"

"My getting all blubbery at the beach," I said.

"First of all, a few tears hardly equals blubbery. And second, no, I don't think they noticed. They were too busy with their impromptu gymnastics training session," Jeremy said. "I think the milk is boiling."

I broke out of his embrace and reached for the pan before the milk could scald. I dumped some cocoa into the pan and whisked it into the milk. Jeremy leaned against the counter and watched me.

"So . . . I was thinking," I said slowly. "Maybe Rose is right."

"Right about what? That she should be crowned Imperial Leader of the World? Because I have to say, I don't think she'd be a particularly benevolent dictator," Jeremy said. "She'd force us all to be her slaves. In fact, she'd probably keep us chained to her throne."

"No, not that. Although, yes, I agree, the thought of Rose in power is terrifying. But I was thinking about what she said earlier at the beach. About how we should adopt a baby. I think . . . ," I began, but then stopped and swallowed hard, trying to quell my nerves. "I think maybe we *should* think about it."

Jeremy nodded, but didn't say anything for a few beats.

"We always said adoption was a possibility," he said finally.

I realized I'd been holding my breath, and let it out in a whoosh. "We did," I agreed.

"But we wanted to try IVF first," Jeremy said. "We wanted to pursue that for as long as it was a viable option."

"That's just it. I don't think it is a viable option," I said. I was trying to keep my voice steady, but I could hear the pain seeping in around the edges of my words. Jeremy heard it, too. His face creased with worry, and he reached for me.

"No, I'm okay," I said. "I just . . . I just really want to be a mom. And I think that adoption is the only way it's going to happen for us. So maybe it's time we looked into it."

Jeremy inhaled deeply. Finally, he nodded. "Okay. Let's do it."

Two
JEREMY

I sat at my out-of-the-way table at SciCon, trying not to yawn. The plum table assignments had been given to the rock stars of the sci-fi community—minor actors from hit television shows, comic book artists, computer game developers. As the writer of a series of paperbacks with middling sales, I'd been placed so far away from the action I might as well have been in the parking lot. I perked up as a pair of twenty-year-old geeks dressed as Captain Picard and Spock from *Star Trek* passed by.

"I'm telling you, I totally saw Tricia Helfer by the laser exhibit," Spock said. "Caprica Number Six in the flesh."

"No way. That wasn't her," Captain Picard replied. "That was just some blonde chick in a Caprica Number Six costume."

"I'm telling you, it was her. The *real* Six," Spock insisted.

They glanced in my direction. I smiled winningly.

"Hi," I said. I held the bowl out. "Hershey Kiss?"

India had talked me into bringing the candy with me, despite my protests that I wouldn't use it. I held out for about an hour. After watching convention stragglers trailing past my table without once glancing in my direction, I finally gave in and broke out the Kisses.

"Thanks, dude," Picard said as they each grabbed a handful of Kisses. Neither one even glanced at my book display or at the cardboard sign that read, JEREMY HALLOWAY, AUTHOR OF THE FUTURE RACE SERIES. Instead, they walked off in the direction of the stage, where characters from *Star Trek: Deep Space Nine* were scheduled to appear.

A robot passed by, headed in the opposite direction from the Trekkies. "Kiss?" I offered, shaking the bowl. The robot didn't speak. He—or she, it was impossible to tell—held up one silver hand and pointed toward its masked head. "Oh," I said sympathetically. "Yeah, I guess it's hard to eat when you're in costume."

The robot shrugged and kept moving. I slumped back in my chair and swallowed back another yawn. It had been a late night. The chaise lounge had not made a comfortable bed, and the situation got even worse after the storm blew in at around two in the morning. Luckily, the kids hadn't wanted to stay out in the tent once it started thundering, so we moved indoors. Miles slept in the guest room, Rose and Luke unrolled their sleeping bags on the sofas in the living room, and I managed to get a few hours of sleep in my bed.

But at daybreak, just as the first fingers of light were stretching into the room, I woke up with something sharp jabbing me in the side and something else waving disturbingly close to my face that—after I started awake—I belatedly realized was a foot. The two younger kids had relocated to our bed—or, more specifically, to my side of our bed—at some point during the night. Rose had fallen asleep upside down in the bed, with her feet on my pillow. Luke was lying across his sister, his legs looped over her back and his knee lodged firmly in my side. Both of them were snoring softly. I gave up on sleep at that point and headed downstairs to make pancakes and extra-strong coffee.

But, tired as I now was, I had a feeling my inability to focus on pitching my books had more to do with my and India's conversation the night before.

Adoption.

I hadn't lied to India. I did think we should look into adoption. I just didn't have any idea how we were possibly going to afford it. After three rounds of IVF, we were broke. We already had a large second mortgage on the house, and my career was not exactly taking off at the moment. Actually, India didn't know that. I hadn't told her about the low earnings statements I'd received from my publisher a few weeks earlier, figuring she had enough stress to deal with—but I was all too aware of it. And I knew adoptions weren't cheap. A college buddy—Dave, who when I knew him was famed for his ability to eat four pizzas on his own in a single sitting—and his wife had adopted a little girl from Russia two years ago, and when I ran into him at our ten-year college reunion, he'd said that the process had cost about forty grand.

Forty thousand *dollars.* Needless to say, we did not have forty thousand dollars. In fact, we owed more than that to the bank. A lot more.

But the expression on India's face when she broached the subject of adoption—a mixture of relief, elation, and desperate hope—had stopped me from bringing up our strained finances. She'd been through too much over the past few years. Month after month of disappointment, followed by first a grim infertility diagnosis and then the IVF failures, had taken a toll.

I wanted kids, too, of course. I always had. But for me, it was more of a hazy, indefinite future goal. I had vague images of wearing scrubs in the delivery room while I reminded India to breathe and, later, cheering from the sidelines of my kids' soccer games. For India, it went deeper than that. She longed for a baby. And Rose was right, India would be an amazing mother. She'd always loved kids. She'd even chosen to have her photography studio specialize in children's portraiture.

So if adoption was the only way for us to have a baby, I was all for it. I just didn't yet know how the hell we were going to swing it.

A crowd of women, all wearing matching neon pink T-shirts

emblazoned with MIDDLE EARTH BABES in black block letters, approached. I sat up straighter, and smiled at them. Most of them ignored me, although one of the women—in her fifties, with heavy blonde highlights and a large handbag slung over her shoulder—peered at my sign through a pair of reading glasses perched on the end of her nose.

"Jeremy Halloway," she said out loud. She examined me. "Is that you?"

"It is," I said.

"You look different in person than you do in your picture," she said. She studied my author photo again. "Oh, I see what it is. You have more hair in the photograph."

Feeling somewhat deflated, I tried to laugh it off. "At least I don't get carded anymore."

Ignoring my joke, she picked up one of my books and began to page through it.

"That's the sixth book in my Future Race series," I explained.

"Do you have to read the first five to understand what's going on?"

"No, each book is written to stand alone. But the first five books provide the backstory," I said.

She held the book up. "Are you giving these out for free?"

"No. You have to buy it. But I'll sign it for you," I said, holding up one of the Sharpie pens I'd brought with me that morning and had yet to use.

"No, thanks," she said, dropping the book onto the middle of the table, rather than returning it to the top of the stack. She helped herself to a handful of Kisses and, without another word to me, turned away and hurried off to catch up with the rest of her group.

I returned the book to its place and moved the bowl of Hershey's Kisses back from the edge of the table. If people kept insisting on taking handfuls, I would run out before lunchtime.

"Hey," I said as I walked in the garage door, which opened onto the kitchen.

"Hi, honey," India said. She was standing at the counter, chopping an onion into a neat dice. "How was SciCon?"

"I sold three books," I said.

"That's all?" India asked sympathetically.

"Your Hershey's Kisses were a big hit."

India opened the refrigerator and pulled out two bottles of Amstel Light. She popped the caps off, handed one to me, and then clinked her bottle against mine.

"Did you get the kids home in one piece?" I asked.

India nodded. "They were so sticky, though. Especially Luke."

"He did pour nearly a whole bottle of maple syrup on his pancakes," I said.

"Maybe I should have made him take a bath before I brought him home."

"Or thrown him into the pool."

"Mimi didn't seem to notice. Then again, she said she had three martinis last night and was still feeling pretty fuzzy," India said, grinning.

"Did they have fun in South Beach?"

"They had a great time. She said to pass on her thanks a million times over for watching the kids." She picked up her knife and went back to dicing the onion. "I told Mimi what we talked about last night. You know. About how we were considering adoption."

"You did?"

"Do you mind?" India glanced up at me.

"No, it's just I didn't know we were at that point yet."

"What point?"

"The telling-people point," I said.

"It wasn't people. Just Mimi. Oh, and my mom."

"Your mom?"

"I dropped off her tent on my way home from Mimi's," India explained.

"Why does your mom own a tent again?" I asked.

"I'm not sure. I think a friend gave it to her," India said vaguely. "You know, back when Mom was talking about driving across country. I think she was planning on camping out along the way. Nothing ever came of it."

"I'm shocked," I said dryly. Georgia, India's mother, was a sixties-era hippie, and a present-day flake. She wore caftans, wrote poetry, and was overly fond of wine.

"Anyway, Mimi knows an adoption attorney," India continued.

"Why? Is she planning on getting rid of one of the kids?"

"No, but she knows everyone in town. Or if she doesn't, she knows someone who does. Anyway, she gave me this lawyer's name and number." India held up a yellow Post-it note with Mimi's scrawled handwriting. "I was going to call him for an appointment."

I blinked. "Oh," I said.

India frowned, causing three vertical lines to appear on her forehead. "Is that okay? I thought we decided we wanted to look into this."

"No, it's fine," I said quickly. "Make an appointment. We'll go talk to Mr. Baby Lawyer Man."

"You're not going to call him that, are you?" India asked. "Like the time you called my gynecologist Dr. Crotch. To his face."

"You thought that was funny," I said.

"I did. Dr. Seagle didn't," India said.

"I'm pretty sure Dr. Seagle has never found anything funny in his life."

"You're probably right," India conceded. "Anyway. Are you sure you're cool with this?" She lifted the Post-it note again.

I registered the hope shining on India's face. "Yes. Definitely cool with it."

India turned her face up to mine. I leaned forward and kissed her. "I'm so glad we're doing this. It just feels right. Don't you think?"

What could I say?

"Absolutely," I said.

India and I first met on the beach. I had brought Otis, who was at the time a six-month-old bundle of fur and energy. I'd learned the hard way that if I didn't take him out for a long run every morning, he'd get back at me by eating my furniture. He'd already gnawed his way through a coffee table and two of the four legs on my sofa. So I'd bring him to the beach, unhook his leash, and let him bound up and down at the water's edge in a blur of black and white fur. This wasn't technically allowed, so we always went early, when the lifeguard stands were still boarded up and the beach was more or less deserted. Besides, Otis never bothered anyone. He loved to chase the waves and then turn tail and run when they came back at him.

I was sitting on the sand, drinking coffee out of a Dunkin' Donuts cup and watching Otis play, when he turned too quickly, lost his balance, and fell, snout first, into the sand. I laughed, and then turned when I heard someone behind me laughing, too. A woman. My first impression was of her hair—kinky blonde curls rioting out of control. Her grin was wide, her eyes crinkled up at the edges, and her nose was on the snub side. She was wearing a faded T-shirt and denim cutoffs, and her bare legs were long and tan. Then I noticed the camera with the long, professional-looking lens strapped to her chest.

"Damn, the paparazzi found me again," I said. I put a hand up, pretending to block a shot of my face. "When are you people going to stop harassing me?"

She laughed again. But she lifted her camera up after all, aiming it at Otis. She took a few shots and then walked over to where I was sitting. "He's gorgeous. Is he a puppy?"

I stood up, dusting sand off my bottom. When I first adopted

Otis, a few of my friends kidded me about dogs being chick magnets. I'd laughed it off at the time, but was now quickly gaining appreciation for the theory.

"Yeah. He's six months old," I said, trying to remember if I'd brushed my teeth that morning before leaving for the beach. My mouth tasted of coffee. I hoped it was strong enough to mask any residual morning breath that might be lurking there. I could smell her perfume, or maybe it was just her shampoo, light and faintly floral.

"Is he a border collie?" she asked.

"There's some border collie in there, but he's not a purebred. Just a mutt," I said.

We stood and watched Otis run, barking, at a trio of seagulls who were strutting along the beach. They took off in alarm well before he got anywhere near them.

"The great hunter," I said dryly.

Otis turned back, grinning, and loped toward us. He ignored me and headed straight for the blonde, jumping up on her with large sandy paws.

"Otis! Get down!" I ordered.

Otis ignored me. Obedience was not his strong suit. The woman just laughed and petted his damp, sandy head. Her fingernails were short and unpolished. For some reason, I found this incredibly sexy. It was probably because the last girl I'd dated—who'd turned out to be a complete pain in the ass—used to file her long nails into talonlike points and paint them the color of dried blood.

"It's okay, really. He's a sweetheart," she said.

Later, I liked to tell India that this was the moment when I decided I was going to marry her. It's a lie but not terribly far off from the truth, which is that this was the moment when I developed a massive crush on her. Hell, she was a pretty blonde with a goofy grin, and she liked my dog even when he was filthy and badly behaved. Who wouldn't get a crush on her?

"This is Otis," I said, suddenly feeling self-conscious.

"Yeah, I figured that out when you called him Otis," she said, smiling at me over Otis's shaggy head. He fell back and leaned shamelessly against her legs while she bent over to pet him. She looked up at me. "I'm India, by the way."

"India? That's an unusual name. Is that where you were born?"

India laughed. "Knowing my parents, they'd be more likely to name me after the place I was conceived."

I wasn't sure how to respond to this. Luckily, India continued. "No, my parents were major hippies back in the day. I'm lucky they didn't name me Moonbeam or Star." She smiled.

"I'm Jeremy," I said. I nodded at her camera. "Are you a photographer?"

"Actually, no, I direct porn films," she said, without even pausing. "I'm just out here scouting locations for my next film."

I gaped at her, and she laughed at me. "Tell me you're not that easy," she said.

"Sadly, I think I am," I said sheepishly.

"It's okay. You have a great dog. That makes up for a lot," she said, and grinned up at me again. Her eyes were squinting against the sun, and I again noticed that her smile was slightly lopsided. It was the sort of smile that was impossible not to return.

The adoption lawyer, Mike Jankowski, had an office in a tall black building in downtown West Palm overlooking the Intracoastal Waterway. He was in his fifties, with thick silver-streaked hair, a sun-reddened face, and a protruding stomach. He wore a short-sleeved tropical print shirt that made me instinctively wary of him.

"Call me Mike," he said jovially when he came out to the reception area to greet us.

Mike ushered us back to a conference room, where India and I sat side by side at a long table, our backs to the window and its water view.

"Can I get you anything? Coffee, soda, water?" Mike asked.

"No, thanks," I said.

"Water, please," India said.

I was suddenly incredibly thirsty and wished I had asked for a drink, too. I'd always thought you were supposed to refuse in these types of situations, that it was offered more as a courtesy than with any actual intent. Before I could ask for a Coke, though, the lawyer left. I wondered if India would mind if I shared her water.

I could tell she was nervous. She sat with her shoulders hunched forward and her hands clasped in her lap. Her eyes were open wide, and she was blinking rapidly.

Mike returned to the conference room. "My assistant will bring your water right in." He looked at me. "Are you sure I can't get you anything?"

"If you have a Coke, that would be great," I said.

"Sure," the lawyer said, and left again.

India gave me a slightly exasperated look.

"What?" I asked.

"Why didn't you just ask for a drink the first time he asked?"

"I wasn't thirsty then."

Mike returned and took a seat across the table from us. "You're interested in a domestic adoption," he said.

"I think so," India said, glancing at me. I nodded encouragingly. "To be honest, we're just starting to look into adoption."

"There are a lot of factors to consider. So many it can be overwhelming," Mike said.

"Yes," India and I said together.

India hesitated. "I've heard that it can take a long time to find a birth mother," she said.

"It depends. There's no hard-and-fast rule, but I'd say that normally it can take anywhere from nine to eighteen months," Mike said.

India let out her breath. "That seems like a long time," she said. "I mean, I know you don't have a nursery full of babies here in the law firm—"

Mike chuckled. "No, I don't. That would make things easier, wouldn't it?"

"I just didn't know it would take so long," India said.

"It might not," Mike said. "It all comes down to the birth mother. One who thinks you two are the perfect adoptive parents could walk in here tomorrow. Or it could take quite a bit longer. There's no science to it. All I can say is that for a standard adoptive couple—and by standard, I mean there aren't any other issues we have to deal with—the average waiting time is usually around nine to eighteen months."

"Would you mind telling us a bit about your background?" India asked.

While Mike outlined his experience (extensive) and the services that he offered (finding a birth mother, taking care of the necessary paperwork, clearing any legal impediments that might spring up along the way), Mike's assistant came in with the drinks. She placed the bottle of water in front of me and the glass of Coke in front of India. India, who was listening intently to Mike, didn't seem to notice the mistake, and took a sip out of my soda. When she put it back down, I quickly switched our drinks and then guzzled my Coke.

"Do you have any questions?" Mike asked, after he'd been talking for what seemed like an inordinately long time.

India looked at me expectantly. I tried to think of something intelligent and insightful to ask.

"Can you give us a basic overview of the process?" I asked.

India gave me an approving look. Excellent. I was acing Lawyer Interviewing 101.

"First you'll fill out a placement profile for me. It has a number of detailed questions about your tolerance for various situations. For example, if you want to work only with birth mothers who don't have health issues and whether you're comfortable staying in touch with the birth mother after the adoption is finalized," Mike said.

"What do you mean by 'staying in touch'?" India asked quickly.

"Almost all private adoptions are open these days. That basically means that the birth mother knows who you are, and vice versa. Some birth mothers want it stipulated in the contract that they will get updates and pictures. Some even have it written into the adoption contract that they will be allowed to see the child at set intervals," Mike explained.

India and I exchanged a nervous look.

"But other birth mothers prefer not to stay in touch. They find it easier to move on with their lives that way. And you get a say in it, too, of course. If you're not comfortable with continued contact, you can choose to work with only a birth mother who doesn't require it. These are all things you should think about when you're filling out the questionnaire.

"Your next step is to have a home study, where a social worker will come to your house and talk to you, and make sure that you'll provide a safe and suitable home for the child. And, finally, you'll create an adoptive-parent profile, which is basically a way to sell yourselves to potential birth mothers. It should tell who you are, the sort of life you lead, why you want to be parents, and will include photographs of the two of you," Mike said. "But before we get to all of that, the first decision you have to make is who you're going to hire to facilitate your adoption. Of course, I hope you choose to hire me, but I understand that this is an important decision, and you might want to talk to other attorneys or adoption agencies before making your choice."

This seemed like a good time to jump in with my main question. "How much do you charge?" I asked.

Mike smiled. "I probably don't have to tell you, adoption is not inexpensive. I charge three hundred dollars an hour, and require a two-thousand-dollar retainer to start. If there aren't any legal complications, the legal fees will normally be in the neighborhood of five thousand dollars."

Five thousand dollars? Not nothing, but not nearly as much as I thought it would be. But then Mike continued.

"Of course, there are other expenses, some of them quite significant. The law in Florida allows for adoptive parents to pay for a birth mother's expenses, including medical and reasonable living expenses, such as rent, groceries, and clothing. As you would probably guess, many women who are considering putting their babies up for adoption are not financially secure. Occasionally, we'll have a teen mom who's still living with and being supported by her parents. But that tends to be the exception, not the rule, so you should plan on covering her living expenses."

"But that could be..." I did some quick math in my head. "Thousands of dollars."

Mike nodded. "I tell clients to budget about three thousand a month for it."

I wondered if this number gave India the same stomach-sickening wrench it gave me. Three thousand dollars times the nine-month gestation period was a grand total of $27,000. Which, along with Mike's fee of $5,000, got us up to $32,000. And that was for a noneventful adoption. What if an event came along? What if the birth mother required an emergency C-section, or ended up in the hospital for a month?

"The good news is that you can use the time it takes to find a birth mother to get your finances in order. If you don't have that sort of money readily available to you..."

"We don't," I confirmed.

"Then perhaps you could look into getting help from your family, or perhaps refinancing your home," Mike suggested. "You'd be surprised how resourceful you can be when you have to be."

Even if India and I subsisted on ramen noodles and boxed macaroni and cheese for the next eighteen months, that was not going to make a dent in the $32,000—at a minimum—that we'd have to come up with. I looked at India, sure that she would be reaching the same conclusion, and braced myself for the inevitable look of despair and hopelessness. I wondered if we had enough left over in our emotional stores to ride out yet another devastating blow.

But to my surprise, India wasn't at all upset. Instead, her face had a glowing intensity to it, her eyes bright and her cheeks flushed.

"That's true," India said. "It would give us the time to figure out how we're going to pay for everything."

"Do you have any other questions?" We didn't. Actually, I did—primarily where the hell was I going to come up with thirty-two grand in the next six months?—but I knew Mike wouldn't have that answer for me.

"Think it over, and let me know if you'd like to go forward," Mike said.

"We definitely will," India said, standing to shake Mike's hand.

"What do you think? I liked him," India said, once we were back in my ancient Honda Civic, heading home. "Did you like him?"

"Sure," I said. "He was . . ." I groped for the right adjective.

"Knowledgeable," India supplied. "I agree. He seemed like he really knew what he was talking about. Mimi said he's the best in town."

I nodded and drummed one hand on the wheel.

"I'd feel comfortable signing up with him," India said. "Would you? Or do you want to interview other attorneys?"

"If he's the best in town, we should probably stick with him."

"I agree. He's perfect."

"Except for the shirt," I said, expecting India to laugh. I knew she shared my opinion of tropical print shirts.

But all she said was "Mmm," and I knew she hadn't heard me. She was too lost in starlit dreams of roly-poly babies with gummy grins and jelly bellies.

I hesitated, glancing sideways at her. I knew it was time to bring up the obvious obstacle to all of this, but it was a subject that had to be broached carefully. "The problem is," I began.

"I know," India said, cutting me off. "The money. We don't have thirty thousand, or however much it's going to be."

"No, we don't. Even the two thousand he wants as a retainer would be a stretch right now," I said. "Maybe in a few months, maybe after I get the next royalty check from my publisher."

I didn't add that that money was already earmarked for our next few mortgage payments.

"I was thinking..." India paused.

"What?"

"We could ask your parents," she said.

My hands tightened on the steering wheel. I had never had a close relationship with my parents. We got along fine on a super-ficial, see-you-once-a-year-at-Thanksgiving level. But you didn't have to dig very deep to hit the undercurrent of tension. My parents had not approved when, five years ago, I gave up my job in corporate development to write full-time. My second novel had just been published, and I'd signed a new contract with my publisher. I was thrilled. My parents were not. In fact, there had been an ugly scene when I told them. My mother had actually cried, and my father had been in a tight-lipped fury over the money he'd "wasted" on my education.

"When it goes pear-shaped, don't come to me for a loan," he'd told me.

Not if. *When.*

At that moment, I'd decided that I would never ask him for

anything, ever again. India knew all of this, of course, although she hadn't been present for the big confrontation.

"I don't think my parents have that sort of money," I hedged. My parents were not wealthy, at least not the sort of wealth where they could easily write us out a check for thirty-two thousand dollars.

"I'm not suggesting we ask them for all of it. Just enough to put down a retainer, until we can remortgage the house. And we'd pay them back, of course," India said.

I breathed in, and let the air out slowly.

"It's not as easy as you're making it sound," I said.

"I know," India said. She reached for my hand. "But I don't think it's unusual for family to help cover the cost of an adoption. If my mother had any money, I'm sure she'd help us out."

"If your mother had any money, she'd find a way to lose it before she could give it to us," I said tersely. "Or she'd end up giving it all to an abused-elephant rehab center, or whatever bullshit charity she's into at the moment."

India didn't argue with me. She knew what I said was true.

"And second, if we ask my parents for money, we're going to have to tell them what we need it for," I said.

"So what?"

"My parents aren't the most pro-adoption people in the world," I said.

"Seriously? Your parents are anti-adoption?" she asked. "You're kidding me, right? Who the hell is against adoption? It's like being anti-puppy."

"Actually, they don't like dogs much, either," I said. "Look, it's not that they're anti-adoption, at least not for other people. But when it comes to them, to their family, to me, I don't think it would be their first choice."

India let go of my hand. "It wasn't our first choice, either," she said quietly.

"I know," I said. I drew in a deep breath, and, after several long beats, I said, "Okay."

"Okay what?"

"Okay, I'll talk to them."

"Are you sure?" India asked, her brow puckering with worry.

I nodded. "What's the worst that can happen? That I'll be confirming all of my dad's predictions that giving up my corporate job was the worst mistake I could possibly make, and that I'd end up a washed-up failure, crawling to him for money? It'll probably make his year. You know how he loves to be right."

"You are not a failure," India said sharply. "And you're not crawling anywhere. You know what? Forget I suggested it. We'll find a way to raise the money ourselves."

"Hey, I was just kidding," I said. "I'll handle it. Don't worry."

To my mother's credit, she hardly said anything negative at all when I called to tell her about our adoption plans. There was only one moment of loaded silence, after which she asked in a somewhat tremulous voice if we were planning on adopting "one of those Chinese babies," which made me thankful that India wasn't privy to the conversation. In the end, my mother—after a brief consultation with my father, out of my hearing—agreed to lend us five thousand dollars. It was enough to get started.

Once Mike's retainer was paid, there was a ton of paperwork for us to fill out, but India threw herself at it with enthusiasm. She spent night after night sitting at our dining room table, pen in hand, filling out forms.

After a long debate, we decided that we would be comfortable sending the birth mother a yearly photo and written update, but that we did not want to have any post-adoptive meetings, at least not until the child was old enough to decide if that was something he or she wanted to do.

Next came the home study, which we were both dreading.

India insisted we purge all alcohol from the house and put child locks on every single drawer and cabinet door in the kitchen and two bathrooms, which meant that every time I went to get an aspirin, I had to struggle to remember how to open the door to the medicine cabinet. I kept pointing out that the social worker was unlikely to ask to see evidence of childproofing, considering it would be at least a year before we had an actual baby, but India insisted.

"I want this to go well," she said nervously. "What do you think I should wear?"

"Definitely clothes. I'm sure they look down on nudists," I said, in an attempt to inject some levity into the proceedings.

India rolled her eyes.

"What?" I said. "All I did was suggest no full-frontal nudity."

"You have to promise me that you won't make any stupid jokes in front of the social worker," India said.

"Okay, okay. I promise I won't mention anything about nudity," I said. "Or our voracious porn habit. Or the meth lab we have set up in the garage."

India pointed at me. "That's exactly what I'm talking about."

The home study wasn't nearly as bad as we feared. A frighteningly efficient social worker named Brenda came over to grill us on why we wanted to adopt, what our parenting style would be (I almost made a joke about how sparing the rod spoiled the child, but with a truly heroic effort, managed to stop myself), and what sort of child care we'd arrange for the baby. India surprised me by having good answers to all of these questions. If it had been up to me, I would have been left stuttering and probably making the exact sort of joke India had banned.

The only time things got tricky during the interview was when Brenda asked us how our extended family felt about our adoption plans. I glanced quickly at India, but she remained unflustered.

"My mother, who lives in town, is very enthusiastic," India said. "And Jeremy's parents have assisted us with the financial side of things."

I was impressed. She somehow managed to not lie and yet still portray our parents as normal and supportive.

"Speaking of your finances, how are you planning on covering the cost of the adoption?" Brenda asked. She was fortyish, plump-ish and black, with long braids caught back in a ponytail.

"We're going to refinance our house," India said.

"I thought I read in your paperwork that you've already done that once." Brenda flipped through our file. "Right. To cover the cost of your infertility treatments."

"The bank agreed to extend our home equity loan," I explained. It was true, the bank had extended the loan, although not by much. But between the bank and my parents' loan, our adoption budget was up to fifteen thousand dollars. "And I'm looking into taking on some freelance work."

I held my breath while Brenda made a notation on her paperwork. Then she looked up at India, smiled warmly, and said, "Have you begun childproofing your house yet?"

After Brenda left, I wandered outside to water the hibiscus trees I'd recently planted in a line outside our front door.

"Hey," a voice said. I looked up and saw Kelly Emmett crossing the street, bottle of beer in hand.

"Hey, man. What's up?" I said.

Kelly held out his beer-free hand for me to bump, which I did, even though this ritual always made me feel slightly ridiculous, like we were pretending to be sixteen even though we were both in our thirties.

Kelly bought the house across the street from ours about a year after we moved in. He'd recently gone through an ugly di-vorce, and shared custody of his now-preteen daughter with his ex-wife. The ex-wife had been replaced by a steady stream of tan, slim, young women, a phenomenon India could never figure out.

"What do they see in him? He's not that attractive," she'd always say, after sighting yet another gorgeous girl leaving Kelly's house. "And he's way too old for her."

"But he is rich," I said. It wasn't clear where his money had come from—I never asked—but Kelly was definitely loaded. He owned a popular martini bar on Clematis Street, drove a new Lincoln Navigator, and had a huge boat that he kept docked at a local marina.

"He's thirty-nine going on eighteen," India would say, rolling her eyes, as though all the money in the world couldn't make up for his immaturity. Then she'd grin at me. "I like 'em poor and grown-up."

"Hey, I'm rich in potential," I'd protest.

Kelly had thinning dark hair, shoulders that sloped forward, and was today wearing Wayfarer sunglasses, an Ed Hardy T-shirt, plaid shorts, and flip-flops.

"A group of us are heading out on the boat this weekend," he said, taking a swig of his beer. "You should come with, it's going to be a blast."

"Oh, yeah? Who's going?" I asked.

"A few of my buddies, some of the chicks from the bar," Kelly said.

I could just imagine how India would feel about my spending a day out on Kelly's boat with a group of bikini-clad cocktail waitresses while she stayed home and worked on our adoptive-parent profile.

"Can't," I said apologetically. "Too much to do around here."

"Sure, I know how it is. I used to have a wife, too," Kelly said. He laughed and took another swig of beer. "She always pitched a fit when I wanted to go out and have some fun."

"India's not like that," I said mildly.

"Sure, whatever," Kelly said.

Just then, a white Miata pulled in to his driveway. The door opened, and a tall, leggy brunette climbed out, shaking back her long hair and dusting off her practically nonexistent skirt.

"Hey, babe! I'll be right over," Kelly called out. The brunette waved and then sashayed into Kelly's house. We both gazed after her.

"New girlfriend?" I asked.

"Who, Caitlyn? No, she's been around," he said vaguely, as though not really sure where she came from and how long she'd been there.

"What happened to . . . ?" I asked, struggling to remember the name of the last one. "Rebecca?"

"Rachel." Kelly shrugged. "Didn't work out. She wanted to get married, and there's no way in hell I'm going down that road again. Plus, Ashley thought she was a bitch," he said. Ashley was Kelly's daughter. She was twelve, and dressed like she was twenty-five. In fact, not unlike the way Caitlyn was outfitted. "Caitlyn's less complicated. She doesn't even want to stay the night."

A sense of déjà vu swam up. I could swear I'd had this conversation before. And then I realized, I *had* had this conversation before. Back in college.

I gave the hibiscus one final squirt of water. "I have to get going."

"Right. The Marlins game is on," Kelly said.

I don't follow baseball, or football, for that matter. The only professional sport I ever watched was the occasional televised tennis match. But because I was wearing a Marlins hat the first time I met Kelly—a gift from India, who thought the fish on it was cute—he'd gotten it into his head that I was a baseball fan. No matter how many times I'd tried to tell him otherwise, I hadn't been able to dispel this myth.

"Right. The Marlins are on. Don't want to miss that game," I said, and began to coil the hose.

"Later, bro," Kelly said, and scuffed back over to his house and the waiting Caitlyn.

India was at her usual spot at the dining room table, with all of our adoption paperwork in front of her. Brenda had added a stack of papers to the pile, and India was poring over it all, a pen brandished in one hand. Her blonde hair was rising up from her head in a halo of frizz, as if it were as stressed out as she was.

India looked up when I came in. "How's Kelly?" she asked.

"Same as usual."

"Was that a new girlfriend?"

"Are you spying on the neighbors again? Keep it up and I'll get you a pair of binoculars for your birthday."

"Ha-ha. I just happened to be looking out the window when she pulled up."

"I didn't meet her, but he said her name's Caitlyn."

India snorted. "Which means she's twenty-three, tops."

"There's an age limit on Caitlyns?"

"There might as well be. All of those names—Madison, Brittany, Kayla, Brianna, Taylor, Tiffany, Alyssa. It automatically means you were born after 1984. Which also means she's way too young for Kelly." India dismissed the topic with a disgusted wave of one hand. "So I was thinking—you should write our adoptive-parent profile."

"Why me?"

"You're a professional writer."

"I write science fiction," I pointed out. "Did you want a few space aliens or genetic mutants worked into the profile?"

"No. I want you to make us sound amazing, like the sort of parents any pregnant woman would be thrilled to hand her baby over to," India said.

"So I shouldn't mention the S&M dungeon in the basement?"

"And no smart-assery."

"That's not even a word."

"See? I didn't know that. That's why you have to write it. Just talk about what great people we are."

"Are we?"

"Yes, goddamn it, we are." India smiled. "And make sure you include something about Otis."

Otis, who was lying under the dining room table at India's feet, thumped his tail when he heard his name.

"What about him?" I asked doubtfully. Otis was known for two things—his ability to fall asleep on his back with all four paws sticking up straight in the air and a startling enthusiasm for eating his own shit. I couldn't imagine either one would hold much sway over potential birth mothers.

"The idea is to make us sound like the all-American couple. Otis is a selling point; he makes us look nurturing. We need to talk everything up—our house, our jobs, our friends, our family."

"Our family? Am I allowed to lie?"

"No. But we can package creatively," India said. "It's a fine line. You don't want to exaggerate too much, but you want to make sure we sound like the perfect couple to hand a baby over to. So focus on how kind and loving we are—"

"Kind and loving? This morning you said something about wanting to rip my face off."

"You forgot to buy coffee! And we were entirely out! You know I can't function without coffee. And you can't hold anything I say while in a state of extreme caffeine withdrawal against me," India exclaimed.

"You probably don't want to put your insane caffeine addiction in the profile, either. It's not pretty."

"Yes. Just put in warm, fuzzy things, like our Christmas traditions and stuff like that."

"Do we have any Christmas traditions? Other than your mother getting drunk and losing track of when she put the turkey in the oven, which usually ends up with someone getting food poisoning? Then there's that time she set the Christmas tree on fire," I said. Both India and I snorted with laughter at the memory.

India's mother, Georgia, had insisted on tying real candles to the boughs of the tree, in an attempt to re-create an authentic Dickensian Christmas. The fact that the tree was artificial didn't in any way dampen her enthusiasm for the project. Moments after she lit the candles, the tree went up in flames, with noxious, carcinogenic clouds of black smoke billowing out until I sprinted in with a fire extinguisher. No one was seriously hurt, although Georgia's eyebrows were singed off. For weeks after, she went around with a pencil-drawn arc over each eye that gave her a permanently startled look.

India suddenly stopped laughing and her face crumpled with worry. "Oh, God. What woman in her right mind is going to give a baby to us?" she said plaintively. Tears sparkled in her eyes. "We have no experience with babies! And our families are insane!"

I gathered India in my arms. She felt soft and warm pressed against me. My heart cracked open.

"We'll be great parents," I said firmly, stroking her hair. "And somewhere out there, there's a woman who will see that."

"Do you really think so?" India asked. She leaned back and looked up at me. The tears had smudged her mascara and left red streaks on her cheeks.

"Yes," I said. "And when we find her, we'll just make sure that she never meets our parents."

Three
LAINEY

In the bathroom of the tiny apartment she shared with her boyfriend, Lainey Walker stared at the home pregnancy test stick she'd just peed on.

"Shit," she said, and grabbed the box to read the directions again. A straight line meant the test was negative, a plus sign was positive. She looked back at the test stick, praying that this time she'd see a straight line. The plus sign was still there, an unmistakable bright blue.

Lainey let out her breath in one long stream. "Well, isn't that just fucking great."

Lainey tossed the stick in the small plastic garbage can by the toilet and then sat back down on the closed lid of the toilet. There was no way she could have a baby. Not now. Not when she was so close to getting out of here, to putting her big plan into motion.

She'd thought it through carefully. First, she'd get together as much money as possible. Second, she was going to move to L.A. And third, she would get cast in a reality television show, which would turn her into a star. She wasn't even going to bother trying to get into movies. It was impossible to break into the business that way, unless you had an in. And since Lainey didn't have a daddy who was a director or a boyfriend who was a producer, she knew it was next to impossible to land a commercial, much less star in a movie.

But reality shows were wide open. You just had to know how to package yourself and look amazing in a bikini. Lainey had decided she was going to nab the role of the Girl Next Door. At first, she'd thought she'd go for being the villain—it was a flashier role that would get more attention—but then decided she didn't want to get typecast so early in her career. The villains became Internet jokes; the Girls Next Door landed jobs co-hosting *The View*.

But first Lainey had to find the right show. The survival ones were out—she didn't have any survival skills, and besides, those people all started looking nasty once they'd spent a few days away from makeup and hair conditioner. The talent shows, where you had to dance or sing, wouldn't work since Lainey couldn't do either.

Her best bet was probably one of those looking-for-love shows, where a group of women competed for the attention of some walking, talking Ken doll. The only real problem was that you started as just one of a group, so you didn't get any real screen time until you made it into the top three or so. But Lainey was convinced that she could make herself stand out, especially if there was a chance to appear in a bikini. She just needed a shot—one shot—and she'd make it work. And it was now or never. Lainey was already twenty. The way she figured it, her prime bikini years were numbered.

But a baby was definitely *not* part of the plan. She stood and leaned toward the mirror over the sink, puffing her cheeks out to see what she'd look like fat.

Gross, she thought, blowing the air out. *There's no way in hell that's going to happen.*

And there was also no way in hell she was going to pay for an abortion out of her L.A. fund. She tossed her long dark hair over her shoulders and marched out of the bathroom, down the short dingy hallway and into the tiny living room. Travis was sprawled on the couch, watching an episode of *The Simpsons* and breathing loudly through his mouth.

When they'd first met—at the gym, both waiting for the leg press machine—Lainey had thought Trav was hot. Sure, his features were a bit too thick to be considered handsome—his nose was wide and his lips were fleshy—but his ripped arms and perfectly defined abs made up for it. And even if he wasn't the smartest guy in the world, Trav took care of himself and made a good living as a salesman at the local Toyota dealership. This was a stark contrast to her previous boyfriends, so Lainey had been willing to overlook his less-than-sparkling intelligence.

But that was before the steroids. One of Trav's bodybuilder friends had gotten him started. The drugs made Travis's chest and arm muscles pop out like a superhero's, but they also gave him a cavemanlike brow ridge and caused an ugly rash of acne to spread over his face, shoulders, and back. Lainey had thought that the side effects might be a deterrent to Trav's continued juicing, but he seemed almost fascinated with his zits. He'd spend hours staring into the bathroom mirror, squeezing them until green pus erupted out. It was revolting. Even worse, he was irritable all the time and picked fights with Lainey for no reason. And he never wanted to go out anymore—all he did was go to work, go to the gym, and then return home to zone out in front of the television. Lainey was fed up with him.

And now the dumbass had gone and gotten her pregnant.

"I need to talk to you," Lainey said.

Trav didn't look up from *The Simpsons*. "What about?"

"Turn the TV off."

Trav didn't respond, nor did he turn the TV off. He didn't even lower the volume. Her irritation boiled over into hot anger.

"Hey, asshole, I'm talking to you," Lainey said.

Travis finally looked up at the word *asshole*, his expression sullen. "What?"

"Do you remember when you told me that I wouldn't get

pregnant? I told you to pull out, and you said you didn't have to because that steroid shit meant you couldn't get me pregnant."

"Yeah. So what?"

"So your great plan didn't work out so well. I'm pregnant."

Travis looked at her blankly. Lainey closed her eyes and shook her head. He was even dumber than she'd thought. She wondered if he'd always been this stupid, or if the steroids were melting his brain.

"Preg-nant," she said, sounding the word out.

"No way," Travis said, and the color drained from his face. *"Dude.* What are you going to do?"

What are *you* going to do. Very nice, Lainey thought. Not that she'd expected a marriage proposal, but *still.* A little fucking support would have been nice.

"I'm going to get rid of it. Obviously."

As the specter of fatherhood faded, Travis looked relieved. "Good," he said, his eyes drifting back to the *The Simpsons.*

"Oh, no. You don't get off that easily," Lainey said, crossing her arms. "You're paying for it."

This did get his attention. "How much?"

Lainey shrugged. "I'm not sure. I think it's around ..." Lainey paused. She was about to say six hundred, which is what she knew for a fact one of her co-workers had shelled out for her abortion. But Lainey was pretty sure Trav wouldn't insist on coming to the clinic with her, so she could probably get away with inflating the figure. "Eight hundred," she said instead.

"Eight hundred? Are you kidding me?"

Trav used to buy Lainey things all the time. He'd even surprised her on her birthday with a Dooney & Bourke purse she'd been drooling over. Now, he got pissy if she asked for twenty bucks to pay for takeout. She knew he made a good living, but from what she could tell—and she'd made a habit of monitoring his bank account—he was spending over a thousand dollars a month on his drug habit.

"This is all your fault," Lainey snapped. "If you wore a condom, like I told you to, this wouldn't have happened."

"I don't like condoms. Why can't you go on the Pill?"

"I tried the Pill. It made me gain weight."

Travis glared at her. "What if I don't have the money?"

Lainey crossed her arms and stared him down.

"How much do you think eighteen years of child support is going to cost you? You know they deduct that straight from your paycheck, right? Doesn't leave a lot of money left over for your drugs, or gym membership, or your entrance fees to those stupid bodybuilding competitions."

Trav's face was no longer pale. Instead, it was slowly turning a mottled shade of red.

"Why are you being such a bitch?" he demanded.

"Why are you?" she retorted. "I know steroids shrink your dick, but I didn't know they turned you into a whiny little girl."

Travis stood suddenly, his shovel-like hands clenched into fists. Lainey wondered if he was going to hit her. She wasn't afraid. He had slapped her once, and she'd responded by first kneeing him in the groin and then, when he was doubled over with pain, clipping him in the jaw with a neat right hook.

But Trav didn't hit her. Instead, he spun around and punched the wall, leaving a dent in the drywall. He let out a roar of pain and shook his hand. "Shit! That really fucking hurt!"

Lainey rolled her eyes and turned away. *What an idiot.* "I'm calling the women's clinic. The sooner I get this taken care of, the better."

Lainey's eyes fluttered open. Where the hell was she? And what was that smell? It reminded her of visiting her grandmother in the nursing home before she died, a depressing combination of bleach and urine. But then the fog began to lift, and piece by piece, it slowly came back to her.

She'd been at the clinic. Sitting in an exam room. They'd given her a flimsy paper gown that gaped open, covering nothing. After the doctor examined her, the nurse came in to draw blood. The last thing Lainey could remember was watching the tip of the needle prick through the thin skin of her inner arm, and the blood bubbling up into the needle... and then everything had gone black and fuzzy.

Lainey lifted her head and glanced around. She was still there, in the clinic, in the same exam room she'd been in when she met with the doctor. She was also still wearing the paper gown, although someone had laid a scratchy yellow blanket over her.

Lainey felt a tightness on her arm. She looked and saw there was a Band-Aid there, holding down a cotton ball. She picked at the Band-Aid, but it stuck to her arm hair. There was a knock on the door.

"Come in," Lainey said.

The door opened, and a middle-aged woman with a kind face and short dark hair speckled with gray came in.

"How are you feeling?" the woman asked her. "I'm Rosemary. The nurse had to go see another patient, but she asked me to keep an eye on you. Should I call her back?"

"I'm fine," Lainey said, not entirely truthfully. She was still pretty woozy. "What happened?"

"You fainted," Rosemary said. When she smiled at Lainey, the edges of her eyes and mouth creased up like the folds of a fan. "You don't have to get up right away. Feel free to lie there as long as you want."

"It's okay," Lainey said, swinging her legs off the cot and sitting upright. "You're not a nurse?"

"No, I'm a volunteer counselor."

"Are you here to counsel me?" Lainey asked. Her chin lifted defiantly, as though daring Rosemary to try.

"If you want to talk, I'd be happy to listen," Rosemary said. She gestured toward a task chair that was floating adrift in the middle of the exam room. Lainey shrugged. Rosemary seemed to take this as acquiescence and sat down, resting both feet flat on the floor and folding her hands in her lap.

"Look. I'll just tell you up front: I want to have an abortion. You're not going to talk me out of it," Lainey said.

Rosemary looked surprised. "I'm not here to talk you out of anything. I support every woman's right to make choices about her reproductive health."

"Oh," Lainey said, her indignation deflating. "Then what do you want to talk about?"

Rosemary smiled. "It doesn't work that way. I'm here to listen, if you'd like to talk."

Lainey shrugged again. "There's no point."

Rosemary nodded, but didn't say anything. Lainey waited for some sort of reaction, and when none was forthcoming, she began to talk again, just to fill the silence.

"I don't want kids. I definitely don't want one now, and maybe not ever. And besides, my boyfriend is sort of a jerk. He wasn't always, but lately . . ." Lainey trailed off. She was pissed at Trav, but even so, she didn't want to get him in trouble for his illegal steroid use. She picked at the Band-Aid, but it stayed firmly in place.

Rosemary nodded. "Have you discussed your decision with your boyfriend?"

"Yeah. Trust me, this is what he wants, too." *Not that his opinion counts for anything,* she silently added. She wrapped her arms around herself, pressing them tightly across her stomach. Then, wondering if that would bother the baby, she released them. *Was the baby big enough to feel something like that?* she wondered. It was a weird thought—that pressing her own arms over her own stomach would affect someone else. No, that was stupid. The baby was probably too small to feel anything.

"Do you have a good support system?" Rosemary asked. Lainey must have looked confused, because she added, "Your mother, a sister, a close friend?"

Lainey made an irritated sound in her throat. She didn't need a support system; she needed an abortion and a bus ticket to L.A. "Look, just so you know, I don't really do this."

"Do what?"

"The touchy-feely, talking-about-my-feelings crap."

Rosemary laughed. "Okay. I'll keep that in mind," she said.

Lainey stood, wanting to change out of the paper gown and into her real clothes, and then to get the hell out of there. "I should get going. Am I all done here?"

"The nurse practitioner is going to want to talk to you to make sure you're feeling well enough to leave. Then, just make an appointment on the way out," Rosemary said. She reached into her pocket and handed Lainey a business card. She wrote a phone number on the back. "Call me if you change your mind about wanting to talk."

"Sure," Lainey said. She took the business card, fully intending to throw it out as soon as possible.

"I can't believe you're pregnant," Flaca said. She was sitting on a faded floral upholstered chair with her feet propped up on the coffee table, while Lainey painted Flaca's toenails dark blue.

Flaca Reyes was roughly as wide as she was tall, with massive breasts, long, shiny dark hair, and tattoos covering both arms. Lainey had spent much of her childhood at Flaca's house, escaping first her parents' escalating arguments and then, after her dad moved out, her mother's spiral into alcoholism. Flaca was one of eight siblings, and although she'd complained bitterly about the lack of space and privacy while growing up, Lainey had envied her. Some of the best moments of her childhood were spent sitting at the Reyeses' kitchen table, eating Mrs. Reyes's empanadas hot from the pan and listening to the good-natured arguments breaking out between Flaca and her siblings.

Flaca was now living with her fiancé, Luis, a mechanic who fixed up classic cars in his spare time. Flaca's parents liked to pretend that the two weren't actually living together out of wedlock, a fiction Flaca maintained by not allowing Luis to keep anything at the apartment, other than the single dresser drawer he was allotted in their bedroom. Luis was storing all of his belongings at his parents' house until after their wedding.

"I know," Lainey said. She looked up from her polishing job. "Do you have anything to eat? I'm starving."

"I thought you said you felt sick," Flaca said.

"I do. I'm sick and hungry at the same time, all the time. Isn't that weird?" Lainey said.

"Angelina was the same way when she was pregnant," Flaca said. "She'd pig out, throw it all up, and then pig out some more."

Angelina was Flaca's oldest sister, and had gained seventy-five pounds when she was pregnant, most of which she never lost after the baby arrived. Lainey shuddered at the thought of that happening to her.

"There's a box of cereal in the cupboard," Flaca said. She got up and, hobbling on her heels so as not to smudge her newly polished toes, went into the kitchen to retrieve the box. She came back in the living room and handed it to Lainey, who ripped it open and dumped a small pile of Cap'n Crunch out on the coffee table.

"You've definitely decided to have an abortion?" Flaca asked. There was no condemnation in the question. Flaca was Catholic by birth but pragmatic by nature.

"Yes." Lainey paused. "Something weird happened when I went to the clinic."

"What?"

"I fainted."

"Again?" Lainey had accompanied Flaca to the tattoo studio when she was having Luis's name inked on the back of her neck. The tattoo artist had barely begun, just touching the needle to Flaca's skin, when Lainey slid off her chair in a dead faint.

Lainey nodded. "They were drawing blood," she said, shuddering at the memory.

"Damn, girl, what is it with you and needles?"

"I don't know. I can't help it," Lainey said defensively. She shoved a handful of cereal into her mouth.

"You okay?"

Lainey shrugged. "Fine. I mean, still pregnant, but otherwise fine."

"Do you think it was a sign? You passing out like that?"

"A sign of what?"

"That you should have the baby," Flaca said. She lifted her heavy eyebrows in a meaningful way.

Lainey snorted. "A sign from God? Please. You know, you should let me tweeze your eyebrows. I keep telling you, it would really make your eyes pop."

"You know how you feel about needles? That's how I feel about having my hair ripped out by the roots. And don't change the subject," Flaca said. "I really think this could be a sign."

"I don't believe in signs."

"I do. The first time Luis and I went out, there was a huge full moon in the sky, even though it was still light out. I knew then that we were meant to be together."

"You're getting married because of a moon?" Lainey teased. She adored Luis and would have killed Flaca if she hadn't decided to marry him. "You know that's crazy, right?"

"No it's not. And it's not the only reason I'm marrying him. I was just paying attention to the signs that God was trying to tell me something," Flaca said.

"If God wanted me to keep this baby, he'd send me a winning lottery ticket. Now, *that* would be a sign. And even then, I still wouldn't want it. The baby, I mean. I'd take the money."

"I don't think God works that way."

"Too bad. I could use the money for my L.A. fund. In fact, it's too bad you can't sell babies."

"Well . . . ," Flaca said, and bit her lip thoughtfully.

"I was just kidding."

"I know. But do you remember Crystal Owens? She was a year ahead of us at school."

"Yeah, sure. She used to go out with Jason Tucker. Remember when he got loaded at that party and tried to stick his hand up my shirt? Crystal got in my face about it, warning me to stay away from her man. As if I'd have any interest in that freak," Lainey said, with an eye roll. "He was a total troll. They're not still together, are they?"

"No, they broke up ages ago. But don't you remember, she got knocked up senior year?"

"That's right. I'd totally forgotten about that."

"She gave her baby up for adoption."

"She did? How did I not know that?" Lainey finished painting Flaca's nails and capped the bottle of polish with a flourish.

"I think she kept it pretty quiet. Anyway, from what I heard, the family who adopted the baby paid her for it. They even rented her an apartment and paid her bills."

Lainey stared at her friend. "Seriously? They gave her money?"

Flaca nodded. "I heard she had enough afterward to get a new car," Flaca said. She wiggled her toes for Lainey to see. "What do you think of this color? Damn, girl, you give the best pedicures."

Lainey shrugged off the praise. She'd be thrilled to never see the inside of another nail salon. Currently, she was working at one in the mall that was owned and run by a Korean family. Lainey was the only native English speaker employed in the place, and she was pretty sure the other nail technicians talked about her while she was sitting right there. They were always giving her sly, sidewise looks and giggling behind their hands. "Crystal seriously bought a new car?"

"Yeah. It was just one of those little shitty Kias, but still." Flaca shrugged. "Better than nothing, right?"

Lainey wondered what a new Kia cost. It had to be at least ten grand, right? That would definitely pay for a bus ticket to Los Angeles, and cover a few months of living expenses if she was careful. Would that be enough time for her to get discovered?

"How much money do you think I could get?"

"I don't know. Probably a lot. There are a lot of rich people out there who want to adopt. I've seen, like, whole episodes on *Oprah* about it. The women have careers or whatever, and by the time they get around to having babies, it's too late," Flaca explained.

"So they're desperate," Lainey mused. "Desperate enough to pay a lot of money."

"Definitely," Flaca agreed. "And you know, the kid would be totally set up for life. It would probably have a nanny and a pony."

Lainey shrugged this off. She was far more interested in the idea that this pregnancy—which she had, right up until this very moment, seen only as a problem that needed to be dealt with—might actually be an easy way for her to make some money. True, it would mean she'd have to be pregnant for months and months, and would get really fat in the meantime. But that would be temporary. She could lose the weight. Lots of movie stars had babies, and were skinny again a few weeks later.

"How would I find one of these rich, desperate women?" Lainey asked.

"Seriously?" Flaca asked.

"What? It was your idea!"

"But it's a really big deal. A huge, life-changing deal. A few minutes ago, you were sure you were going to have an abortion."

"A few minutes ago, I didn't know having this baby would make me rich," Lainey retorted.

"But don't you think it'd be hard to go through a whole pregnancy, feeling the baby kick, and then at the end, hand it over to a couple of complete strangers?" Flaca asked. She shook her head. "I don't know if I could do that."

But Lainey was caught up in fantasies of bloated bank balances and the glamorous new life it would buy her in Los Angeles—meeting movie stars, attending glittering parties, finding a rich guy to fall in love with her. Her entire life would change for the better.

"I don't think it'd be hard at all," she said.

Lainey almost lost her nerve when Rosemary answered the phone.

"This is Rosemary," a familiar, pleasant voice said.

"Yeah, um, you probably don't remember me, but my name is Lainey. I was at the clinic last week and I passed out when they were taking blood, and you gave me your card."

"Of course I remember you," Rosemary said warmly. "How are you, Lainey?"

"I'm okay. I was thinking about not having an abortion after all. But I don't want to keep the baby, either," Lainey added quickly, lest Rosemary get it into her head to knit the baby some booties, or whatever it was that old ladies did with their free time.

"You're considering adoption?" Rosemary asked.

Lainey searched the words and tone for even the merest trace of being judged. But then, deciding there was none, she said, "Yeah, I guess so. But the thing is, I don't know how to do that."

"You have several options. I would recommend that you use some sort of intermediary. A lawyer, an adoption agency, even a good not-for-profit group," Rosemary said.

Lainey did not like the sound of *not-for-profit*.

"I think I want to go through an attorney," Lainey said, figuring that this was probably how rich people adopted babies. Rich people always had lawyers.

"There are several good adoption attorneys in town, but there's one in particular that I've gotten good feedback on."

"That would be great," Lainey said, picking up a pencil to write down the lawyer's name on an unpaid cable bill. *Mike Jankowski, 555–0400.*

"What's this?" Trav asked when he got home from the gym that night. Lainey was sitting at the coffee table, eating pizza right out of the delivery box, which she'd paid for with a twenty she'd found in Trav's sock drawer. It was one of his favorite places to stash money, although why he continued to put it there, when Lainey just helped herself to it, she didn't know. Maybe he forgot about it. Either way, she was glad—she'd been craving pepperoni all day.

Lainey glanced up and saw that Trav—still sweating and smelling like a gym rat—was holding the cable bill.

"It says *Mike Jankowski*," he said.

Lainey let out an excited gasp. "You learned to read! Good for you," she cheered sarcastically.

"Who is he?" Trav asked, ignoring her sarcasm.

"Why? Are you jealous?"

Trav snorted, and dropped his gym bag on the ground. "As if. In fact," he hesitated, "I've been thinking. After you get the... well, you know."

"You can't say the word *abortion*?"

"Fine. After you get the abortion, I think you should move out," Trav said.

Lainey stared up at him, the pizza slice frozen en route to her mouth. "Are you kidding me?" she asked.

"Come on, Lainey," Trav said, sitting in the La-Z-Boy recliner. It had always grossed Lainey out that he'd lounge there after working out before he'd showered. The gray microfiber uphol-stery was starting to smell. "This—the two of us—it isn't working out. We both know that, right?"

Lainey didn't know what was more irritating: the fact that Trav had beaten her to the breakup, or that he was now talking to her in a soothing, sympathetic voice, as though she might be upset. As though he had the ability to break her heart.

"Let me get this straight: I'm pregnant with your baby, and you're kicking me out of our apartment," she said.

"My apartment," Trav said. "I pay the rent. And you don't have to go right away. Stay until you have the abortion."

The irritation quickly became a hot, buzzing anger that filled Lainey's lungs and choked in her throat. She hadn't planned on using her decision to keep the pregnancy as a weapon to bludgeon Trav with. If anything, she was hoping he wouldn't interfere or do anything to screw up the adoption. But that resolve was swept away in her rage.

"I changed my mind," Lainey said. She smiled maliciously at Trav's look of dumb incomprehension. "I'm not going to have an abortion after all."

The color drained from Trav's face. "What?" he asked. "What do you mean?"

"I mean I'm going to have the baby. I canceled my appointment at the clinic," Lainey said.

She stretched out her legs and took a bite of the pizza. She took her time chewing and swallowing.

Trav sat heavily on the end of the couch, looking like he might cry.

"Why?"

"I changed my mind."

"But you don't want a baby," Trav said. His voice was now a whine, which Lainey found both irritating and satisfying.

"Relax. I'm not keeping it," she said.

"What?" Trav's head snapped up, and he turned to stare at Lainey with something that looked very much like hatred. "So you're just fucking with me? You're lying to me?"

"No, I'm not lying. And drop the 'roid rage, I'm not in the mood. I'm going to give the baby up for adoption. That guy's name I wrote down on the cable bill? He's a lawyer," Lainey said. "An adoption lawyer. I'm going to see him tomorrow."

"But you said you *wanted* to have an abortion. I gave you the money for it," Trav said.

Typical, Lainey thought. All he cared about was his eight hundred bucks. He'd turned into such a cheapskate.

"I'm going to use that money to hire the lawyer, genius," Lainey lied. She'd checked that out when she called Mike Jankowski's office to schedule the appointment—she wouldn't have to pay a dime. But she was fairly sure that Trav wouldn't know that, so she'd decided to add his eight hundred to her Los Angeles savings. She figured she deserved it, just for having to put up with his steroid-induced mood swings.

"Jesus, Lainey. You can't make these decisions on your own," Trav said.

"Why not? It's my body. It has nothing to do with you. I'm going to have the baby and put it up for adoption. It's not like I'm asking you to raise it or anything."

"Why?"

"Because I think you'd be a shitty parent."

"No, I mean why are you doing *this*. Having the baby. What do you get out of it?"

Lainey shrugged and took another bite of her pizza. "Nothing. I just think it's a good thing. The baby gets a shot at a decent life, and some sad couple out there who can't have a kid gets to have one."

Trav let out an incredulous bark of laughter.

"What?" Lainey demanded.

"You've never done anything for anyone else in your life."

"That's not true! I gave Flaca a pedicure today."

"Yeah, you'll do shit for Flaca," Trav admitted. "But not for anyone else."

"Look, if I want to have this baby, I will. And there's nothing you can do about it," Lainey snarled. She kicked at Trav with one bare foot, but he jumped out of the way before she could make contact.

"Yeah, well, there is," Trav said. "You can get out of my apartment."

Lainey stared at him. "What?"

"Yeah. I want you out. Now."

"Now?" Lainey's voice was shrill. "Where am I supposed to go at this time of night?"

"I don't know, and I don't care," Trav said. "I just don't want you here."

"Then *you* should leave!"

"This is my apartment. I pay the rent. You never pay a fucking dime for anything. In fact, where'd you get the money to pay for this pizza?" he asked.

"I have a job," Lainey retorted.

"You stole it from my sock drawer, didn't you!"

Lainey was so surprised he'd caught on, that she didn't rebuff his accusation quickly enough. "No," she said finally. "Fuck off."

Trav snatched up the pizza box. "Then this is my pizza," he said.

"I'm pregnant with your baby!" Lainey stood, her hands balled at her sides.

"You just told me it has nothing to do with me. It's your body, remember? So get your shit, and get your body out of here," Trav said.

"Fine. Whatever," Lainey said. As she passed by him, she reached out and knocked the pizza box out of his hands. Deep-dish pepperoni spattered onto the graying vinyl floor and, even better, down the front of Trav's black sleeveless moisture-wicking gym shirt.

Lainey knocked on the door of her mother's house. She was clutching a kitchen garbage bag containing all her possessions, which bumped uncomfortably against her shins. To make herself feel better, Lainey tried to picture herself as a television star with a complete set of Louis Vuitton luggage. The fantasy didn't have the calming effect it normally did.

The porch light wasn't on, although that didn't necessarily mean that no one was home. It could have blown out weeks, even months ago. Lainey's mother, Candace, rarely got around to such mundane tasks as changing lightbulbs. Lainey knocked again. This time, she could hear an unintelligible squawk of conversation, followed by footsteps approaching and the metallic jingle of a chain lock being unfastened. The door swung open, and a back-lit Candace peered out at her daughter.

Candace was a large, blowsy woman. She had meaty shoulders and arms, and a bloated face that was bare of makeup. Her hair was her one vanity. Although it was too long and, Lainey thought, too blonde, Candace put a lot of effort into styling it—curled bangs, feathered-back sides, lots of volume on top.

"Hi, Mom," Lainey said. "Can I come in?"

"Baby!" Candace exclaimed. She swung open the door and folded Lainey into her arms. Candace smelled as she always did: a potent combination of Aqua Net and gin. Lainey allowed herself to be hugged for a few beats, but then stiffened and stepped away.

"What are you doing here, sugar?" Candace asked. The words were slightly slurred, but still comprehensible, which Lainey took as a good sign.

"Trav kicked me out," Lainey said. She dropped her garbage bag full of clothes on the ground. "Do you mind if I stay for a few nights? Just until I find a new place."

Candace peered at her daughter. "He kicked you out?"

Lainey nodded. "He's an asshole," she said by way of explanation.

"Come on in," Candace said, turning to start down the short hallway. "We're all in the living room."

"Who's here?" Lainey asked, her heart sinking. She'd noticed the cars parked at the curb, but had hoped they belonged to one of the other houses. The street was mostly made up of duplexes, all tightly squeezed in on too-small lots, each with only a single driveway.

"Al, of course, and his friend Richie." Al was Candace's live-in boyfriend, and as he was a complete loser, he had a lot in common with every other boyfriend she'd ever had. He sponged off Candace for every dime he could get out of her. Candace wasn't wealthy, but she did have a steady job at the Florida Department of Transportation that she'd managed to keep despite her drinking problem.

Lainey followed her mother down the hall, into the tiny, cramped living room. The house was a mess, littered with empty soda cans and discarded chip bags. There was a funky odor, too. A mixture of unwashed male and stale beer. Al was stretched out on a recliner, drinking a can of Budweiser. He had greasy hair that was prematurely gray and a scrawny build. His friend, who was the size of a baby whale, was lounging on the brown sofa, his feet propped up on the coffee table. They were both absorbed in the Gators game blaring on the television.

"Hey, girl," Al said. "This is Richie. This is Candace's kid, Lainey."

"Hey there," Richie said, leering at Lainey in a way that he obviously meant to be sexy. Lainey rolled her eyes. As if. Richie's thick curly hair had receded back to display a shiny forehead, and he'd cut his sideburns into muttonchops. Behind his thick glasses, he had small, piggy eyes. She was fairly sure that he was the source of the unpleasant smell.

"You want something to drink? A beer or something?" Candace said, passing through the living room, into the kitchen. Lainey followed her, mostly wanting to get away from Richie, who was now looking at her like she was a lollipop he'd like to cram into his mouth.

"No. Just some water," Lainey said.

"What's this about you and Trav?" Candace asked. She stuck a smudged glass under the tap and, once it was full, passed it to Lainey.

"I'm pregnant," Lainey said.

Candace stared at her and, for a moment, looked surprisingly sober. Then she shook her head, sighed, and sipped from a glass containing a bright yellow liquid. Gin and diet Mountain Dew— her mother's favorite cocktail. Actually, this was a good sign, Lainey thought. She only really had to worry when her mother switched to whiskey, which she drank straight.

"I thought you were smarter than that," Candace said.

"You're one to talk," Lainey said. Her mother had given birth to Lainey when she was sixteen, four years younger than Lainey was now.

"That's why you should know better," Candace retorted.

"I'm not keeping it," Lainey said.

"Make Trav pay for it," Candace said immediately.

"I'm going to have it. I'm just not going to keep it. I'm putting it up for adoption," Lainey said.

Candace, who had been in the middle of lighting a cigarette, stopped and peered at Lainey. "You are?"

"Why does everyone find that so hard to believe?"

"You're just not the type, I guess," Candace said. She inhaled deeply on the cigarette and then, without removing it from her mouth, blew the smoke out one corner of her mouth.

"Obviously I am," Lainey said. She waved away the smoke. "And can you please not smoke around me? I *am* pregnant, after all."

Candace shrugged and continued to puff on her cigarette. "So that's why Trav kicked you out?"

"Yep. Well, that, and the fact that he's a dick."

"Trav's not so bad. Didn't he buy you that nice handbag?"

"Yeah, he's a real prince. So can I stay here for a few nights?"

Candace shrugged. "We don't have any room. If you haven't noticed, this isn't exactly Mar-a-Lago. Richie's got all of his stuff stored in the second bedroom. You can't even open the door to get in there."

"I can sleep on the sofa."

"Richie's got the sofa," Candace said. "He's staying here for a while."

"Since when?" Lainey demanded.

"Since he lost his job and couldn't pay his rent," Candace said.

"Now it's not just Al sponging off you, but his friends, too?" Lainey asked, her eyebrows arched. Her mother just shrugged. "Jesus, Mom, I'm pregnant and I've got nowhere to stay. Shouldn't your daughter come before your scumbag boyfriend's freeloading friends?"

"Watch your mouth, little girl," Al said as he ambled into the kitchen, heading straight for the refrigerator. He pulled out two beers.

"Don't tell me what to do, asshole," Lainey said. She could feel her temper flaring again.

"I won't be insulted in my own house," Al said. He puffed his thin chest out.

"It's not your house, it's hers." Lainey thrust a chin in Candace's direction. "So I'll speak to and about you however I fucking please."

Al looked at Candace, who said, "Cut it out, Lainey."

Lainey laughed without humor. "That's right. Take his side. You always do. Doesn't even matter who the guy is, it's always the same."

"Hey, buddy, you getting me a beer or what?" Richie shouted from the living room.

Al gave Lainey one last triumphant look and shuffled back out of the kitchen.

"Why do you put up with him?" Lainey demanded. "He's disgusting."

Candace didn't say anything. She didn't need to. Lainey knew why. Her mother would always do whatever it took to keep a man, no matter how greasy and worthless he was.

She's pathetic, Lainey thought as she felt something inside of her harden. *And there's not a chance in hell I'm ever going to end up like her.*

"That's it, then? You're going to let that fat piece of shit stay here instead of me?" Lainey said.

"I just can't kick him out without notice."

"Fine." Lainey slammed her glass of water down on the kitchen table. "I'm leaving."

She turned and marched back through the living room, ignoring the two men as she passed and headed to the front door.

"You don't have to go off in a huff. We'll figure something out," Candace said, trailing behind her.

"No, thanks." Lainey threw open the door and marched out into the warm evening, letting the screen door slam behind her. She'd go to Flaca's for the night. And tomorrow she had an appointment with the adoption lawyer.

It's all going to work out fine, Lainey told herself. It almost always did.

Four

INDIA

I stared at a tiny silver cell phone resting on the kitchen table, willing it to ring.

"Staring at it isn't going to make it ring," Jeremy said. We were sitting at the kitchen table, still wearing our pajamas. Jeremy was reading the paper while devouring his morning bowl of Frosted Mini-Wheats.

"I know," I said, still not taking my eyes off the phone.

The cell phone was the infamous birth-mother phone. It was standard for every adoptive couple to have one, a phone dedicated to a single purpose: for prospective birth mothers to call. Mike Jankowski had told us to always keep it charged, turned on, and nearby, because you never know when a birth mother will see your profile and decide to make the first tentative contact. Birth mothers don't leave messages, Mike had warned us, so we had to be prepared to take the call whenever it came.

While I knew Jeremy was technically right—the phone wasn't any more likely to ring while I stared at it—I had to believe we'd get a call soon. After all, we had the most kick-ass parenting profile out there. I knew—I'd become semi-obsessed with studying other couples' ads posted on adoption websites.

Our profile was elegant and simple, but warm at the same

time. Between my photos and Jeremy's text (which I'd had to rewrite extensively), we looked and sounded like something out of a magazine. I'd even managed to make Otis look noble by snapping a shot of him when his head was lifted high and his ears were perked up. No one had to know that at that moment Jeremy was standing behind me, waving a cookie in the air.

"Maybe we should name it," Jeremy suggested.

"You want to name our birth-mother phone?"

"We could call it the Bat Phone," he said.

"I think the Fetus Phone would be more appropriate."

"The Bun-in-the-Oven Hotline?"

"Too much of a mouthful. How about the Stork Cell?"

"That sounds like a prison for wayward birds," Jeremy said.

We grinned at each other. And just then, a phone rang. Jeremy and I both stared at the cell phone in wonder. But then I realized it wasn't ringing; the house phone was. I sighed and picked up.

"Hello?"

"Hey, India, it's Mike Jankowski."

"Hi, Mike. Have any pregnant women desperate to give us their baby hanging around?"

"As a matter of fact, I happen to have one sitting here in my office who wants to talk to you."

"Are you serious? I was kidding!"

"I wasn't. How fast can you and Jeremy get here?" Mike asked.

I opened my mouth, but no sound came out. Jeremy frowned. "Are you okay?" he mouthed at me.

"India?" Mike asked. "Are you still there?"

I cleared my throat and attempted to regain my composure. "I'm here. We'll be there in half an hour."

Jeremy and I broke speed records for dressing (both of us), putting on makeup (me), and letting Otis out before he peed on the bedroom rug again (Jeremy). Once Otis was back in the house, I threw some kibble in his dish, and Jeremy and I sprinted for the car.

"I'll drive," Jeremy said.

"Let me," I countered.

"No way. I hate it when you drive."

"You have control issues," I said. "Do me a favor, and try to hide that from the birth mother. She's not going to want to hand over her baby to a control freak." I attempted to pry the car keys out of his hand.

Jeremy tightened his grip on the keys. "Seriously? You think *I'm* the control freak in this scenario?"

"Okay, fine, you drive. But hurry!"

On the way to the law office, Jeremy asked me questions I didn't have the answers to.

"What's her name?" he asked.

"I don't know."

"How old is she?"

"I don't know. Would that make a difference?"

"Maybe," Jeremy said. "What if she was one of those freakishly old women who get pregnant in their sixties? That would be weird, wouldn't it?"

"I highly doubt she's sixty," I said. My chest was so tight with anxiety it was hard to breathe. I felt the urge to roll the window down and stick my head out into the wind, the way Otis does when he rides in the car, but suppressed it. I didn't want to mess up my hair.

"It's possible, though," Jeremy said.

"No. It's not," I said. "Women in their sixties don't get pregnant by accident. They have fertility treatments. They do IVF. They use donor eggs. As we're all too aware of, it's a long, expensive, and frequently unpleasant process. A woman who's gone through all of that isn't likely to give up her baby at the end of it."

Jeremy considered this. "Maybe you're right," he conceded. Then he brightened. "Unless—just hear me out—*unless* her husband dropped dead of a heart attack, and she decided she was too old to raise the baby on her own!"

"Can we not talk about this right now?"

"Sure. Whatever." Jeremy was quiet for a few minutes. "You know what else would be weird? If the birth mother was pregnant with twins and wanted to adopt the babies out to two separate families. So we'd have one baby, and somewhere out there would be its identical twin. They'd grow up without ever knowing each other, and then one day, they'd bump into each other—at the grocery store, or gas station—and think they were meeting their clone. Wouldn't that be freaky?"

"The Parent Trap," I said.

"What?"

"It was a movie. Hayley Mills starred in it, playing twin sisters. The parents divorced when the girls were babies. One grew up in Boston with the mother, the other in California with the father, and they never knew about each other. Then the girls ended up at the same summer camp. Instead of being devastated by the discovery that their parents had been lying to them for thirteen years and developing an eating disorder or a drug problem like any self-respecting teenager would, the two Hayleys spend the rest of the movie trying to get their parents back together. I can't believe you've never seen it. It's a classic."

"Chick flick," Jeremy said dismissively. "It would be way cooler if it turned out that one of the twins was recruited by the government to be an assassin. And then the other twin didn't know anything about it until she was falsely accused of a murder her assassin twin had actually committed. That's a movie I'd want to see."

"Honey?"

"Yes?"

"I'm about two minutes away from asking Mike Jankowski if he does quickie divorces on the side."

"You might want to keep that to yourself. I have a feeling it wouldn't go down so well with the birth mother," Jeremy said.

By the time we reached the lawyer's downtown office, I could feel sweat dripping down my back. Between the drumroll of my heart and the sickly sensation in my stomach, I was feeling much like my sixteen-year-old self when out on a first date with Kevin Thorn. In fact, that was exactly what meeting with a birth mother was like—a nonsexual version of dating. We were checking her out, too, although we were the desperate ones, so our opinion didn't matter as much. What she thought of us was far more important. In high school terms, she was the star football player who was heading to Harvard with a full sports scholarship, while we were the shy girl with the small breasts, thick glasses, and an intimate knowledge of Jane Austen's collective works.

The receptionist—moon-faced with a wall of eighties-era bangs hairsprayed into place—looked up when we entered the office. We'd been there several times before, but she never seemed to remember us.

"India and Jeremy Halloway," I reminded her. "We're here to see Mike. He's expecting us."

She didn't smile—she never did, at least not that I had ever seen—but instead just punched a few buttons on her phone and said into her headset, "Mike? Mr. and Mrs. Halloway are here. . . . Okay." She looked up at me. "He'll be right out."

Jeremy took my hand and squeezed it. I squeezed it back. Were we really about to meet our baby? Well, not the actual baby, obviously. But the baby would be there in the room with us, even if he or she was out of sight.

Don't get your hopes up, don't get your hopes up, I silently chanted. *The birth mother may not like us. We may not be what she has in mind.*

Mike came out. He was wearing a blinding red Hawaiian shirt with big yellow flowers.

"Hi there," he said jovially, shaking Jeremy's hand and giving me a half hug. "Let's step into the conference room."

As we followed Mike back through the office, my heart started to pound again, and my stomach cramped with nerves. *This is it,* I thought. *This is a moment I'll never forget for the rest of my life.*

I hadn't given a lot of thought to what our baby's birth mother would look like. I was too consumed with fantasies inspired by innumerable BabyGap ads, featuring babies with big grins, round eyes, Nordic-knit hats. I knew this was ridiculous; life was not a BabyGap ad. And babies in South Florida rarely, if ever, wear Nordic-knit hats.

When I did occasionally wonder about the birth mother, I pictured her as a fresh-faced schoolgirl who'd gotten knocked up by her seventeen-year-old boyfriend. She'd be frightened and tearful, and he'd be wearing a varsity letter jacket. I wasn't even sure if kids still wore letter jackets these days; in fact, I was fairly certain they didn't. Still, the picture stuck.

But when Mike opened the door, the conference room was empty.

"Did she leave?" I asked, unable to keep the disappointment tinged with despair out of my voice.

"She's waiting in my office," Mike said. "I wanted to talk to you alone first, to prepare you before you meet her."

"Prepare us for what?" Jeremy said. "What's wrong with her?"

I was glad he said it, because although it sounded ungracious, it was exactly what I was wondering. What if there *was* something wrong with her?

"Nothing," Mike said soothingly. "But do you remember what I told you about how nearly every birth mother we deal with is in crisis?"

Jeremy and I exchanged an alarmed look. I knew we were both picturing the same thing—a woman with a needle full of heroin stuck in her arm. Or popping Haldol while muttering about how the CIA was bugging her thoughts and looking around for a tube of tinfoil to make a hat out of.

"Yes," I said, trying to stay calm. "We remember."

"This woman is no different."

"How old is she?" I asked.

"She's twenty. And she's in a difficult situation. I just want you to be prepared for that before you meet her."

"Mike, you're pretty much freaking us out," Jeremy said. "Just tell us what the issue is."

Mike nodded. "She's homeless," he said.

"You mean she lives on the street?" I asked.

Every news story I had ever read about homeless drug addicts flooded back to me. Suddenly, the sheer helplessness of my position terrified me. I wouldn't just have to worry that the birth mother was taking her prenatal vitamins and eating plenty of green leafy vegetables. I'd have to also pray that the baby—*my* baby—wouldn't be born addicted to crack.

"Don't you have any nice knocked-up teenage girls back there?" I blurted out. "I mean, I keep hearing about the terrible teen pregnancy problem we have in this country. Where are they all?"

Mike and Jeremy looked at me, both startled. Mike cleared his throat.

"I'm sorry. That was inappropriate. I'm just a little nervous," I said.

"I understand. You want a healthy baby," Mike said.

"Yes," I said, relieved that he had instantly understood my concerns. "That's exactly it. We just want a healthy baby."

"But, all things being equal, we'd definitely prefer a pretty baby over an ugly one," Jeremy chipped in. "And if you could find us one with superpowers, that would be even better."

I elbowed Jeremy in the side, harder than I meant to.

"Ouch! Yikes, I was just kidding," he said.

"From what the birth mother tells me, she has not been living on the street," Mike said. "Her boyfriend, who apparently does not support her decision to carry the pregnancy to term, kicked her out of their apartment yesterday."

Anger quickly displaced my fear. "He made her move out because she's pregnant?" I asked. "What a jerk!"

"So that means she's going to need a place to live," Jeremy said.

"Yes, and quickly," Mike said. "I know you wanted some more time to get your finances in order before you took on the cost of the adoption, and I should tell you that if you don't want to work with this birth mother, I do have other couples who would jump on this chance. So there's no pressure if you're not ready. But she did pick out your portfolio, and wants to meet with you first."

"That's great," I said. She'd liked our portfolio best! I knew it rocked! "Can we meet her now?"

"Sure, I'll go get her," Mike said.

Once he'd left, Jeremy looked at me. "Nothing like the hard sell," he said.

"What do you mean?"

"If we don't jump on this, someone else will? No pressure there," Jeremy said, shaking his head.

"I think Mike was just being honest. He was saying that we *shouldn't* feel pressured, because if we don't decide to go forward with her, someone else will," I said. "Besides, I think we should go forward if we like her. Don't you?"

"You heard what he said. She needs a place to live immediately. How are we possibly going to pay for that right now?" Jeremy asked.

"I don't know. We'll think of something."

"India." Jeremy sighed. "We have to be realistic."

But before he could continue, the door opened. Standing there, framed in the doorway, was a remarkably pretty girl dressed in a tight blue tank top and low-rider jeans. She was tall and lean, with high cheekbones and a square chin. Her eyes were so dark they almost looked black in the office light. Almost involuntarily, I glanced down at the girl's abdomen, looking for signs of a bump, but it was so flat as to be almost concave.

Is she really pregnant? I wondered.

"I'm not showing yet," the girl said, reading my thoughts.

"Right. Sorry," I said.

Flushing, I stood so quickly the wheeled chair I'd been sitting on careened off and bumped into the glass wall behind me. I wiped my hands quickly against my skirt and then reached forward to offer my hand. She hesitated for a moment before shaking it. Her reluctance made me wonder if I'd done the wrong thing. Should I have hugged her instead? Surely that would have been too forward, too familiar?

"Hi, I'm India Halloway. This is my husband, Jeremy," I said, gesturing to Jeremy, who was also standing.

"I'm Lainey," she said.

"You've met? Excellent," Mike said, walking briskly into the conference room, a folder in his hand. "Why don't we all take a seat and get started?"

Mike sat at the head of the table, and Lainey sat to his left. Jeremy and I returned to our seats across from Lainey.

"Normally at this point, I like to encourage you to get to know one another and ask any questions you have," Mike said genially, as though we were all meeting at a cocktail party. "India, why don't you begin. Tell Lainey a bit about yourself."

My heart jumped and then began racing. This was it. Time to sell myself. "Sure." I gave Lainey what I hoped was a confident smile. "I'm a portrait photographer. I have my own studio, which I opened five years ago."

Lainey nodded. "I saw your pictures. In that profile thingy."

I'd included some examples of my work in our portfolio—mostly shots of older kids, romping on the beach or sitting in the back of the antique Ford pickup truck I used as a prop, but also some baby portraits. My favorite was a black-and-white close-up of a delicious little baby boy with wide, serious eyes. I knew all too well how pictures could manipulate—the most fractious family in the world could look idyllic and happy if I snapped the shot at just the right moment. But I thought it was important to show potential birth mothers my passion.

"I have complete control over the hours I work," I said. "If—when—we are able to adopt, I plan on taking some time off to be with the baby."

I thought the flexibility both Jeremy and I had with our jobs would be a good selling point. But Lainey just stared at me, her dark eyes inscrutable.

"Jeremy and I have been married for seven years," I continued. "We started trying for a family two years ago, but we found out that I can't get pregnant."

"What's wrong with you?" Lainey asked.

The bluntness of her question surprised me, until I realized she probably wanted to make sure I didn't have any health issues that might affect my ability to parent.

"My body went into early menopause," I said.

"Early menopause," Lainey repeated, and frowned. "I didn't know that could happen."

"I didn't, either," I said ruefully. "But otherwise, I'm very healthy. Jeremy and I both are."

I glanced at Jeremy.

"Very healthy," he echoed. "India power walks every day. And I ride a bike. Well, sometimes I do. It depends on how work is going. Sometimes, if I'm under a deadline, I let the exercise slack a little."

Jeremy always got chatty when he was nervous. I wondered if Lainey was having the same effect on him that she was having on me. There was something about her that put me off balance. Maybe it was just a case of reality not meeting expectation. She was certainly not the hormonal, tearful girl I'd pictured when Mike told us she was in crisis.

"Jeremy's a writer," I explained.

"What do you write?" Lainey asked.

"Science fiction," Jeremy said. "I write a series called Future Race. Have you heard of it?"

Lainey shook her head.

"It's set in the future when extensive genetic manipulation has resulted in people having evolved into several different subspecies. And these different subspecies are at war with one another," Jeremy said. "One group basically wants to live in peace, but other groups aspire to world domination."

I thought I saw interest flare in Lainey's dark eyes. She leaned forward in her seat.

"Cool," she said. "Is there going to be a movie made out of it?"

"No," Jeremy said. "Although I did once get an email from a producer who seemed interested."

"Really? What happened?"

"Actually, nothing," Jeremy said. He smiled wryly. "I never heard back from him again."

Lainey sat back and crossed her arms, clearly disappointed. Jeremy and I exchanged a nervous glance.

I cleared my throat. "So, let's see, what else can we tell you?" I began to rattle off the rest of our background information—where we grew up and went to school, where our parents lived, what our hobbies were—until I realized that I'd been talking for what felt like a long time, and began to worry that I was rambling.

"Jeremy and I can't wait to be parents. It's something we've always wanted, always dreamed about," I said. I took Jeremy's hand. "To be honest, adoption wasn't the path we thought we'd be taking to parenthood, but the more we think about it, and talk about it, the more excited we both are about the idea. So I really want to thank you for considering us."

Lainey looked at me, and I wondered if I'd come on too strong. It's a fine line. It's hard to say *Please, please, please give us your baby* without looking desperate. Then again, we were desperate. But Mike smiled at me as though I'd said just the right thing.

"Do you have any questions for Lainey?" Mike asked.

"When did you find out about your pregnancy?" Jeremy asked.

"Two weeks ago," Lainey said.

We waited for her to go on, and when she didn't, I said, "Have you seen a doctor yet or had any prenatal care?"

"Not really. I went to the women's clinic, but I was planning to get an abortion," Lainey said.

"Do you mind if we ask why you changed your mind and decided on adoption instead?" Jeremy asked.

"When I was at the clinic, the nurse drew some blood, and I fainted. My friend Flaca thought it was a sign that I shouldn't get an abortion," Lainey said.

I felt a twinge of discomfort. If she changed her mind so quickly, she could change it again. I tried to think of a tactful way to feel her out.

"Are you sure that adoption is the right choice for you?" I asked carefully.

"Yes, I'm completely sure," Lainey said.

I nodded, relieved at her self-assurance. I didn't want to talk her out of it, after all. "Do you have any health issues that you know about?"

"I never get sick," Lainey said.

I wasn't sure how to ask the next question—or if she'd give me a truthful answer—but I felt I had to ask. "Do you take recreational drugs? Or drink?"

"Never," Lainey said firmly.

I breathed in, relief filling my lungs, and looked at Mike for guidance. He smiled at me reassuringly.

"Lainey, do you have any questions for India and Jeremy, or is there anything else you'd like to share with them?" Mike asked.

"How soon can I get an apartment?" Lainey asked. "Right now I'm crashing at my best friend's place."

Jeremy and I glanced at each other. I could feel my heart rate kick back up.

"Are you saying . . . you're interested in . . . I mean, you'd consider letting us adopt your baby?" I asked.

"Yeah." Lainey looked surprised. "Isn't that why you're here? Don't you want it?"

Mike cleared his throat. "At this point, it's really more about getting to know one another. This is the time to ask any questions you might have."

"Yes, we want the baby!" I said quickly.

"India," Jeremy said quietly.

I looked at him and bit my lip.

"Excuse me, Mike," Jeremy said. "Is there somewhere India and I could talk privately for a moment?"

"Absolutely," Mike said, standing quickly. "Lainey, are you thirsty? Why don't we go find you a drink? Would you like some bottled water?"

After they left, closing the door behind them, I looked beseechingly at Jeremy. "Don't you think she seems perfect? She's young and healthy, and she doesn't seem at all conflicted about putting the baby up for adoption."

"I know, but India . . . ," Jeremy said. He ran a hand over his head, causing his hair to ruffle up like feathers. "I don't think we can afford this right now. We don't have the money. Maybe if I get some freelance work, and we're really careful, we'll be able to save up. But right now, I don't see how it will work."

"There has to be a way to make it work," I said. Tears of frustration burned in my eyes.

"Please don't make me be the bad guy here," Jeremy said gently. He took my hand. "I can't snap my fingers and change the reality of our situation."

"What if I took on more work? I could try to get some jobs shooting weddings. They pay well."

"You hate doing weddings. The bridezillas always drive you crazy."

"I don't care. I'm willing to do whatever it takes. I'll even go to those awful bridal expos to drum up business."

"You could. But it would take months to expand your business. You heard Lainey. She needs a place to live now."

A place to live now. It was too bad she couldn't just move in with us, I thought. But, no, that was crazy. Or was it?

"I think I might have just had the most brilliant idea ever," I said slowly.

"What?"

"What if Lainey stays with us?"

"You mean in our house?"

"No, of course not. She wouldn't be comfortable with that. But she could stay in the guesthouse."

"The guesthouse," Jeremy repeated.

"Why not? It has its own bathroom and kitchenette," I said, growing more enthusiastic with each passing moment. "We can fix it up for her, get it furnished."

"It's my office," Jeremy said.

"You can work in the house for a few months. You did before, when we were renovating."

"A few months? She's not even showing yet. It'll be a lot longer than that."

"Jeremy, think about it—it's the perfect solution. Between saving on her rent, and my picking up some weddings, we might just be able to swing this," I said.

"And have a stranger living in our backyard?"

"She's not a stranger. She's the mother of our future child."

"She's a stranger," Jeremy said firmly. "We know next to nothing about her. What if she's on drugs, or has sketchy friends who like to steal things? What if her boyfriend is some sort of a psychopath?"

"She said the boyfriend kicked her out. I doubt they'll be hanging out together," I said. "And you heard her. She said she doesn't do drugs."

"So she says," Jeremy said.

"Look, I hear what you're saying. You're worried that we don't know much about her. But we could set some rules ahead of time, and just do it on a trial basis," I said. "If we run into a problem, we'll deal with it then."

"You don't even know if she'd want to live so near us. There are probably lots of couples out there who'd be happy to rent her a condo," Jeremy said.

"But for whatever reason, she chose us. Out of all of the adoptive-couple profiles, she liked ours the best. You heard her. She wants *us* to adopt her baby. The least we can do is ask her. All she can say is no," I pleaded.

Jeremy hesitated, but finally he nodded. "Let's just run it by Mike first."

I could tell Mike wasn't thrilled with the idea. "It's unorthodox," he said.

"You told us to get creative," I argued. "Besides, this way we'll be able to look after Lainey. Make sure she's eating properly, getting enough sleep."

"It's possible that knowing you're nearby might keep her from engaging in negative behavior," Mike admitted. I was pleased that he saw the wisdom in this, until Mike continued. "But there's another factor I think you're missing. What if you get too close to her? Or she to you?"

"What exactly are you saying? Birth mothers who get to know the adoptive parents are less likely to go through with the adoption? Or that she would go through with it, but might then be stopping by the house every day for the next eighteen years?" Jeremy asked.

"Actually, no. Lainey has specified that she doesn't want to have any contact with the child or the adoptive parents after the adoption is finalized. She doesn't even want a yearly update or photo. So that will be written into the contract," Mike said.

I glanced at Jeremy. I could tell he was somewhat mollified.

"If either of you has a better solution for how we can cover her living expenses, please tell me. Because we don't have an extra three grand a month right now, but we do have an empty guest cottage," I said.

Mike spread his hands, a motion of defeat. "We might as well present the idea to Lainey. But be prepared that she might not want to do this."

I nodded, my nerves jangling. Jeremy didn't say a word, although when Mike left to fetch Lainey back, he gave me a long look.

"What?" I said.

Jeremy just shook his head. "This worries me," he said.

"If you're really against this, we don't have to do it," I said.

"I'm not saying I'm against it. I'm just concerned."

"Should I go stop Mike before he talks to Lainey?"

Jeremy sighed and ran a hand through his hair. "No. Let's give it a try."

"Are you sure?"

"What's the worst that can happen? Wait, no, don't answer that," Jeremy joked.

Mike returned, leading Lainey back into the conference room.

"India and Jeremy have a proposal to make," Mike said, once they were seated. "They want to make it clear that they're not putting any pressure on you to agree to this, and that the decision is totally up to you. If you're not comfortable with the idea, just say so."

I wasn't sure if I should be annoyed with Mike for what could be read as a caution, or grateful that he was delivering our proposal in such a way that Lainey wouldn't feel pressured. I folded my hands on the table, and attempted to look maternal, while Mike explained our proposal. When he was finished, Lainey looked from Mike to us, and then back at Mike again.

"Okay," she said. "When can I move in?"

"Really?" I asked, barely believing it. She hadn't even hesitated.

Lainey shrugged. "I just need a place to stay for a while. Is your guesthouse nice?"

"Yes, very nice," I said. "It's right off the swimming pool. It has two rooms—a bedroom and a sitting room—and a private bath. There's a little kitchenette in the sitting room." I decided to leave out the fact that for now, at least, the sitting room was actually Jeremy's office.

"Yeah, it's fine with me," Lainey said, with another shrug.

"Lainey, do you mind if I ask what your plans are after you have the baby?" Jeremy asked suddenly. I tensed. What if she took the question the wrong way? What if Lainey thought he was implying that she'd be a freeloader and would never leave?

"I'm moving to Los Angeles. I've been saving up to go. I do nails," she added.

"Nails?" Jeremy asked.

"Manicures, pedicures, you know. I work in a place at the mall," Lainey said.

"What are you going to do in L.A.? Are you going to work in a salon there?" I asked. Then, worried that I might be offending her by underestimating her ambition, I added, "Or are you planning on opening your own salon?"

Lainey blinked and then shook off this suggestion. "No way. I'm not going there to work in another salon. I'm going to be on television. On a reality show."

"You mean those shows where people eat bugs?" Jeremy asked. "I saw one where they had to eat camel lips. I think that would be worse than the bugs. The lips were actually still *hairy*. Imagine what it would be like to eat that. I mean, you're putting it in your mouth, you're chewing . . . and you can feel the camel's lip hair."

Lainey stood suddenly, clapped both hands to her mouth, and rushed from the room.

"What just happened?" Jeremy asked.

"I think you made our birth mother throw up," I said.

Jeremy looked sheepish. "Sorry. I didn't realize it was going to have that effect on her," he said.

"Should I go check on her?" I asked.

Mike shook his head. "I'm sure she just needs a few moments to compose herself," he said. "Now, are you sure you're ready to go forward? I know that Lainey's living arrangement means we have to move somewhat quickly, but we can always put her up in a hotel for a few nights while you all think it over, and perhaps take the time to get to know one another."

As sensible as this advice sounded, I felt a wrench of panic. If Jeremy and I took the time to think it over, then Lainey would, too. What if she changed her mind about us? What if she looked through more adoptive-parent profiles and found a couple she liked better?

"No, we're sure. At least, I think we are," I said, glancing at Jeremy. "Are we?"

Jeremy nodded. "We might as well give it a try," he said.

"Try what?" Lainey asked. We all looked up to see her standing at the door of the conference room. She looked a little pale, but otherwise seemed okay. She was young, I realized. Only twenty years old. But her poise made her seem older. When I was her age, I was a sophomore in college and in the middle of a phase where I wore all-black clothing, blood-red lipstick, and listened to nihilistic music.

"The living arrangements India and Jeremy suggested. If you're still interested, of course," Mike said.

Lainey nodded, and shrugged. "Yeah, sure."

As much as I wanted to bank on her agreement, I hesitated. "Are you sure you don't want to take some time to think about all of this?" I said. "I'll tell you right now, we'd love to adopt your baby, but we understand if you need some time to make your decision. We don't want you to feel pressured."

I knew I was giving her an out, but if she was going to change her mind—if she decided to terminate the pregnancy, or keep the baby rather than giving it up for adoption—I'd rather she did so now rather than six months from now when we were attached.

But Lainey shook her head. "I don't need any time," she said firmly. And then, as if she'd read my thoughts, she added, "And I'm not going to change my mind."

My hands started to shake. It was surreal. After everything that we'd been through, after all the months of trying and the constant failure, it was finally happening. We were going to have a baby. This was happening. It was really, really happening.

I was going to be a mother.

Five
LAINEY

As soon as Lainey saw the Halloways' house, she knew she'd been screwed over. She stood on the sidewalk, waiting as Jeremy unloaded the garbage bags that served as her luggage out of the trunk, and stared up at the house.

It was a lot smaller than she had expected. A *whole* lot smaller. When India had told her they had a guesthouse, Lainey had assumed the Halloways lived in a mansion, maybe on the water, with a housekeeper and a big swimming pool in the back. Instead, they were parked in front of a pink stucco granny house that wasn't much bigger than Candace's cinderblock duplex. Admittedly, it was tidier than Candace's house—the landscaping was lush and green, the lawn newly mown, the paint fresh—but still. Definitely not a mansion. Not even close.

They're not rich, Lainey realized.

Anger began to pulse through her. She knew that she couldn't sell the baby outright to India and Jeremy—the old lawyer guy had made *that* clear enough, he'd only told her about four zillion times—but *still*. She'd assumed that they'd funnel a good chunk of cash her way under the table. Did they really expect her to spend the next six months getting fat and stretched out for nothing?

"What do you think?" India asked nervously.

Lainey turned to look at her. India had seemed nice enough at the attorney's office. A bit tense and twitchy, but okay. But Lainey could feel her resentment growing, quickly sharpening into hatred. These people had known she was desperate with nowhere to live, and they'd taken advantage of her.

"There's a playground just down the street, and the beach isn't too far away," India said. "And there are all sorts of neighborhood activities. We have a big block party every year on the Fourth of July, and there's trick-or-treating at Halloween, and at Christmas people go all out with their decorations. The light displays are gorgeous."

Lainey stared at India, wondering why she was telling her all of this. Did India expect her to get dressed up in a costume and go trick-or-treating? Or hang out with their neighbors? What sort of weirdos were they anyway?

"It's the perfect place to raise a family," India continued.

Lainey suddenly realized India was talking about the *baby's* future, not hers. Another surge of anger washed over her. The Halloways were getting what they wanted. They were getting the baby. But what was she getting out of this?

As India blathered on about the benefits of raising a child in this neighborhood, Lainey glanced around, wondering what exactly was supposed to be so great about it. All of the houses were small and old, and it didn't seem even remotely glamorous. Maybe she should have moved to Los Angeles and had the baby there, where it could have been adopted by movie stars. She noticed the car in front of the house across the street from the Halloways' house. Lainey squinted: It was a Cadillac Escalade. That wasn't a cheap car. Weird. Why would someone who could afford that car live in such a small house?

"Flamingo Park is a historic neighborhood," India continued. "Most of the houses here were built in the 1920s. It's actually hard to find a house to buy here—when one goes on the market it frequently sells the same day it's listed."

"So, what, the houses here are worth a lot of money?" Lainey asked.

"Well," India hesitated. "The houses are usually valued at a higher price per square foot than most in the county. They're on the small side, but you should see some of the interiors. There are homes here that have been photographed for magazines."

"So you *are* rich," Lainey said, relieved.

"What?" India looked startled.

"Ready for the grand tour?" Jeremy asked, shutting the trunk.

"Sure," Lainey said, shrugging.

The house might be small, but Lainey had to admit that it was pretty nice inside. The living room had matching sofas with white slipcovers, glossy black tables, a large sisal rug, and pots of orchids. On the walls were black-and-white photos of beaches. The television was shitty, though—it was the old kind, small and boxy. Trav had a big flat-screen, so large it dominated one whole wall of the living room in their apartment.

"India took those," Jeremy said, when he noticed Lainey eyeing the photographs.

"That's the beach where Jeremy and I met," India said.

Lainey nodded, but didn't say anything.

"You're not afraid of dogs, are you?" India asked.

Lainey shook her head, although truthfully, she wasn't a fan. Dogs had always grossed her out, with their constant drooling and musty stink.

India left the room, and Lainey heard her talking to someone, and a moment later, the sound of nails scrabbling on tile. A shaggy black and white dog lumbered into the room, heading straight for Lainey. She backed up a few steps, but the dog kept coming. He raced right up to her and began snuffling at her knees and feet.

"This is Otis," India said, reappearing.

"Does he bite?" Lainey asked, holding her hands up.

"Just don't make any sudden moves," Jeremy warned. "And avoid direct eye contact."

Lainey looked at him in alarm.

"Kidding! I was just kidding," he said quickly. He smiled sheepishly and balled his hands into the pockets of his khaki pants. "Otis is a lover, not a fighter."

Otis sat down heavily, panting. His long, shaggy tail thumped on the ground. Lainey tentatively patted his head, which he seemed to like.

Lainey noticed that India kept staring at her intently, while Jeremy seemed to be looking anywhere but at her. Normally, it was the other way around—men stared, while the women tried to ignore her. Was everything upside down here? Rich people living in small houses with crappy TVs, men who didn't pay attention to her? The whole thing was weird.

Jeremy disappeared while India showed her around the rest of the downstairs of the house. There was a dining room with a big table surrounded by black chairs, a kitchen with white cupboards and butcher-block countertops, a small bathroom papered with floral wallpaper. Lainey looked at everything, but said little, so India filled the silence by chattering nervously about all the work they'd done since they'd moved in—hardwood floors that were refinished, walls that were knocked down, bathroom fittings that had been replaced.

"Jeremy and I did most of the work ourselves," India said. "I never thought I'd be such a whiz with a table saw. So, would you like to see the guesthouse?"

Lainey shrugged. "Sure."

"I have to warn you—Jeremy's been using it as an office, so we'll have to move things around a bit. He's out there now, clearing out his stuff," India said.

India opened the kitchen door that led to a patio. Lainey was relieved to see the pool. It was just a small, kidney-shaped pool, not the waterfront Infinity one she'd expected, but it was better than nothing. Back behind the pool was the guesthouse. It was a miniature version of the main house, painted the same stupid shade of pink, and surrounded by bougainvillea bushes. Jeremy came out with a laptop under one arm and a box under the other.

"Where should I dump this?" he asked India.

"The dining room," she replied.

Jeremy nodded. "I brought your things inside," he said to Lainey.

"And here's your new home," India said, opening the door, and standing back so Lainey could enter the guesthouse ahead of her.

Like the main house, it was smaller than she'd expected, but even so, Lainey had to admit—to herself, at least—that it was pretty nice. The interior was painted a soothing shade of sage green with crisp white trim. There was a small living room with a kitchenette along one side, and a door off the living room that opened onto a bedroom furnished with a queen-sized canopy bed draped in gauzy white curtains. The only furniture in the living room was a desk, a mostly empty bookshelf, and a leather arm-chair with a matching ottoman.

"Like I said, we'll have to move some things around," India said. "Obviously, Jeremy's desk will have to go, and probably the bookshelf, too. We have a love seat in our bedroom that will fit perfectly in here." India pointed to the space the desk occupied. "And you'll also need a coffee table, and a few lamps. We'll make it nice and cozy for you."

"Where's the TV?" Lainey asked.

"There isn't one in here, but you can watch our TV whenever you want," India said.

No TV? This was even worse than she'd first thought. Lainey suddenly felt exhausted, and she yawned without bothering to cover her mouth.

"You're tired," India said instantly. "Why don't you lie down and rest?"

"Yeah, I think I will," Lainey said. She was supposed to be at the salon, two hours into an eight-hour shift, but she'd blown it off. It would probably mean she'd be fired, but now that she had a free place to stay and—hopefully—a steady source of cash, who cared? Her body ached, and she could feel twinges of nausea prickling in her stomach and throat.

"We're so happy to have you here," India said. She stepped forward and put her arms around Lainey in an awkward embrace. Lainey stood stiffly, not returning the hug.

"Let me know if you need anything," India said, stepping back. She smiled nervously at Lainey, and then finally left, shutting the door behind her.

It took Lainey a long time to wake up. She felt like she was swimming slowly through murky, dream-filled water. When she finally was able to open her eyes, it took her a few beats to remember where she was and how she had gotten there. Then she remembered: the pregnancy. The adoption. The Halloways.

Lainey sat up. Her new bed was incredibly comfortable, so much so that she'd fallen asleep as soon as she crawled under the fluffy white duvet. But now she felt hot—she kicked the duvet off her legs—and was overcome with a stomach-gnawing hunger. What time was it? She glanced at the clock on the bedside table. No wonder she was hungry. It was already six o'clock. She'd been asleep for hours.

She got up, headed into the other room, and poked around the kitchenette. There wasn't much in the way of food there. Only a single package of chocolate cookies. Lainey opened it and devoured several of them, licking the crumbs from her fingers. Then she left the cottage and headed over to the main house, skirting around the perimeter of the rinky-dink pool. A long pink raft floated dejectedly in the middle of the water.

When Lainey got to the back door, she hesitated. What if the dog attacked her? Sure, they'd claimed he wasn't vicious, but people always said that. When Lainey was a kid, a family who lived down the block had a pit bull they kept chained in their front yard. They insisted their dog was harmless, but every time Lainey passed by, walking to and from school, the dog would lunge against the fence, barking and snarling at her, foam spraying from his mouth. She'd once seen him catch a squirrel and eat it whole.

Lainey knocked instead. No one answered, and the dog didn't come rushing in, so Lainey opened the door and walked in. There were signs of dinner preparations in the kitchen. Three raw steaks sat on the counter, lettuce leaves were resting in a colander in the sink, a pot of peeled potatoes bubbled on the stovetop, a pan of brownies sat cooling on the counter. Interestingly, the sight of the raw meat didn't make Lainey feel like retching, as the chicken breasts Flaca had Shake 'n Baked the night before had.

It was all so homey, Lainey thought. Were they putting on a show for her benefit, or did they always eat like this? Was this what the kid had to look forward to, a life of steaks and home-baked brownies? Lainey felt another surge of resentment. Why didn't she have this sort of life when she was growing up? Where would she be now if she had? Probably not knocked up by a steroid-addicted gym rat.

Otis suddenly came scrabbling into the kitchen, his leash still attached, and headed straight for Lainey. The dog jumped up on her, leaving two muddy paw prints on her shirt. Lainey let out a shriek of surprise.

"What's wrong?" India asked as she rushed into the kitchen. "Otis! Get down! Oh, God, Lainey, are you okay?" She grabbed Otis's leash and dragged him away. "Bad dog! Here, sit down, Lainey. Can I get you anything? A glass of water?"

"What's wrong?" Jeremy asked, appearing in the doorway to the kitchen.

"The hellhound jumped up on Lainey."

"I'm fine," Lainey said as India handed the leash to Jeremy.

"He always gets excited at dinnertime," Jeremy explained.

"Otis, you should know better," India scolded. "You could have hurt the baby."

The dog looked unrepentant. He sat down heavily and, licking his chops, stared fixedly at the steaks. India shook her head at him.

"Otis flunked out of obedience school. Seriously. The instructor asked us not to return. She said Otis was a bad influence on the other dogs," Jeremy told Lainey.

Lainey nodded unsmilingly. At the realization that India's concern was for the baby and not for her, Lainey felt something harden inside of her. No matter how nice or sympathetic India acted, Lainey reminded herself that she couldn't get sucked into thinking it was for her benefit. Everyone had an angle. India was no different.

The doorbell rang, and Otis started barking and pulling on his leash.

"Who could that be?" India wondered out loud.

Everything—the house, the dog, the rich aroma of the baking brownies—suddenly made Lainey feel like she'd walked onto the set of a television sitcom. What now? A neighbor stopping by to deliver homemade cookies? Hearing voices at the door, Lainey trailed after India and Jeremy. In the front hall, they were greeting a couple. The woman was curvy and wore a mustard yellow sundress and very high red heels. A cloud of dark hair swirled down to her shoulders. The man was short—shorter than his wife in heels—and neat, with close-cropped thinning hair, a long, elegant nose, and expressive brown eyes. He was holding a bottle of wine.

"What are you guys doing here?" India was asking.

"Don't tell me you forgot," the dark-haired woman said, laughing.

"Forgot what?" India asked.

"Dinner tonight? You invited us over? Is any of this ringing a bell?"

India gasped and covered her mouth with her hands.

"She forgot us," the woman said, sighing and turning to her husband. "We managed to get a babysitter for once—no small miracle, considering the reputation our children have among the local babysitter circuit—and she forgets all about us." The woman then saw Lainey and smiled at her. "Hi, I'm Mimi."

"Oh! I didn't see you there, Lainey," India said. She looked momentarily distracted. "Lainey, these are good friends of ours, Mimi and Leo Carrera. This is Lainey. She's going to be staying with us for a while."

India tripped over the explanation, almost, Lainey thought, as though she were embarrassed by Lainey's presence.

"Hi," Lainey said flatly.

"Staying with you?" Mimi turned to look at India for further explanation. India looked from Mimi to Lainey, clearly unsure of how to proceed.

"They're adopting my baby," Lainey announced. But this didn't seem to clarify matters for Mimi and Leo. They gaped at her with twin expressions of incomprehension.

"You're having a baby?" Mimi finally asked.

"I'm pregnant," Lainey clarified. "They're going to adopt it after it's born."

Mimi gasped, spun around, and pulled India into a hug. "You didn't tell me you'd found a birth mother!"

"It all happened very quickly. Just today," India said.

"No wonder you forgot about dinner!" Mimi turned to look at Lainey again. "And you're staying here? For the duration of your pregnancy?"

Lainey wasn't sure what Mimi meant. "Until I have the baby," she said.

"Is that common? For the birth mother to live with the adoptive parents, I mean," Mimi asked India.

Jeremy shook his head. "No. Highly unusual, in fact."

"It's a creative solution," India said. "Lainey needed someplace to live, and we have the guesthouse."

"I thought you work back there?" Leo asked Jeremy.

"Worked. Past tense," Jeremy said.

"Ah," Leo said. "Sore subject?"

"Of course not," India interjected. "Anyway, why are we all standing at the door? Come in, have a drink."

"Why don't we go, and we'll just do this another night," Mimi offered. "You have enough on your plate at the moment without having to feed us."

"Absolutely not," India said. "I'll just send Jeremy out for some extra steaks. We have more than enough of everything else. Besides, we should celebrate having Lainey here with us!"

Lainey had never been to a dinner party before. There had been some family barbecues over the years, where everyone drank too much and someone always ended up starting a fight.

Dinner that first night at the Halloways' house couldn't have been more different. They ate in the dining room, used cloth napkins, and wine was served with the meal. The wine actually caused a tense standoff, when Jeremy offered Lainey a glass and India sharply reminded him that Lainey couldn't drink. Mimi chipped in that she'd indulged in the occasional glass of wine while pregnant, until Leo caught her eye and shook his head slightly. Lainey rolled her eyes.

"I don't want any wine. I don't drink," Lainey announced.

"What, never?" Mimi asked. She leaned forward, intrigued.

"Never. It makes you bloat," Lainey explained.

"Lainey's planning to go into the entertainment industry," India explained. "She's saving up to move to Los Angeles."

"Really? What are you going to do there?" Mimi asked.

"I'm going to star in a reality television show," Lainey said.

Mimi looked impressed. "Wow! Which one?"

Lainey immediately regretted announcing her plans. She felt stupid now, having to admit, "I don't know yet. I'm going to audition once I get there."

Mimi studied her. "I could definitely see you on one of those shows," she said, twirling her wineglass.

This was the first time anyone had ever said this to Lainey. "Really?"

"Absolutely. I bet you're really photogenic. You have great features. Very well defined."

"Thanks," Lainey said. She suddenly realized that everyone was looking at her. She stared down at her plate, feeling like she couldn't catch her breath.

Her dining companions seemed to sense her discomfort. Mimi spooned a dollop of mashed potatoes on her plate and said, "We went to the movies last weekend."

"What did you see?" Jeremy asked, obviously eager to change the subject.

"Some weird French film. It was called *La Dame en Bleu.*"

"You didn't like it?" India asked.

"No, it was terrible. It had subtitles, and, as you know, I have a very strict rule against subtitles," Mimi said, waving her fork in emphasis. "I don't go to the movies to read."

"Philistine," Leo said, smiling at his wife. "I liked it better than Mimi. It was French, so of course it ended in madness and death."

"This is one of those areas where Leo and I will never agree. He likes depressing films. I prefer my movies to have happy endings," Mimi said.

"Mimi likes car chases and explosions," Leo added.

Mimi nodded enthusiastically. "That's right. And lots of sex, too."

"I like anything from the eighties. That was the golden era of Hollywood moviemaking," India said.

"What are you talking about? Isn't that when *Porky's* came out?" Leo asked, laughing at her.

"Okay, that was a terrible movie," India admitted. "I was thinking more along the lines of *Heathers* and *Ferris Bueller's Day Off.*"

"Oh, I love *Ferris!*" Mimi agreed. "The eighties are also when all of those great Tom Cruise movies came out: *All the Right Moves*, *Risky Business*, *Top Gun.*"

"I'm going to have to stop you there," Jeremy cut in. "*Top Gun?* Terrible movie."

"And totally gay," Leo said.

"Gay? How is *Top Gun* gay?" Mimi demanded. "It had that yummy scene between Tom Cruise and what's-her-name."

"Kelly McGillis," India said.

Mimi pointed at her. "Yes! Thank you."

"Totally gay," Leo said. "Right, Jeremy?"

"I'm afraid I'm going to have to side with your husband on this one," Jeremy said.

"Are you serious?" Mimi exclaimed.

"The locker room scene with Maverick and Iceman," Leo said. "You could tell they were about thirty seconds away from dropping their towels," Leo said. "And Kelly McGillis was a virtual man."

"Actually, I read a theory somewhere," Jeremy began.

"Somewhere?" India repeated.

"Fine. I read it on the Internet," Jeremy admitted. "But that doesn't mean it's not true. Anyway, this—" he cleared his throat, "—*source* theorized that *Top Gun* is actually an allegory about Maverick choosing between a heterosexual path, symbolized by Kelly McGillis's character, and a homosexual life, symbolized by Iceman and Goose."

"You are totally ruining this movie for me," Mimi complained.

Jeremy and Leo sniggered, but India continued with her thesis. "Anyway, the eighties was the era of John Hughes. *Weird Science. Uncle Buck.* And, most importantly of all, the Molly Trilogy."

Lainey had no idea what any of them were talking about. At least she'd heard of Tom Cruise and *Top Gun,* although she'd never seen the movie. But who was John Hughes? And what was the Molly Trilogy? Not that she was about to ask. Instead, she forked another piece of steak in her mouth, even though her appetite had vanished, replaced by another wave of nausea.

"The Molly Trilogy!" Mimi repeated in rapturous tones. "Those were the best movies."

"Chick flicks," Jeremy said.

"Trilogy?" Leo frowned. "*Sixteen Candles, Pretty in Pink...* what was the third?"

"*Isn't she ... pretty in pink,*" Jeremy sang, while pouring himself another glass of wine.

Lainey glanced sideways and caught India studying her. India smiled encouragingly. Lainey stared back down at her plate. The steak was oozing bloody red juices onto the plate. Her stomach lurched unpleasantly.

"*The Breakfast Club,* of course," Mimi said.

"*The Breakfast Club,*" Leo repeated. His thick eyebrows drew down. "But that wasn't really a Molly Ringwald movie. It was more of an ensemble cast."

"She was one of the leads," Mimi said.

"The greatest movie of the eighties is not in dispute," Jeremy announced.

"He's going to say *This Is Spinal Tap,*" India muttered to Mimi, who rolled her eyes.

"*This Is Spinal Tap,*" Jeremy said, raising his wineglass in a toast to the table.

"See?" India said.

"Boy movie," Mimi said. "If a girl movie is a chick flick, what do they call boy movies? Dick flicks?"

"My high school boyfriend made me watch *Spinal Tap* fifteen times," India said.

"One time is too many," Mimi said. She smiled at Lainey. "Don't you agree, Lainey? Boy movie, right?"

"I never heard of it," Lainey said.

Her four dining companions stared at her.

"Are you serious?" Leo asked.

India quickly came to Lainey's defense. "It was way before her time."

"If you're going to live here, we're going to have to remedy this deficiency in your education immediately," Jeremy said.

"The bigger the cushion, the sweeter the—" Leo began singing. He stopped abruptly. "Ow! Did you just kick me?" he asked Mimi, affronted.

Mimi raised her eyebrows and tilted her head toward Lainey. "Considering we've just met Lainey, I think now is not the time to sing pornographic lyrics in front of her, honey."

"Oh. Sorry," Leo said to Lainey.

Lainey nodded and shrugged. She still had no idea what they were talking about. And the pressure of trying to keep up, to make some sense out of the conversation, was exhausting.

"Not that my wife will believe this—she thinks that I like only foreign movies with subtitles," Leo began.

"Depressing foreign movies," Mimi interrupted. "Particularly ones that are meant to be deeply profound, but really just don't make any sense at all. They're cinematic versions of those modern paintings that are just a blank canvas with a black dot in the middle and everyone thinks that this somehow makes them deep."

Leo continued, ignoring her. "But I've always been partial to Bill Murray's earlier work: *Meatballs, Stripes, Caddyshack.*"

India and Mimi both groaned and began to argue with the men. But Lainey couldn't take it anymore. She stood abruptly. All conversation came to a sudden halt as the Halloways and Carreras stared up at her.

"I'm tired. I'm going to go back to my room," Lainey said.

"Of course," India said quickly.

"I was the same way during my pregnancies. I could never stay awake past eight o'clock," Mimi sympathized.

"Do you need anything? Do you want to take a brownie back with you?" India asked, also standing.

Lainey wondered if India was planning on escorting her back to the guesthouse. "No, I'm fine. I just want to go to sleep." Her stomach gave another queasy shift.

"Good night," everyone chorused.

"Nice to meet you," Mimi said.

Lainey, turning to leave, didn't respond. She was fairly sure that if she opened her mouth, she'd throw up right there, in the middle of the living room.

Six
JEREMY

I hated working in the dining room. It was too open, too exposed. Every time India walked by, or Lainey went into the kitchen to scrounge around for snacks, or Otis scratched himself, I was interrupted. Writing fiction requires a suspension of reality—you have to submerge yourself in your made-up world in order to create it. It was impossible to do this with the constant distractions.

So I did the only thing I really could do under the circumstances: I spent most of my time surfing the Internet. I was particularly fascinated to discover a sci-fi fan site that had a message board dedicated to my series, Future Race. The board was called FutureRaceFanatics, and had two dozen posters, including at least five who seemed to be regular commentators. They discussed all manner of Future Race lore—characters, plotlines, speculation on future books. The amazing thing was that these readers had found all sorts of symbolism in the books that I hadn't consciously placed there.

My favorite poster went by the handle HippyChick and had a grinning skull with a bowtie as her avatar. She posted things like:

> HippyChick: Book Four just proves what a GE-
> NIUS Jeremy Halloway really is!!!! I especially

loved how Acton turned out to be the killer! I actually gasped out loud when I read that, because I was sure that Yael—the guy with three arms—was going to turn out to be the bad guy! I also loved how it foreshadowed the Griff/Juliet romance of Book Five. I'm so hoping that they'll stay together, even though their differential DNA means that they won't be able to have kids.

She also defended me from detractors. One poster—Xerxon—posted the message board equivalent of a drive-by shooting, calling Book Five—*The Battle at Quad Vector-Nine*—"a derivative, wholly unoriginal series that rips off both *X-Men* and *The Terminator* and yet isn't half as interesting as either." HippyChick took him out with a flamethrower:

> HippyChick: Only a COMPLETE MORON could read these BRILLIANT books and call them UNORIGINAL!!!! Obviously you don't have the BRAINS to grasp the complexities of a series like Future Race!!!! Ugh, I won't even waste my time on you. Go back to your comic books, and stay off our boards, you TROLL!!!!!!!

I liked her spunk. I considered posting on the boards, and thanking them for their kind words and support, but decided against it. I didn't want to be caught Googling myself. It lacked dignity.

The phone ringing interrupted my cyber-sneaking. I made sure to close the browser before answering, in case India or Lainey came in and saw what I was reading. It was yet another downside to working in the dining room—my computer screen was in full view for anyone passing by to see. It wasn't like I spent my time surfing porn sites, but it reminded me unpleasantly of what it had been like to work in an office—always having to be on edge that your boss would walk in at any moment and catch you goofing off. The whole point of being self-employed was the freedom to slack without censure.

"Hello," I said.

"Hey, yourself," a familiar voice said. It was my brother, Peter. He was two years older, worked in the thrilling field of podiatry, and lived in Jacksonville, less than a mile away from our parents' house. Whenever I spoke to Peter, and he brought up his new car, or flat-screen television, or the trip he was taking with his dim-witted wife, Stacey, I tried to remind myself of how I, too, had once had a lucrative job—soul-sucking, it was true, but lucrative, or at least more lucrative than my current career—and had given it up to live my dream of being a writer. It always made me feel a bit better, at least right up until my monthly mortgage statement arrived.

"What's up with you? Anything new?" Peter asked. And then, without waiting for a response, he continued, "Stacy and I have some big news!"

I knew what he was going to say even before he completed his announcement.

"Break out the cigars, little bro! Stacey's pregnant!"

"Wow. Congratulations," I said, wondering if there was any possible way I could hide my sister-in-law's pregnancy, along with the future child, from India.

"It's crazy, isn't it? Can you believe it? Me, a dad," Peter said. "Mom's ecstatic. She's already going crazy buying crap for the baby, and we don't even know if it's a boy or a girl yet."

So our mother knew. That meant it would only be a matter of time—days, certainly, maybe even hours—until India found out. I sighed. I was going to have to break the news to her before my mother got to her first.

When India arrived home, I followed her into our bedroom, where she was swapping her black knit top and khakis for a T-shirt and faded denim cutoffs. I sat down on the edge of the bed, watching her change.

"I had the most amazing idea today. It just came to me while I was doing a shoot at the beach," India said, as she pulled a T-shirt with the caption THAT'S HOW I ROLL screen printed across the chest. "It was a mom-and-daughter portrait. The little girl was about three, and her mom was pregnant. It was pretty cute. The girl was wearing a pink and green sundress, and the mom was wearing green jeans with a pink polo," India said. "It gave me the most amazing idea for a show."

"Portraits of people wearing color-coordinated outfits?" I asked. "Preppies on the beach?"

"Pregnant women!" India said. "I'm going to do a series of tummy portraits."

"Tummy portraits?" I repeated, suddenly picturing photos of naked women with swollen stomachs and heavy, pendulous breasts.

"A lot of photographers are doing them. Ever since Demi Moore posed pregnant on the cover of *Vanity Fair*, it's become popular among women, even regular suburban moms, to have a pregnancy portrait taken. I haven't done a lot of them myself, but I was thinking it would be a great area to branch into. I could do a whole series and then have a show at my studio. Who knows, maybe I'll become the go-to person in West Palm, in all of South Florida, even, for maternity portraiture."

She was bright-eyed and pink-cheeked in her enthusiasm. Even her hair seemed to crackle with energy as it danced and bounced off her shoulders.

I looked at her, nonplussed.

"What?" she asked.

"You're not seriously considering this," I said.

"Why wouldn't I be?"

"Um, because it's a terrible idea?"

India fisted her hands against her hips and frowned at me. "That's pretty much the opposite of supportive," she said.

"India." I sighed. "Just last month, we had to leave the Palm Beach Grill before we'd even had dinner because there was a woman with a newborn baby sitting at the next table. The month before that, you refused to go to that baby shower for your friend Mona."

"Not friend," India qualified. "She's a distant acquaintance. And really, it's tacky to invite people you hardly know to your shower just to get extra presents."

"My point is that you—understandably—have a hard time being around pregnant women. So why voluntarily put yourself in a position where you're photographing their pregnant stomachs?"

"I photograph babies all the time," India countered.

"Pregnant stomachs are different. It's almost like . . . well, fetishizing them."

"It is not." India rolled her eyes, grabbed a stack of laundry off the bed, and walked into the closet to put them away. "I'm just thinking of creative ways to expand my business. You're the one who's always saying we need to make more money."

"You're really going to go with that line of argument? That you're doing this for the money?" I asked.

India turned around to meet my gaze. Her expression was defiant. "So maybe I'm not. Maybe I want to celebrate our baby, our unconventional pregnancy. What's wrong with that?"

"You're planning to photograph Lainey?"

India nodded, her eyes brightening. "If she'll let me. I'd love to take a series of photographs of her, documenting the changes in her body as she goes through the pregnancy," she added.

"Have you talked to Lainey about it?"

"No, not yet. I just got the idea today. Why? Do you think she'll mind?"

I shrugged. "I have no idea. Who knows what Lainey thinks about anything? She isn't exactly easy to read."

"I know what you mean. I think she's just overwhelmed by everything. She's had some pretty big changes to adjust to lately. Breaking up with her boyfriend, the unplanned pregnancy, moving in here. It's a lot for one person to process."

I knew how she felt. It was a lot for me to process, too.

"I talked to Peter today. He had some news," I said carefully. India, still in the closet, had turned to sort the dirty clothes in the hamper. Her back visibly stiffened.

"Stacey's pregnant," she guessed.

"Yep," I said.

India turned around slowly. She didn't look upset. Then again, I'd seen her impassive when faced with the troop of power walking, stroller-pushing mothers who lapped our block every morning, only to discover her quietly crying in the kitchen ten minutes later.

"How far along is she?" she asked.

"I have no idea."

"You didn't ask?"

"Men don't ask about things like that," I said. "In fact, men don't really talk about pregnancy at all, if we can help it."

"Why not?" India asked.

"Fear. I once asked a co-worker at my old job who was hugely, enormously pregnant, if she was overdue. Apparently, she still had three months to go. She glared at me every time she saw me after that. I can't tell you what a relief it was when she finally went on maternity break."

"Coward," India said.

"Yes," I said. "Yes, I am. Anyway, I think Peter said the baby is due sometime in the summer."

"Late summer or early summer?"

I shrugged. "I've told you everything I know."

"Our baby is due in June," India said.

It felt weird to hear her calling the baby, the one still residing in Lainey's womb, *our baby*. "It's not a contest," I said. "It's not like the first one to have a baby wins."

"Of course it is," India said. "Your mother will think it is. Have you told her about Lainey yet?"

"No," I said.

"Why not?"

"I haven't talked to her. Besides, I make it a policy never to tell my mother anything. It's a strategy that's been working well for me ever since I hit puberty," I said.

"Does she know about Stacey?"

I nodded, trying to ignore the dread currently spreading through my gut.

"What did she say?"

"Peter said she's excited," I said cautiously.

"Then we should tell her our news, too. I'm sure she'll be even more excited to hear she has two grandchildren on the way," India said briskly. She scooped up an armful of dirty laundry and, stepping out of the closet, transferred it to the plastic laundry basket we used to ferry clothes downstairs to the laundry room off the kitchen.

"You have met my mother," I said.

"What is that supposed to mean?"

"It means I think you should manage your expectations."

"You mean she's not going to be as excited about our baby as she is about Stacey and Peter's?" India asked.

"Hey," I said softly. "I'm not the enemy here. I'm not responsible for my mother. And I don't know, maybe she will be excited. But..."

"But don't get my hopes up?" India asked. She sighed. "Don't worry, they're not." She squared her shoulders and lifted her chin, a fighter steeling herself. "You're coming with us tomorrow, right?"

This sudden non sequitur threw me.

"Coming where with who?" I asked, trying—and failing—not to sound suspicious.

"Seriously, do you ever listen to me?" India asked.

"All the time. Just last night, you were going on and on about how hot and studly I am," I said. "I heard that."

India rolled her eyes, but didn't resist when I reached for her and pulled her toward me. Since I was sitting and she was still standing, this meant my head was nicely positioned between her breasts. She let her cheek rest on the top of my head, and I stroked her back. It was the closest contact we'd had in days, and I could feel the first stirrings of desire.

"So tell me again—what's tomorrow?"

"Our first appointment with the OB/GYN."

Oh, no, I thought. Had I agreed to go? When? Why?

"You will come, though, right?" India asked. She linked her fingers together behind my neck, and her touch made me shiver.

The honest response to this would be *No*. Or even *Do I have to?* I was pretty sure neither would go over very well, so I instead said, "Is it important that I be there?"

"Yes," India said.

"Then I guess I'll go," I said without enthusiasm. "Wait...I'm not going to have to be in the room when the doctor examines her, am I? Because that would be weird."

"You're going to be in the room when the baby is born," India said.

"I am?"

"Aren't you?"

She pulled away and looked down at me.

"I really don't think I'm comfortable seeing her...you know. Her business," I said.

"And what business is that?"

"You know." My face was flaming.

"No. What?" India giggled.

"Everything up inside," I hissed. I considered myself a modern man. On occasion, I purchased tampons for India. But I was not—nor, hopefully, would I ever be—the sort of man who was comfortable accompanying a woman he barely knew to a pelvic exam.

"You won't be able to see that! Not unless you get down next to the doctor and peer up inside her with a flashlight!" India was now laughing so hard she was shaking.

"Wait—do we know what the doctor's office is going to charge?" I asked, trying to remember how much we had in our checking account and if it would be enough to cover it.

"It's not going to cost anything. Or, at least, it won't cost us anything," she said.

"Why?" I asked. I knew Lainey didn't have health insurance through her job. If she even still had a job. As far as I could tell, Lainey hadn't gone to work since moving in to the guesthouse. India was thrilled—she worried that it wasn't safe for the baby to be around the noxious nail salon fumes. I was less pleased. We'd already agreed to pay Lainey a monthly stipend, with Mike laying out the guidelines for what was allowed. Even so, I suspected that an unemployed Lainey would want more than we were already paying her, and kept expecting her to approach us—or, more likely, India—with a demand.

"Don't you remember? Mike found out that Lainey qualifies for Medicaid. He helped her get the paperwork filled out, and recommended a good obstetrician who accepts Medicaid patients."

"Was I in the room when this was being discussed?" I asked.

India thought about it. "Actually, you might not have been," she admitted. "But I definitely told you about it afterward."

"I don't think so. I would have definitely remembered hearing that something related to this adoption is free," I said. I eyed India, still hopeful that she'd step back into my arms, which would maybe lead to more interesting activities. But instead, she turned, heading for the door.

"Where are you going?"

"I have to get dinner started," India said. "Do you think Lainey would like a cheese and onion frittata? I think I could sneak some spinach into it without her noticing."

Before I could answer, she was gone.

I could tell Lainey was nervous. As we waited to see her doctor— sitting all in a row, with India in the middle—Lainey had her arms and legs crossed, her right foot bouncing rhythmically in the air. I tried to figure out if she was bouncing along to a song playing in her head, and if so, which one—I'm partial to tapping along to EMF's "Unbelievable" myself—but quickly gave up. She probably listened to music by Justin Timberlake, or whoever else is big with the kids these days. Nothing I would know.

"It'll be fine," India said soothingly. "I think it's basically like having a Pap smear."

"What's that?" Lainey asked.

"You've never had a Pap smear before?" India asked.

Lainey shook her head, and shrugged. "I don't even know what that means."

"It's a test they do to see if you have cervical cancer," India explained. "Have you ever had a pelvic exam?"

This time Lainey nodded. "When I went to the clinic for the abortion."

India flinched involuntarily. I glanced around at the waiting room, which was decorated for the holidays. There was a fake tree with blinking multicolor lights set up in one corner, red and white paper bells hung from the reception desk, and cutouts of Santa were taped to the wall.

There were five other women there, all obviously pregnant, although there was a lot of variation in stomach size. Some were so hugely round they looked like they'd swallowed a baby elephant. Others were just a bit bloated, as though they'd gone overboard on the Szechuan chicken and fried rice at the all-u-can-eat Chinese lunch buffet. One of the larger women—so big she had to sit with her feet splayed out to either side while her enormous protruding stomach rested on her thighs—looked as though she might be ready to pop at any minute. She caught me looking at her, and I quickly averted my eyes, pretending I had been looking at the clock over her head.

"Lainey Walker," a nurse called out.

Lainey stood quickly. India stood, too, and glanced down at me. "Are you coming?"

"Right," I said, getting up.

The nurse led us back to a small, rather utilitarian office—laminate desk, matching five-shelf bookcase, framed diplomas on the wall—and told us the doctor would be with us shortly. India and Lainey sat in the two available chairs; I stood off to one side. The doctor came in almost immediately.

"Hello, I'm Dr. Jones," she said, smiling.

Dr. Alice Jones looked to be in her mid- to late thirties. She was black, with closely cropped hair and silver-framed glasses, and wore no makeup or jewelry. She didn't seem at all surprised to see the three of us there together, and shook each of our hands in turn. I wondered if this was common—the adoptive couple tagging along to the exam—or if she'd been informed ahead of time.

"I'm sorry there's not an extra chair," Dr. Jones said to me. "I can try to find one for you."

"That's okay. I'm good," I said.

She sat behind her desk and flipped open a manila file that contained the paperwork Lainey had filled out in the waiting room. "I see you didn't put down the date of your last period," Dr. Jones said.

"I couldn't remember," Lainey said.

"That's fine. We'll do a sonogram today and see if we can get an idea of how far along you are," Dr. Jones said. "Have you been taking prenatal vitamins?"

Lainey shook her head.

"I'll give you some samples before you leave. Let me know which you like the best, and I'll write a prescription for you. So, do you have any questions for me?" Dr. Jones looked up. "Any of you?"

Lainey and I both shook our heads this time, but India—sitting on the edge of the chair, her back poker-straight—had come prepared with a list of questions she'd gotten out of *What to Expect When You're Expecting*. She'd actually taken to carrying the book around with her, and it was now worn and dog-eared from frequent use.

"How long have you been in practice?" India asked.

"I've been here for two years. Before that, I did my residency in obstetrics at Jackson Memorial in Miami," Dr. Jones said.

"How often will we see you, and how often will we see the other doctors in this office?" India asked.

"There are five physicians here in this office, along with two midwife practitioners. I'll be Lainey's primary doctor, but she will have the opportunity to meet the other doctors and midwives. We like to do that so if, for some reason, I'm not available when she goes into labor, she'll have already met the doctor on call."

"Is that likely?" India asked.

"We all like to attend the deliveries of our own patients. I'll make every effort to be there," Dr. Jones replied.

India went on to ask about prenatal testing, childbirth classes, developing a birth plan (whatever that was), the odds of a cesarean, what hospital Lainey would give birth in, and who would be available to answer phone calls, should we have any concerns while at home. Dr. Jones answered each question equably and competently. Lainey sat in absolute silence, and I did likewise, shifting from foot to foot, wishing India would hurry up and finish. I wasn't sure what the point of this all was anyway—there were only so many obstetrical practices in the area that accepted Medicaid, and Mike had assured us that this was the very best of the lot.

Finally, India ran out of steam. "That's all we have for now," she said.

"Anyone else? Lainey? Jeremy?"

Lainey and I shook our heads in unison.

"All right. Lainey, you come with me. We'll do the exam, and then when it's time for the sonogram, India and Jeremy can join us," Dr. Jones said.

Cool relief trickled through me. I wouldn't have to be present for the examination. Once Dr. Jones had ushered Lainey out of the office, and India and I were alone, I claimed Lainey's vacated chair. India turned to me.

"So?" she said.

"So what?"

"What did you think?"

I shrugged. "I really didn't want to be in there during the exam anyway."

"I meant what do you think of the doctor?"

"She seems nice. And her glasses are really cool," I said.

"Her glasses?"

"Yeah, didn't you notice? They were rectangular. Very funky," I said.

"Oh, good. That's right here on my list of what to look for in an obstetrician. Funky eyewear. Check."

"Really?"

"No. That was sarcasm."

"That's too bad. It should be on your list."

"Jeremy?" India said.

"Uh-oh."

"Why *uh-oh*?"

"You only call me Jeremy when you're mad at me."

"That's not true."

"Yes it is," I said. "Usually you call me honey or snookums."

"I have never, ever called you snookums," India said.

"Maybe not, but when you call me Jeremy, that usually means I'm in trouble," I said. "So why are you mad at me?"

"I'm not mad. I'm concerned."

"About what?"

"The jokes, the obsession with Dr. Jones's eyewear," India began.

"I'm not obsessed. I just liked her glasses. And I always joke around."

"I know. But there's a time and a place for it. And when we're interviewing our birth mother's doctor, it really isn't the best time or place. She's the person who's going to be responsible for the safe delivery of our future child. It feels like you're checking out."

"Checking out on what?" I asked.

"Everything." India made a sweeping gesture with her hand. "The adoption. Getting to know Lainey. Interviewing the doctor."

"I'm here, aren't I?" I pointed out.

"Yes, but you've barely said anything. You didn't ask Dr. Jones a single question," India said.

"That's because you asked everything anyone could possibly want to know," I said. "There was nothing left."

"It's more than that," India continued. "You just don't seem present. It was one thing when you let me handle all of the paperwork leading up to the adoption."

"I wrote our adoptive-parent profile," I said indignantly.

India just looked at me.

"What?" I asked.

"You wrote it in the style of a movie trailer. 'Meet India and

Jeremy Halloway. They're about to embark on the biggest adventure of their lives: parenthood,'" India said, reciting the profile by heart in a way that made me suspect she'd been harboring a grudge about it for some time.

"I was trying to make us stand out from all the other prospective adoptive parents. I was trying to give it a good hook," I said.

"I had to rewrite the whole thing," India said peevishly.

So she *had* been holding a grudge.

"But it worked. Lainey picked us," I said.

"I know."

"Then why are we fighting about it now?"

"We're not fighting. We're talking. I just need you to be with me on this," India said.

"I am with you," I said. "I'm here, aren't I?"

"Are you?" India asked.

The door to Dr. Jones's office swung open, and a nurse stuck her head in. "Dr. Jones said you can come in now if you'd like to be present for the sonogram."

India stood. "Yes, we definitely would," she said quickly.

We followed the nurse down the hall. She knocked briefly on a closed door, then opened it without waiting for a response. Lainey was inside, sitting up on an exam table. She was wearing a yellow cotton hospital gown and had a blue paper blanket spread over her lap. Dr. Jones was sitting on a wheeled stool, scribbling in the ever-present chart. She looked up at our entrance and smiled at us.

"Come on in," she said.

"Is everything okay?" India asked, looking from Dr. Jones to Lainey.

Lainey shrugged—this seemed to be her default reaction to everything today—but Dr. Jones said, "So far, so good. We'll have a better idea once we get a picture."

There was a sonogram machine, complete with a small television, set up next to the examination table.

"Where would you like us?" India asked.

"Right back here," Dr. Jones said. She stood, and gestured for us to move to the far end of the table, next to where Lainey's head would be once she lay down. "I'll turn the monitor so that you'll be able to see. Lainey, lie back and put your feet up."

Dr. Jones switched off the lights while Lainey got into position, resting her heels in the stirrups and lying back with her knees bent and legs spread. Dr. Jones fiddled with the machine for a few moments, flipping switches and adjusting the monitor toward us.

"Do you have a good view?" she asked.

"Yes," India said.

Dr. Jones rolled her stool over and sat down between Lainey's legs. Embarrassed, I stared at the television screen. Lainey had the paper sheet spread over her lap, so even if I looked—which I had no intention of doing—I wouldn't be able to see anything, but I still felt vaguely lecherous just for being in the room.

Suddenly, a blurry picture appeared on the black-and-white screen. It was almost triangularly shaped, although the top was sawed off and the bottom was curved. In the middle, there was a bubble, and inside the bubble . . .

"There's the fetus," Dr. Jones said, pointing. "Here's the head, the torso, this is the leg." The blob moved. "There's a hand. Do you see?"

India gasped. I turned to look at her. She had both hands pressed over her mouth, and her eyes glittered with tears. A lurch of panic seized me.

"Is it okay?" I asked. "Is it . . ."

I was going to say *alive*, but couldn't seem to form the word.

"So far, so good. Do you see this here?" The doctor pointed at something that looked like a flickering grain of rice. "That's the heartbeat."

I stared at it and waited for a sense of divine knowledge to hit me, a feeling that *this was my child*. It didn't come.

"Lainey, look," India said, squeezing Lainey's shoulder.

"Cool," Lainey said. She sounded bored. "Is it a boy or a girl?"

"It's too early to tell," Dr. Jones said.

"Can you tell how far along Lainey is?" India asked.

"The measurements I took are telling me the fetus is twelve weeks, four days old," Dr. Jones said.

I glanced down at Lainey, wondering if this revelation was causing her to remember the fateful night that the baby was conceived. But she appeared uninterested in what she was seeing. And so, so young. Despite her heavy makeup—black eyeliner, caked-on foundation, maroon lipstick—she looked much younger than her twenty years.

"Jeremy, look," India breathed.

I looked at her. She was staring so intently at the monitor, she didn't seem to notice the tears that were running freely down her face. I glanced at the screen again. It looked exactly as it had before.

"What?" I asked.

"The baby was waving his—her—foot around," India said.

"How can you tell?" I asked.

"Well, it's stopped now," India said. "But isn't it amazing?"

"I can't see anything," Lainey complained. "It just looks like a blob to me. A blob with a head."

I privately agreed, but decided it would be smarter not to say so out loud. Then suddenly something caught my eye.

"Hey! Do you see that?" I asked, pointing at the screen. "Is that what I think it is?"

"What?" India asked. She leaned forward over Lainey to get a better look.

"Look! It's a boy!" I said excitedly.

Dr. Jones laughed. "That's the arm," she said. "Not the penis."

I could feel my face turning hot, especially when India and even Lainey began giggling, too.

"Don't worry," Dr. Jones said. She winked at me. "All of the new dads make the same mistake."

I thrust my hands into my pockets, determined to keep my mouth shut for the duration of the exam. Maybe for the whole pregnancy. Even so, I couldn't help but wonder: *But do all of the new dads feel like actual dads? Or do they all feel like frauds, too?*

Seven

INDIA

"I wish we could have brought Otis with us," Miles said.

Miles, Rose, Luke, and I were standing outside the tiger exhibit at the zoo at Dreher Park. The tiger was prowling around his habitat, looking out of sorts. I knew how he felt. Between Lainey's presence in the guesthouse, my heavier workload, and the stress of worrying about the adoption, I'd been feeling out of sorts lately, too.

"They don't allow dogs at the zoo," I said.

"Why?" Luke asked. He leaned forward, mashing his nose against the plexiglass barrier that enclosed the tiger's habitat.

"Because to that tiger, Otis would look like dinner. A cheeseburger on a leash," I said.

"Really?" Rose asked. "But Otis runs pretty fast. The tiger wouldn't be able to catch him."

I shook my head. "Trust me, Otis wouldn't stand a chance."

"Actually, that would be pretty cool," Miles said.

"What? Otis being eaten alive?" I asked.

"No, not Otis. But they should put a deer or something in here, so people could see how a tiger hunts," Miles said.

"Gross," Rose said.

I agreed with Rose. "I don't think the zoo wants small children traumatized by a bloodletting," I said.

"I wouldn't mind seeing it," Luke said. "It would be like the show *When Predators Attack*."

"Does your mom know you watch that?"

All three kids nodded.

"It's educational," Rose explained.

"The circle of life," Miles said. "And it's really cool. Last week, they showed a crocodile eating a wildebeest. Did you know that crocodiles have the strongest bite of any animal? And that they sleep with their mouths open?"

"No, I did not know that," I said.

"And when they hunt, they look like this," Luke said. He slouched forward, pretending to be a crocodile floating in the water. Then, with a roar, he leapt forward and grabbed Rose. She screamed.

"Shhh," I said. "Rose, stop screaming. Luke, stop pretending to eat your sister. Come on, let's go see the giant tortoise."

We began walking through the simulated jungle that led out of the tiger habitat.

"India?" Rose asked.

"Yes, honey?"

"I was thinking. If you decide not to adopt that baby, you can have Luke," Rose said.

"Hey!" Luke said, scowling at his sister.

"It only makes sense," Rose told him. "India and Jeremy don't have any kids. And we have one extra in our family."

"I am not extra!" Luke said.

"Yes you are. We already have one boy and one girl. We don't really need you."

"If you took Luke, I'd get to have our room to myself," Miles mused.

"Okay, guys, that's enough," I said. "As much as we would love to have him, you can't give me Luke. Your mom wouldn't like it. Now, come on."

"Rose offered to give Luke to Jeremy and me today," I told Mimi later. We were standing in her kitchen. I was leaning against the counter, drinking an iced tea and watching while Mimi prepared chicken salad for lunch.

"Do you want him?" Mimi asked.

"Absolutely," I said.

"He's yours," Mimi said, adding a dollop of mayonnaise to the chicken salad. "Taste this. Is it too dry?"

"No, I like it like that. You don't mean it about Luke."

"Want to bet? Look at this," Mimi said. She opened a kitchen drawer, which contained broken shards of china.

"What is that?"

"The Wedgwood vase my grandmother gave Leo and me for a wedding present. It was a family heirloom. Luke and Rose were playing with their light sabers yesterday, and *crash*."

I gasped. "No. And you let them live? Why are you saving the pieces?"

"I thought maybe Leo could glue it back together," Mimi said.

I looked down at the fragments. "I don't think that's going to happen."

"I know." Mimi sighed. "But I couldn't bear to throw them out. And it's just as much my fault as it is theirs. I should have kept it packed away in bubble wrap until the kids had finished their *Star Wars* phase. Are you sure you want kids, India? It's like living with savages."

"I was sure until I saw your vase," I said. I smiled. "No, I'm sure. Besides, we have one on the way, so it's too late to back out."

"So, how's it going with the birth mother?" Mimi asked. "Has she stolen anything from you yet?"

"Mimi!" I said. "Lainey's not like that."

"How do you know what she's like? You don't really know anything about her," Mimi said, continuing to stir the chicken salad.

"I do too know her," I insisted. "Or, at least, I'm getting to know her."

Five weeks had passed since Lainey moved in, and I'd been doing my best to break through her defenses. It was hard. Lainey was not a people person. At least, I hoped that was what it was, and not that she just didn't like me.

"I'm still not sure you should have let her move in to your guesthouse."

"Why? I think it's working out great," I said. Okay, so maybe *great* was an exaggeration. But it wasn't a disaster, either.

"For all you know, she could be a sociopath. She could sneak into your house in the middle of the night, stab you to death while you're sleeping, and then set your bed on fire to cover up the murders. Do you really want that to happen? Do you want your house burned down while you're dead?" Mimi asked, pointing her fork at me.

"If I'm dead, I suppose I wouldn't mind so much about the house fire. And you have got to stop reading those true-crime books. They're warping your mind."

"Say what you will, but I have always been a fantastic judge of character," Mimi said.

This was actually true. At every wedding Mimi had ever attended, she'd predicted with almost perfect accuracy whether the marriage would succeed. Her only failure so far was the Hendersons—he was a doormat, she was overbearing—who were still together, despite Mimi's pronouncement that they wouldn't make it to their second anniversary. Whenever I pointed the Hendersons' enduring marriage out to her, Mimi would just shrug and say, "Give it time."

Still. Just because Mimi could predict the chances of a marriage succeeding between two people she knew didn't mean that she could meet Lainey one time and see right into her soul.

"She's just a kid that's gotten into a tight spot," I said.

"Hardly a kid. Didn't you say she was twenty? That's old enough to vote," Mimi pointed out.

"But not old enough to drink," I countered.

Mimi snorted. "She doesn't drink. Remember? She doesn't want to look bloated in her bikini."

"So now not drinking is a character flaw?"

"Of course not. But excessive vanity is."

"I don't think Lainey had the easiest childhood," I said. "I haven't gotten a lot of details from her, but she mentioned that her mother drinks. Let's face it, she comes from a different world than we do." I reconsidered. "Then again, maybe not such a different world. My mom isn't exactly a teetotaler."

Mimi waved this off and reached for the salt. "Your mom isn't a drunk. She's just an enthusiastic drinker," she said, shaking salt over the chicken salad. "I think this is done. Let me cut up some avocado, and then I'll call the kids."

"That sounds like semantics to me. Why give my mom a pass?"

"Your mom never forgot to pick you up from school or feed you when you were growing up, did she?"

"Dinner was certainly late on occasion. But you're right, I wasn't neglected."

"Anyway, what bothered me about Lainey when I met her is that she seems so hard-edged. And she seemed completely detached from the whole situation. I'm not entirely sure she gets that she's going to be handing over an actual baby."

"Don't forget that was the same day she moved in. I'm sure she was feeling overwhelmed," I said.

Mimi put down the knife she'd been slicing avocado with and fixed me with a penetrating look.

"What?" I asked, instantly defensive.

"Do you want me to be blunt?"

"When are you ever not blunt?"

"How do you know she's not just mercenary? That she won't

use this situation—and your desperation—to get as much money out of you as possible?"

"What money? We don't have any money."

"Trust me, I bet she *thinks* you have money," Mimi said.

I reached for my iced tea and gulped it down, wishing it was something stronger. Unfortunately, I had to work after lunch, and I've found that most mothers don't appreciate it if you show up drunk to their child's photo session.

"You're making her sound like some sort of scam artist. She's just a kid," I said. I put up my hands defensively. "I know, I know, she's twenty. But in my book, that's still a kid. When I was twenty, I was a sophomore in college. The most I had to worry about was finishing the reading assignment for my English Lit class before heading out to a kegger. An unplanned pregnancy, putting the baby up for adoption. That's a lot for someone her age to deal with. I think we have to give her credit that she didn't take the easy way out of the situation."

"I agree. But that doesn't mitigate my concerns," Mimi said. "I'm telling you, I don't trust her. Something about Lainey pings my radar."

"But I have to trust her. She's the one with the baby. If I want to be a mom, what other choice do I have?" My voice cracked, and I suddenly realized my eyes were hot with tears.

"I know." Mimi reached over and squeezed my hand. "Just do me a favor and keep your eye on her. Okay?"

"Actually, you have a point."

"You don't have to sound so surprised," Mimi said, rolling her eyes.

I smiled, glad to feel some of the tension dissolving. "What I mean is that I have been wanting to get to know Lainey better. She does have a hard shell, which makes it difficult. But I'm going to make more of an effort. And I want her to get to know Jeremy and me, too, so that she'll see what good parents we'll make." I reconsidered. "Although Jeremy isn't exactly being cooperative on that front."

"Uh-oh," Mimi said. "That doesn't sound good. What's going on?"

"You think Lainey's detached. Jeremy's even worse. He's completely checked out," I said.

"Do you think he's changed his mind?"

"No. At least, he says he hasn't. But this is a big thing. Shouldn't he be a little excited about it?" I asked.

Mimi shrugged. "He's a man," she said. "The only things that excite them are sandwiches and sex."

"Is that a saying, or did you just make that up?"

"I made it up just now, but I think I might have it embroidered on a pillow. Take Leo. When I was in labor with Rose, and experiencing the most horrific pain of my life, he was out in the parking lot talking to his broker on his cell phone. And he didn't even make it to the hospital at all when I delivered Luke," Mimi said.

"That wasn't his fault, though. You went into labor three weeks early, and he was out of town on a business trip," I reminded her.

"Still. Men check out. It's what they do. It's how they cope. We're the ones in there getting emotional, and bloody, and slogging through it," Mimi said. "It's our burden as women."

"You really do have a fascinating viewpoint on the relationship between the sexes," I said. "But I'm not letting Jeremy off the hook that easily. I'm going to make him slog through this with me."

"Good luck with that," Mimi said. "Will you call the kids? Lunch is ready."

Rose and Luke came galloping into the kitchen, light sabers in hand.

"You two! No light sabers in the house," Mimi exclaimed. "Did you learn nothing from yesterday's incident?" She rolled her eyes at me. "I've changed my mind. You can have them both. Just leave me Miles. He's semi-civilized. Or, at least, he will be until he hits puberty in a few years."

The following Saturday, I decided it was time to put my get-to-know-Lainey-better plan in action. Steeling myself, I knocked on the door to the guest cottage. I knew Lainey was home—her Nissan sedan was parked in the driveway—but she didn't answer right away. I waited, noticing the pot of impatiens next to the door were drooping, and made a mental note to water them. I knocked again. This time, I heard the heavy fall of footsteps, and a moment later, the door opened. Lainey looked as though she'd been napping. Her eyes drooped, and her hair—usually brushed and glossy—stuck up at the back of the head.

"What's up?" she asked, yawning.

"Did I wake you? I'm sorry," I said.

Lainey shrugged, but didn't say anything. I found her habit of staying silent when politeness dictated a response unnerving. More so than when she came out with the occasional crass comment.

"I wanted to see if you were up for a shopping trip," I said.

Lainey blinked. "You mean groceries?" she asked, clearly unenthused by the idea.

"No. Maternity clothes," I said. "I know you're barely showing, but I thought it might be fun to pick up a few things now."

Lainey's eyes were dark, almost black, and so inscrutable I could never tell what she was thinking. When she watched me like that, was she judging my pared-back Saturday uniform—khaki shorts and a navy blue T-shirt, riotous curls tamed into a ponytail, face bare except for a swipe of cherry ChapStick? Or was she looking for clues that would illuminate what sort of a mother I'd be to her baby?

Although now that I thought about it, she hadn't yet seemed

all that interested in what kind of parents Jeremy and I would be. Maybe it was just a combination of fatigue and hormones. Or maybe it was self-preservation. I couldn't imagine how hard it would be to carry a baby to term and then hand it over to another woman to raise. Deep down, Lainey had to be an amazingly strong woman.

"Come on, it'll be fun," I coaxed.

Lainey nodded and shrugged again—I was starting to really tire of the shrug, but tried to tell myself it would be good practice for parenting during those difficult teen years—but she finally said, "Okay, I guess."

It wasn't enthusiastic, but it was a start.

"Do you see anything you like?" I asked.

I'd been dying to go shopping at Pea in the Pod ever since Jeremy and I had first started trying to conceive. I'd been once before, with Mimi when she was pregnant with Luke and shopping for a cocktail dress. I'd laughed at the irony of a cocktail maternity dress, but it turned out there were racks of them, thus showing yet again how little I knew about all things pregnancy related.

"I don't know," Lainey said, looking around at the round-bellied mannequins dressed in cashmere sweaters and wide-legged wool trousers. "These aren't the sort of clothes I usually wear."

She had a point—everything displayed in the front of the store did seem geared more toward professional women. A smiling salesgirl came forward to greet us.

"Do you have any casual clothes?" I asked. "Jeans, T-shirts, anything like that?"

"Right this way," the salesclerk said, leading us to the back of the store.

"Perfect!" I said when I saw the racks of denim, graphic T's, and cute little sundresses. I pulled out a pair of skinny, dark denim jeans and held them up to Lainey. "These would be adorable on you!"

Lainey looked nonplussed. "But how will I be able to tell if they'll fit me once I'm bigger?"

"We have belly pillows in each dressing room. You just tie it on, and you'll be able to see how the garment will fit once you've started showing more," the salesclerk chipped in.

"Really?" Lainey looked surprised, then—amazingly—she actually smiled. At least, it was almost a smile: One corner of her mouth definitely quirked upward. "That's sort of cool."

I was so excited by this first flash of enthusiasm from her, I began pulling clothes off the racks. Cotton sundresses, wrap T's, denim skirts, more jeans. "You have to try this. Oh, and this! And isn't this great?" I said, pulling a jersey empire-waisted dress out and holding it up to Lainey.

"You want me to try on all of these?" she asked, looking down at the armful of clothes I'd handed her.

"I'll take those and put them in a dressing room for you," the salesclerk offered.

Lainey modeled outfit after outfit for me. She was so tall and leggy she looked great in everything.

"What do you think of this?" Lainey asked, showing off an elegant ivory cotton sweater over a denim pencil skirt. She turned to look at herself in the mirror, her neck an elegant arc, her eyebrows arched. My fingers itched for my camera.

"Would you mind if I took your picture?" I blurted out.

I'd been trying to work up the nerve to ask Lainey to model for my planned maternity portraiture exhibit for a few weeks, but kept chickening out. I fully expected her to cross her arms, stare down her nose at me, and reject the idea.

But Lainey stopped, mid-twirl, and looked at me. "What, now? Here?" she asked.

"No, no," I said. "In my studio. I'm putting together a show of portraits of pregnant women. My plan is to shoot each woman at different stages in her pregnancy, and, when possible, of the baby with the mother. I'd like to include you in the show."

"You're going to take a photo of me with the baby . . . or you with the baby?" Lainey asked.

I don't know what was more unsettling—the question and all that it implied, or the cool, appraising look Lainey was giving me.

"The show will be held before you give birth, so neither, actually," I said carefully.

"Oh," Lainey said. "Sure, I guess."

She'd acquiesced surprisingly quickly. "Really?"

"Why not." She shrugged. The wall was back in place. "Do I have to be naked?"

"It's up to you. Some of the pregnant women I've photographed have bared their bellies. But if that makes you uncomfortable, you could just wear whatever."

Lainey shrugged, and turned to stare at herself in the mirror. "I don't care. I'm not against full nudity, but only if it advances my career. You know: *Playboy* but not Internet porn."

"Um, right. Good for you," I said, trying to sound supportive. "But no, this wouldn't be at all like that. The portraits will be very tasteful, very artistic."

"Okay. Whatever." Lainey brightened. "You said they're going to be part of a show? Will anyone famous see them?"

"I doubt it. The show is going to be at my studio," I said apologetically.

"Oh," Lainey said, looking disappointed. She turned back to study her reflection in the mirror. "Still, I guess I can use the photos in my portfolio. If I don't look too fat. What do you think of this skirt?"

"It's very cute," I said.

"Can I get it?"

"Sure," I said. Hopefully, I'd be able to hide the Visa bill before Jeremy saw it.

After Pea in the Pod, we hit Mimi Maternity and then took a lunch break. Lainey was hungry, and I was reeling from the seven hundred dollars I'd just spent on maternity clothes. I knew Jeremy would freak when he found out about it. But, I reasoned, this was what prospective adoptive parents had to do to keep the birth mother happy. I'd been haunting adoptive-parent online chat boards, and from the stories I'd read there, a shopping spree was the least of it.

Other prospective adoptive parents bought their birth mothers cars and furnished their apartments, or sent them on beach vacations. Laws on what you were allowed to do varied by state, but most of the adoptive parents reasoned that things like cars and furniture fell under the category of living expenses, while restful, stress-reducing spa days and vacations could qualify as medical care. Everyone knew that this was stretching the limits, from acceptable expenses to what could be considered the outright purchasing of a baby. But none of them cared. They were all willing to do whatever it took to get one. And Jeremy and I simply didn't possess the resources many of these couples had.

Luckily, I'd recently been referred some wedding jobs. A few had come by word of mouth—brides who'd been unhappy with the photographer they had hired, and were looking for a last-minute replacement. I'd also scored a few jobs from another photographer I knew, Joanie Boyle, who had broken her arm on a skiing trip. So while our financial crisis wasn't completely solved and I was stuck spending the next five Saturdays in wedding hell—tearful brides, bossy mothers, bitchy bridesmaids—the extra money I was making would help with the expenses.

"How's your sandwich?" I asked.

"Fine," Lainey said, wolfing down a turkey and cheese panini. She was ignoring the spinach salad I'd also ordered for her—"You have to try one, they're delicious here!"—and was instead chasing each bite of sandwich with a greasy handful of french fries. At least she was taking her daily prenatal vitamin, I thought. I gave her one every morning with a freshly squeezed glass of orange juice.

"You said you're developing a portfolio?" I asked. "Have you done any modeling?"

Lainey shook her head. "Not my thing," she said. "I just wanted to have some photos so that when I go on casting calls, they can see how I look on film."

I nodded. I had no idea how casting calls worked, but her reasoning was sound enough.

"Would you like me to photograph you?" I offered. "Not just the pregnancy photos. I could also do some head shots."

"You'd do that?"

"Of course." I smiled at her surprise. I got the feeling that Lainey wasn't used to anyone doing anything for her. Maybe that was why she was so guarded.

I picked up my turkey on whole wheat, and took a bite without tasting it. As I chewed I watched Lainey from beneath my lashes, trying to figure out what was going on. She was scowling down at her plate. I put the sandwich back down and said, "Is something wrong, Lainey?"

She shook her head.

"You seem down. Are you not feeling well?"

"I said I'm fine," she said testily.

"Do you like your new clothes?" I asked, trying to coax her out of the sullen mood.

Another shrug.

"What is it?" I asked.

"It's just . . ." Lainey heaved out a sigh and brushed her hair back over her shoulders. "These are the nicest clothes I've ever had, and they don't really count. I won't be able to wear any of them after I have the baby."

Anger rose like bile into my throat. I had just spent *seven hundred dollars* on this girl—more money than I had ever spent on clothes for myself at one time—and she was sighing and tossing her hair around as though this were some great injustice. The ingratitude of it staggered me.

But then I tried to remind myself that she'd been through a lot lately: discovering that she was pregnant. Breaking up with her boyfriend. Being forced out of her home. Finding herself alone in the world. Moving in to the guesthouse of strangers. It would be a lot for anyone to take in, much less someone so young.

My anger ebbed, cooled by an unexpected rush of empathy. Of course this was all overwhelming for her. The shopping bags propped up on chairs and resting on the ground by our feet were full of clothes that had tummy panels and empire waists. What twenty-year-old wanted that?

"You know, there are some great stores in this mall," I said, trying to remember if we'd paid off my Bloomingdale's card. "Maybe we could pick up a few things for you to wear after you have the baby?"

I was rewarded by the first genuine smile I'd seen from Lainey all day. It transformed her face, turned her from merely pretty to a true beauty. She didn't have classical features—her jaw was too blunt, her nose a smidgen too wide, her lips too thin—but altogether, they made for an arresting combination. It was a face that would photograph beautifully.

"Really?" she asked.

"Sure," I said, grinning back at her. "We're here to have fun, right?"

When we got home from the mall, laden with shopping bags and our feet aching, we found my mother sitting at the kitchen table, peeling an apple with a paring knife. Otis was under the table, lying down on his side with his head resting on my mother's feet.

"Jeremy let me in," my mother said by way of greeting. She

had her long gray hair tied back in a braid and was wearing a floor-length celery green linen dress. Glasses were hanging at her neck, suspended by a beaded chain.

"Where is he?" I asked.

"Hiding, I think. He said something about taking Otis for a walk, but he apparently forgot to take the dog with him, and I haven't seen him since," Mom said. "What have you two been up to?"

"Shopping," Lainey said succinctly. She sat down in the chair opposite my mother, tucking one foot up under her leg, and watched as my mom slowly rotated the apple against the knife so that the peel fell away in a perfect coil. "That's so cool. How do you do that so it's all in one piece like that?"

"Practice and patience," Mom said. She used the paring knife to slice the apple into chunks, and fanned them out on a plate with a flourish.

"Show-off," I said, taking one of the apple slices and popping it into my mouth.

"Can I try?" Lainey asked.

My mother handed Lainey the knife and an apple. Lainey slid the knife against the apple, hacking off a chunk. "Shit," she said.

"Here, watch me. It's all in the wrist," Mom said, taking the apple back and demonstrating.

Lainey took another stab at peeling the apple. This time, she managed to turn it all the way around before breaking the peel off. "Oh, no! I almost did it that time," she said.

"Good!" Mom said, beaming at her.

I looked from one to the other, trying to figure out what was going on. For Lainey, this was practically gregarious. Then again, it wasn't uncommon for my childhood friends to gravitate toward my mother. Maybe she had a mysterious appeal to the twenty-and-under crowd that I'd been immune to at that age. Or maybe my friends were just hoping she'd break out her stash.

I checked my watch. "I have to get to the studio," I said.

"On a Saturday?" Mom asked.

I just nodded. I didn't want to talk about the extra work I'd taken on to help cover the adoption expenses in front of Lainey, in case it made her uncomfortable. "Have fun peeling apples," I said, keeping my voice light. "Should I expect a pie to be waiting here when I get back?"

"Not unless you like being disappointed," Mom said. "What are you working on?"

"I'm putting together the proof book for the McKinley wedding I shot last weekend. They're coming in Monday to get it. And I need to edit some photos I took for the show," I said.

"What show?" Mom asked.

I rolled my eyes.

"What?" she demanded.

"I've already told you about it," I said. "I swear, you're as bad as Jeremy."

"Tell me again."

"What's the point? You'll just forget about it again," I said irritably. My mother's memory had always been awful—probably a consequence of living through the sixties—but she'd been getting even worse lately.

Lainey turned to gaze at me, and I immediately regretted snapping at my mom. It made me look petty and mean-spirited, which were not traits I wanted our birth mother to associate me with. I needed to always appear serene, warm, maternal. Lainey could still change her mind, I reminded myself, as an oily dread twisted in my stomach. Once a birth mother gave her consent to give her baby up for adoption, it was irrevocable. But, as Mike Jankowski had explained to us, consent couldn't be obtained until forty-eight hours after the birth. It meant I had twenty-four weeks—plus forty-eight hours—to convince Lainey that I would be the perfect mother. I couldn't afford to let my guard down, not once.

"I've been taking fish oil capsules," Mom said.

"That's good," I said, forcing my lips up into a smile.

Mom frowned at me. "Why are you grimacing like that? Don't. It makes you look like you're one broken nail away from a nervous breakdown."

I would have killed my mother right then and there, except that I had a feeling that would probably make an even worse impression on Lainey.

"What does fish oil do?" Lainey asked.

"It's supposed to improve your memory. And it's good for your skin," Mom said.

"Really? How?"

"It's chock-full of omega-3 fatty acids. Wonderful stuff, you can't have too much of it. It keeps your skin clear, your cholesterol down, your brain working," Mom enthused.

"Maybe I'll try it," Lainey said. "Being pregnant is making me break out. See?" She pointed to a tiny, barely noticeable red bump on her chin. "Isn't that gross?"

"Fish oil will definitely help," Mom said, examining the pimple.

"I think you should check with Dr. Jones before you start taking anything," I cautioned.

"I'm sure it's fine. It's just fish oil," Mom said.

"Even so," I said.

When I was thirteen, my mom tried—unsuccessfully—to convince me to smoke pot to relieve menstrual cramps, so she was not someone I wanted giving medical advice to our birth mother. In fact, I was now having a terrifying vision of Mom talking Lainey into taking massive doses of fish oil and the baby being born with gills and covered in scales. I made a mental note to Google *fish oil birth defects* and decided to change the subject.

"The show I'm doing is going to feature portraits of women in different stages of pregnancy," I said.

"I'm going to be in it," Lainey said.

I smiled at her. "That's right."

My mother gave me a penetrating look. I wondered if she, like Jeremy, was going to lecture me on how masochistic it was for an infertile photographer to take maternity portraits. But instead, she said, "That's an excellent idea."

"It is?" I said, surprised.

"Of course! It's a celebration of love and life and the ultimate female experience!" My mother placed a hand across her breast, as though she were about to recite the Pledge of Allegiance. "It's very powerful."

"That's what I thought," I said, glancing sideways at Lainey. She was attempting to peel another apple.

"I'm going to write a series of poems to go along with your photographs," Mom announced importantly. "All in free verse, each celebrating a different aspect of pregnancy. We'll hang them on the walls next to the portraits, thereby creating both a visual and textual experience! What do you think?"

I knew what I thought: I hated the idea. The last thing I wanted was for people to be distracted from my photography by trying to make sense out of a series of poems with titles like "The Spermatozoon Strikes" and "My Journey Out: Meditations on a Birth in Process."

"You write poetry?" Lainey asked, unexpectedly perking up.

"I do," Mom said, coyly patting her gray curls.

"Cool," Lainey said. "Are they in, like, books?"

Mom sniffed. "Modern-day publishing houses are corporate, profit-driven behemoths. They don't support art, only crappy commercial pap."

Unfortunately, Jeremy chose this moment to enter the kitchen, unseen by my mother and Lainey, who were both sitting with their backs to him. At the phrase *crappy commercial pap*, he arched his eyebrows at me.

Sorry, I mouthed. Jeremy shrugged, and silently backed out of the kitchen before Mom saw him.

"These days, I only read the classics. And even then, I check them out of the library. I have some of my poems here," Mom said, pulling a spiral notebook out of the battered cotton tote she used as a handbag. "Would you like to read one?"

"Sure," Lainey said, reaching for the notebook.

"My friend David from poetry club is going to teach me how to set up a website, so I can self-publish my own poetry, as well as the works of other poets."

"Cool," Lainey said again, flipping open the notebook and leaning forward over it.

"I have to get going. Have fun, you two," I said.

I tried not to let it bother me that neither one of them looked up when I left.

Bam-bam-bam.

Lainey woke suddenly. *What the hell is that?* she wondered. She sat up and blinked blearily at the alarm clock: 10:53. Lainey yawned and rubbed her eyes, and then flopped back down on the bed, determined to go back to sleep.

Bam-bam-bam. It was coming from the front door of the guest-house.

"I'm coming," Lainey said irritably. She slid out of bed and stalked to the front door, which she yanked open. "What do you want?"

She'd expected to find India standing there, making yet another annoying attempt to become Lainey's best friend. But it wasn't India. Instead, a small dark-haired girl was standing there. The girl, who was staring up at her with a frank curiosity, was wearing a black T-shirt emblazoned with a glittery skull, a lime green tulle skirt, and purple-and-pink-striped stockings. Otis was behind her, sitting on his haunches, panting loudly.

"If you're trick-or-treating, you're a couple of months late," Lainey told the girl.

"I'm Rose," the girl said.

"Okay, Rose. Do you want to tell me why you're knocking on my door at the crack of dawn?"

"It's not the crack of dawn. It's almost lunchtime. Why aren't you wearing pants?" Rose asked.

Lainey looked down at herself. She was wearing panties and an extra-large T-shirt she'd stolen from Trav. It was screen printed with CAN YOU COME BACK IN A FEW BEERS?

"Can I come in?" Rose asked. "Jeremy used to let my brothers and me play Little Red Riding Hood in here." Without waiting for Lainey's permission, she stepped around her and walked into the cottage. "It looks really different now. It's a lot messier than it used to be when it was Jeremy's office."

Lainey glanced around. The place was a mess. Piles of discarded clothes were heaped on the floor and leather chair, empty soda cans littered the coffee table, and piles of magazines—*People, Us, In Touch Weekly*—were stacked on the counter. Rose pushed aside a bra and a maternity shirt to clear herself a space on the sofa.

"Hold on," Lainey said. She grabbed a pair of sweat shorts off the leather chair and pulled them on. "Who are you again?"

"I'm Rose Carrera. I'm eight. Are you really pregnant?"

"Yeah. How do you know India and Jeremy?"

"They're my godparents. Are you going to give them your baby?"

"That's the plan. So, what, are you over here visiting them or something?" Lainey asked.

Rose nodded. "My mom is having her highlights done, and my dad and brothers went to my older brother's soccer game. I didn't feel like going, so India said I could hang out here," she said.

"And where's India now? Does she know you're out here?" Lainey sat down in the leather chair.

"No. She went to the store. She left Jeremy in charge, but he's on the computer. I thought you might want to play with me," Rose said, with the air of a queen bestowing a great favor on a peasant.

"Oh, you did, did you?" Lainey crossed her arms, and attempted to stare Rose down. The younger girl didn't seem at all fazed.

Rose nodded. "We could play Little Red Riding Hood. One of us has to get into bed and pretend to be the wolf. And then Little Red Riding Hood comes in and says, 'Oh, what big ears you have.'"

"I know the story," Lainey said. "I don't think so, kid." She yawned, and her stomach let out a loud gurgle.

"Are you hungry?" Rose asked.

"I'm always hungry. It's the baby. He's a pig."

"I don't think you're supposed to call a baby a pig," Rose said disapprovingly. "And how do you know he's a boy?"

"I don't," Lainey said.

"Rose? Where are you?" It was Jeremy, calling for the little girl outside. Lainey got up and opened the door to the guesthouse.

"She's back here," Lainey called to him.

Jeremy crossed the backyard, and hesitated at the front door.

"Rose, I've been looking everywhere for you."

"Hi," Rose said. "Did you think I was lost?"

"Nah. I'd never get rid of you so easily," Jeremy teased her.

Rose stuck her tongue out at him. Jeremy mimicked her.

"Big meanie," Rose said.

"Little twerp," Jeremy said. He glanced at Lainey. "Did she wake you up?"

Lainey shrugged. "It's okay."

"Lainey's hungry. She said the baby is a pig," Rose said.

"Tattletale!" Lainey said.

Rose smiled sweetly. "But India said we didn't have any food in the house."

"Did she? Well, it just so happens that I know where India hides all of the good stuff," Jeremy said. "Follow me, ladies."

When India arrived home twenty minutes later, Jeremy, Lainey, and Rose were sitting at the kitchen table, eating corn chips dipped in salsa and M&M's.

"This is healthier than it looks," Jeremy said. "The chips have fiber—I checked—and the salsa counts as a serving of vegetables."

"And the M&M's?" India asked, putting two bags of groceries up on the counter.

"They provide tasty goodness," Jeremy explained. He stood and began helping India unload the groceries.

"I see you've met Rose," India said, smiling at Lainey.

Lainey nodded and stuffed a chip in her mouth.

"After lunch, Lainey and I are going to play Little Red Riding Hood in the guesthouse. I'm going to be the wolf," Rose announced.

"We are? I don't remember agreeing to that," Lainey said.

Jeremy grinned. "You might as well give in now. When it comes to Rose, resistance is futile."

Lainey shrugged. "Okay, fine. But I want to be the wolf."

Rose considered this. "Deal."

"Now that we've worked that all out, who wants a sandwich?" India asked.

That evening, Lainey stood on a stool in the living room of Flaca's apartment while Flaca pinned a topaz blue satin bridesmaid dress on her.

"I look like a blue tent," Lainey said.

"I'm trying to figure out how much room to allow for your stomach to grow," Flaca said. She stood back, frowning as she considered this. "I should have had my mom come over to pin this. She's the one who will be doing the alterations. Do you think your boobs are going to get any bigger?"

"Who knows?" Lainey said, shrugging.

"Don't shrug! You'll make the pins fall out."

Lainey stilled. "My boobs are getting huge, aren't they? They're almost as big as yours."

"You always said you wanted a boob job," Flaca said.

"First of all, I don't get to keep them. And second, pregnant boobs are heavy. They hang low like cow udders. Moo."

"You're really not that big yet. How far along are you?"

"Only twenty weeks," Lainey said mournfully. "Which means twenty long weeks of swelling to go." She arched her back. "I need to sit down. My feet hurt."

"Hold on," Flaca said. She unzipped the dress and carefully lifted it off over Lainey's head. "There. You can sit down now."

Lainey pulled on her maternity shorts and T-shirt while Flaca folded the dress and set it aside.

"Do you want a drink?"

"Just water," Lainey said.

Flaca went into her kitchen and returned with a glass of water and a soda. Lainey looked at the soda longingly.

"Do you want one?" Flaca asked, popping the can open.

"Yes, but I'm not supposed to drink soda," Lainey said. "India would probably have a heart attack if she saw me."

"So what is she like, anyway?"

"She's okay, I guess. She tries too hard to be friends with me, which gets old. Did I tell you she wants to take my picture?"

"No. Why?"

"She's a photographer, and I guess she's having a bunch of pregnant women model for her. When they're done, she's going to have a show of the photographs at her studio. She asked me to be in it," Lainey explained.

"That's kind of weird, don't you think? Photographs of pregnant chicks?"

"I don't know. The way India described it, I thought it sounded kind of cool."

"Are you going to do it?" Flaca asked.

"I guess so. I mean, why not, right?"

Flaca nodded. "I guess it could be fun. When is she taking your picture?"

"Tomorrow sometime."

Lainey leaned back on Flaca's sofa, tucking a cranberry red throw pillow behind her head. She yawned luxuriously.

"Tired?" Flaca asked sympathetically.

"At least I'm not throwing up anymore, which is a nice change after the three-month puke-athon. Doesn't it suck that we're the ones who have to go through this? Men have it so easy."

"Speaking of men," Flaca said, glancing sideways at Lainey, "I wasn't sure if I should tell you this or not, but I saw Trav at the bar the other night."

"Do you really think Trav qualifies as a man?" Lainey asked.

"No, you're right. He's really more like one of those monkeys. You know, the ones with the big heads and long arms? What are they called? Not apes."

"Baboons!" Lainey said gleefully. "Oh, my God, you're right! He does look like a baboon!"

"Only dumber," Flaca said.

"Obviously," Lainey agreed. "He really is an idiot. I don't know how I stayed with him as long as I did."

Flaca hesitated. "When I saw him, he was with some girl."

Lainey's eyes narrowed. "Who?"

"I don't know her. She was really muscular, though. You know, like one of those bodybuilder chicks."

Lainey laughed bitterly. "Why am I not surprised? She's probably some skank he picked up at the gym."

"So you're not mad?" Flaca asked. She let out a deep breath. "Good. I thought you'd be pissed off. I almost didn't tell you."

"I *am* pissed. I'm pissed that asshole is out partying with some slut, while I can't even stay awake past nine o'clock. It's not fair. I hate him."

"I do, too," Flaca said. She held out her soda, and she and Lainey clinked their drinks together.

"I just want this pregnancy to be over, so I can get on with my life. I'm so sick of it," Lainey said.

"Do you know what you're having yet? A boy or a girl?"

"No. India decided she wanted to be surprised, so we didn't find out." Lainey rolled her eyes. "Lame."

"I've never understood that. Who cares about being surprised? Wouldn't you rather know if you should be buying pink or blue baby stuff?" Flaca asked.

"Well, supposedly India's not buying anything. At least, that's what she tells Jeremy." Lainey smirked. "But I know she's lying."

"What? How?"

"I found a shopping bag full of baby stuff in the back of her closet, behind the Christmas decorations."

"What were you doing in her closet?"

"I was bored," Lainey said. "I had nothing else to do, and I'd already looked through the rest of the house. Besides, people always hide the best stuff in their closets."

"You're evil, girl."

"I know, but I'm okay with that," Lainey said, grinning.

Flaca suddenly looked up sharply. "You've never gone through my closet, have you?"

Lainey's smile grew wider.

"Oh, my God! You have! You bitch!" Flaca whacked Lainey over the head with a throw pillow. "Just so you know, that stuff is all Luis's. He likes to get his freak on, you know?"

"The black faux-leather teddy is Luis's? He *is* pretty freaky." Lainey laughed and dodged another blow.

"Okay, so the teddy is mine. But Luis bought it for me." A red flush crept over Flaca's face and neck. "But the movies are all his. I swear."

"Yeah, right. Face it, he's not the only freaky one."

Flaca took another wild swing with the pillow.

Lainey shrieked and ducked. "Hey! Stop hitting the pregnant girl!"

"Where do you want me?" Lainey asked, shifting uncomfortably from foot to foot. India was flitting around her studio, adjusting a camera on a tripod, setting up an enormous octagonal-shaped light box, straightening out the black backdrop. The room they were in was large and windowless, and filled with camera equipment and props.

"Just a minute," India said, again fiddling with the camera. She glanced up. "Are you tired? You can go sit in the reception area, if you want, while I get set up here."

"No, I'm okay." The truth was, Lainey was fascinated by how focused and serious India was. It was so different from the ingratiating, hovering India she normally saw at home.

India dragged a white chaise in front of the backdrop. "Go ahead and sit down," she said.

"Like this?" Lainey asked, reclining back on the chaise and fluffing her hair up with both hands.

"I'll pose you in a minute. Let me just get a light reading," India said. She checked the light level and then spent a few busy minutes getting the light boxes positioned correctly, before turning back to Lainey. "Okay. Now. Turn your shoulders here. And your head this way," India said, maneuvering Lainey into position with a light touch of the hand. "There. Hold that."

It felt awkward holding herself in such an artificial position. India returned to her position behind the camera and began snapping pictures. She'd give Lainey instructions—"Raise your chin a bit. No, not quite that much. There! Perfect! Hold it!"—and then, after snapping a few quick shots, would return to pose her again, occasionally having Lainey stand so India could push the chaise into a different position. Lainey posed with her head resting on her arms, lying back with one hand draped near the baby bump, leaning back against the chaise. It didn't seem very glamorous. Every time Lainey tried to strike a sexy pose—bending forward to show cleavage, or opening her mouth seductively—India would stop her.

"Are you sure I shouldn't be wearing something dressier?" Lainey asked. At India's direction, she was wearing her maternity jeans and a white tank top.

"No. This is perfect. I want you to look casual," India said with such authority Lainey didn't question her further.

The photo session was relatively short; after thirty minutes India announced that she had enough.

"You did a great job," India said. "You're a natural."

And although Lainey thought India might just be buttering her up again, she couldn't help feeling a flush of pleasure at the compliment. No one had ever before told her she'd been a natural at anything.

"Do you take all of your pictures here?" Lainey asked.

"It depends. I do all of the formal portraits here, but I actually prefer working in natural light," India said. "I do a lot of shoots at the beach, or at the nature preserve."

"Why? Is natural light better?"

"I think so. It's actually what I'm known for. I prefer the effect, although it can be less predictable. That's why some photographers prefer working with artificial lights." India gestured to the light boxes. "The results are more consistent. But these lights are really just meant to replicate natural light, so I figure why not use the real thing."

Lainey remembered the photos hanging on the Halloways' walls. Candid shots India had taken of Jeremy wading in the surf, Georgia sitting in a garden, wearing a big hat and laughing up at the camera, Otis asleep on his back with all four paws sticking straight up. They looked like pictures out of a magazine.

"So why did you take my picture inside?"

India opened her mouth to speak, but then stopped and frowned. "You know, I'm not sure. Most of the maternity portraits I've seen are posed. Actually, much more so than I just did with you—they often have lots of dreamy special effects, smudged edges, the subject dressed in a flowing white dress. Really not my style at all. I guess I assumed that most women would want their maternity portraits to be, well, not formal, but definitely stylized." The frown deepened, and India started muttering to herself. "But you're right, maybe it's silly to do that just because it's what other photographers do. I should just shoot the show in my style. Forcefully bring my perspective to this project. Hell! Why didn't I think of that before? I should know better!" India exclaimed, growing more animated by the moment. Her eyes were bright and her cheeks flushed. She suddenly stopped and smiled at Lainey—a smile of such real pleasure, Lainey was taken aback.

"Thank you," India said warmly. She grabbed Lainey's hand and squeezed it.

"What for?" Lainey asked, staring down at their linked hands. The familiarity made her uneasy. She pulled her hand back, out of India's grasp.

India didn't seem to notice the rebuff. "You made me realize exactly what I've been doing wrong. Come on. Let's go to the beach," India said, grabbing her camera bag. "I'm going to kick it old school, and use my Leica."

"What . . . now?" Lainey asked.

"Yes, now! The light will be perfect."

"But I'm hungry. It's almost dinnertime. I could kill or die for some ice cream."

India looked at her thoughtfully. "I'll tell you what: I'll stop and buy you an ice-cream cone on the way, *if* you promise not to drip it on your shirt."

"Can I have chocolate?" Lainey asked hopefully.

But India shook her head. "Vanilla," she said strictly. "You're wearing a white shirt. Chocolate would be flirting with disaster."

"Fine," Lainey said, sighing. Even though she pretended she was giving in, she felt a secret thrill of excitement at the prospect at being the subject of one of India's black-and-white photos, of seeing herself in magazine-photo perfection. "But I want chocolate sprinkles."

"Deal. But hurry. I want to get there before we lose the light."

The beach shoot was such a success that, to celebrate, India stopped off at Hunan Palace on the way home for takeout. She urged Lainey to order everything that sounded good, and they ended up leaving with three heavy, steaming bags of food. When they got back to the house, India laid the food out on the coffee table, after giving Otis strict instructions that he was to stay away. He went as far away as his bed, where he lay down, staring intently at the food and drooling conspicuously. Lainey and India sat on the floor, eating right out of the boxes and watching a reality makeover show, where the hosts bullied a frumpy middle-aged woman into throwing out all of her clothes and getting blonde highlights.

"Why did she have to throw out her sweatpants?" India asked indignantly. "What's she supposed to wear when she's vegging out at home?"

"She was wearing those sweatpants to work," Lainey pointed out.

"Still. They could have left her one pair to watch TV in." India groaned, pushing a carton of kung pao chicken away from her. "I'm stuffed. I can't eat another bite."

"I can," Lainey said, digging into the vegetable fried rice. She tipped the box toward India. "Look at me, I'm voluntarily eating vegetables."

India giggled and took a sip of red wine. "Good, then I don't have to nag you for another twelve hours."

It was the most relaxed Lainey had ever seen India. The tense lines around her eyes were gone, and her smile was genuine.

"What does it feel like?" India asked. "Being pregnant, I mean."

Lainey considered. "Better now that I don't feel sick all the time. But it feels a little weird when the baby moves around." She shrugged and rested a hand on her bump.

"Does it hurt?" India asked.

"No. It's more like having a little ocean inside of you, with an octopus swimming around inside of it. Most of the time I don't feel it, but then every once in a while it bumps up against me," Lainey said. When India laughed, Lainey looked up, suspicious that India was laughing at her. But then she saw that India wasn't mocking her. She was tickled at the idea.

"I had no idea," India said. "I never thought to ask my friends when they had babies. I guess I assumed that I'd find out when..." She stopped suddenly, her smile vanishing.

The silence that followed made Lainey feel uneasy. She picked up one of India's hands and studied the short square nails with a professional eye.

"You should let me do your nails for you," Lainey said. "I could make them look a lot better."

India stared ruefully at her nails. "I never take care of them. I'd like to claim it's easier to work with short nails, but the truth is, I'm just lazy about it."

"You can keep them short, but they'd look better with polish," Lainey advised. "I'd probably recommend going with a pinky beige for a natural look. Or you could go the other way, and do a really dark red. That would be hot."

"I've never thought of myself as a red-nail-polish kind of a woman," India mused.

"Why not try something new?" Lainey said, releasing India's hand.

India shrugged back. "You're right, why not?"

They fell silent for a few minutes, both watching the television. It wasn't awkward, though, Lainey thought. It was an easy silence. Almost like when she hung out with Flaca.

"You said you've done other photo shoots at that beach. Do you have any pictures here?" Lainey asked.

India looked up and smiled. "You really want to see them?"

"Sure," Lainey said.

India stood and walked over to one of a pair of bookshelves that flanked an enormous mirror, and pulled out a large book bound in black leather. It was one of a dozen, lined up neatly on a shelf. India paged through it, then put it back and chose another.

"Here they are," she said. India brought the book to Lainey and then sat cross-legged on the sofa with her wine.

Lainey began to slowly page through the book. Each page held one black-and-white photograph, all taken at the beach, although the subject matter varied. A wide expanse of ocean with low dark clouds swirling over. A close-up of a starfish covered with white ridges. Ribbons of sand intercut with thousands of broken shells. A little girl with a headful of ringlets throwing a stone into the water. An even smaller boy with serious dark eyes standing barefoot on the beach, holding out a shell to the unseen photographer. A dog, soaking wet from the belly down, romping in white foaming waves.

"Is this Otis?" Lainey asked, holding the book up for India to see.

India nodded. "I took that photo the day Jeremy and I met. In fact, I shot that with my very first Leica. I had to work two jobs to save up for it."

"What's a Leica?"

"It's a very high-quality film camera. Not many photographers use film anymore. I don't use it much, myself. Everything's digital these days, so you do all of your editing on the computer. But sometimes you just can't beat real film."

Lainey turned the pages of the album slowly. "Where did you learn to do this?"

"College," India said. "I went to the University of Florida."

"Did you always know you wanted to be a photographer?" Lainey asked.

India considered this. "Not always, no. When I first started school, I planned to go into graphic design. But I was never very passionate about it. Then, during my second semester freshman year, I took an Intro to Photography course on a lark. And I just fell in love. It was just so freeing, I suppose. It gave me the power to capture a single perfect moment. I was hooked. I can't imagine doing anything else with my life."

"I've never heard anyone talk about their job like that before," Lainey said.

"That's just it. It's not just a job to me. I remember when I was little, my dad told me that if I could find a way to make a living doing something I loved, I would have a happy life. And while I don't think it's quite as simple as that, there's a lot of truth in it," India said. She twirled the stem of her wineglass slowly around in one hand. "My dad was an old hippie— worse than my mom, if you can believe it—but he occasionally made a lot of sense. He passed away when I was in college. But I guess you already knew that—it was in our adoption profile."

Lainey, who had not read their adoption profile closely, hadn't known.

"My dad left when I was a kid," Lainey said. She felt shy sharing this, as though she were a child trying to make friends by breaking a chocolate bar in half and offering up one of the pieces.

"Where is he now?" India asked.

"I don't know. He's never stayed in touch. Sometimes he sent me a birthday card, although it was always, like, three months late," Lainey said with a forced laugh.

India did not laugh along with her. Instead, her eyes opened wide with sympathy. "Are you serious? That's terrible. I'm sorry."

Lainey shrugged and looked away, wishing she hadn't said anything. The back door opened and then thumped shut. Otis— who'd been stretched out on his rectangular cushion, keeping one watchful eye on the cartons of Chinese food, ever hopeful that an egg roll would happen his way—leapt to his feet, stretched, and padded out of the room. A moment later, Jeremy appeared, framed in the doorway, Otis wiggling with happiness at his feet.

"Hi," India said, looking up. "Where've you been? You missed dinner."

"I was working at the library. I guess I lost track of time," Jeremy said. He still had his green canvas messenger bag slung over one shoulder.

"Are you hungry?" India asked.

"No, I grabbed a sandwich while I was out."

"Sit down and join us. I'll pour you a glass of wine," India said.

"No, thanks. I'm going to go upstairs and take a shower," Jeremy said. He gave Lainey a half-smile and then disappeared back into the hall.

Lainey stood. The warm, intimate mood had disappeared. Suddenly, she felt awkward and out of place, as though she didn't belong there.

"I should probably go," she said abruptly.

"You don't have to," India said. She patted the couch. "Stay and watch TV. I think there's another makeover show coming on.

Maybe this time the hosts will make the lady cry when they tell her all of her clothes are ugly."

"I'm too tired," Lainey said, feigning a wide yawn. "I'm about to fall asleep. I'll do your nails tomorrow, okay?"

"Sure. Okay," India said, nodding, watching Lainey get to her feet. "See you tomorrow."

Nine
JEREMY

The thing about B2, is that yeah, okay, so it's dark and stuff...but that's also the beauty of it. JH clearly wanted Rogan to come face-to-face with his demons—his mother deserting him when he was a baby, his dad dying in the Dust Wars, the brother that raised him turning out to be a spy for the Ice Race—and come to terms with all of that before he duels Pilot at the end of the book.

I reread HippyChick's post on the FutureRaceFantatics online message board, before hitting the Reply button. The shorthand of the board had taken a bit of getting used to at first—"B2" meant Book Two of the Future Race series, entitled *The Dark Dust,* "JH" was me—but now I was an old hand. I drafted my response.

You really nailed that. It was necessary for Rogan to reach his lowest point—which came when he discovered that his girlfriend, Trixie, was having an affair with his traitorous brother, and had been passing on information to the Ice Race about Rogan's whereabouts—in order for him to shed

his skin, and transform into a new man. A harder
man, it's true, but also a much tougher, much
deadlier warrior. The warrior who, in fact, is finally
able to kill Pilot.

I typed, my fingers flying over the keyboard, and hit the Post Reply button. The page reloaded with my new post at the end, written under my online alias, Magnus. I waited a few minutes, and another reply popped up from HippyChick.

Magnus, you ROCK! You totally get where JH is
coming from! Are you totally PSYCHED for B7???
The title of the book hasn't been announced yet,
but I read on JH's website that it's going to focus
on Griff stepping up to take Rogan's place, now
that he's dead. I thought up an AMAZING name…
THE WARRIOR'S APPRENTICE.

It actually wasn't a bad title, I thought. Better than anything I'd come up with so far; the working title was currently INSERT KICK-ASS TITLE HERE. I'd been hoping inspiration would strike while I was in the process of writing, but I hadn't been doing much of that lately. I was only forty-eight pages into the manuscript, stuck at the point where Griff's teen son, Lorcan, is kidnapped by a band of traveling metal collectors (metal being a rare commodity in the Future Race world). It wasn't that I worried about Lorcan's fate—Griff would, of course, save him, but not before Lorcan ended up in the hands of Griff's nemesis, Tertia, the wily female head of the Bixan clan, thus setting up a sexually-charged-albeit-not-consummated Mrs. Robinson scenario. It was more that I'd run out of steam. And rather than banging my head against my keyboard while I tried to think of a new laser-powered weapon system that could be deployed against Griff and his ragtag group of freedom-loving followers, I found it was far more pleasant to pass my time reading the nice things that HippyChick and the other FutureRaceFanatics had to say about my books.

At first, I'd avoided the temptation of posting on the board. But eventually I found myself drawn in when HippyChick and another regular, BobaFett36, were debating whether Future Race was supposed to be an allegory for World War II, and I had to jump in with my opinion that no, it was definitely not. I hated allegorical storytelling. Of course, I couldn't admit to being me. For one thing, I'd look like an asshole if I admitted to lurking on a website for fans of my books. And for another, they might not believe that I was me, but just some loser claiming to be me, and run me off. So I created an online alias for myself—Magnus—and posted on the allegory thread.

The problem was that once I had started, I found it hard to stop. Internet message boards were oddly addictive. They allowed you to carry on in-depth conversations without having to go to the trouble of actually talking to anyone. Also, you could contain your conversations to just those areas that you found interesting—you weren't forced into having to listen to someone bore on about his diet, or the dream he'd had the night before, or how much he hated his boss.

I hit the Reply button and was about to tell HippyChick how much I dug her proposed title, when I heard the metallic clink of our mail slot being opened, and then the thump as the mail fell into a basket India had nailed to the door.

Otis, who'd been sleeping on his bed in the corner of the dining room, jumped to his feet with a startled bark.

"Easy, killer," I said.

When we'd first moved in, there hadn't been a basket in place, so the mail would just fall to the floor in a pile. This was how we discovered Otis's fetish for envelope glue, although not before he'd eaten both the utilities bill and a birthday card to India from my mother, which we later learned—when my mother took me aside after Thanksgiving dinner to complain that India had never thanked her—had also contained a gift certificate to Hickory Farms.

Glad to have a legitimate excuse to take a break from writing, I stood, stretched—was it normal for my back to make that popping sound?—and went to collect the mail. It was the usual assortment of bills, junk mail, glossy catalogues, and requests from our respective alma maters for donations. I pulled out the Visa bill and our mortgage statement, and then headed to the kitchen, where India was readying dinner. I dropped the rest of the mail straight into the recycling bin.

"Anything for me?" India asked, not looking up from the carrot she was dicing with a deadly looking chef's knife.

"Nothing good," I said. "Not unless you're planning on donating a new student union building to the University of Florida."

"Mmm, not this year," she said.

Backtracking to the dining room, I first opened the mortgage statement—confirming that yes, we still owed a monstrously large sum that we couldn't ever hope to repay to the bank—and then the Visa bill, which I expected to contain the usual higher-than-strictly-necessary balance.

And then I read the impossibly high number on the bill.

"What?" I muttered aloud.

I stared down at it, trying to make sense of the numbers I was seeing there. There was no way we'd spent nearly fifteen hundred dollars in a single month. Was there? No, of course not, I thought, relief trickling through me. It must be a mistake. Either that, or we were victims of credit card theft. And if that was it, Visa would refund the money that had been illegally charged.

I looked at the list of charges, expecting to see charges for computer or electronic stores or pornography websites, and suddenly felt like I'd been sucker punched. $424 at Pea in the Pod. $285 at Mimi Maternity. $190 at The Gap. $390 at Coach.

Wait, Coach? I had a vague memory of something to do with

Coach. An overheard snippet of conversation between India and Lainey about a handbag. A handbag Lainey was carrying. That's right, now I remembered! India was complimenting Lainey on the handbag. A *Coach* handbag.

Realization dawned. Lainey must have stolen our credit card and gone shopping with it!

Oh, God, I thought. India was not going to take this well. She probably wouldn't even want to report it to the police and risk upsetting Lainey, but without a police report, the credit card company surely wouldn't cover the loss, would they? Or was it even legal to report it? Did it count as fraud when the perpetrator was your future baby's birth mother? Knowing India, she'd want us to just swallow the additional debt, to pretend it hadn't happened, rather than risk upsetting Lainey. But if we didn't confront it—confront Lainey—what would stop her from doing it again? Did I really have to sit by and say nothing while this woman torpedoed our credit and drove us even deeper into debt we couldn't afford?

I fisted my hands on top of the dining table to stop them from shaking. "India, can you come in here for a second?" I called.

I could hear the rhythmic beat of India's knife slicing through vegetables, readying them for pasta primavera, followed by the muffled clank of a knife being set down on the counter. A moment later, India appeared in the doorway, wiping her hands on a dish towel she'd fashioned into an apron by tucking it into the waist of her jeans.

"What's up?" she asked.

"Is Lainey here?"

"No. She went to the movies with my mom," India said.

This momentarily distracted me. "With your mom?" I repeated. "Why?"

India laughed. "I know, right? They're like the new Odd Couple. I don't really get it, but they seem to love hanging out together."

I refocused. "Look at this," I said, pushing the Visa bill across the table to her. Her face went pale and her eyes widened before she'd even picked it up.

"I can explain," India said quickly.

"You can explain," I said, confused by her reaction. "You mean you *knew* about this?"

"Of course I knew. What did you think?"

"I thought Lainey stole our Visa card."

India frowned. "That's terrible. I can't believe you think she'd do something like that."

"What else was I supposed to think?" I retorted, my voice ringing with frustration. "That you'd be stupid enough to run our Visa bill up to its limit?"

"Excuse me?"

"The fact that you're not denying it leads me to believe that yes, you really were that stupid." I was light-headed with anger, but even so, I had a distant feeling that this might be going a bit too far. The fact that India's blue eyes were flashing—always a danger sign—supported this.

"Please calm down," India said.

But I couldn't calm down. "Do you not get that we're in a financial crisis? Seriously, do you not get that? We owe a *lot* of money. More than we can pay off anytime soon. We have no savings left. None. And every month, the bills coming in are more than we make. Which means every month, I have to figure out what I can get away with not paying and still avoid having our water or power turned off or our mortgage foreclosed." I could hear my voice rising into a near-shout, but I couldn't stop myself. "And while I'm conducting this horrible balancing act, you're off buying, what?" I looked down at the Visa bill, now crumpled in my hand. "A four-hundred-dollar handbag? God knows what at The Gap? Seven hundred dollars of maternity clothes? Do you not see how insane that is?"

India crossed her arms and glared at me. "And do you have any idea what couples in this very city are willing to pay for a healthy baby? A Coach handbag is the least of it. There are birth mothers out there getting cars and apartments and bank accounts. It doesn't matter if it's legal or not, or if it's moral, it's happening. What if Lainey finds out? Do you want her to dump us and run?"

"We have a contract," I said.

"Which means nothing, as you well know! She has the right to change her mind at any time up until the point that the adoption papers are signed. Do you get that? *At any time.* And she can't even sign the papers until forty-eight hours after the birth."

"And so, what? You're going to let her hold us hostage until then?"

"Stop being so dramatic. She's not holding us hostage. She didn't ask for anything. I offered to get her that stuff," India said.

"Why would you do that?"

"I told you. I want to keep her happy," India said.

"Even if it means driving us into bankruptcy? Because that's where we're headed. We could lose our home, India. Is that what you want?"

"Of course not. But I don't think things are as bad as you're making them out to be. We both have good jobs. With all of the extra work I'm doing, my earnings this year are up," India said.

"Which would be great, except for the small fact that you're giving all of that extra money to Lainey to replace her income!"

"So now I'm the bad guy because I don't want our birth mother inhaling nail polish?"

"I'm not saying you're the bad guy," I said. "But it's simple math: We can't spend money we don't have. The end."

"Aren't you up for a new contract with your publisher? Why don't you ask for a larger advance?" India suggested.

"I can't do that."

"Why not?"

The last shreds of my self-control dissolved. "Because right now, I'll be lucky to have any advance at all."

India stilled, her hand resting on the back of a black dining chair. "What does that mean?"

I suddenly remembered—a moment too late—that I hadn't told India about the latest crappy royalty statement; that I had, in fact, been purposely keeping this information from her. Partly, I didn't want to upset her, not when she was already under so much stress, first from the failed infertility treatments and now the pending adoption. But that wasn't the whole truth. I also hadn't wanted to admit my failure. I stared at the table, unable to look her in the eye.

"My books sales are down. The last time I spoke to my editor, he wasn't what I'd call optimistic about the future of the series," I said.

"Why didn't you tell me?"

I shrugged. "You've had enough to worry about lately. I didn't want to add to it."

"You didn't want to add to my worries," India repeated.

She stared at me, blinking in a dazed way. My anger softened. I knew what she was going to say before she even said it: We were a team. She always wanted to know what was happening with me, good or bad. We loved each other and that was all that mattered.

But what she actually said was "What the hell sort of a pathetic excuse is that?"

"What?"

"You've been lying to me?"

"I didn't lie," I protested.

India snorted. "Please. Don't even try to argue that holding back that sort of information from me wasn't deceptive. Especially in light of the constant, never-ending discussions you insist on having about our finances."

My anger flared up again. "So let me get this straight. To you, this," I held up the credit card bill again, "is an acceptable thing to do. But my not telling you about a work problem that hasn't even happened yet is unacceptable?"

India was gazing at me as though I were a stranger. "Why can't you be with me on this?" she asked. Her voice was no longer angry, but instead was tinged with such sadness I went cold. I had a sinking feeling that this was one of those Big Moments, that whatever I said next could make or break us, and I had no idea how to make it better.

"I don't know what you need from me," I said helplessly.

India pressed her lips together, and her eyes filled with tears. I wanted to stand up and take her in my arms, to hold her and smooth away her sadness, but I couldn't. I was too angry, too overwhelmed by the situation. So I just sat there, with the table and what felt like a vast space between us, and looked helplessly up at her.

"Jeremy," she began.

But before she could finish, the kitchen door opened and shut. Georgia's voice rang out, mingling with Lainey's laughter. There was the clatter of footsteps across the hardwood floors, and then Georgia and Lainey—giggling together like a pair of teenagers—appeared behind India, framed in the doorway to the dining room. Lainey looked from India to Jeremy, and her smile slowly disappeared.

But Georgia, clearly oblivious to the tension, said, "What's for dinner? I hope there's something more than those vegetables in the colander. Lainey's craving garlic bread."

India attempted a smile for Lainey's benefit. "You are?"

"No, Georgia is," Lainey said. "I hate garlic bread."

"Traitorous girl," Georgia bellowed. "That's the last time I buy you the extra-large popcorn at the movies."

"You should have gotten me the Raisinets, too," Lainey said, throwing Georgia an evil grin.

"I'll go finish dinner. And if you play your cards right, and stop griping about the vegetables, I'll make you your garlic bread," India said. "But someone's going to need to go to the store for French bread. We don't have any."

"I'll go," Lainey offered. "I'm still craving Raisinets."

"Thanks. Let me get my purse and I'll give you some money," India said.

Without looking at me, she walked out of the room, with Georgia and Lainey trailing in her wake.

I wandered outside. Before I even saw him, the rhythmic thud of a basketball on pavement told me Kelly was out shooting hoops. He was wearing a sleeveless gray T-shirt and long baggy shorts, and was dribbling the ball with a practiced ease.

"Hey," I said, walking up his driveway.

"Hey," Kelly replied. He bounced the ball to me. I dribbled a few times, then took a shot. The basketball rolled around the rim and then fell out.

"Great," I said flatly.

Kelly crowed with laughter. He retrieved the ball, bounced it back and forth between his legs, and then took a shot. The ball swished through the net.

"And that's how it's done. Nothing but net," Kelly said, throwing me the ball.

I bounced the ball twice and took another shot. This time it rattled on the frame, but eventually fell in. This gave me a ridiculous rush of pleasure.

I knew why Kelly annoyed India so much. With his expensive toys, young girlfriends, and gobs of disposable income, it was hard not to resent how easily everything came to him. Even his job, managing his hip downtown bar, was glamorous. But although I wouldn't admit it to India upon pain of scrotum waxing, a small part of me envied Kelly. His success, his money, even the women. His life seemed so easy. And so unlike mine.

"Who's the hot chick I keep seeing coming and going from your place?" Kelly asked.

It took me a minute to think of who he was talking about. "You mean Lainey?"

Kelly shrugged. "I've just seen her from a distance. Dark hair, long legs, nice ass."

"Lainey," I confirmed.

"What's the story with her?"

"She's pregnant. We're adopting her baby."

Kelly whistled and shook his head. "Are you serious?"

"Yeah," I said, hoping I wouldn't have to go into detail about our infertility. And, if I did, I wondered how I could make it clear that it was an issue with India, and not me, without violating India's privacy. Ever since one of India's book club friends had, after too many glasses of wine, laid a sympathetic hand on my arm and asked if my sperm count was low, I now worried that everyone immediately assumed the fault lay with me.

"She's pretty hot for someone who's knocked up," Kelly said. "Is she single?"

"Dude," I said. "Do not hit on our birth mother."

"Why not? Pregnant sex is hot. At least, it is until they get huge. But there's that period right in the middle, when their tits get really big and they're up for it, like, all the time," Kelly said. "In fact, it was the only time my ex-wife was ever up for it."

I caught the basketball Kelly tossed to me. "That is way too much information."

Kelly laughed. "There she is now," he said, looking across the street toward our house. Lainey was leaving, the infamous Coach handbag slung over one shoulder. She glanced over in our direction and nodded once. I raised my hand in a listless wave. Kelly lifted his chin and called out, "Hey there." Lainey climbed into her dented car and pulled out of the driveway.

"Smoking hot," Kelly said, watching her drive away.

I shook my head and turned to take another shot at the basket. This time the ball whistled through the air and sank straight through the net without touching the rim.

I wanted to talk to India, but she successfully avoided me for the rest of the evening. Georgia decided to hang around after dinner, and she and India ended up watching some insipid television show with Lainey about people who were set up on blind dates. It didn't seem very realistic, and I couldn't stomach Georgia's ongoing commentary about how it was a fascinating insight into modern youth and good research for her poetry, when it was clear that she was really just delighted to ogle the shirtless young men and their washboard abs. I retreated to the dining room, closing the folding doors behind me.

I was just getting settled in to discuss theories about the plots of upcoming Future Race books with the FutureRaceFanatics board when there was a knock on the door.

"Come in," I said. I expected it to be India, wanting to finish our talk. I was surprised when Lainey slid open the pocket door and walked in.

"Hi," she said.

"Hi."

Lainey wandered around the dining room, looking at the pictures on the wall—a series of framed botanical prints India had unearthed at a thrift store—and a collection of conch shells on the sideboard. She picked one up and lifted it to her ear.

"Do you hear the ocean?" I asked.

"No," she said.

"I never could, either."

Lainey put the shell down. "What do you do in here?"

"What do you mean?"

"You spend all of your time shut up in here," Lainey said.

"I'm working," I said, wondering why she was making me feel

defensive. Surely I didn't owe her an explanation for how I spent my time.

"So, what, you're writing a book?" Lainey asked.

I nodded. She glanced at my computer screen, where the FutureRaceFanatics website was on display. Damn. I'd forgotten to minimize it.

"What's that?" Lainey asked. Before I could answer, she walked swiftly around the table—she moved surprisingly fast for a pregnant woman—and leaned over to squint at the screen. "Future Race Fanatics?"

"Yeah. It's just a message board," I said. I reached for the mouse, but Lainey had stepped closer, blocking my access. I couldn't even reach around her; her rounded stomach was in the way.

"What sort of a message board?" she asked.

"It's nothing, really. Just a forum where people discuss books," I said. "Aren't you watching that show with India and Georgia?"

"No, it was boring. What kind of books do they discuss?"

"Actually, it's a board about my books," I admitted.

"Really? Cool," Lainey said. "I want to see what they wrote."

Before I could protest, she had dragged a chair over, settled herself in, and taken hold of the mouse. She began scrolling down, reading the thread I'd just opened.

"Make yourself at home," I said.

Lainey ignored my sarcasm. "Wow, they really like your books. Except for this guy."

"What guy?" I asked.

"Someone called Xerxon. Nice name." Lainey snorted. "He basically thinks your books suck."

So my old nemesis was back. Xerxon had posted quite a few unflattering critiques of my work on the boards, but he hadn't been around in a while. I thought HippyChick had driven him off.

"That goes along with the job. Not everyone's going to like

everything I write," I said, trying to sound magnanimous, even as I leaned closer to read what Xerxon had written.

> Haven't you idiots ever seen *Battlestar Galactica*? The whole premise of *Battlestar Galactica* is that humans are trying to escape killer robots, known as the Cylons. JH basically rips that off in book six, by having Griff and Juliet running away from the Titans, who have amped up their brains with artificial intelligence chips. That's why JH sux. All of his books are totally unoriginal.

"What? Future Race isn't anything like *Battlestar Galactica*," I said indignantly. "For one thing, *Battlestar Galactica* takes place in space. For another, it's a post-apocalyptic story. The only thing that *Battlestar Galactica* and Future Race have in common is that they both have artificial intelligence plotlines. But show me a sci-fi book that doesn't have an artificial intelligence plotline! It's practically required, along with a rogue protagonist and a spunky love interest. In fact, you could argue that *Battlestar Galactica* is derivative of *Star Wars*. I wonder what Xerxon would say to that."

But Lainey wasn't listening. She had clicked the Reply button, and started to type surprisingly fast, considering she only used two fingers.

"What are you writing?" I asked. I leaned forward to read.

> Xerxon is obviously a loser who doesn't have a girlfriend and so he spends all of his time stuffing Twinkies in his mouth and insulting people. I bet he's 15 years old and a virgin.

Lainey hit the Post key before I could stop her.

"I can't believe you just did that," I said.

"Trust me, this will totally get under his skin. Nothing annoys a nerd more than being called a virgin," Lainey said.

"How do you know that?" I asked. As an ex-nerd myself, I knew this was true, but I had a hard time picturing Lainey spending much time hanging around with geeks.

"I went to high school," Lainey said.

"Where you apparently spent your time tormenting nerds," I said.

Lainey clicked the Refresh icon for the webpage. There was a new post. We both leaned forward to read it. It was written by HippyChick, who was thrilled that someone was helping her flame Xerxon. She posted a message highly supportive of Magnus, including a liberal usage of exclamation points.

"That chick has issues," Lainey commented.

"Yeah, but she's on our side. And she's a fan," I said. "So don't insult her."

"Don't worry, I won't," Lainey said.

Xerxon didn't take long to respond. By the fourth time Lainey had refreshed the page, he had posted.

> I have a girlfriend, and she's really hot. So if any-
> one's a loser, it's you. Loser.

"I think you succeeded in getting under his skin," I said.

"I'm just getting started," Lainey said.

She started typing again, rattling off yet another insult. This time, Lainey wasn't content with maligning Xerxon's virility. She went on to insult his mother, hypothesize that his obesity was likely caused by an unhealthy dependence on deep-fried fast-food products, and finished by suggesting that he had immoral intentions toward various barnyard animals. HippyChick was jubilant. Xerxon was outraged, and began yelling—signified by his typing in all capital letters—that he'd have us banned from the Future-RaceFanatics board.

"I probably will get banned for this," I said ruefully.

"Because I called him a chicken fucker?" Lainey said.

"Yeah. I'm guessing that will probably do it. Boards like this usually have rules about not attacking fellow posters."

"Sorry," Lainey said. "I guess I had some pent-up aggression I needed to release. It's the hormones."

"By all means release it. I'd hate to see what you're like if you get any more pent up than that," I said.

"So, this is where you disappeared to. What are you guys doing in here?" Lainey and I looked up. India was standing at the door, holding a pint of rocky road ice cream in her hands. "Do either of you want ice cream?"

"Absolutely," Lainey said, springing to her feet. "I'm starving."

"I'm shocked," I said.

Lainey rolled her eyes, but smiled. She headed out of the dining room toward the kitchen, plucking the ice cream out of India's hands as she passed.

"What were you two doing?" India asked.

"Surfing the net," I said. "Lainey was giving me a lesson in how to get back at my critics. Remind me not to get on her bad side."

"Okay." India hesitated. "Thanks."

"For what?"

She glanced over her shoulder to make sure Lainey was out of earshot. "For spending some time with Lainey. Making an effort."

I nodded. I didn't know that was what I'd been doing, but as long as I was being praised, I wasn't about to argue.

"No problem," I said.

"And I'm sorry," India continued. "I should have talked to you before I spent all that money. It was a stupid thing to do. I guess I got carried away in the moment."

"I understand," I said, although I didn't really. But I also didn't want to fight anymore.

"Good." India smiled. She tilted her head in the direction of the kitchen. "Do you want to join us for some ice cream?"

I glanced at the computer, where the FutureRaceFanatics board was still up. I had been thinking I'd refresh the board a few more times and see how the havoc Lainey had wrought played out. But ice cream sounded good, too.

"Sure," I said. "Why not?"

Ten
INDIA

I had what I thought was a brilliant idea—I offered Lainey a job.

Now that she was halfway through her second trimester and her marathon bouts of nausea had finally subsided, Lainey's energy rebounded. Her hair was shiny, her skin was clear, and her stomach had popped out, so perfectly round it looked like she'd stuck a beach ball up under her shirt. I tried very hard not to stare at it. For the past few years, just the sight of a pregnant woman had felt like a razor blade slicing up my soul. But now, seeing *this* pregnant stomach, carrying *my* baby, brought an unexpected peace.

And so, noticing that Lainey was clearly feeling better and starting to get bored, I asked her if she'd be interested in working at the studio.

"Really? Me?" she asked, looking surprised when I brought it up one night after dinner. She and I were sitting in the living room, curled up on either end of the slip-covered sofa, watching TV. Jeremy was, as usual, locked away in his office, supposedly working, but more likely wasting time on the Internet. Every time I passed by, I saw that he had a browser open and was typing away on some sort of chat board. I wondered briefly if this was something I should be concerned about, but then put it firmly out of my mind. I had enough to worry about without adding to the pile.

"Yes, you," I said, smiling at her surprise. Sometimes Lainey seemed like such a kid—thrilled with a treat, happy at being included. Then, other times, I occasionally caught a chilling glimpse of the hardness Mimi had warned me about. I still couldn't tell if Lainey even liked me, although she did seem more relaxed around me than when she first moved in.

"But I don't know anything about photography."

"You don't have to. You'd be more of an assistant, really. You could help out on the shoots, help me with the kids. You were great with Rose when she was here visiting. That's what gave me the idea," I said.

Lainey had spent hours with Rose, first playing along with one of Rose's complicated make-believe games—it didn't matter what the story line was, the games all consisted of Rose telling you what to do and say—and then retiring to the living room to watch *Mary Poppins* together.

Lainey hesitated. "I don't know."

I tucked my feet up beneath me. "It was just an idea. If you're not interested, it's not a big deal."

"Well, okay. I guess I could try."

"Really?"

"Sure, why not?" Another of her trademark shrugs. By now, I could predict the shrug's arrival with such accuracy, I could have shrugged in perfect unison with her.

"Great," I said. "I'll be glad to have the help."

"I'm getting bored sitting around all the time with nothing to do," Lainey said.

"What did you used to do with your free time?" I asked.

"I worked," she said. "And I went to the gym a lot. Almost every day."

"We could ask Dr. Jones if you can start exercising now that you feel better," I suggested, although I immediately regretted it. Signing Lainey up for a gym membership—and thereby taking on yet another Lainey-related expense—would almost certainly annoy Jeremy. Especially considering Jeremy and I had had to drop our health club membership when the expenses related to the fertility treatments began piling up.

"I guess. I don't belong to that gym anymore. I'd have to find a new one."

"Why? Is it too far away?"

"No, but Trav—my ex—works out there," Lainey explained.

It was the first time Lainey had ever mentioned her ex-boyfriend to me. Part of me wanted to hear more about him, as our baby would inherit half of his genes. Was he smart, handsome, talented? Did he have an ear for music, or a natural affinity for languages, or the ability to throw a curveball? But at the same time, hearing his name for the first time filled me with dread. What if Lainey had started missing Trav? What if they reconciled and decided to keep the baby?

"Have you heard from Trav since you moved out?" I asked carefully.

Lainey snorted. "God, no. He tried to call me when I was staying at Flaca's, but that was just because he wanted his iPod back."

"Why? Did it get mixed up with your things when you were packing?" I asked.

Lainey looked at me with an almost pitying expression. "No. I took it to piss him off."

"Oh," I said, taken aback. "Did you ever give it back to him?"

"No way! Look, he knocked me up and then kicked me out. I deserved that iPod. Men are all assholes, anyway."

"Not all men," I said gently.

"Right," Lainey scoffed.

"No, really. I know it seems like they're all jerks when you're twenty, but some of them improve with age."

Like Jeremy, I thought, softening toward him. I realized just how much I'd been missing him. Everything had changed so much lately, and as a result, he and I hadn't been spending much time alone together. With the weddings I'd taken on, I was working a lot more, and Lainey had gotten in the habit of joining us for dinner every night.

What we need is a weekend away together, I thought. *A chance to be alone so we can reconnect.*

"My mom has had a lot of boyfriends, all of them a lot older than twenty. And they're all dicks, too," Lainey said.

"Okay, so maybe not every guy will improve. But a lot do," I said. Then, suddenly worried that she might take this as advice that she should reconcile with Trav on the off chance that he might not be such a bastard by the time he hit thirty, I hurriedly added, "But that doesn't mean you should put up with being treated badly, of course."

"So, what? I should date only older guys?"

"Maybe," I said. "Why, is there someone you're interested in now?"

"It's not like they're beating down my door. Not when I look like this," Lainey said, looking down at her swollen abdomen with disgust.

"I think you look beautiful," I said sincerely. It was true. Lainey had been a pretty girl before, but pregnancy had softened her. Her face was filling out along with her body, easing the sharp angles.

"You're crazy," Lainey said, although she gave a small smile. "Was Jeremy a jerk when he was twenty?"

"I didn't know him when he was twenty," I said.

"How old were you when you met?"

I tried to remember. "I think I was twenty-seven, so that would have made Jeremy twenty-eight."

"So you were old," Lainey said so bluntly I had to laugh.

"It doesn't seem like it now," I said. The person I had been at twenty-seven was like a stranger to me now. She had ambitions of becoming a world-famous portrait photographer, the sort whose work was prominently featured in magazines like *Vanity Fair.* She wasn't thinking of marriage, and certainly not of children. In fact, she'd have been shocked to learn just how baby obsessed she would become, I thought suddenly.

Or to know just how far Jeremy and she could drift apart.

"Hey," Jeremy said.

I was lying in bed, reading. Otis was up on the bed, too, his head hooked over my foot. I looked up, surprised by Jeremy's voice. I hadn't heard him come into the bedroom. Lately, he usually didn't come upstairs until after I'd gone to sleep.

"How did Lainey's first day of work go?" Jeremy asked.

"Fine," I said. And it had gone surprisingly well. Lainey had answered the phone, arranged a few appointments, and then assisted while I did a studio portrait of a five-year-old little boy and his toddler sister. Lainey stood behind me with a puppet of Count von Count from *Sesame Street* and did a surprisingly good imitation of the Muppet's voice: "One, two, *two* little children, ha-ha-ha!" The children were transfixed, and I took several excellent photographs of them beaming up at the camera.

"I wanted to talk to you about something," I said. "Two somethings, actually."

"What's that?"

"The first is that we haven't discussed baby names yet."

"That's true. Do you have any ideas?"

"What do you think about Lily?"

"For a girl or a boy?" Jeremy asked.

"Ha-ha. I was thinking of Liam for a boy," I said.

"Lily and Liam." Jeremy nodded. "Those are both good names."

"Don't you want to throw out a few ideas?" I asked. "That's how this normally works. I suggest the name Agatha, and you say there's not a chance in hell that we're going to name our daughter Agatha, and suggest Maude instead. And then we go back and forth."

"I would never suggest the name Maude," Jeremy said. "And I like the name Lily. It's pretty."

"Yes, it is. But there are other names. I like Madeline, too. And Sophia. And for boy names, I also like John and Christian. Unless you want to name him after you. Jeremy Junior."

"No, no juniors. Every junior I knew growing up was an ass-hole. Even worse were the number guys—Hugo the Third, Boris the Fourth."

"You grew up with a Boris?"

"No," Jeremy admitted. "It was just an example."

"Do you have any other ideas?"

"How about Boris?"

"No," I said. "But that's how it works. One of us pitches a name, and we both have veto power."

"Can I think about it?" Jeremy said.

I was disappointed at his lack of enthusiasm, but I nodded. "Sure, make a list. Anyway, the other thing I wanted to talk to you about is, I was thinking maybe we could go away for a weekend. Just the two of us. Now that Lainey's working for me, she can cover for me at the studio. I mean, she can't do photo sessions, ob-viously, but she can cover the phones and handle any customers that stop by. And I have a wedding-free weekend coming up at the end of the month. We wouldn't have to go anywhere expensive," I added quickly. "Maybe we could just drive down to the Keys for a few days. I found some good deals on hotels online."

"That's not a bad idea," Jeremy said. He sat on the edge of the bed, nudging Otis over. Otis groaned, but moved grudgingly.

"We'll go for walks on the beach and eat crab sandwiches."

Jeremy's eyes softened. "That sounds amazing. Do you think Lainey can handle the studio by herself?"

"She was great today."

"I never asked. How much did you agree to pay her?"

I hesitated. "Fifteen dollars an hour," I admitted.

To my surprise, Jeremy didn't seem outraged by this, even though it was more than I'd ever paid any other part-time employee I'd had over the past few years. In fact, he looked rather pleased about it.

"You don't mind?" I asked.

"Why would I? I can finally work without Lainey coming in and out of the house forty times a day, banging the kitchen cupboards and playing the television at full volume, and you've figured out a way to offset a portion of the money we're giving her. Even if it's just in the form of a tax deduction, every penny helps," Jeremy said cheerfully.

"I thought the adoption expenses were already tax deductible?"

"Partially, but the amount you can deduct is capped," Jeremy said. He looked thoughtful. "Maybe you should give her a raise. Pay her, like, thirty dollars an hour, so we can get an even larger tax break."

"Is that really a good idea?"

"Why wouldn't it be? It's money we'd be giving her anyway, right?" Jeremy said cheerfully as he stood and began to change into his pajamas.

"I guess that depends on what you mean by 'giving her anyway,'" I said carefully.

Jeremy, who'd been pulling his T-shirt off, froze. "Please tell me that you're not paying her above and beyond what we were already giving her. Please tell me you're not paying her salary replacement *and* a salary."

I held my book up higher, effectively covering my face from his sight.

"India!"

"What?"

"Don't pretend that you can't hear me when I'm talking to you," Jeremy snapped.

I put the book down. His cheeks were flushed and his lips were pressed together in a tight, white-edged line.

"I can hear you," I said carefully. "But can we talk about this calmly?"

Jeremy took a deep breath in, exhaled, and then, speaking in a deliberately calmer voice, he asked, "Are you paying Lainey money above and beyond the allowance we already agreed to pay her?"

I swallowed. "Yes," I admitted.

Jeremy closed his eyes and ran both hands through his hair. Then he turned abruptly away and continued the process of putting on his pajamas. He walked into the bathroom, shutting the door behind him, and I could hear the muffled sounds of toothbrushing and gargling. Five minutes later, he returned, although still not looking at me.

When I couldn't bear the silence any longer, I said, "Aren't you going to say anything?"

"What would you like me to say?" Jeremy asked coldly as he tossed his dirty clothes into the hamper.

"You're obviously angry at me. We should talk about it."

"Why?"

"Because that's what mature married people do when there's a problem."

"You don't talk to me," Jeremy said. He climbed into bed and yanked the covers up to his waist.

"Of course I talk to you."

Jeremy snorted. "Right. Like the way you talked to me before you agreed to give Lainey even more money on top of what we can't afford to be paying her now?"

I hesitated. "Okay. Maybe I should have discussed that with you first. But I told you, it's important that we keep Lainey happy."

"Yes, you have told me that," Jeremy said. He picked up a book and turned away, curling onto his side with his back facing me.

I stared at his stiff, angry form, turned away from me. "I thought we both wanted this. I thought we agreed we wanted to go forward with an adoption. Covering the birth mother's expenses is part of what's required."

"It's not the money. Well, it's not just the money," Jeremy said.

"What is it, then?"

"I didn't know it would be like this," Jeremy said quietly.

"Like what?"

Jeremy finally rolled over so he was lying on his back, staring up at the rotating ceiling fan. "This whole adoption thing is out of control. It's taken over our lives."

"No, it hasn't," I disagreed. "I know it's taking more time and resources than we might have originally thought. And I know it's been a little awkward having Lainey basically move in with us. That's why I suggested the weekend away. I thought we could use some time to ourselves."

"It's more than that," Jeremy said. "I feel like . . ." He stopped and waved a hand helplessly.

"What?"

"I feel like I'm drowning," Jeremy said.

The air left my lungs, and it was a few long beats before I remembered to start breathing again. "What are you saying? That you don't want to go through with the adoption?"

"I don't know what I want anymore," Jeremy said quietly.

I closed my eyes and curled my hands into fists. This wasn't happening, I thought. Not now. Not when we were so close to finally having a baby.

Jeremy continued, "Everything's changed so much, so quickly."

"That's just how it works. You wait and wait, and then you finally find a birth mother, and suddenly everything changes," I said.

"I think it was a bad idea to have Lainey move in to the guest-house. It crossed a line."

"It's unorthodox, I admit. But maybe it was meant to be."

"Meant to be?" Jeremy repeated dubiously.

"Maybe. I absolutely believe that this baby, Lainey's baby, was meant for us. So maybe whatever we have to go through to bring him or her home was meant to be. Maybe Lainey needed to come here, and meet us, to know that we would be the best choice," I suggested.

"Except that she made the decision to give us the baby about five minutes after she met us. She didn't exactly put a lot of thought into it," Jeremy said.

"Maybe she instinctively knew this was meant to be, too," I said. Jeremy gave a grunt of disbelief. "What, you don't believe that's possible?"

"I don't think there's some divine plan for us to have this baby, no," Jeremy said.

We lay there in silence. Otis rolled over on his back, sighed heavily, and began to snore.

"If you were unhappy with the situation, you should have said something before," I finally said.

"Before what?"

"Before I got my hopes up," I said. My throat felt thick and raw, and I could feel a sob pressing up in my chest. I swallowed hard, trying to hold it back.

"Look. I'm not saying I've changed my mind, or that I want to tell Lainey she has to move out. I just need you to know that I've been feeling overwhelmed. Something has to change."

Hot tears stung at my eyes. Where were we supposed to go from here? Unlike Jeremy, I was one hundred percent sure that this baby, Lainey's baby, was meant to be ours. If Jeremy didn't feel the same way, what happened then?

"I can't do this right now," I finally said.

"You're right. I probably shouldn't have brought it up right at bedtime," Jeremy said. "We can talk about it later."

I nodded, even though that's not what I had meant. It wasn't talking about it tonight that was the problem. It was talking about it at all. Jeremy rolled over and turned off his light. I did the same, although sleep was out of the question. I lay awake, staring up into the darkness long after Jeremy's breath had deepened into sleep.

Jeremy and I didn't continue our conversation the next day. After breakfast, Jeremy holed up in the dining room with the pocket doors closed, while I headed to my studio intending to spend the day compiling the album for the Farrell wedding and, if there was time, sorting through the maternity photos I had taken for my upcoming show. Lainey didn't come to work with me. She went off with my mother to have her tarot cards read by one of Georgia's poetry club friends. I was glad for the chance to be alone, and to lose myself in my work.

The wedding album went quickly, so I was able to turn my attention to the maternity proofs after lunch. I'd decided to feature ten women in the show, including Lainey. Dr. Jones had been helpful, sending a few of her patients my way. I'd asked each model to agree to pose at four different sessions, and in return, I would give each woman a copy of the portraits I used in the show. It was an agreement they'd all been pleased with. So far, each woman had sat for me three times, and I now had to go through the proofs, picking out which ones I wanted to use.

I marveled at how one of the models, Yasmin, had changed in the five weeks between sessions. At her first sitting, I'd photographed her at a local park, reclining in the grass. She'd been drawn and pale, and was barely showing. At the second shoot, perched in the bed of my old Ford pickup, she had transformed— her breasts were full, her stomach was rounded, her skin was glowing. But another model, Laura, was just the opposite. At her first sitting, she'd been about six months along, and blooming with the same sort of vitality I'd recently noticed in Lainey. But just three weeks later, she'd been exhausted and huge when I photographed her at the beach. In my favorite picture, she'd draped a striped towel around her shoulders and was staring down at her sandy feet, her eyes shuttered.

I'd been right to move the shoots from the stark white background and artificial light of my studio to the outdoor settings. The pictures didn't look like the sort you'd find on a greeting card—they were grittily real. All of the emotions associated with pregnancy, the joy, discomfort, worry, anticipation, were reflected in my models' faces.

After work, I stopped off at the grocery store, and by the time I got home, it was already dusk and an early moon was hanging full and low in the sky. It was what my mother had always called a "child's moon," because it was visible while children were still awake to see it. Both my mother's and Lainey's cars were parked in the driveway. Jeremy's was not.

"Hello?" I called out.

"I'm in here," Mom called out from the living room. The television wasn't blaring, which, I surmised, meant Lainey wasn't there. I was correct. My mother was alone, sitting on the sofa, reading a romance novel. I wasn't sure how this fit in with her bleak view of the publishing industry or her claims that she only read classical literature. I was fairly sure that none of the classics had cover art featuring a shirtless Fabio.

"Hi," I said. "Where is everyone?"

"Lainey's in her room, napping. Jeremy went out for a drink."

"He went out for a drink?" I repeated. Jeremy had never been much of a drinker. He'd occasionally go out for a beer if he had an old college buddy in town visiting, but that was about it. I felt a twinge of guilt. Was this a result of our upsetting talk the night before? Had he felt the need to drown his sorrows? "Do you know where he went?"

"He said something about a martini bar. I think he went with your neighbor from across the street."

"He went out with *Kelly?*"

Mom shrugged. "I guess so."

My eyes narrowed. I knew all about Kelly's bar, the Dirty Martini. Or, at least, I knew what Mimi had told me about it, and she's always had top-notch information. The Dirty Martini was the current hot spot for the young and horny. Jeremy wasn't drowning his sorrows; he was getting an eyeful at the local meat market.

"Are you hungry? I bought a rotisserie chicken at the store, and I'm making butternut squash risotto," I said, stalking back to the kitchen.

My mother trailed after me, still holding her trashy romance book, marking her place with one finger. I pulled the butternut squash out of the shopping bag, and began hacking it apart with my largest carving knife. It was an excellent way to channel my aggression.

"Is everything okay?" Mom asked.

"Fine," I said through gritted teeth.

"You don't seem fine. You seem angry."

Butternuts were a pain in the ass to slice, but according to the Bradley pregnancy diet—which I was preparing for Lainey, despite her insistence that french fries count as vegetables—a well-balanced pregnancy diet should include five servings of yellow or orange vegetables per week. Lainey categorically refused to eat anything orange, so I'd taken to sneaking her weekly ration in where she wouldn't suspect it, for example, adding pumpkin puree to homemade brownies. The squash in the risotto was harder to hide, but if I grated enough Parmesan cheese over the dish, maybe she wouldn't notice it.

"I'm not angry. I'm pissed off."

"There's a difference?"

"Yes," I said. "One makes you want to reevaluate your life. The other makes you want to hack things up with big knives."

"Do you want to talk about it?" Mom suggested.

"Not really."

"I thought Jeremy seemed out of sorts, too. A bit sad. Did you two have a fight?"

"Not exactly," I said.

"It would be understandable. You're both under a lot of pressure and going through some big changes in your life together. It would be odd if you weren't feeling the strain. Do you have any wine?"

"Check the fridge. There's an open bottle of white in there," I said. "If you'd rather have red, I think there's a bottle in the pantry."

My mom retrieved the red wine from the pantry and, after rummaging around in the kitchen drawers for a corkscrew, opened it. She poured generous servings into two wineglasses, and set one beside me on the counter, with the air of a nurse tending to an ailing patient.

"The important thing is that you and Jeremy talk things out, and don't let small hurts pile up into something more serious," Mom continued.

"I can't talk to him."

"Why not?"

"Because he's not the person I thought he was. Because it turns out that when the going gets tough, Jeremy shuts down," I said.

My mother settled herself into a kitchen chair and took a large gulp of wine. "This all has to be hard on him," she commented.

"On *him*! How is this hard on him?" I said, placing the knife down on the counter with a bit more force than necessary. I wiped my hands on a towel, yanked a pan out from under the counter, and plopped it onto the stove. I splashed some olive oil into the pan and turned on the burner. "What exactly does he do? I'll tell you: He does *nothing*. He spends all of his time closed up in his office."

"He's probably working," Mom said.

"That's just it, I don't think he *is* working. Every time I've gone in there, he's on the Internet." I dumped the cut-up squash in the pan. It sizzled pleasantly, giving off an earthy, caramel fragrance.

"That doesn't mean he's not working at other times. He's an artist, after all. We can't predict when the Muse will inspire us." My mother looked thoughtful as she sipped her wine. "You know, I've never been one to believe in archaic gender constructs, but it is very common for men to feel that they bear the ultimate responsibility for the family finances."

I turned on her, the full force of my anger and frustration bubbling up to the surface. "Oh, really? Then why am I the one working day and night trying to get the extra money we need to cover all of the adoption costs? Why am I the one who has to worry about everything all of the time? I'd love to check out for weeks on end like Jeremy, but you know what? I can't. I have too much responsibility! Oh! And I didn't even tell you! Do you know who called me today?"

"Who?"

"Carol, asking me if I'd like to be included in Stacey's baby shower!"

"That was nice of her," Mom said grudgingly. She and my mother-in-law had endured a strained relationship for years, dating back to my wedding, when words were had about whether a passage from the Bhagavad Gita would be read aloud during the ceremony.

"No, it wasn't! She didn't say, 'I'd love to throw both of you a baby shower.' Oh, no. Her exact words were, 'I'm hosting a baby shower for Stacey in late May, and I thought I'd check with you to see if you want to be included. I don't think it's appropriate to ask

Stacey's friends to get you presents,'" I paused, the words choking in my throat. " 'But we can put your name on the cake.'"

My mother's face darkened with anger. "I hope you told her to stick that cake right up her bottom."

I shook my head. "Of course not. I never do. Because for some insane reason, I never want to hurt her feelings." I gave the pan of squash a vigorous shake. "Besides, if I had turned her down, or hinted in any way that her offer was less than gracious, she would have just made a big stink about it." Tears stung at my eyes, and I wiped them, forgetting that I had squash goop on my hands. "So now I'm going to be forced to spend hours watching a hugely pregnant Stacey open presents, while I just sit there like a great big infertile freak! Not to mention it's the weekend right before my show, so it's about the worst possible time for me to have to drive up to Jacksonville! This is all Jeremy's fault."

"You can't blame Jeremy for what his mother does."

"Watch me."

"This is hard on him, too. The changes, the pressure . . . I'm sure Jeremy is doing his best."

I snorted. "Jeremy is an emotional cripple!"

I was just about to tell my mother how Jeremy had basically admitted he was having second thoughts about the adoption, when a movement by the door caught my eye. I turned my head, already knowing who it was. Lainey. How long had she been standing there? But I already knew: long enough to witness that I wasn't the patient, calm, perfect adoptive-mother-to-be I'd been pretending all along to be. My stomach tightened, and a ripple of fear passed over me.

"Hi," Lainey said. She looked from me to my mother. Otis got up off his bed and, tail wagging, greeted Lainey. She petted his head.

"Hi. Come in and sit down. Can I get you anything? Would you like a cup of herbal tea?"

Lainey wrinkled her nose. "Gross," she said.

"Hot chocolate?" I suggested.

She hesitated. "Do you have any marshmallows?"

"Yes, of course!" I began rushing around, putting the milk in the microwave to heat, getting out the cocoa and the marshmallows. "Did you get some rest?"

"Yeah, I guess," Lainey said. She yawned widely, not bothering to cover her mouth.

"Good for you!" I said cheerily while I spooned some cocoa into the mug.

I could hear myself—I sounded like some sort of a maniacal Stepford wife. What the hell I was doing? Why was I trying to convince Lainey of my perfection, even now after she'd seen me coming unglued? I stared down at the mug, gripping the handle in one hand, while fatigue rolled over me like a damp fog.

"Sweetheart?"

I looked up. Mom and Lainey were both staring at me. My mother's eyebrows were drawn down in concern, and Lainey looked confused.

"Are you all right?" Mom asked gently.

"Yes." But even as I said the word, my head began to shake from side to side. "No."

"You've lost all of your color. Here, you sit down. I'll make the cocoa. I wouldn't mind a mug myself. Do you have any Bailey's Irish Cream to put in it?"

I sat down woodenly, still clutching my wine. I could feel Lainey's dark eyes watching me. I met her gaze and smiled weakly.

"Sorry," I said. "I plead temporary insanity induced by my husband."

To my surprise, Lainey's face lit up with a smile. "I know how that goes," she said. "I was once so pissed off at my ex I dropped his iPod in the toilet."

My eyes went round with surprise. "Really? Wait, I thought you said you took his iPod when you moved out?"

"Oh, I did. I took the new one he bought to replace the one I flushed."

My mother stirred the hot milk into the two coffee mugs, added a dollop of Bailey's to her mug, and passed the virgin one to Lainey.

"You should be careful with revenge," Mom advised. "Even if it's justified, you can still create bad karma."

Lainey and I looked at each other and we both smiled.

"What?" Mom asked indignantly. "It's true."

"Lainey, remind me to rub a crystal over your forehead later to dispel the bad karma," I said.

Lainey giggled into her cocoa. With her face bare of makeup, her hair pulled back in a ponytail, and a genuine smile lighting her face, Lainey looked like a sixteen-year-old, hanging out after school.

Lainey stood. "I want more marshmallows," she announced, retrieving the bag from the kitchen counter and grabbing a handful. She stopped to look into the pan. "India, I think something over here is burning."

I jumped up and ran to the stove. "Oh, no! The squash!" I stared into the smoking pan. "Damn. I think it's ruined. I had the heat up too high."

"Were you doing that thing where you hide vegetables in my food?" Lainey asked.

"You know about that?"

Lainey rolled her eyes. "Duh," she said. "There were orange blobs in the brownies you made the other day. So gross."

I dropped the still-sizzling pan into the sink and ran cold water into it. "Well, dinner's ruined. I vote we order a pizza."

"Can we get it with pepperoni?" Lainey asked hopefully.

I hesitated only a moment, before deciding that if there was ever a time to relax my ban on processed meat products, this was it. "Absolutely. We'll get it with *everything*," I said, and reached for the phone. "And for dessert, we'll eat ice cream right out of the carton. The real stuff, not the low-fat yogurt I'm always pushing on you."

Lainey cheered.

"Excellent," my mother agreed. "I'm glad I decided to stay for dinner." She tossed back the last of her spiked cocoa and then looked up. "You did invite me, right?"

Eleven
LAINEY

Lainey was covering the phone and front desk at the studio while India was at a photo shoot at the beach. She sat perched on a tall stool behind the reception counter, slowly flipping through one of the black leather-bound portfolios of her work that India kept in the waiting room for clients to look at. This one featured pictures of babies. A tiny newborn asleep with one hand flung over his head. A little girl with plump cheeks wearing a fancy bonnet covered in flowers. A mother holding a naked baby up over her head.

Lainey's cell phone rang. She checked the caller ID and blinked. It was her mother. Lainey hadn't heard from Candace since the night Trav kicked her out of their apartment. She considered letting her mother's call go to voice mail, but curiosity overcame her. She clicked the phone on.

"Hello," Lainey said.

"Hi there, stranger," Candace said. "Where've you been? I haven't heard from you in ages."

"I didn't think you cared," Lainey replied.

"What sort of a thing is that to say to your mother?" Candace asked. "Especially since I just called to see how you are."

"I'm fine," Lainey said. "Still pregnant, but otherwise fine."

"That's why I called. How are you feeling?"

"Better," Lainey admitted. "I was really sick in the beginning. It felt like I threw up for four months straight."

"It was the same way for me when I was carrying you," Candace said. "How far along are you now?"

"Almost seven months," Lainey said.

"Have you been to the doctor?"

"Yep. I go every month."

"Good. That's real important," Candace said.

Lainey rolled her eyes. Knowing her mother, Candace probably drank and smoked throughout her pregnancy. What did she know about the importance of prenatal care?

"Have you heard from Trav?" Candace asked.

"No. And I don't want to."

"He wasn't that bad."

"He kicked me out of our apartment because I wouldn't get an abortion," Lainey said flatly.

"Well, yeah, that wasn't his best moment. But the problem with you, Lainey, is that you get in a temper, and you don't give people a chance to make up with you," Candace said.

"I don't want Trav to make up with me. I want him to die a painful death."

"Why? Are you seeing someone else?"

"No. But if the choice is between Trav and being alone, I'd rather be alone," Lainey said, knowing as she said it that this was something her mother would never understand.

There was a long pause. Lainey could hear Candace inhale deeply on a cigarette.

"Is there anything you need?" Candace finally asked. "Diapers or anything?"

"No. I'm fine," Lainey said. "Look, I have to go."

"But you've hardly told me anything. Where are you staying? What have you been doing?"

"I can't talk right now. I'm at work," Lainey said.

"Oh, okay. I guess we'll catch up later," Candace said.

"Bye, Mom."

Lainey ended the call. Resting her hand on her stomach, she drew in a few deep breaths, feeling suddenly dizzy. Her phone rang again. *Please don't let it be my mother again,* Lainey thought. But no. It was Flaca.

"Hey," Lainey said, relieved. "Guess who just called?"

"Trav?" Flaca guessed.

"God, no. It was the Mother of the Year."

"Oh," Flaca said sympathetically. "My mom ran into your mom at Publix a few weeks ago. Mom said Candace looked terrible."

Worry flickered through Lainey. Was Candace drinking? She always drank to some degree, of course, but there had been a few bad episodes over the years—usually precipitated by a bad breakup—where Candace had lost control of her drinking.

"Maybe I should stop by her house and check on her," Lainey said.

"You know what I'm going to say to that, right?"

"You're going to tell me that it's not my job to take care of my mother," Lainey said. Over the years, Flaca had given her many speeches about how she should not enable Candace's alcoholism.

"Exactly," Flaca said. "Anyway, I called for a reason. Are you at work? Can you get on the Internet?"

"Sure," Lainey said. "Why?"

"Check out the website for DiCosta Casting."

"Why?"

"I'm telling you, girl, just look at the website," Flaca said over the phone. "You're not going to believe it."

Lainey tucked the phone between her ear and shoulder. "Hold on, I'm looking it up right now," she said, typing *DiCosta Casting* into the search engine. "Wait, I think I found it. Yeah, here it is."

Lainey clicked through to the website. DICOSTA CASTING was featured at the top in bubbly, neon pink lettering, and below that, it read, THE MOST EXPERIENCED CASTING AGENCY IN MIAMI! SEE WHAT FIFTEEN YEARS OF KNOW-HOW CAN DO FOR YOU!

"Look at the list of casting calls. There's one for a reality show," Flaca said.

"Are you serious?"

Lainey clicked on the link to current casting calls. She scanned over the list; it was mostly for commercials. But then she saw what Flaca had called to tell her about:

CASTING CALL FOR NEW REALITY SHOW!
We're casting for a new reality television show that will be shot here in Miami, and which will air on a major network! Looking for Mr. Right will feature seven gorgeous single women who are still looking for their Prince Charming. Our panel of celebrity matchmakers will help the women sort out the princes from the frogs. The women will live together in a house located in the glamorous South Beach neighborhood. We're looking for people with strong, extroverted personalities, who embrace new experiences and who are ready to take on the notoriety that this high-profile show will bring. Candidates must be extremely attractive and ready to commit to a four-month filming schedule. Open casting will take place on April 15th at the Hyatt Regency located in downtown Miami.

Lainey's pulse picked up, and a warm flush prickled over her body. This was it! This was the opportunity she'd been waiting for! And she didn't even have to go to Los Angeles—the audition was actually within driving distance. As though it sensed her excitement, the baby began to squirm. Lainey didn't think she'd ever get used to the odd, fluttering sensation this gave her, and she absentmindedly dropped one hand to rest on her rounded belly.

"Where did you hear about this?" she asked.

"The radio. They were talking about it on the morning show. Are you going to try out?"

"Absolutely!" Lainey said excitedly. "I have to get one of these spots!" The baby did another back flip—this one so strong she could feel the ripple of movement against her hand—and Lainey's hopes suddenly plummeted. "Wait...April fifteenth? That's two weeks from now."

"I know. It's the day of my wedding."

"Then I can't go," Lainey said, deflating.

"Of course you can. The wedding's not until five o'clock. You'll have plenty of time to get to Miami and back."

"But don't I have maid-of-honor duties?"

"I have five sisters. They can cover it," Flaca said.

Lainey hesitated. "Are you sure? I don't want to let you down."

"I know. And I'm absolutely sure," Flaca said.

"The other problem is that I'll still be the size of a baby ele-phant," Lainey said.

"I think it will make you more interesting—the beautiful young woman who's still fragile after bravely giving her baby up for adoption."

Lainey made a face into the phone. "Me? Fragile? No one's going to buy that."

"It's just your character. That's what they want—people who make good television. And there's also no way they'd cast you as the evil girl that way."

"The evil girl normally gets more airtime," Lainey pointed out.

"Yeah, but everyone hates her forever," Flaca said.

Lainey's enthusiasm began to hum again. "I'm totally going to get this. I can feel it. It's perfect for me."

"I know what you mean. As soon as I heard it, I had this weird, like, sixth sense about it."

"Thanks, Flaca," Lainey said gratefully.

"What have you been up to, girl? I haven't talked to you in forever."

"Same old crap. Still pregnant. Did I tell you India's teaching me how to take pictures? She gave me a camera to practice with."

"You said she was buying you all kinds of stuff."

"She didn't buy it for me. It's an old one she had around here."

"That's pretty lame," Flaca said, clearly unimpressed with this haul. "You're giving her a kid. The least she could do is give you a new camera."

"No, I like it. It's the one India used while she was in school. She said it's a good camera to learn on," Lainey said.

"Now you're going to be a photographer?" Flaca asked.

"I don't know. Why?"

"It's just kind of weird, don't you think? It's not like you've ever been interested in cameras before."

"So?" Lainey asked defensively. "I can't try something new?"

Flaca sighed. "I know you like this chick, but don't forget, you're probably never going to hear from her again after you have the baby."

"What are you saying? That you think she's just using me?" Lainey asked aggressively.

The truth was, she had wondered if this was just what India was doing. Or if not using her, exactly, then humoring her. But it was one thing for her to harbor suspicions, and another altogether for Flaca to give voice to them. It made Lainey feel foolish.

Flaca was not put off by the hostility in Lainey's voice. She snorted. "Of course she's using you. Just like you're using her. I'm not saying it's bad, but don't be stupid. Don't pretend that it's something it's not."

"Look, I have to go," Lainey said abruptly.

"What, now you're pissed at me?"

"No. I just have some work to do." Lainey didn't bother telling Flaca about the four rolls of film she'd taken with her borrowed camera when she'd accompanied India to a wedding two days earlier. India had explained that her favorite shots were candid ones taken in natural light—the bride turning to make sure her veil was straight, the groomsmen laughing over their drinks, the flower girl spinning in circles until her skirt ballooned out around her. Lainey had loaded her camera with black-and-white film, and in between helping India keep track of all her cameras and lenses and organizing the wedding party for their formal portraits, Lainey snapped pictures whenever something caught her eye. India didn't keep a darkroom at the studio, particularly now that so much of her work was done digitally, so they'd dropped off the rolls of film at a local lab that morning. The guy manning the counter had promised her the film would be ready by four.

Then, remembering the original purpose of her friend's call, Lainey softened. "Thanks for the info about the casting call."

"No problem," Flaca said. She hesitated. "So you're really not pissed at me? Because I just don't want you to get hurt."

"No, we're good," Lainey said. "I'll talk to you later."

India came in just as Lainey clicked the off button on the phone. Her curls were bunched on the top of her head in a bun and secured with a pencil. She smiled when she saw Lainey.

"Did you pick up your prints?" India asked.

"I was waiting for you to get back. I'll go over and get them now."

"I can't wait to see them," India said.

Lainey nodded, hesitating. She wanted to tell India about the casting call for the reality show, but Flaca's warnings were ringing in her thoughts. What if India was just pretending to be her friend, humoring her, trying to keep her happy so she didn't back out of the adoption agreement?

"Is everything okay?" India asked. When she frowned, vertical lines puckered between her eyes. She nodded toward the phone, which was still in Lainey's hand. "Did you get some bad news?"

"No, that was just my friend Flaca." Lainey hesitated. She wasn't sure if India would approve of the reality show. But this immediately annoyed her. Who cared if she disapproved? It wasn't any of India's business. And when had she, Lainey, ever worried what anyone thought of her?

"She called to tell me about this casting call they're having in Miami. For a reality show," Lainey said abruptly.

India nodded. "That's what you've been wanting to do."

"Yeah. I'm going to the audition." Lainey felt self-conscious under the weight of India's gaze. She shrugged and tossed her hair back. "It probably won't lead to anything—I'll still be huge— but I might as well try out."

"You definitely should."

Lainey was startled by India's enthusiasm. She'd gotten the distinct feeling that India didn't really approve of her plan to get on a reality show. "Really?"

"You said this was your dream, right? Well, I firmly believe in following your dreams," India said. "When's the audition?"

"April fifteenth."

"Do we have anything on the calendar that day?"

Lainey flipped a few pages forward in the engagement book. "No, that's one of the days you wanted to keep open so you could work on the show."

"Excellent. Then I'll take you down there myself."

Lainey stared at her. "What?"

"I'll drive you down to the audition."

Lainey's eyes narrowed. "Do you just want to keep an eye on me? Are you worried that I'll get stressed out and go into early labor or something?"

India looked genuinely surprised. "What? No. I want to give

you moral support. And if I do the driving, it will be one less thing you have to worry about."

"Oh... okay then," Lainey said. Then, after an awkward pause, "Thanks."

"No problem," India said. "Now go pick up your prints! I can't wait to see them."

On the morning of the casting call, Lainey and India left while it was still dark out. It had rained overnight, leaving behind a thick veil of water droplets on the car. India was worried about traffic—she said it was always worse when the roads were wet—and Lainey wanted to make sure she'd be near the front of the line of hopefuls. They stopped at a Dunkin' Donuts drive-thru for muffins, coffee (for India), and orange juice (for Lainey), and then got on I-95 just as the first pink fingers of morning light were creeping into the sky.

"Are you nervous?" India asked as she sipped her coffee.

Lainey shrugged. "Yeah, I guess. Maybe a little."

A small smile played on India's lips.

"What?" Lainey asked.

"I've just never heard you admit to any sort of vulnerability before. You're so stoic. When I first met you, you intimidated me."

"I did? Seriously?"

"Seriously," India said. "You were just so poised and together. I was never like that when I was your age. You're a strong person, Lainey. Remember that during your audition. They'd be lucky to get you on their show."

Lainey shifted in her seat, uncomfortable under the weight of this praise.

"How long do you think you'll be?" India asked.

"I'm not sure, but Flaca's wedding is at five o'clock."

"So we'll have to leave by one or two o'clock at the latest,"

India said. "Good thing we're getting there early. Hopefully, you'll be at the front of the line."

"Hopefully," Lainey repeated.

She turned to stare out the window. She was too nervous to talk, and after a while, India gave up trying to make conversation. They rode the rest of the way in silence.

The commuter traffic surging down to Miami slowed their progress, so it was nearly nine in the morning by the time India pulled in front of the Hyatt Regency.

"I'll drop you off here and then go look for parking," India said.

"No. I don't want you to wait with me," Lainey said.

She busied herself retrieving her Coach handbag from the floor so that she didn't have to see India's hurt expression.

"Are you sure?" India asked. "Because I don't mind."

Lainey nodded. "I'm sure," she said.

"Okay. I guess I'll go over to the Miami Art Museum. They're having a Charles Cowles exhibit I've been hearing good things about. So, you have my cell phone number, right? Just call me when you're done, and I'll come get you."

Lainey nodded and climbed out of the car.

"Good luck," India called after her, but Lainey shut the door without saying a word.

Lainey waited in line for three hours. The casting call was being held on the second floor of the hotel, and the hallway outside the room where auditions were being held was filled with young hopefuls. Some of the girls had come with friends, and they stood together in loose knots. Others chatted on their cell phones or texted while they waited. After Lainey got her number, she sat on the floor, leaning against the wall to relieve the ache in her lower back.

A woman with a clipboard called out the numbers one by one. When Lainey's number was finally called—sixty-seven—she struggled to her feet, trying to ignore the surprised looks the other girls were shooting her. She could hear a few whispered exclamations of "She's pregnant!" as she passed through the corridor.

"Right in here," the woman with the clipboard said as she ushered Lainey into a small conference room.

The size of the room surprised Lainey. She'd imagined the auditions would be held in a big ballroom with chandeliers and a parquet floor. Instead, it was just a normal, rectangular room, like the one she'd met India and Jeremy in at the lawyer's office, only without the large conference table. Instead, there was a much smaller folding table set up across the far, short side of the room. Two men and a woman sat behind it, their heads bent together in conversation. Lainey hesitated at the door, but the woman waved to her without looking up and said, "Come on in."

Lainey walked in, closing the door behind her.

"Do you have a head shot?" the younger of the two men asked. He had highlighted hair and a dark goatee and wore a tight-fitting V-neck T-shirt. Lainey guessed he was in his late twenties.

She was glad India had suggested she bring a head shot. It was a good one, too, she thought. India had taken it at the studio, and then she and Lainey had pored over the proofs to make sure they selected the best picture. India had also urged her to take one of the shots from their first photo session at the beach, back when she was still hardly showing. Lainey was worried that she looked fat in it, but India had insisted it was beautiful and unusual enough to help Lainey stand out from the crowd. The two pictures were in a manila envelope, which Lainey clutched in her hands.

Goatee Boy and his two associates—the woman had short blonde hair and black-framed glasses; the second man was balding and had a receding chin—finally stopped talking, and looked up at Lainey for the first time. All three gawked at her.

"Oh, my God! Are you pregnant?" Goatee Boy asked.

The blonde woman rolled her eyes and sighed impatiently. "The casting call clearly said that we're looking for single people to live in a house for four months. You're wasting our time."

"I am single," Lainey said quickly.

"Yeah, well, we aren't looking for new mothers. Thank you. On your way out, please ask the next girl to come in."

Lainey could feel the opportunity slipping away, and she grasped for it, panicked that she'd come all this way to be dismissed after two minutes.

"I'm not going to be a mother. I'm not keeping the baby," she said quickly. "I'm putting it up for adoption."

"Really?" The older man—Lainey thought he looked a bit like a turtle, with his small eyes and chinless face—looked up at her, his eyes thoughtful as they roamed over her body.

"It doesn't matter. This is a show about dating, not about getting over postpartum depression," the blonde woman said.

"She is very pretty," Turtle Man said.

Lainey thought that he was probably the one in charge, for the blonde woman shut up and Goatee Boy narrowed his eyes, examining her with renewed interest.

"She'd photograph well," Goatee Boy said. "Her cheekbones are divine."

"When's the baby due?" Blonde Woman asked.

"June," Lainey said.

"That's two months. And another two more before we start filming," Turtle Man said.

"Doesn't it take most women longer than that to lose the weight?" Blonde Woman said.

Lainey felt a surge of antagonism toward this woman, with her sharp, judgmental eyes and thin lips.

"I have a great metabolism," Lainey said. "I never put on weight. In fact, I have a hard time keeping weight on."

This wasn't exactly true—she'd always exercised like a fiend to avoid getting fat—but it was fun to see the flash of jealousy cross over Blonde Woman's face. Lainey guessed that Blonde Woman probably had to subsist on turkey and cottage cheese to wedge herself into her size-eight jeans.

"It could be an interesting plotline," Goatee Boy said. "The birth mother who's overcoming the heartbreak of being separated from her child, now looking for love and a second chance. I bet it would resonate with viewers."

"It could alienate them," Blonde Woman argued. "This show is supposed to be glitzy. Hot girls, sexy guys, cool clubs. She'd be a downer."

Lainey was stunned. She knew her body had changed, but *this* was how people saw her now? *I'm still young!* she wanted to shout. *Young enough to walk around in a bikini, and hang out in clubs, and get hit on by every straight guy in Miami!* And it was beyond annoying how they all kept talking about her as though she wasn't there. Lainey fisted the hand not clutching the photographs, until the nails cut into her palm.

"You could be right," Turtle Man said. "On the other hand, it could be inspiring. And parents' groups might just love it."

"Parents' groups would love a young unmarried mother?" Blonde Woman asked skeptically.

"One that's lived with the consequences of her actions *and* who selflessly put her baby up for adoption? Absolutely they'd love it. They might even endorse the show," Turtle Man said.

"I don't think we need the Moral Majority's approval," Blonde Woman said.

Turtle Man gave her a cold look. "You'd rather they condemned us?"

"Yes! That's great press! Just think of all of those teen girls out there, dying to see what's happening on our show that's causing their parents' heads to spin around!"

"Maybe if it were 2002 again. Kids today are jaded. They've already seen the envelope pushed to the edge," Goatee Boy argued. "A show that parents would actually approve of might just be fresh enough to get some media attention. I can see *Entertainment Weekly* and *Seventeen* doing stories on her." He thrust his chin in Lainey's direction.

"Then why don't we just do a show about Mormon schoolgirls saying their prayers every night?" Blonde Woman snapped. "I'll tell you why: It's boring. No one wants wholesome television. And if they do, well, that's what *Little House on the Prairie* reruns are for."

"Enough, you two." Turtle Man ended the argument by raising one finger in the air. Goatee Boy and Blonde Woman both fell silent. "What's your name?"

"Lainey Walker," Lainey said. She handed Goatee Boy the questionnaire she'd already filled out, along with the envelope containing her photographs.

Turtle Man glanced over her paperwork. "You haven't done any television before?"

Lainey shook her head. "No."

"What's your availability? We're planning to start filming in August, and it's a four-month commitment. You'd have to agree to live on set, be filmed twenty-four/seven, and have limited contact with friends and family. Would you be willing to do that?"

"Absolutely," Lainey said, nodding eagerly.

"You know the basic concept of the show? The idea is for each of the seven girls to work with matchmakers and psychologists and image consultants in order to find her Mr. Right. In fact, that's the name of the show: *Looking for Mr. Right.* So we want to make sure our cast is actually single. We don't want to have a situation where a cast member is having her dates filmed, only to find out she's got a boyfriend or husband back home."

"I don't have a boyfriend or a husband," Lainey said.

"What about the father?" Turtle Man asked.

"He's out of the picture," Lainey said. Blonde Woman smirked, obviously not believing this. Lainey glared at her. "No, *really*. I haven't seen him in months."

"All right. Thank you for coming in," Turtle Man said.

"That's all?" Lainey asked. "You don't want to ask me any more questions?"

"Not at this time," Turtle Man said. "If we're interested, you'll hear from us in a few weeks. If you don't hear back, it means you didn't make the cut."

Lainey nodded, understanding that she was being dismissed. Who knew if she'd ever have an opportunity like this again? A sense of urgency swelled inside of her, and she took a step forward.

"Just so you know, I really want to be on this show. I'll do whatever it takes," Lainey said, wishing she had the words to make a more compelling case, to make them see just how perfect she would be.

But Turtle Man just nodded at her, and then Blonde Woman murmured something in his ear, diverting his attention away from Lainey. Goatee Boy busied himself flipping through the pile of questionnaires on the table in front of him. Realizing she'd been dismissed, Lainey turned and left.

By the time India pulled up in front of the hotel, Lainey was exhausted. Her body was always burdensome under the weight of the baby these days, but now her limbs felt especially heavy and stiff. It took all of her energy to climb into the car.

"We'll be back in plenty of time for the wedding," India said brightly. "How did it go?" Then she saw Lainey's expression, and her face creased with concern. "Oh, no. What happened?"

Lainey just shook her head. India put the car into gear and

headed for home without saying another word. Lainey stared out the car window, watching the passing urban landscape without seeing it. In her mind's eye, she was back at the audition, while the three producers sneered at her and dismissed her. Lainey waited for rage to flood her. But instead, she just felt an unbearable sadness. It pushed down on her, filling her throat and lungs, smothering her under its weight. Her eyes began to sting, and before she could find a way to stop them, tears started to trickle down her cheeks.

India had been so busy focusing on merging into the highway traffic, she didn't immediately notice Lainey's distress.

"Why won't this jerk let me over?" India muttered, glaring up at her rearview mirror. "Look at this guy! He's totally boxing me out!" She glanced in Lainey's direction, clearly hoping for some solidarity on road jackassery. "Oh, my God, are you crying?"

Lainey didn't—couldn't—respond. Instead, when she opened her mouth, another sob ripped through, and suddenly she was crying uncontrollably, her body shuddering, her arms wrapped around herself.

"What's wrong?" India asked. She reached over to pat Lainey's leg. "Here, let me pull over."

India yanked the steering wheel to the right, making a quick exit off the highway. It took another few minutes—during which time Lainey continued to sob—before India was able to pull in to the parking lot of a McDonald's. She put the car in park and then turned to Lainey.

"Please tell me what's wrong," India begged. "Do you feel sick?"

Lainey shook her head, and wiped her nose on her sleeve.

"Here," India said, retrieving a crumpled tissue from her bag. "It's clean, I promise."

Lainey blew her nose and then pressed her fingers against her closed eyes, attempting to stem the tears. Amazingly, it worked.

Her breathing gradually slowed down. Her hands dropped into her lap with a dull thud. A moment later, she felt the warm pressure of India's hand holding hers. Lainey surprised herself by not grabbing her hand away.

"They hated me," Lainey finally said, her voice ragged.

She expected India to launch into the fakey-nice routine—*I'm sure they didn't, who would hate you?*—but instead, India simply said, "Why?"

"Because they thought I was a whore," Lainey said. She sniffled into the tissue.

"They called you a whore?" India asked, her voice suddenly sharp.

Lainey shrugged and shook her head. "Not exactly."

"What did they say to make you think that?"

"They—well, one of them, and she was a total bitch, by the way—didn't like that I was pregnant. It seemed to gross her out." Tears began to leak out of Lainey's eyes. "And can you blame her? Look at me! I'm huge! I'm disgusting!"

"You're not disgusting. You're pregnant," India said calmly. "This is what you're supposed to look like."

"I can't believe this is happening to me! I can't believe I blew what could have been my big break by doing something so stupid! Why did I have to get pregnant and ruin my life?"

India was quiet for such a long time that Lainey turned to look at her for the first time. India was resting her chin on her hand, the elbow propped against the steering wheel, staring out the window. Although the car was pointed toward the fast-food restaurant, facing the drive-thru, India didn't appear to see the crumpled dollar bills being handed to cashiers and warm paper sacks and shakes being handed back in return.

"Life is weird, isn't it?" India finally said. "You see this pregnancy as the worst thing that could have happened to you, while I see it as my big chance to fill the hole in my life."

"I wish I could just give it to you. Not just the baby, but the big belly, the stretch marks, the swollen ankles. All of it," Lainey said with such vehemence that India couldn't help but laugh.

"I'd take it if I could. But, for whatever reason, that's not the way it happened." India sighed and pushed a handful of her wild curly hair back from her face. "You said that one of the producers didn't like you. Were there others? What did they say?"

"One of them—the guy who seemed like he was in charge— seemed to think they could work the whole pregnancy and adoption thing into the show. Like, make me out to be some sort of pitiful girl who's lost her way and was getting over her broken heart," Lainey said, rolling her eyes.

"What an asshole!" India exploded. Then she thought about it and started to laugh.

"What?" Lainey demanded.

"Just the idea that anyone would think of you as pitiful," India said, giggling. "You're maybe the least pitiful person I've ever met."

Lainey began to laugh, too. "And like Travis could break my heart. *Please.* He has more zits than brain cells."

"I'm sorry it didn't go well. I know it doesn't seem like it now, but it will all work out in the end. Everything happens for a reason," India said.

Lainey stared at her. "Do you really believe that?"

"No," India admitted. "But my mother always says that."

Lainey sniffled into the tissue. "Yeah, well, I don't know if you've noticed, but your mom is sort of nuts," she said, and they both started to giggle again.

"I suppose we should get home," India said. But Lainey was eyeing the drive-thru window.

"Any chance we could stop for a burger first?" she asked hopefully. "I'm starving. And I'll need my strength for my upcoming maid-of-honor duties."

Lainey, feeling like a blue satin whale, sat alone at a round table at the reception. Dinner was being served buffet-style, and even though Lainey was starving, she couldn't bear the idea of standing in line right now. After standing all evening, first through the ceremony and then for the endless photographs, her feet were aching. She kicked off her heels under the table, which helped. High heels and pregnancy did not go together.

"Hi, baby girl," Candace said, sitting in the chair next to Lainey. Her words were slurred at the edges. "I brought you a plate."

"Thanks," Lainey said without enthusiasm, although she accepted the plate. She'd been avoiding her mother all evening. She hadn't seen Candace since the night her mother had refused to evict Al's rotund friend from the couch, although they'd talked several more times on the phone. Despite Flaca's warnings about not enabling her mother's alcoholism, Lainey had taken to calling her mother every few days, just to check on her and make sure that her drinking wasn't getting out of control. So far, she had seemed okay. But tonight, Candace had clearly taken full advantage of the open bar. Her eyes were bloodshot and her skin was a florid red. Lainey just hoped that her mother wouldn't do anything to embarrass herself, or offend the Reyes family.

"Is that your camera?" Candace asked, nodding to the Nikon on the table in front of Lainey.

Lainey nodded. "I'm going to make an album for Flaca as a wedding present."

"Doesn't she have a professional photographer?" Candace asked.

Lainey had accompanied India on enough wedding gigs to know that this wedding photographer wasn't doing a very good job. The pictures were all posed awkwardly, and in all of the outside shots, he had his subjects standing so they were squinting into the setting sun.

"It's just something I want to do for her," Lainey said, shrugging.

"This is delicious," Candace said, pointing to her plate with her fork. "What am I eating?"

"Mrs. Reyes's specialty: Cuban roasted pork with onions," Lainey said, taking a bite. It was the food of her childhood. Flaca's mother had made roast pork every Sunday, and Lainey had always had a standing invitation to join the family for meals.

"Marisa made all of this food?" Candace asked, clearly impressed.

Lainey nodded. "Mostly, although Flaca's aunts and sisters helped. Did you try the rice and beans?" The more starches her mother ate, the better, Lainey thought. It might soak up some of the alcohol.

"No, but I'm definitely going back for more." Candace looked her daughter over, her eyes lingering on Lainey's rounded stomach. "You're carrying all out in front. That means it's a boy."

Lainey shrugged. "I don't know what it is."

"It's a boy," Candace said confidently. "With boys, you carry out in front. With girls, you put on weight all over. When I was pregnant with you, every last bit of me was swollen up. Even my fingers."

Lainey thought this sounded like bullshit, but didn't bother saying so.

"Can't you ask the doctor to tell you what you're having?" Candace went on.

"India didn't want to know the baby's sex."

"Who's India?"

"I told you. She's the adoptive mother," Lainey said.

"Why does she get to decide? You don't need her permission to find out if it's a boy or a girl."

"She's going to be the baby's mother, so it's her decision," Lainey said.

Candace clicked her tongue and shook her head.

"Have you heard from Trav?" she asked.

"Don't start, Mom," Lainey said wearily.

"What? It's just a question. You don't have to answer if you don't want to."

"I don't," Lainey said.

"I'm going to get some more of this pork dish," Candace said. She stood, swaying slightly. "Do you want anything else?"

"No, thanks," Lainey said. These days, no matter how hungry she was when she started eating, Lainey felt stuffed after just a few bites. Then she'd be starving again a half hour later. She supposed it was the baby. The bigger it got, the less room there was in there for food.

The band had started to play again, and people were slowly making their way to the dance floor. Flaca and Luis—who had already danced their first dance to Selena's "I Could Fall in Love" before dinner—were back out in the middle of the dancers, bopping away to a cover of "Last Dance." Flaca looked lovely. At her mother's insistence, she wore a long-sleeve wedding dress to cover her tattoos. The top of the gown clung to Flaca's curves before belling out in an A-line skirt. She was glowing with happiness, laughing with Luis as he showed off his dance moves.

Lainey watched them, laughing herself as Luis struck a ridiculous disco pose. As happy as she was for her friend, it was hard to look at Flaca and Luis together, their happiness shining as brightly as the sun, without feeling a twinge of jealousy.

Will I ever have that? Lainey wondered. It didn't seem likely.

The baby, perhaps sensing the music, began to somersault around, and Lainey rested her hands on her abdomen.

"Don't you go starting up. And we are not dancing. I'm

so enormous, I'd take up the whole dance floor," she told the baby. "But if you calm down, I promise I'll get you a piece of cake."

The baby stilled and then gave a little wiggle, as though it understood exactly what Lainey had said.

Lainey laughed and patted her stomach. "That's more like it," she said.

Twelve
JEREMY

I heard car doors slam, followed by the high-pitched giggle of girly laughter. I spun around in my desk chair, currently parked behind the dining room table, and peered out the window. Kelly and his latest girlfriend had emerged from his hulking SUV and were headed up to the front door of his house. She was a ponytailed and short-skirted blonde I hadn't seen before, certainly not the same girl who had been hanging on Kelly when he'd talked me into going to the Dirty Martini a few weeks ago. It hadn't been a fun night. The bar was full of energetic twenty-year-olds; I'd felt decrepit in comparison.

Maybe Kelly had it all figured out, I thought. He lived on his own—his daughter was only there one or two nights a week—in a house unencumbered by marital strife. He had an apparently limitless supply of twenty-four-year-old girls to keep him company. He spent his weekends tooling around on his boat. Sure, Kelly was a shallow prick, but he seemed like a happy shallow prick.

I still didn't know what had gotten into me the night I told India I wasn't sure if I wanted to go through with the adoption. It wasn't even true. I'd just felt momentarily overwhelmed by the financial sinkhole we were in, and before I knew it, the words just sort of came out. India and I hadn't talked about it since. In fact, we'd barely talked about the adoption at all. India hadn't asked me once to accompany her and Lainey to their now biweekly doctor's visits, or brought up the topic of baby names again. She also hadn't mentioned the weekend away. When I asked her about it, she was evasive, saying that she was overbooked at work, and besides, we really couldn't afford it anyway.

India instead spent that weekend painting the second bedroom, which was going to be the baby's nursery, a soft green with a gender-neutral circus theme. I offered to help put together the crib and dressing table, both of which had arrived in flat boxes. We were both quietly polite to each other as we worked, but it was hard to ignore the distance between us that had never been there before.

I also couldn't help noticing that as the space between India and me spread, she and Lainey had grown closer together. It wasn't just that they spent a lot of time together, now that Lainey was going to the studio nearly every day, but also that there was an intimacy between the two of them that hadn't been there before. Over dinner, Lainey and India would talk about a photo shoot they'd done or India's upcoming show, while I just sat there, unable to contribute to the conversation. Then there were the pamphlets India had gotten for Lainey from the local community college. I'd wandered in on enough conversations to know that India was trying to persuade Lainey to take some photography classes, maybe even pursue an associate's degree. I couldn't help but wonder where she'd be living while she attended these community college courses. Was India planning on letting Lainey remain here, living in the guesthouse, even after the baby was born?

Although I worried about this, I didn't ask India about it. I wasn't at all sure I wanted to hear the answer.

I turned back around in my chair and tried to focus on the

character outlines I'd spent the morning working on. It was busy-work, but it made me feel productive and, hopefully, would spur on my elusive inner Muse to do something other than sit on my shoulder and blow raspberries at me.

"Hey."

I looked up to see India standing in the doorway. She brushed her hair back behind her ear.

"Do you have a minute?" she asked.

"Sure," I said.

"I don't want to interrupt you if you're in the middle of something." India looked poised to flee.

"No, I'm not doing anything important," I said. To prove my point, I capped my red pen and set it down on top of the still-unedited pages. Then I gave India my friendliest smile.

"What?" she asked, looking alarmed. "Why are you looking at me like that?"

"Like what?"

"Like you're the Big Bad Wolf getting ready to eat me."

I pressed my lips together.

"Now you look like you're trying not to throw up."

"Was there something you needed?"

"Stacey called," India said portentously.

"What did she want? She never calls."

"And thank God for that," India said. "You wouldn't believe how hard it was getting off the phone with her. She insisted on describing every single symptom of her pregnancy to me. It's as though no woman in the history of the world has ever been pregnant before."

"Very annoying," I agreed.

"It gets worse," India said. "Brace yourself. They're coming here this weekend."

"Here here? To our house?"

India nodded. "They're driving down to Fort Lauderdale to

look at some boat Peter is thinking about buying. They want to stop by on their way back north."

I felt a twinge of jealousy. Peter was making enough money to afford a boat? On top of the mortgage for the five-bedroom McMansion he and Stacey had settled into three years earlier? The news stung, especially now that I had to think twice about whether I could afford to eat lunch out at Chick-fil-A.

"Anyway, she said they'd be driving back up through West Palm in the late afternoon," India began.

"Very subtle," I said.

"Exactly. There was no way of getting out of inviting them for dinner." India winced. "Oh, well, I suppose it could be worse."

"How so?"

India smiled. "At least your mother isn't coming with them."

That night, over dinner, India tentatively suggested that Lainey sign up for a Lamaze class.

"I saw a flyer for it at Dr. Jones's office," she said. She looked hopefully across the table at Lainey, who was tucking into a bowl of chicken-and-white-bean chili. "What do you think?"

Lainey reached for the corn bread. "No way. Pass the butter."

India handed over the butter dish and also nudged a bowl of sautéed collard greens toward Lainey. Lainey ignored the greens, but helped herself to a large dollop of butter, which she smeared on her corn bread.

"You want to be prepared for the birth," India tried again.

"First of all, I'm having drugs," Lainey had said. "And second, those classes are stupid. I already know how to breathe."

"Mimi said that Lamaze was useful," India said. I think she knew in her heart that this was an argument she wasn't going to win, but clearly felt obligated to pursue nevertheless.

"I thought Mimi had C-sections?" I asked, reaching for the collard greens.

"Only with Luke," India said.

I privately thought Lainey was right—the classes were stupid. I'd never been to one, but had seen so many of them in television sitcoms and comedy movies that I had the general idea. Basically, it always went down like this: A hugely pregnant wife guilt-trips her husband into attending the birthing class with her. The instructor is a new age hippie with a weird name and fanatical ideas about childbirth. The other couples include one set of eager beavers who volunteer to answer every question, a Jersey girl with spiked hair who curses out her hapless husband, and a humorless lesbian couple. The husband goofs around, winning himself a lecture from the hippie instructor about the spiritual beauty of the birthing process, until he's squirming on his mat and his wife is hissing at him to be quiet. Then the class takes a break, and all of the pregnant women jump to their feet and waddle off to the cookie table to exchange complaints about pregnancy discomfort and idiotic husbands.

Pretty grim stuff.

India opened her mouth, but before she could continue to make her case, Lainey sighed and said, "Look, I'll make a deal with you. If you promise not to say the word *Lamaze* to me ever again, I'll eat some of those collard greens." She pointed to the dish.

India weighed this over for about five seconds, before reaching the obvious conclusion that she had no chance of ever talking Lainey into attending a birthing class. She pushed the bowl of greens across the table to Lainey.

"Are you going to be around Saturday night?" India asked Lainey.

Lainey shrugged. "I was going to go out clubbing, but then I suddenly remembered: I'm the size of a hippo and I can't stay awake past eight. So, yeah, I guess I'm free."

I wondered if all pregnant women were this crabby, or if it was just ours.

India just smiled indulgently. "Since your clubbing plans are out, would you like to have dinner with us?"

"I always have dinner with you," Lainey said.

This was true, even though there was a serviceable kitchen in the guest cottage. India probably worried that if left to plan her own meals, Lainey—and our fetus—would subsist on Cheez Whiz and Funyuns.

"Jeremy's brother and his wife are coming over. I want you to meet them," India continued.

"Why?" Lainey and I said at the same time. We looked at each other. Lainey's lips twitched up in a smile.

"I just thought it would be nice for you to meet," India said defensively. "Stacey—my sister-in-law—is pregnant, too. Their baby and our baby will be cousins. They'll grow up together."

"Aren't you leaving out one not-so-insignificant detail?" I asked.

"What?" India asked.

"Stacey is a pain in the ass."

This got a laugh from Lainey.

"No, she's not," India objected.

My eyebrows shot up, and I stared at her with incredulity.

"That's just a little harsh," India said. "Stacey's not so bad. She's just . . ."

India groped for a word that would encompass Stacey's shallow, grasping personality.

"Shallow and grasping?" I suggested.

"Insecure," India said.

"She sounds like a blast," Lainey said. "Thanks for the offer, but I think I might be coming down with a migraine on Saturday."

I laughed. "Maybe I will, too."

"What about me?" India asked.

"You're the one who invited them over."

"What choice did I have? They basically invited themselves over. What would you have done?"

"What's the point of having caller ID if we don't use it? Always, *always* check before you answer." I rolled my eyes at Lainey. "Okay, here's the deal. Stacey and Peter are a pain in the ass. They like to talk about how much money they have, what they spend it on, what they're planning to spend it on, and what their friends spend money on. I just want you to know what you're signing up for. It's not going to be a fun evening."

Lainey shrugged. "What the hell? I'm in."

"Really?" I asked.

"How could I pass up meeting them when you've made them sound so..." Lainey smirked at me, and I knew she was well aware that I'd been trying to talk her out of coming, not for her own sake, but because I really didn't want her there adding an awkward element to what would already be a tiresome evening. *"Interesting."*

Stacey had a voice that was a cross between a bassoon and a slide whistle. It started loud and deep, and then, as she grew excited, would slide up into a higher, nerve-jangling pitch.

"Look how BIG I am!" she shrieked, when India and I opened the front door. "Can you BELIEVE it?"

"Yes," India said sweetly. "You're huge."

Everyone hugged and kissed, except Peter and me, who were not and had never been the sort of brothers who hug. We shook hands instead. Stacey was hugely pregnant, much bigger than Lainey was. I had to lean over her bump to hug her. India led everyone into the living room, while I took drink orders—mineral water for Stacey, a Scotch and soda for Peter.

"So my OB/GYN told me he didn't think it was a good idea for me to drive down here, but I told him he was crazy if he thought I was going to let Peter go look at a boat all on his own! As if! If I wasn't there, Peter would have ended up buying it right on the spot!" Stacey yammered on.

"What kind of a boat is it?" I asked, handing Peter his drink.

"A Sea Ray. Only twenty-six feet," Peter said modestly. "Just something to take out on the weekends, catch some fish."

"Like you're going to have time to do that after the baby's born!" Stacey laughed loudly.

Whenever I was around her, I had to constantly fight the urge to press my hands over my ears to blunt out the noise. I handed her the mineral water, hoping she'd start drinking and stop talking. But she just stared at the glass. "Don't you have any lemon?"

"I'll get it," India said, disappearing into the kitchen, and returning a moment later with the lemon, along with a bottle of Guinness for me and a glass of wine for herself.

"We don't have anything stronger?" I murmured as she handed me the beer.

"So, Peter and I have an announcement," Stacey said. She tucked her chin down and looked up coyly. "We've known for a while, but we wanted to tell you in person. We found out we're having"—she paused for dramatic effect and then opened her eyes wide and threw her arms up in the air—"a baby girl!"

Stacey and Peter beamed at us with matching, bleached-tooth smiles. India and I blinked back at them for a few beats longer than what was really socially acceptable.

"Wonderful!" India finally said.

"Great!" I added.

"Isn't it?" Stacey purred. She rubbed her round stomach. "Ooh! The baby is kicking! Do you want to feel, Jeremy?"

To my horror, Stacey pushed her swollen abdomen in my direction. I leaned back. "No, that's okay. I'm good."

Stacey looked disappointed. "Are you sure?"

"It's really cool, bro. You should feel it," Peter chipped in.

"Thanks, but *no*," I said firmly.

"India?" Stacey asked, turning toward her.

If I were a better man, I would have run interference for my wife. As it was, I was just glad that it was her, and not me, being forced to pat Stacey's tummy and say, "Mmm, yes, she is a strong kicker."

"I keep saying I think she's going to be a ballerina," Stacey said. "Don't I, Peter?"

India suddenly brightened. I followed her gaze and saw that Lainey had arrived. She was standing in the doorway, barefoot with her hair pulled back in a ponytail.

"Lainey! Come in, let me introduce you," India said. "Peter, Stacey, this is Lainey Walker, our birth mother. Lainey, this is Jeremy's brother, Peter, and his wife, Stacey."

"Hey," Lainey said without enthusiasm.

"Well, hello there," Stacey said, with the overly bright sort of voice one normally uses with a small child. "It's nice to meet you, Lainey."

Peter held out a hand, which Lainey didn't shake, forcing him to do a jokey wave instead.

I cleared my throat. "Lainey's staying in our guesthouse until the baby's born," I said. I hadn't gone into the details of our unusual arrangement with my family. I figured the less they knew, the fewer things they had to criticize me for.

"When are you due?" Stacey asked.

"June thirteenth," India said.

Stacey looked taken aback. "Really? Wow. I'm not due until the end of July, and you're tiny compared to me."

We were all forced to compare Lainey's and Stacey's girths.

"You're not that much bigger," India lied.

Stacey rubbed her stomach again and looked petulant. "My doctor said I'm very healthy. In fact, I'd be worried if I was too small. It might mean the baby was failing to thrive."

India glanced worriedly at Lainey's smaller belly.

"I have really strong ab muscles. It keeps me from popping out as early. Women with softer abs show sooner," Lainey said authoritatively.

I had to fake a coughing fit to cover my snort of involuntary laughter at Stacey's sour expression. Stacey opened her mouth—clearly prepared to loudly and shrilly defend her pre-pregnancy abdominal definition—but India stepped in.

"You two timed your arrival perfectly. Dinner is just about ready. Why doesn't everyone head into the dining room, and I'll bring out the salad," India said, pointing toward the dining room, which was, for the night, cleared of my office stuff. My computer, files, books, and papers were all stacked in our bedroom closet, behind the dirty clothes hamper.

Peter led Stacey from the room, his hand firmly on her back, as though to prevent any last-minute predinner swooning. Lainey turned to flash a smile at me. I grinned back at her. Maybe it wouldn't be so bad having her around for dinner, after all.

The strain from the predinner abdominal-strength comparison lasted well into the salad course. Peter and I filled the space as best we could—I asked some more questions about the boat, he questioned me about the new book I was writing—but we were already back to babies by the time India brought out the mahi-mahi and roasted corn salad.

"Carol and I have been planning the menu for our baby shower. I know it's officially *our* baby shower." Stacey made bunny ears around the word *our*. "But we didn't think you'd mind if we went ahead and took care of the details."

"No, of course not," India demurred.

"We're going to have chicken salad and these delicious little croissants a bakery in town makes. Then there's going to be fruit salad, and cookies, and a cheese plate. And the colors are going to be pink, of course, because I'm having a girl." Stacey's brow furrowed. "Do you know what you're having?"

"No," India said. "We decided not to find out."

"Do you mind the pink? I supposed we could do something more gender neutral, like green or yellow, it's just that we found these adorable pink floral plates and paper napkins at the party store, and I just had to have them," she said. She smiled at Lainey. "Pink's my favorite color. It's a good thing I'm having a girl."

"But what if I have a boy?" Lainey asked Stacey.

"What do you mean?" Stacey asked.

"You just said you're having a pink shower, right? Pink plates, pink invites, pink everything. I assume the guests are going to bring girl presents, right? So what if I have a boy? India isn't going to want a bunch of baby girl clothes," Lainey said.

"It's okay, Lainey," India said calmly. "We've talked about it. The invite is going to specify that although the shower is a joint shower for Stacey and me, the guests are only to bring presents for Stacey."

"What? But that's total bullshit!" Lainey said.

Stacey's eyebrows arched so high they disappeared under her bangs. "Excuse me?"

"Who would want to have a baby shower and not get presents?" Lainey asked.

"Lainey, it's fine," India said.

"No it's not. It's bullshit," Lainey said again.

"She has a point," I said. I'd thought the whole concept of a joint shower was doomed for disaster, ever since India had first told me about the plan.

"None of the women attending the shower know India. Well, except for a few of Carol's friends, but mostly it will be my girlfriends who will be there. It would be weird to ask them to bring presents for India," Stacey explained.

"You're right, it would be strange," India said. "Really, it's fine, Lainey. Would anyone like some more salad?"

"Then why are they bothering saying it's your shower at all? If it's all pink, and all for Stacey, why bother putting your name on the invitations?" Lainey demanded.

"Carol wanted me to be included," India explained.

"It doesn't sound like it to me," Lainey muttered.

There was an awkward pause.

"So, Lainey, what do you do?" Stacey asked.

"What do I do when, Stacey?" Lainey shot back.

Stacey blinked and then tried again. "I meant, what do you do for a living?"

"At the moment, I'm a mule for a heroin dealer, but I'm hoping to get promoted to the position of assistant dealer." Lainey held up one hand and twisted her fingers together. "Fingers crossed."

Stacey and Peter stared at her.

"She's joking," India said. "Lainey's a manicurist, but she didn't want to be around the nail salon fumes while she's pregnant, so now she's working at my studio."

"Are you a photographer, too?" Peter asked Lainey.

Lainey hesitated. "Not exactly. I'm learning."

"She's being modest. Lainey is a natural," India said proudly.

"That's great," Peter said. "That way this isn't wasted time for you. You're learning a skill. It's like they used to do in the olden days. What was that called? When a younger boy—no offense, ladies, but it was mostly men going into the workforce those days—would work for an established craftsman in order to learn the trade?"

"Apprentice," I said.

"Right. She's like your apprentice." Peter winked at Lainey. "You're a multitasker."

Stacey stared down at her mahi-mahi, looking alarmed. "India, I should have asked you. Is there mercury in this fish? Oh, wait, you probably don't know about mercury, do you? I mean, since you've never been pregnant."

India cleared her throat. "Lainey isn't my apprentice. She's just doing me a favor by helping out at the studio," she said evenly. "And the mahi-mahi does not have mercury in it. I checked. Now, if you'll excuse me, I'll go get another bottle of wine."

India stood and walked into the kitchen, letting the door swing behind her.

We all stared after her.

"I'm going to go help her...find the bottle...uncork it," I muttered, and shot out of the room after her.

India was standing in front of the open refrigerator, staring into it, her arms crossed in front of her chest.

"Everything okay?" I asked.

India didn't answer me. I moved closer, concerned that close proximity to Stacey might have pushed India over the edge.

"Honey?" I tried again.

"Everything's fine," India said. "Or it will be, right up until I get arrested for stabbing Stacey with a butter knife."

"Not a butter knife. It would be too hard to pierce the skin. If you're going to stab her, commit to it. Use a chef's knife."

But when India turned to look at me, tears were glittering in her eyes.

"Why is it that a horrible, selfish, shallow woman like Stacey can get pregnant, but I can't? How does that happen?" she asked quietly.

I shook my head. "I don't know."

"It's not fair."

"No, it's not."

We looked at each other. India's eyes had a tendency to change color depending on the light she was in and what she was wearing. When she was dressed in dark colors, or near the ocean, her eyes deepened to indigo. Today, they were a pale blue, the color of faded denim. I held out a hand, and after a beat, India took it.

"Should we go back in?" I asked.

India sighed. "I suppose we have to. It would be rude if we snuck out the back door and made a run for it, right?"

"Probably. But completely understandable."

"I guess we have to go back in. We can't desert Lainey."

"Something tells me that Lainey can take care of herself just fine. But if we are going back, make sure you bring the extra bottle of wine. We're going to need it," I said.

The rest of dinner passed uneventfully. Whenever possible, and despite Stacey's determined efforts, I tried to steer the conversation away from the following topics: pregnancy, baby showers, baby clothes, baby cribs, baby gymnasiums, baby play groups, pregnancy weight gain, post-pregnancy weight loss, breast- versus bottle-feeding, why my books hadn't been made into movies yet, why India hadn't yet been tapped to shoot a photo spread for *Vanity Fair*, new boats, new cars, vacations to Bermuda, and Peter's virility. Exhausted, I finally let Peter run with one of his pet topics—the hassles of running a podiatry practice—until Lainey began to yawn luxuriously.

India stood up and began clearing the plates. "Would anyone like coffee with dessert?" she asked.

"I can't," Stacey said. "Caffeine isn't good for the baby. It was so hard to give up, too. Can you imagine waking up in the morning without a cup of coffee? I nearly died the first week!"

"There's the silver lining in our infertility struggles. We'd both be miserable if you had to give up coffee," I said to India.

India rolled her eyes at me. "I can make decaf," she offered.

"Actually, decaf isn't all that much—" Stacey began.

India cut her off. "Peter?"

"None for me, thanks," Peter said affably.

"Lainey?"

"Sure, I'll have some," Lainey said.

"As I was just saying—before India interrupted me—decaf coffee isn't good for the baby, either. The chemicals they use to decaffeinate it are proven carcinogens," Stacey said so peevishly we all turned to look at her. Her cheeks were very red, and she was blinking rapidly. "I don't know why everyone keeps talking over me tonight," she added petulantly.

I half expected Lainey to tell Stacey to stick her carcinogens up her ass, or something along those lines. But to my surprise, it was India who had reached her breaking point.

"Well, Stacey, maybe if you were a little more sensitive to other people's feelings and a little less self-absorbed, people would want to hear what you have to say," India said. Her voice was calm enough, but an angry red flush was creeping up over her cheeks. That was always a danger sign. I wondered how much wine she'd had to drink.

"What is that supposed to mean?" Stacey asked sharply.

India thumped the stack of plates she was holding down on the table. "Stacey. I'm infertile. This is a painful topic for me. So why on earth do you think it's appropriate to announce, not once, but three separate times over the course of one dinner, that you and Peter got pregnant the first month you tried? Or that you'd like to have three more kids after this one, because you read in a magazine article that it's hip to have four children?"

"So I'm not allowed to talk about my pregnancy in front of you?"

"I didn't say that. I'm just asking that you be a bit more thoughtful before you speak," India said.

Stacey rolled her eyes at Peter. "Your mother was so right about how oversensitive she is. First I have to deal with her taking over my shower, and now I'm not even allowed to talk about our baby in front of her."

"Excuse me? *I'm* taking over *your* shower?" India repeated.

"It's supposed to be *my* special day, with *my* friends, and *my* presents, and *my* colors. First I have to put up with your name being on the invitations. And you obviously hate the pink theme, so I'll probably be asked to give that up, too. It's not fair!" Stacey wailed, and she burst into tears.

Lainey was staring at Stacey as though she'd just descended from an alien spaceship. "Is she always like this, or is it the hormones?"

"No, she's pretty much always like this," India said.

"You're right, Jeremy. She is a pain in the ass," Lainey commented.

"Excuse me?" Stacey's voice was so high pitched that Otis—who had been lurking under the table, ever hopeful that some mahi-mahi would fall his way—slunk from the room with his tail down.

"You said Stacey is a pain in the ass?" Peter asked me, his back stiffening.

"I have some good news for you, Stacey. The shower? It's all yours. All of it—the nauseating pink theme, your annoying friends, the present whoring. I'm out. And for the record, I never wanted to be part of your stupid shower in the first place. When Carol asked me, I only agreed to participate because I didn't want to hurt her feelings," India said.

"Oh, *please*! You just didn't want me to have my special day!"

I thought I heard Lainey mutter something along the lines of "Batshit crazy." But no one else seemed to. Her voice was drowned out by India.

"Stacey, I'm going to give you some unsolicited advice. I know this is going to come as a shock to you, but there is a world out there that exists beyond you and your special fucking day. In fact, most people have problems that are bigger than the color scheme of a baby shower. And those of us who live out here in Grown-Up Land understand that. Perhaps it's time you joined us," India said.

"Excellent," Lainey said approvingly.

"I knew you didn't like the pink theme!" Stacey cried.

"Of course I don't like the pink theme! I'm not a Barbie doll!"

India's uncharacteristic outburst had shocked me into silence. I cleared my throat and said, "Look, why don't we all just calm down."

"Tell that to your wife," Peter snapped. He pointed at India in an aggressive way I didn't care for. "She's getting Stacey upset."

Stacey wept dramatically into her white dinner napkin.

"India's not the one who started this," I said mildly.

Peter snorted. "Please. Stacey's right. India is too sensitive."

That was it. No one had the right to call India oversensitive. Especially to her face.

"It's not just the constant pregnancy talk. It's all the little digs," I said. " 'Morning sickness is so hard! Oh, but sorry, India, I guess you wouldn't know about that.' 'Breast-feeding reduces the risk of getting breast cancer. But don't worry, India, you probably won't get cancer. You don't have a history of it in your family, do you?' 'India, you're so lucky you're not going to have to deal with stretch marks! I wish I could have hired someone to be pregnant for me!' " I shook my head with disgust. "Seriously, Stacey, are you incapable of thinking before the words start coming out of your mouth? Can't you just shut your piehole for once in your life?"

"This is starting to remind me of my family," Lainey remarked.

Peter stood up so quickly his chair toppled over behind him. "Don't talk to my wife like that," he said.

"Oh yeah?" I said, with a casual bravado that disguised the fact that my pulse had ticked up a few notches. Peter and I hadn't fought like this since we were kids, and he—being older, bigger, and stronger—had pretty much always whipped my ass back then. "I think I just did."

"That's it. Outside," Peter said, jerking his thumb toward the back door.

"Sit down, Peter. I'm not going to fight you."

"Are you chicken?" Peter asked.

"Are you eight?" I retorted.

Stacey had forgotten to pretend-cry; she, Lainey, and India were watching us, their heads swiveling like spectators at a tennis match.

"Jeremy's right. We should all just take a deep breath and calm down," India said.

"Shut up, India," Peter snapped.

The force of the anger swelling up within me took me by surprise. Suddenly, I was standing, too, my fists clenched at my sides. "Don't tell my wife to shut up," I said.

"I'll tell her whatever the hell I want," Peter said. His jaw was clenched so tightly I could see a muscle pulsing. Suddenly, what I wanted more than anything was to hit him, right there on his stupid, perfect nose.

"Outside," I said, and before I could think it through, I turned and stalked to the back door.

"Cool," Lainey said. "A fight!"

"What?" India said. "No! This is crazy!"

I turned around to see if Peter was following me. He was trying to, but Stacey was holding him back.

"Peter, let's just go," she said.

"Who's chicken now?" I jeered.

Peter shook Stacey off with more vigor than strictly necessary. She stumbled back a few steps, although she managed to keep her balance. He strode outside after me, the women following close behind him. I headed past the pool, to the postage-stamp-sized lawn next to Lainey's guesthouse. I rolled up the sleeves on my oxford shirt, and turned, raising my fists in front of me. Peter shed his yellow cotton sweater and began jogging in place to warm up. Lainey, Stacey, and India had gathered on the pool patio, Stacey standing several feet away from the other two.

"Jeremy, please stop. This is insane!" India called out.

"I'm going to teach you about respect, little bro," Peter said, dropping one shoulder and feinting forward.

I dodged back, my fists still up. "If you're going to start giving lessons in manners, I suggest you start with your wife."

"Hit him, Peter!" Stacey hollered, distracting me just long enough that I didn't step back when Peter swung at me. His fist connected with my left shoulder, sending pain vibrations down my arm.

"Ow!" I exclaimed. "That really hurt!"

Peter swung at me again, but I was ready for him. I ducked and stepped to one side, and he fell past me. When he turned back around, I was ready. I took a wild swing at him, but misjudged and ended up punching his fisted hand. This time, the pain that erupted was so intense it caused my eyes to water.

"Christ!" Peter said, shaking his hand. "Didn't you ever learn how to fight?"

"Jeremy, you hit like a girl!" Lainey said.

I was tired of being criticized. I took another swing at Peter, but my arm just swished through the air as he stepped back. He moved forward suddenly and punched me in the gut.

"Ugh," I grunted, doubling over as waves of nausea hit me.

"For Christ's sake, Jeremy, step into it," Lainey shouted. Still sick from the gut punch, I looked over at her, and she demonstrated, turning her torso as she punched the air.

I imitated Lainey's movements and succeeded in landing a punch on Peter's left shoulder. He grunted, and I felt a rush of adrenaline. It had worked! I looked back over at Lainey for more advice.

"Hit him again!" she yelled, demonstrating another low blow with her left, followed by a high, fast punch with her right.

Without thinking, without wondering if could pull it off, I did exactly as I was told—landing a hard blow to Peter's abdomen, followed by a quick clip to his jaw. He made a low, guttural sound, staggered backward, and fell heavily onto the lawn.

"Yes!" Lainey cheered.

Stacey screamed and rushed forward. "Peter! Oh, my God, Peter! You killed him!"

Christ, had I killed him? I wondered. Fear spread through me. But no. Peter was already getting up, propping himself up on his elbows. I stared down at him, feeling an odd mixture of shame and pride for having actually knocked him down. I held a hand out to Peter, offering to pull him up. Peter ignored me, choosing instead to struggle to his feet, amidst Stacey's weeping.

"That's it, we're leaving," Stacey said, wrapping one arm around Peter's waist, as though he'd need her support to stand. She pointed a finger at me. "You just stay away! I'm not going to let you beat him up anymore!"

"Sorry," I mumbled. I glanced down at the back of my right hand. My knuckles were bleeding and raw. I flexed my hand and then flinched. It really hurt.

"Can't we all just go inside and talk this through?" India tried one last time.

But Peter and Stacey ignored her. They turned to leave, Peter's arm draped over Stacey's shoulders.

"Shouldn't you at least help him into the car?" India asked me.

"Peter, do you want some help getting to the car?" I called after them.

Peter didn't answer, but Stacey turned around and shot me a filthy look.

"Guess not," I said to the retreating backs.

As soon as they were out of view—although probably not out of earshot—Lainey whooped and thumped me on the back. "That was awesome," she said. "That was a wicked right cross. I didn't know you had it in you!" She beamed at me.

India just stared at me, shaking her head. "You are ridiculous," she said. But she was smiling as she said it. She noticed me shaking my hand, and took it gently in her own. "You're bleeding."

"My war wound," I joked.

"Come on inside, I'll get you patched up," India said.

"Aren't you going to call me your hero?" I asked, following her.

"Lainey, are you coming in?" India asked, turning back. "We haven't had dessert yet."

But Lainey was stifling a yawn. "No, thanks. After all that excitement, I'm beat," she said. "I'm going to bed. See you tomorrow."

"Good night," India and I said together.

India finished brushing her teeth and spat toothpaste into the sink. "I hate to admit it, but that felt good."

I passed her a face towel. "Watching me fight Peter?"

"No. Well, that, too—he had it coming. But I meant standing up to Stacey. It was cathartic. And it means I won't have to go to her hideous baby shower, so bonus." India smiled at me. "I didn't know you could fight like that."

I blew on my bruised knuckles. "I have hidden depths."

"Yes, you do," India said, stepping closer to me. She kissed me softly on the cheek.

"What was that for?"

"Thank you."

"For what?"

"For looking out for me," India said. She smiled at me. "Are you coming to bed?"

"You're not still mad at me?"

"Do I sound mad at you?"

"No," I said carefully. "But maybe you're *so* angry, you're now plotting some sort of long-con revenge on me. It starts off with you suggesting sex, and ends with me curled in a fetal position praying for my mortal suffering to end."

"That's an attractive image," India said. "Have you always been this paranoid?"

"Yes. I just hid it well for the first seven years of our marriage. Look." I took in a deep breath to quell my nerves. "I didn't mean what I said that night about not being sure I wanted to go through with the adoption. I was just a little freaked out, and it all came out wrong."

"That's what my mom said," India said. "I told her about our talk that night, and she said you were probably just overwhelmed and that I should cut you some slack. Don't look so surprised. My mother can be surprisingly perceptive."

"I guess so."

"Anyway, I was upset for a while, but I'm okay now. And I appreciate that you stood up for me tonight. Hell, you got into a fistfight for me."

This was true. My hand was still throbbing. "So all I need to do to impress you is to punch my asshole brother?"

India grinned wickedly. "It's a start. Now are you coming to bed?"

I had been planning to floss my teeth, but it took me less than two seconds to decide good oral hygiene could wait a night. I dropped the dental floss back in the drawer and closed it firmly shut.

"Absolutely," I said.

Thirteen

"Lower. A little lower," I told Miles. He was holding up the very last photograph to be hung for my show that evening. Miles had spent the afternoon at my studio, helping me hang photos. In return, I'd promised him an unlimited supply of junk food and a video game he'd been pining for. "Wait, that's too low. A little higher."

Miles blew out a long, martyred sigh and lifted the picture up a half-inch.

"Right there!" I darted forward to mark the spot with a pencil. "Okay, you can put it down."

"Finally," Miles said. "My arms were about to break off."

"No one said that *Mutant Martians* was going to come cheap," I said.

"It's called *Mutant Zombies from Hell*," Miles corrected me. "And it's the best game ever. My friend Crunch has it."

"You have a friend named Crunch?" I asked.

Miles nodded.

"I really hope that's a nickname," I said. "Go rest your arms. There's a package of Oreos in my office."

Miles bounded off in search of chocolate while I nailed in a picture hanger at the marked spot. Once it was secure, I carefully hung the photograph and then stepped back to admire the effect.

Stripped of equipment and props, my studio made a pleasingly stark gallery. I stood in the middle of it and looked around at the exhibition of my maternity portraits. I'd had the pictures framed simply, with white mats and thin black frames, and with Miles's help, each series had been hung in a chronological grouping. A flat stomach, a gently curved stomach, a full round belly. A woman pregnant in one photograph and holding her baby in the next. A small boy gazing up at his mother's swollen belly, and then smiling down at his new baby brother, with their mother blurred in the background. There were ten series in all, including Lainey's, beginning with that first photo shoot on the beach to a portrait I'd taken of her just last week, in which she sat on the rickety wooden stairs at the end of the boardwalk, her knees bent in front of her, gazing contemplatively out at the ocean. Maybe I was biased, but the photographs of Lainey were my favorites. I thought I'd managed to capture how her tough façade would sometimes slip away, giving a glimpse of the vulnerable young woman underneath.

"I look fat," Lainey complained from behind me.

I started and turned. I hadn't heard her come into the gallery.

"I thought you were home napping," I said.

"I couldn't sleep," Lainey said, scratching her stomach. "I'm too uncomfortable. Every time I lie down, the baby starts squirming around."

"Mimi says that the last few weeks are the worst," I said sympathetically. "Can I get you anything? A cold drink? A chair?"

"You can talk to your future kid, and tell him or her that it's time to move out. I want my body back," Lainey said grumpily. She rubbed her lower back and glanced around at the display. "You got them all up?"

"What do you think?"

I was normally confident in my work, and had put on a number of shows over the years. But this one was different. The women in these photographs all had something I didn't—couldn't—have.

Was my longing transparent? Or had it given me a unique perspective on the subject matter?

Lainey looked thoughtfully over the photographs. She'd seen them all before, although not hung all together like this. She walked over to the series that ended with the new brothers.

"I like this one," she said. "This kid is funny. He has an old face. Like he's wise or something, you know?"

"That's exactly why I picked that photograph. There were others where he was smiling at the camera, but there was something about his expression in this shot that seemed special," I said.

"It's the light, too. The way it's falling over them."

"That's the nice thing about natural light," I said. "You can't manipulate it, like you can with artificial light, but you get these amazing results."

Lainey nodded thoughtfully. "Did you see those candids I took at the Wagner wedding? I picked up the prints earlier and left them on your desk. There's a good one of the bride looking over her shoulder and laughing at something one of her bridesmaids was saying."

"I did. It was a great shot," I said, feeling as proud of her burgeoning talent as I was of my show. The photograph she was referring to was extraordinary. The bride had not just been laughing—she'd been lost in hilarity, her head thrown back, her eyes screwed shut. She was ethereally beautiful in her mirth. "The client's going to love it. I'm putting it in the front of her album."

When Peter had referred to Lainey as my apprentice, his patronizing tone had annoyed me. But there was some truth in it. She had learned a lot during her time at the studio. Still, while I could take credit for teaching her the mechanics of how cameras worked, how to judge the light, even how to placate an overanxious mother-of-the-bride, Lainey had a feel for the work that couldn't be taught. An understanding of what to look for in your subjects, when you should draw closer and when it was better to hang back, the perfect moment to press the shutter button. Lainey was a natural.

"I think you're ready to start taking on a few jobs on your own," I said, keeping my voice neutral.

"Really?"

I nodded, and smiled encouragingly. "Absolutely."

Lainey rubbed her swollen belly. "But I'm due soon," she said.

It was a simple statement of fact that belied the layers of complications. Once the baby was born—Lainey's due date was only two weeks away—what then? Would Lainey move out of the guesthouse? That had always been the agreement—that she would move out and that we wouldn't have any further contact after the adoption was finalized. Still, I felt uncomfortable kicking her out. Where would she go? Could I really drive her to the bus station and buy her a one-way ticket to Los Angeles? But at the same time, how could she remain in our lives once the baby was here?

"Hey, Lainey," Miles said, reappearing with the bag of Oreos in hand. He held it out to her. "Want one?"

"Thanks," Lainey said, taking a cookie. "What are you doing here?"

"Helping," Miles said, through a mouthful of cookie.

"Yes, you're clearly hard at work," Lainey said, smiling at him. Miles grinned back at her.

The bell on the front door jingled. "Anyone need three cases of cheap-but-not-too-cheap wine?" Jeremy asked, struggling under the weight of the boxes as he came in. "Because if so, I'm your guy."

"Thank God," I exclaimed, rushing to help him. "I thought you'd forgotten."

"Nice. Glad to see you're keeping the faith," Jeremy said. He grunted as I slipped the top case of wine out of his arms. "Where do you want these?"

"Over there," I said, nodding toward a long table, already draped with a starched white tablecloth. Rows of wineglasses were set up on it.

"Is this all you're serving? Just booze?"

"No, we'll also have bottled water. In fact, it's back in my office, so when you have a minute, would you bring it out? And my mom is bringing hors d'oeuvres."

Jeremy flinched. My mother did not have a stellar reputation for her culinary talents.

"No, it'll be okay," I assured him. "I ordered platters from the deli. She's just picking them up. Oh, and someone has to take Miles home. Maybe my mom will do that."

"Can't I stay for the party?" Miles asked indignantly.

"Do you want to stay?" I asked, surprised.

"No," he admitted. "But it's nice to be asked."

"What happened to Georgia's poetry?" Lainey asked. "I thought she'd written a poem for each series of portraits? She read one of them to me. It was . . . interesting."

I flushed with guilt, but Jeremy just laughed.

"India told Georgia that the poems would upstage the pictures, and the show would be more powerful if it remained a wordless event," Jeremy said.

"Some of her poems were really over the top," I said defensively. "I don't want the C-word in big, twenty-four-point font next to my photographs."

Lainey laughed—everything Georgia did seemed to delight her—and Jeremy snaked a hand around my waist and gave me a squeeze.

"Everything looks great," he murmured in my ear. "And you look fantastic."

"You think?" I smoothed down the sapphire blue slip dress Mimi had practically forced on me. I rarely dressed up, but Mimi had insisted that this was not the night to show up in jeans.

"I definitely think," Jeremy said. He gave me one last squeeze and then turned to set up the bar.

When I turned back around, I noticed that Lainey had gone still and quiet, one hand resting on her swollen abdomen and her face inscrutable.

"Maybe you should go sit down," I said. "You look pale."

Lainey glanced up and smiled briefly. "I'm fine. The baby's just kicking a lot."

"It'll be a while, at least an hour, before anyone arrives."

"No, really, I'm fine," Lainey said, waving me off.

Mom breezed in then, empty-handed.

"The food has arrived," she announced portentously.

"Where is it?" I asked, frowning. "Where are my trays?"

"Out in the car, waiting for Jeremy to bring them in," Mom said. "And you'd better hurry. Otis is in the car, too, and he was sniffing at them."

Jeremy hurried off to save the food. My mom took his place at the table, deftly uncorked a bottle of red, and poured herself a generous glass.

"This looks nice," she said, sipping at her wine and looking around the room. "They're really quite powerful, aren't they? All of this naked femininity surging forward. And you," Georgia said to Lainey, "photograph like a dream."

I took the glass away from her. "No wine yet. I need you to take Miles home," I said.

Mom looked sadly after her glass, but sighed and nodded. Jeremy came back in, sweating and carrying the trays. He also had Otis, straining on his leash and sniffing the air excitedly.

"What exactly was the reasoning behind bringing Otis?" he asked my mother.

"Why should he be left out of the festivities?" she asked. "Besides, I put his nicest collar on."

Otis sat down and began to gnaw enthusiastically at an itchy spot on his back leg. Jeremy stared down at him and then looked at me.

"I'll take him home with me," Miles offered.

"Thanks," I said gratefully. I glanced at Jeremy. "Please tell me Otis didn't get into the food."

"No, although not for lack of trying. I think the Saran Wrap confused him. Otis has never been a brainiac," Jeremy said.

"Poor Otis. You're unfairly besmirching his reputation," Georgia said reprovingly. She sighed, and glanced around the room again. "I have to say, I think my poems would have been a nice touch. I know you were worried about being upstaged, India— and I'd never want to do that to you—but I still think they would have worked well together. There's such a synergy between photography and the written word."

"India, should I start opening the bottles now, or wait until the first guests arrive?" Jeremy asked, winking at me.

"Definitely now," Georgia said. She jingled her car keys. "As soon as I get back from taking Miles home, we'll get the party started."

When you're hosting an event, there's always that stark, scary moment when you worry that no one will show up. So when seven o'clock rolled around and the studio was still empty, save for myself, Lainey, Jeremy, Mimi, Leo, and my mother—who was now noticeably tipsy, face flushed and voice merry—I began to experience the first pangs of terror.

No one is going to come, I thought, my stomach shifting sourly. *I'll have gone through all of this work, put in all of this time, and no one will bother to show up.*

But then, to my great relief, the guests began to arrive, first slowly and then at a steady trickle. Suddenly, the studio seemed filled to capacity. Laughter and chatter mingled, and guests crowded around first the photographs and then me, congratulating me on the show. Several people asked about my availability—

one was getting married and shopping for a wedding photographer, another was expecting a first grandchild and wanted to have a portrait taken of her daughter-in-law. But one couple took me aside to inquire if the photographs were for sale.

"Absolutely," I said, delighted.

"I think that series there would look wonderful on the blank wall in our living room," the woman said to her husband, pointing to the group of black-and-white close-ups of one woman's bare torso. "Don't you agree?"

Her husband nodded enthusiastically. "It's what we've been looking for."

I was jubilant. I'd hoped to get bookings—that had always been the best outcome of my previous shows—but actually selling photographs was an unexpected bonus.

"You, my dear, are a hit," Jeremy said, appearing beside me. He looked especially handsome tonight in a charcoal jacket over a crisp white shirt. His cowlicks were sticking up, as usual resisting all his efforts to gel them down into place. His hair drove him crazy, but I loved the ruffled effect. "I've had crowds of people complimenting me on my talented wife."

"And what did you say?"

He smirked. "I told them I taught you everything you know."

"Liar." I laughed.

"Guys, we have a little situation," Mimi said, appearing out of the crowd. She looked lovely, dressed in a creamy confection of layered sheer silk. I coveted her strappy silver sandals, which added four inches to her height.

"What's wrong?" Jeremy asked. "We're not out of wine already, are we?"

"No. I think Lainey just went into labor."

Leo drove us all in his cavernous Suburban to the hospital. I felt oddly calm. Lainey, too. She sat quietly, breathing deeply, turned inward.

Jeremy, on the other hand, was freaking out.

"Don't stop for the red, don't stop for the red! Man, what are you doing? Do you want her to give birth in your car on the side of the road? Do you really want to set up flares, and hope that the placenta won't stain your upholstery?" Jeremy roared.

"The four cars ahead of me all stopped for the light," Leo pointed out.

"It's okay, we'll get to the hospital in plenty of time," Mimi said soothingly.

"Aren't we supposed to get a police escort in this sort of situation? I'm calling 911," Jeremy said, grappling with his cell phone.

"There's no point. We'll be there before they could get a patrol car—or, more likely, an ambulance—dispatched to us," I said.

Jeremy ignored me. "Hello, 911? Yes, I'm with a woman who's in labor. We're on our way to the hospital, and we're stopped at a red light. Do I have permission to run the light?" He paused, scowling into the phone. "What do you mean you can't give permission over the phone to override traffic laws? What good are you?"

I plucked the phone out of Jeremy's hand. "Please excuse my husband. He's just a little panicked right now. But everyone's fine, and we're almost at the hospital."

The 911 dispatcher—a woman with a deep voice—chuckled. "My husband was the same way when I had our first baby. Men can't keep it together when they're about to become daddies," she said. "Good luck to you, ma'am. I hope you have an easy delivery."

She thought I was the one in labor. I don't know why this surprised me—it was the obvious conclusion—but her words flattened me. The fact that I wasn't the one going through this—the contractions, the broken water, the outward push of the baby—made it suddenly all seem like make-believe to me. I felt like an impostor, the artificial sweetener of mothers.

"Thank you," I said, and hit the off button on the phone. "You're in luck, Jeremy. The dispatcher has an idiot husband, too, so they're not going to arrest you for making harassing phone calls."

"Harassing? Did she say that? Give me the phone back, I'm going to—oh, thank God, the light's green. Lainey, are you timing your contractions?"

"No," Lainey said. "I'm not wearing a watch."

Jeremy glanced at his wrist. "Shit, I forgot my watch. Leo, do you have a watch?"

Leo reluctantly unbuckled his watch and passed it back. Jeremy stared at it intently. "All right, Lainey, tell me the next time you have a contraction. I'll start timing them."

The night passed by in flashes, slowing down and speeding up in turns, making it all seem somehow unreal. Going from the darkness of the night into the hyper-bright hospital. Waiting patiently while Lainey was checked in by a nurse in Labor and Delivery. The long hours that stretched by, interrupted by Lainey's gasps of pain as yet another wave of contractions washed over her, and the occasional visit by the attending doctor to check how dilated she was. Lainey and I passed the time watching a *Project Runway* marathon on cable television, while Jeremy asked Lainey how she felt every five minutes, until she finally lost her temper and threatened to ban him from the room. The arrival of Dr. Jones, looking crisply professional in her scrubs and white jacket, assuring us that everything looked fine. Lainey finally getting the green light to push. The rush of activity as a nurse-midwife appeared to assist the doctor. Lainey's cries as she worked through the contractions. Jeremy's hand tight on my shoulder. The midwife's no-nonsense encouragement. Dr. Jones's quiet efficiency. Lainey's tremendous effort as she endlessly strained and sweated and groaned.

And then, finally, just as the sky was starting to lighten into a new day, Dr. Jones announced, "I can see the head. Come on, Lainey, you're almost done."

A now sobbing and exhausted Lainey gave one final great

push. And suddenly there he was, sliding out into Dr. Jones's waiting hands. He was surprisingly long, and covered in blood and white slime. His eyes were shut, his mouth opened in an outraged squawk. Tiny hands closed into fists. His head was slightly squashed.

He was the most beautiful thing I'd ever seen.

"Look at him," Jeremy breathed, as Dr. Jones held up our son for us to admire. He clasped my hand tightly, and tears streaked down his face. "Isn't he amazing?"

Hours later, we were still staring at him. Liam Christian Halloway had been bathed, dressed in a soft white one-piece kimono, and swaddled in a striped blanket, before being handed to us. As though he were ours. Ours to keep. Our son.

Jeremy and I took turns holding him, snuggling his wee body, admiring every last inch: the snub little nose, the curve of his cheek, the dark downy hair, the tiny shell ears. I'd had the presence of mind to grab my Leica before we left my studio, and snapped photos of Liam lying in his bassinet and cradled in Jeremy's arms.

"Can we unwrap his swaddling?" Jeremy whispered. "I want to see his feet."

I hesitated. "I don't know. What do you think? I don't want to get in trouble."

We giggled over this and then, feeling rebellious, unwrapped the blanket that swaddled him. Liam's feet were plump and round, and his toes were very short, like a row of pink candies. I ran one finger over them, marveling at the perfection.

"I wonder how Lainey is," I said. We'd been moved into a separate room shortly after the birth. Lainey needed to rest, the midwife explained, and it was better if we began bonding with the baby out of her presence. I was glad. As grateful as I was to Lainey, as much as I loved her for this gift, right now I just wanted to be alone with my husband and son. A perfect trio. A family.

"She's probably exhausted," Jeremy said. "I can't believe what she just went through."

"I know. She was amazing," I said, and this time, I only felt the smallest twinge of jealousy. I was too happy, too in love, to give it any more energy than that. Now that he was here, in my arms, I no longer felt like an impostor mom. I felt like an actual, real live nag-your-kid-to-eat-vegetables and lift-a-car-off-your-trapped-child mom.

"When can we bring him home?" Jeremy asked.

"The on-call pediatrician has to sign off," I said. "And we have to wait for Lainey to sign the papers, which she can't do for forty-eight hours. So it will be at least two days, but hopefully not longer than that."

"I can't wait," Jeremy said softly. He reached out and put his finger inside Liam's tiny hand. Liam's hand reflexively curled up.

"Who's your daddy?" Jeremy cooed. "I am. I'm your daddy." He looked up at me. "Is that just unbearably nauseating?"

"Oddly enough, no." I smiled back at him.

The door to the room opened, and a nurse walked in. She wasn't one of the nurses who'd assisted with the birth. She wore flamingo pink scrubs, had short dark hair streaked with gray, and looked very stern. The nurse glanced at Liam, lying unswaddled in his bassinet. Jeremy and I exchanged a guilty look.

"I'm sorry we unwrapped him," I said, hurriedly pulling the blanket up over the baby.

"We wanted to see his feet," Jeremy explained.

"I gave him a bottle an hour ago," I said. I had been shyly proud of this. Liam had sucked down the formula like a champ. I thought I'd done well, too, cradling him so that I supported his head with one arm while holding the bottle with the other hand. "How's Lainey doing? Can we see her yet, or is she still sleeping?"

The nurse hesitated, her lips pursed. She had gold-rimmed eyeglasses perched on her nose, and reminded me alarmingly of my foreboding third-grade teacher, Mrs. Simms. I suddenly realized she wouldn't meet my eyes, and felt the first cold ripple of fear. Something was wrong. Was it Liam? He'd been with us for hours, but maybe a blood test or something had come back, and now she was here to tell us he was ill.

"I'm here to take the baby," the nurse said. "His mother wants to see him."

"I'm his mother," I said sharply. What was she talking about? Lainey? Did Lainey want to see the baby? I didn't mind if she did, of course—it was only natural that she'd want to meet him. But shouldn't I be the one to take him in to her?

The nurse sighed and finally looked directly at me. "You don't understand. The baby's mother has asked for the baby back. I think you should know that she's having second thoughts about the adoption."

Fourteen
LAINEY

After it was over, everyone left. A nurse took the baby away to be washed and evaluated in the nursery. India and Jeremy followed the baby out, barely looking back at Lainey as they departed. The nurses buzzed around for a bit, and Dr. Jones checked to make sure that the placenta was all out and that there wasn't any tearing that necessitated stitches. But once she was cleaned and resting comfortably, Lainey was left alone in the hospital room. The television was on and turned to a cable news station, the sound muted. Lainey watched the silent flickering picture—the female anchor with her white-blonde hair and glossy lips, the male anchor dapper in his suit.

They looked, she thought, like the sort of people who glided through life without any problems.

The nurse-midwife had instructed her to get some sleep, and Lainey thought she would—she'd never felt so wrung out, so bone-achingly exhausted, in all of her life. But instead, she just lay there, numbed and sore, and feeling as though some essential part of her had been removed and taken away.

Lainey finally picked up the phone and dialed Flaca's number.

"Hello?" Luis answered, his voice thick with sleep.

"Is Flaca there?"

"Lainey, is that you? What's wrong?" Luis asked, sounding more alert.

"I'm in the hospital. I just had the baby," Lainey said.

"Oh, man. Are you okay? Wait, here's Flaca."

A moment later, her friend was on the line. "You had the baby? How are you? How do you feel?"

"I'm fine," Lainey said. And then she burst into tears.

Candace arrived two hours later.

"Hi, little girl," Candace said, beaming from the doorway. She was as blonde and blowsy as ever, but Lainey could see subtle changes in the landscape of her mother's face. Lines that hadn't been there before, puffiness around the eyes, looseness at the chin. It was hard to believe Candace was only thirty-seven. She looked easily fifteen years older.

"What are you doing here?" Lainey demanded.

"What do you think?" Candace swept in. Lainey saw that her mother was holding a plastic pack of Pampers with a pink bow stuck to the top. "My baby girl just had a baby!"

"Did Flaca call you?" Lainey asked.

"No. I had to hear about my new grandbaby from Flaca's mother. You should have called me as soon as you went into labor," Candace said.

"It doesn't have anything to do with you," Lainey said flatly. She kept expecting to feel a hot rush of rage at Candace's presumption, but Lainey was too tired, too empty, too numb to feel anything other than a distant contempt for her mother.

"Of course it does! You couldn't keep me away from my grandbaby." Candace dropped the pack of diapers onto an empty chair and looked around. "Where's the baby?"

Lainey closed her eyes. "With India and Jeremy. I've already told you. They're adopting him."

"I think we need to talk about this before you rush into making a decision that you can't take back," Candace said. She pulled a chair next to the bed and sat down.

"The decision's already made. I agreed to it months ago," Lainey said. She opened her eyes and tried to focus on her mother's face. But she was so, so tired. Everything seemed to have gone fuzzy at the edges.

"I thought the mother has the right to change her mind," Candace said.

Lainey nodded. "We sign the papers forty-eight hours after the delivery."

"See? That means nothing's set in stone. You have two whole days to make up your mind," Candace said.

Lainey felt like her limbs were so heavy they could sink right through the bed. "I've already made up my mind."

"But that was when you thought you were going to have to go through this on your own. Now I'm here. You and the baby can move in with me," Candace said.

These words—*you and the baby*—caused Lainey's heart to leap and her stomach to tighten. The baby . . . her baby . . . only he wasn't hers now.

"Where's Al?" Lainey asked.

A shadow crossed Candace's face. "Long gone. And I'm just rattling around in that house all by myself. There's plenty of room for you two. I was thinking, we could set up a nursery in the second bedroom, and put up a swing set in the backyard for the baby. Maybe even get one of those little wading pools."

Lainey hesitated at this vision of Candace acting like the mother Lainey had always wished she would be when she was growing up. A mother who didn't drink, who didn't always put her boyfriends first. But she swallowed it back and shook her head hopelessly. "No, Mom. It's over. The decision's been made." As she spoke she was startled to find that she was starting to tear up again.

"There's more," Candace said. She took a deep breath, let it out in a slow, loud exhale, and said, "I'm on the wagon. Clean and sober."

Lainey looked sharply at her. "Really?"

Candace nodded proudly.

"Oh. Well...good for you," Lainey said. She looked down, smoothing the rough hospital blanket over her legs.

Candace rifled through her handbag and pulled out a tissue. She handed it to Lainey. "So, what was it?"

"What was what?" Lainey asked. She pressed the tissue against her eyes, hoping it would stop the tears from spilling out.

"Was it a boy or a girl?"

"A boy." Lainey thought of that last wrenching push, the sharp pain that felt like she was being ripped in half, and then looking down and seeing Dr. Jones holding the baby up, bloody and covered with something that looked like white paste. When he cried, his mouth had been lopsided with anger. His outrage at being pushed out into the world had made Lainey smile. He was a fighter, just like her. "They said he was perfect. Very healthy."

"I bet he's beautiful," Candace said. "You were a beautiful baby."

Lainey's throat felt like it was closing. "He was," she said, wondering why she was speaking in the past tense. He wasn't gone; in fact, he was probably just a few rooms away. A wave of longing seized her then, so strong it took her breath away.

Candace hesitated. "Trav came with me," she said.

"What! Where?"

"He's out in the waiting room. I called him. I thought he had a right to see his baby. He was worried you wouldn't want to see him," Candace explained. She clasped her hands together in her lap. "So I said I'd talk to you first."

"He's right. I don't want to see him."

"You should at least talk to him."

"You talk to him. And tell him from me that he can fuck off," Lainey said.

"Lainey, it's his baby, too," Candace said.

"No it's not. He kicked me out of the apartment when I told him I wasn't having an abortion, so I think he's pretty much given up any rights he might have had."

"He's really sorry for how he acted, and how things ended."

"I don't give a shit what he feels. I can't believe you brought him here!" Lainey was feeling a bit more like herself for the first time. Her anger at Trav—and now at Candace, too—allowed her to momentarily think of something other than her aching sadness. "Why can't you just stay out of it? This has nothing to do with you."

"Nothing to do with me? This is my grandson! My first grandbaby! It has everything to do with me."

"Mom, I'm not keeping him." Sorrow began to rip at Lainey again. She thought of India and Jeremy. They'd both cried when they first saw the baby. Lainey had never believed in love at first sight—it was, she thought, a bullshit theory—but seeing them at that moment, their twin expressions of joy as they stared at him, she wondered if she'd been wrong. Maybe it did exist. "The couple adopting him . . . they're great. They'll give him a really good home. He'll be—" Lainey swallowed, trying to push back the welling grief. "Happy there."

"No one can give him what you can. You're his mother," Candace said stoutly.

"What would I do with a baby?"

"You're older than I was when I had you," Candace pointed out.

Lainey laughed bitterly. "Is that supposed to be an argument in your favor?"

Candace frowned. "I may not have been the best mother, but I did love you. I loved you more than anyone else could have. You don't give away your blood, Lainey." Her face softened. "And having you and the baby move back home with me would be like a second chance. We could be a family. A real family."

Lainey stared at her mother, pain and possibility blooming inside of her. What if Candace was right? What if this baby could be a second chance? For both of them. And the idea of getting him back . . . Lainey was suddenly filled with desperation to feel his weight in her arms, to see his wide eyes looking up at her, to run her fingers over his soft skin. Should she have insisted on holding him, just for a few minutes? Could she still?

"I don't know," Lainey said, her heart starting to pick up speed. "I promised India and Jeremy."

"Who are they to you?" Candace scoffed. "They're not family."

"They've been good to me."

"Of course they were. They wanted your baby," Candace said.

"No, it was more than that."

"Baby girl, they played you. If they really cared about you, where are they now? I found you lying here all by yourself," Candace exclaimed. "And after what you've just been through."

A bubble of doubt rose inside Lainey. It was true, they had left her alone. The birth had been thrilling, and scary, and painful, and after going through all of that, India and Jeremy had just left her. India hadn't even checked up on her to see how she was feeling. They had deserted her.

"You don't owe those people anything," Candace continued.

"They gave me a place to stay. And money and clothes and things."

"I thought you were working for her."

"Yeah. So? It's not like I was a slave. She paid me more than I was making at the nail salon."

"It's not like they were giving you money for nothing, baby girl." Candace laughed. "She really played you, huh?"

"What's that supposed to mean?"

"They stuck you out to live in a back house and put you to

work at her business. And somehow she still managed to convince you that she was doing you a favor!"

"She never said that," Lainey said, although she couldn't help wondering if Candace was right. Had she been played? Had India and Jeremy taken advantage of her? Had India just been pretending that she cared about her, Lainey, while all along using it to cover that they were giving Lainey less than she was entitled to? And all along, had they planned to take the baby and then shut the door firmly in her face?

"It's not like you'll ever hear from them again," Candace continued, as though reading Lainey's thoughts. "Once they get that baby, you'll be out of their lives like that." She snapped her fingers. "They're not going to want you hanging around."

Lainey could feel the beat of her heart starting to pick up, the muscles in her jaw tightening, an angry heat rising up to fill her lungs and throat. Candace watched her daughter carefully.

"There's no shame in changing your mind," Candace said. "He's your baby, not theirs. You don't have to sign those papers."

"I would like to see him again," Lainey said softly.

"I'll go get the nurse," Candace said triumphantly.

The thing that most amazed Lainey was how peaceful she felt while holding her son. The rest of the world fell away, until there was just him and her. A perfect pair. She searched his little face— the wide eyes, the snub nose, the rounded chin—and tried to see herself or even Trav there. But the baby was already, at the tender age of only a few hours old, his own person. She gazed at him, enthralled by his absolute presence, his energy, the knowing look in his eyes as he stared back up at her.

"That's right. You know me, don't you?" Lainey said softly to him. "I'm your mama."

"He looks just like you did when you were born," Candace said, leaning over to look at him.

Lainey barely noticed her mother. She let Candace hold the

baby for a few minutes, but then, growing anxious, had insisted on having him back. And as soon as he was with her again, her mother ceased to be an irritation. Even when Trav came in, a pathetic bouquet of wilting daisies clutched in one hand, Lainey had felt nothing more than a flicker of annoyance. She held their son up for his father to see, and said proudly, "Isn't he beautiful?"

"Let Trav hold him," Candace urged.

Lainey cut her eyes toward Trav, not at all sure he was up to the task. But he shook his head vigorously and held his hands up. "I'm afraid I'll hurt him."

Candace chuckled. "Babies are tougher than you think," she said.

But Lainey tucked a protective arm around her son, glad that he wouldn't be leaving her, not even for a moment. It wasn't a decision she had to consciously make—now that she had him here, in her arms, she knew she'd never be able to let him go.

"What are you going to name him?" Candace asked.

"We could name him after my father," Trav said. "James Michael. We could call him Jimmy for short."

"No," Lainey said. "I don't want him named after anyone. He's his own person. He's going to have his own name."

Trav shrugged and nodded. He seemed more intimidated by this focused, contemplative Lainey than he ever had by the louder, more aggressive version he'd once lived with. "It was just an idea," he said. "You pick the name."

"Griffin," Lainey said suddenly. "That's his name."

"Griffin," Candace repeated. "I like it. Where'd you get that from?"

"From him," Lainey said, her eyes never leaving her son's face. "I got it from him."

The bossy nurse in the ugly pink scrubs walked into the room without knocking. Nurses had been in and out since the delivery, checking her pulse and taking her temperature, and once to take blood, so Lainey barely looked up, even when the nurse cleared her throat.

"The couple in the other room—the prospective adoptive parents—asked me to find out what's going on," the nurse said. "They'd like to talk to you."

"No," Candace said quickly. "Tell them it's over, and that they should just go home."

The nurse hesitated. "Do you have an attorney or counselor you're working with? It's really not my job to be the go-between."

"For heaven's sake, I'll go tell them," Candace said, standing up.

"No, Mom. Sit down." Lainey looked at the nurse. "I'll talk to them. But I don't want the baby here when they come in."

"I'll take him back to the nursery," the nurse said, looking relieved to excuse herself. She glanced up. "Should I call security?"

"No," Lainey said, just as Candace nodded and said, "Yes."

"Mom." Lainey shook her head. "We don't need security. They're not like that."

Trav shifted from foot to foot and glanced nervously after the nurse, who had placed Griffin back in his bassinet and was now wheeling him out of the room.

"I probably shouldn't be here when they come in," he mumbled.

At one time, Lainey would have rolled her eyes and called him a spineless dick. But she barely looked up at Trav as she said, "Yeah, you don't have to stay. You go, too, Mom."

"I'm not going anywhere," Candace said belligerently.

"Yes you are," Lainey said. "I need to talk to India and Jeremy alone."

"They'll try and bully you into giving them the baby!"

"No they won't." Lainey pushed the button on the bedside remote that lifted her into a sitting position. She was still wearing a hospital gown that tied in the back, and she was feeling exposed.

"Can you go home and get some clothes for me? A robe or something I can wear here. And something for me to wear home."

Candace hesitated.

"I'll be fine," Lainey said firmly.

"I'll be back in a few hours," Candace said.

"Bye, Lainey," Trav said.

Lainey nodded at him. Trav balled his hands in his pockets and slunk out of the room after Candace. Lainey adjusted her gown and pulled the blankets up to her waist. She wished she'd thought to bring a hairbrush. She had a bag packed back at the guest cottage, but it had all happened so suddenly, they hadn't had time to get it on the way to the hospital. And now Lainey couldn't exactly ask India to go get it for her.

There was a knock.

"Come in," Lainey called out.

The door swung open, and India and Jeremy filed in. India's face was puffy and streaked red with tears. Jeremy was so pale his skin looked translucent. He was holding India's arm, as though she might suddenly fall over.

"Where is he?" India croaked, looking wildly around the room. "Is he okay?"

"He's fine. He's in the nursery," Lainey said.

"What's going on, Lainey?" Jeremy asked.

"I know this isn't what you want to hear, but..." Lainey paused to draw in a deep breath, and looked directly at India. "I'm keeping him."

"What?" India's voice sounded broken, all sharp edges and ripped seams. "What are you talking about?"

"I'm not putting Griffin up for adoption."

"Griffin? You've *named* him?" India said. This seemed to hit her like a physical blow. She wrapped her arms around herself and drooped forward. "But I don't understand. Why are you doing this?" Her voice, already high pitched with emotion, rose into a desperate bleat.

The simmering resentment Lainey had been clinging to vanished. She looked away, unable to face India's pain.

"You've been saying for months that you have no interest in being a mom! How does that just change all of a sudden?" India asked. *"How?"*

Lainey shrugged helplessly. "I don't know. It just did."

Jeremy stepped forward and wrapped one arm around India. "Let's go home," he murmured to her.

"No!" India said. "I'm not leaving without my baby!"

It wasn't until the room suddenly went blurry that Lainey realized that tears had filled her eyes. She blinked, trying to clear them. Jeremy had tightened his grip on India, who had also started to cry.

Jeremy looked up at Lainey. "If you change your mind . . . ," he began, but then stopped, as though the words had died in his throat.

Lainey glanced at him and nodded once, but quickly looked away.

Jeremy turned India around and gently guided her out of the hospital room. When the door closed behind them, Lainey had never felt more alone in her life. She leaned over and pressed the call button. It took the nurse—a different one this time, young and wearing mint green scrubs—five minutes to arrive.

"Did you need something, hon?" she asked.

"Yes. I want my son back," Lainey said.

Flaca came by in the afternoon. She brought a bunch of silver Mylar balloons, which she tied to the arm of the visitor's chair. Lainey was lying in bed, with a sleeping Griffin cradled in her arms.

"Hey, Mama," Flaca said. "How are you feeling?"

"Like I've been run over by a truck that backed up and ran over me again," Lainey said. She smiled wanly. "I'm feeling pain in places where you should never hurt."

"Yeah, well, I suppose that's how it works," Flaca said. She waved her hands. "Okay, come on, let Tia Flaca see him."

Lainey shifted her arms so that Flaca could gaze down at the sleeping baby.

"Wow," Flaca breathed. "He's so tiny."

"I know." Lainey beamed. "Isn't he beautiful?"

"Well," Flaca considered. "His head is a little squashed."

"Flaca!"

"You know me: I always speak the truth. Is it permanent?"

Lainey giggled. "No. I already asked the doctor about that. He said that the head gets a little lopsided from being pushed out. It'll unsquish in a few days."

"Good," Flaca said. "Because other than the head thing, he's pretty damn cute. Can I hold him?"

Lainey carefully placed the baby in Flaca's arms. Griffin didn't wake during the handover. Flaca cooed at him for a few moments, then looked back at Lainey.

"Are you mad that my mom called Candace?" Flaca asked. "If I'd have known she was planning to, I would have asked her not to. Seeing your mom was probably the last thing you needed today."

Lainey shook her head. "No, it's okay. I suppose she would have found out eventually." Lainey hesitated. "She's asked us to move in with her."

Flaca nodded. "She told me. I saw her on my way in. She said she was going to the store to get baby supplies. So you're really doing this? You're keeping him?"

"Yeah," Lainey said. She held out her arms, antsy to have Griffin back. Flaca handed him to her.

"When did you decide?"

"Just today."

"That's awfully sudden."

Lainey narrowed her eyes. "Are you going to try and talk me out of it?"

"No. But I am wondering what the hell you're thinking," Flaca said. "You have no money, no job, no home, and no interest in actually having a baby. So how's that going to work?"

"He's mine. He's meant to be with me. It's like my mom said—you don't give up your blood," Lainey said firmly. She held Griffin closer to her. "And I do have a home. I'm moving in with Candace."

Flaca rolled her eyes. "And how long will that last?"

"She said she's not drinking."

"Yeah, right. I ask again: How long is that going to last?"

"I don't know. Hopefully long enough for me to get my own place," Lainey said. "And a job."

"And where's the baby going to go while you work?"

"I don't know. Day care, I guess."

"Do you know how much day care costs?"

Lainey's temper, already stretched thin with exhaustion and emotion, snapped. "Why are you interrogating me? Jesus, Flaca, I just gave birth. I'm exhausted. I'm sore. I don't need this shit right now!"

"That's my point. Are you really in the best position to be making such a huge decision?" Flaca asked. "As of yesterday, you were one hundred percent behind the adoption. And now, just because your mom shows up sober—for, like, the first time ever—you suddenly change your mind?"

"I told you, I can't explain it. I just know this is what I'm supposed to do. What I have to do," Lainey said.

"I'm worried about you," Flaca said.

"Well, you don't have to worry. I'm fine. I'm better than fine. I'm great."

"I just think you'd better have a plan, that's all I'm saying." Flaca folded her arms and gave Lainey a penetrating look. "So, how'd they take it?"

Lainey looked away, gazing at Griffin's downy head. "It was bad. They were pretty upset."

"Yeah, well. I guess they would be."

The two friends fell silent. Griffin opened his eyes and looked around. He opened his mouth in a wide yawn and blinked confusedly.

"Ohhhh," Flaca said, leaning closer. "Wow."

"I know," Lainey breathed. "Isn't he *amazing?*"

Fifteen
JEREMY

"You've got to eat something," I said, standing in the doorway of our darkened bedroom. India was lying in bed, facing away from me, the white duvet pulled up over her shoulders.

"I'm not hungry," she said.

Otis sat next to me, his ears pricked. At the sound of India's voice, his tail thumped against the ground.

I tried again. "You haven't eaten all day."

India didn't respond. I waited a minute, wondering if she'd change her mind and get up. She didn't. I closed the door and headed downstairs to the kitchen, Otis at my heel.

"Is she coming down?" Georgia asked. She was sitting at the table, her arms folded in front of her.

"I don't think so."

Georgia sighed and pushed her hair back from her face. "Would it help for her to hear that the universe has a plan for everyone and everything happens for a reason, even if it's not immediately clear what the reason is?"

"No," I said firmly. If I had to wrestle Georgia to the ground to prevent her from charging upstairs and bothering India with talk of the universe and its plans, so help me God, I would do it.

"It's so upsetting," Georgia said. "I was sure that this baby was meant to be your baby."

"I know."

"All along, I've had a very strong, very centered vibe that this little soul—well, I say *little*, but really, all souls are limitless in their potential—was meant to be joined with yours. I suppose I could have been reading the energy wrong," she added worriedly.

Normally, this was the point in one of Georgia's visits where I'd escape, muttering an excuse about having to work, or walk the dog, or make an urgent trip to the drugstore to buy deodorant, and let India deal with her mother's insanity alone. But India was not up to it today. And since I didn't trust Georgia not to sneak upstairs in my absence, I was staying put.

"I need to figure out how to help India," I said.

Georgia patted my hand. "India's heart is broken. The only thing that will heal it is time."

I picked up a flyer advertising a local dry cleaner off the stack of mail Georgia had brought in. I crumpled it up and threw it in the garbage with more force than was strictly necessary. "I wonder if Lainey was playing us the whole time—living here free, taking our money—and never had the slightest intention of giving us the baby," I said.

"I don't think so," Georgia said. "For all of Lainey's shortcomings, I don't think she's outright malicious. You have to understand, the mammalian drive for a mother to stay close to her young is quite powerful. And once you add in the hormones and the physical exhaustion of the delivery, it would be a lot for any woman to cope with, much less one as young as Lainey."

I shrugged off this excuse. I was too angry to give Lainey even the smallest benefit of the doubt. She had deliberately allowed India to get her hopes up—she'd sat by while India bought baby clothes, and painted the nursery, and picked out a crib. She hadn't said a word when India drove her to every single doctor's appointment, or cooked all of her meals for months, or ran out for whatever random snack Lainey happened to be craving. Lainey had taken everything she could from India—her time, money, energy, hope. Everything. And in the end, she'd broken India's heart.

"It's unforgivable," I said through clenched teeth.

"You can't think that way. It's not healthy."

"I'm not angry for me," I said. "I'm angry for India."

Georgia looked at me. "Are you sure about that?"

Before I could respond, the phone rang. It had been ringing all day—Mike Jankowski, Mimi, the few select friends I'd given Mimi the green light to tell. And each time the phone rang, I lunged at it, hoping—even though I knew it was pointless, stupid even, to hope—that it was Lainey calling to tell us she'd changed her mind again. That she'd sign the papers. That India's grief would be stemmed before she drowned in it.

"Hello."

"Jeremy, is that you?"

It was my mother. I'd left my parents a message to call us after we got back from the hospital, although I hadn't gone into any of the details on their answering machine.

"Hi, Mom," I said. I glanced at Georgia and indicated I was going to take the call in the other room. She nodded and got up to pour herself a glass of wine.

"What's wrong? You sound odd," Mom said as I walked into the dining room, closing the double pocket doors behind me. Otis followed me and settled down on his circular bed with a contented sigh.

Before I could tell her what happened, my mother continued. "I'm glad you called. I've been wanting to talk to you about what happened between you and your brother. Stacey has been very upset."

I was so emotionally exhausted that it took me several long beats to figure out what she was talking about. Then, suddenly, I remembered: the big fight with Peter. But that had been weeks ago.

"Wait—you just found out about that?"

"Yes. India never did tell me why she dropped out of the shower at the last minute. I thought it was incredibly rude, especially since I'd already sent the invitations out, and so I was left having to explain her absence to everyone. Apparently, Peter forbade Stacey from telling me. I suppose he didn't want her getting upset by thinking about it. That's the problem with men: They always think that talking about things is the problem, when in fact, it's the *not* talking about them that causes trouble."

"Mom," I said, rubbing one hand over my face. "It's been a long day. Can we talk about this some other time?"

"No. I want to settle this once and for all."

"Settle what?"

"I want you and India to call Stacey and Peter and apologize. Today."

"No way! They started it!" I said. Then, aware that I sounded like I was eight years old, I took a deep breath. "Look, you don't know what happened. You weren't there."

"I heard what happened! Stacey said that India was offended simply because she was pregnant. And that because of India's hypersensitivity, you and Peter ended up in a fistfight!"

"If that's what Stacey told you, she's leaving out some crucial details."

"The small details of who said what to whom don't matter. What matters is that Stacey was a guest in your home, and you upset her. She's at the end of a very difficult pregnancy. We should all be supportive and loving with her," Mom said.

"How is her pregnancy difficult?" I asked, wondering if there was a health issue I hadn't been told about, and feeling the first twinges of guilt.

"She's very uncomfortable. Her feet are swollen," Mom said. Then, in a brisker tone, she said, "Why don't you put India on. I think it's time she and I had a talk."

"No, Mom."

"Someone has to talk some sense into her, to explain that she can't be so oversensitive all the time. And let's face it, Georgia's not going to do it," my mother continued, ignoring me.

I thought of India, lying in the darkened room, numb with grief.

"I know it will be tough for her to hear it—no one likes having their faults pointed out to them—but believe me, it's for the best," Mom continued. "If she doesn't know it's a problem, she'll never be able to change. So may I speak to her?"

"No," I said.

"Jeremy," Mom said, in the sort of threatening, do-what-I-say-or-else tone she'd used back when I was ten.

I drew in a deep breath and pinched the bridge of my nose with two fingers. "Lainey—the birth mother of the baby we were going to adopt—went into labor last night. She delivered a baby boy this morning. Sometime afterward, and after India and I had spent time with the baby, Lainey changed her mind and told us she is going to keep the baby. The adoption has fallen through. India is devastated. So, no, I am not going to put her on the phone just now so you can tell her how she's being too sensitive," I said. I kept my voice level—what was the point of shouting?—but even so, the muscle in the outer corner of my right eye started to twitch.

There was a long, stunned pause.

"Oh, no. Oh, dear," Mom said, her voice faltering. "I'm so sorry. How are you two doing?"

"I'm okay. Upset, obviously. And India's . . . not good."

"Did you have any idea this was coming, that the birth mother was having second thoughts?"

"No. It was a surprise," I said. This didn't seem like the right word for what had just happened to us. Surprises were supposed to be good things, happy things—birthday parties, Christmas presents.

"I can imagine," Mom said. She sniffled.

Was she crying? I wondered. It was funny how everyone else—Georgia, Mimi, now even my mother—had cried upon hearing our news, while India and I had remained dry-eyed ever since leaving the hospital. Were we in shock? I wondered.

"What can I do? Why don't I drive down and stay with you for a few days," my mother asked.

"Thanks, but no," I said quickly. "We'll be fine."

"Are you sure? I don't mind. I can do the cooking, take care of the house. I bet India would feel better if her closets were organized."

I almost smiled at this. "Thanks, Mom, but I don't think this is the best time. We'll let you know if we need anything," I said. I hesitated, then decided it was the right thing to do. "And could you tell Peter that for what it's worth, I am sorry about our fight, and that I'll call him in a few days?"

"Of course," Mom said, her voice breaking again.

"Thanks," I said. Peter and Stacey could be awful, but I truly didn't want to have this stupid fight hanging over any of us. My brother and I would probably never be close—we were very different people. But what was the point in having open hostilities? Especially now, when they were on the cusp of welcoming a new life into the world.

I got off the phone with my mother and headed back to the kitchen. I was glad to see that Georgia was still there, and hadn't snuck upstairs in my absence. Instead, she was contemplating her wineglass. When she saw me, she raised it to me in a toast.

"Here's to the future," she said sadly. "May it be brighter than today."

But things didn't get brighter. Over the next two weeks, India sank deeper into depression. She canceled all of her appointments and spent most of her time in bed. I made her buttered toast and hot cups of tea, which she ignored, eating only when I pressured her.

I quietly cleared out the nursery, boxing up the clothes and toys India had accrued, and moved it all to Georgia's garage for storage. I'd half hoped that India would rage at me for doing this—telling me that I had no right to break down the nursery, that we would adopt another baby. But if she noticed, she didn't say a word about it.

I cleaned Lainey's things out of the guesthouse and brought those to Georgia, too. Georgia promised she'd call Lainey on her cell phone and arrange with her a time to collect her belongings. I didn't ask about the details of this transaction. Every time I thought of Lainey and her broken promises, anger burned through me, pulsing at my temples, clenching in my hands.

I had my office back, but I continued to work in the dining room so I could keep an eye on India. Despite all of the stress and trauma—or because of it, perhaps it was my one escape—I'd become oddly productive working there. I'd lost all interest in posting on the FutureRaceFanatics message board. Instead, I turned my attentions to the new book, tapping away on the laptop, churning out page after page.

I was having a particularly industrious work session one afternoon when India stumbled down the stairs, her face puffy and hair sticking up.

"Hi," I said, looking up. Otis sprang up off his bed and, body wriggling with happiness, brought his stuffed hedgehog over to India. For Otis, offering his hedgehog was the ultimate sign of love.

She seemed startled to see me sitting there. "Oh, hi." Otis pushed the hedgehog against her leg, and India reached down to pet him.

"More flowers came for you," I said, nodding toward the newest bouquet sitting on the hall table. We'd already received several bouquets, most of which were now wilting in foggy glass vases. My mother had sent India an enormous orchid nestled in a sea grass basket.

"I don't know why people keep sending flowers. It's not like somebody's died," India said, her voice flat.

"I think people don't know what else to do," I said. "But they want us to know that they're thinking about us."

India shrugged and turned toward the kitchen. I got up, and Otis and I trailed after her.

"Your mother brought some soup over. It's actually not terrible," I said. "I could heat some up for you."

"No, thanks."

"You have to eat something."

"I'm not hungry," India said. She picked up an orange from the fruit basket and stared at it as though trying to figure out what it was.

"They're good. I got them at that produce stand you like," I said. I took the orange from her, placed it on the cutting board, and, with a sharp chef's knife, sliced it into eight wedges. I put the orange segments in a bowl and set it on the kitchen table. "Sit down."

India sat. It wasn't a good sign, I thought. She'd never been one to take orders, especially not from me. But, deciding to take advantage of this unusual deference, I poured some of the soup—split pea with ham, which looked terrible and tasted wonderful—into a bowl, and heated it in the microwave. While the soup was cooking, I got a biscuit out of the pantry and gave it to Otis. He was delighted and lay down in the middle of the kitchen to eat it. When the microwave beeped, I took the soup out and put it in front of India, along with a glass of ice water, and then sat across from her. India ate a few tentative spoonfuls of soup.

"I have some news," I said. "Good news."

India looked up at me, her face blank.

"I got a call from my agent this morning. A production company has made an offer on Future Race. They're interested in developing it into a television series."

For the first time in two weeks, I saw a spark of interest flare in India's eyes.

"Are you serious?"

I nodded. "Yep. You are looking at the creative force behind what could be the next third-rate cable drama series, most likely starring has-been D-list actors who used to be on *Melrose Place.*"

"I loved *Melrose Place.*"

"I know." I smiled at India. She didn't exactly return the smile, but the corners of her mouth twitched. "And the good news is that they're paying me a lot of money for it."

"Really?"

"You don't have to sound quite so surprised," I said.

"Sorry. I meant: Really! How much is a lot?"

"They offered fifty thousand to buy the option. It will be more if the series actually goes into development," I said. I reached over and took India's hand in mine. It felt frail and light. "Do you know what this means?"

"What?"

India looked suspicious, so I blurted it out before I lost my nerve. "We can go forward with another adoption. We'll find another birth mother. Or try an international adoption," I said. I leaned forward, willing her to take this small piece of hope and hold on to it, the way I had been ever since I'd gotten off the phone with my agent.

India's face closed. She withdrew her hand from mine. "I'm not ready to think about that now."

"India," I said. My wife continued to stare down at the table in front of her, her eyes shuttered by lowered lashes. "We can't just..."

"Just what?" she asked, her head snapping up, her voice taut.

"Because I'm tired of people telling me I can't. I can't let this break me, I can't check out, I can't stop living. I'm tired of it!"

"But it's true. We can't just stop living."

India stood, her chair scraping the ground. Without looking at me, she strode away, stiff with anger.

"India," I said.

She stopped and slowly turned around to look at me. I'd never seen her like this before, so beaten down, her pain raw-edged and vast.

"My heart is broken," she said in a voice so low and desperate I had to strain to hear the words. "Do not ask me to act as though this hasn't happened. As though I didn't hold him in my arms, and fall in love with him, and then have him ripped away from me. Because it *did* happen. And I can't just forget it. I can't just forget him. I can't just move on because you want me to." Her hands were fisted at her sides.

"I'm not asking you to move on or to forget him," I said softly.

Neither of us, it seemed, could bear to say his name. Lainey had taken that away from us, too. We couldn't call him Liam anymore, and I wouldn't call him anything else.

And for just a moment, I allowed myself to remember what it had felt like to hold him in my arms, his body so heavy, so substantial, for such a tiny person. The curve of his soft cheeks. The delicious way he smelled of fresh cotton and soap. The wonder in his round, dark eyes.

It was too much to bear. I drew in a deep breath and willed him away.

But India had no interest in sharing my pain. She was too immersed in her own. She turned away from me and stumbled out of the kitchen. A moment later, I heard the soft thud of her feet going up the stairs as she retreated back to her dark cocoon.

Defeated, I rested my forehead on my hands and wondered how the hell we were ever going to get past this.

I had just returned home from the grocery store and was unloading the bags from the trunk of my car when Kelly appeared, basketball in hand.

"Hey, bud. You want to shoot some hoops?" he asked.

Kelly looked like an idiot. He was wearing a long nylon shirt over baggy shorts, just like the kids wore. Actually, the kids also looked like idiots dressed like this, but you could get away with it when you were sixteen. Not so much at thirty-nine.

"No, thanks," I said. I held up my shopping bags. "I have to get the ice cream in the freezer before it melts."

Kelly nodded, and bounced the ball on the ground. "I can wait," he said. "Come over when you're done."

"Actually, I need to work."

"Oh, sure. That's cool." Kelly dribbled the ball a few more times.

I waited for him to leave, and when it seemed clear that he wasn't going to go without prompting, I said, "Did you need something?"

"Lindsay and I broke up," Kelly announced suddenly.

"Lindsay," I repeated.

"My girlfriend," he said.

"I didn't know," I began, and then stopped, trying to remember who he was talking about. Had there been one special girl hanging around lately? It was hard to tell. All of Kelly's girlfriends looked more or less the same. I tried again. "Had you been seeing her for long?"

Kelly nodded morosely, and bounced his basketball again. "Two months," he said, with the gravitas of a man announcing he was nearing his fiftieth wedding anniversary.

"That's too bad," I said.

"Yeah. She met some guy at the bar—my bar, if you can believe that—and then suddenly announced that they were in love.

She said—" He swallowed, as though about to divulge something very painful. "She said I was too old for her."

For a moment, I relished the idea of sharing this information with India, picturing her delight at having been proven right. Then I remembered: That was the old India. The new, depressed India probably would just shrug and go back to staring at the television.

"How old is she?" I asked.

"Twenty-three," Kelly said.

"That's pretty young."

"I thought she was mature for her age," Kelly said. He snorted with disgust. "Guess I was wrong."

I nodded. "I better get inside," I said. I lifted the bag again. "The ice cream."

"Yeah, okay. Another time?" Kelly asked. He dribbled his ball and pretended to shoot it toward an imaginary hoop.

"Sure," I said.

"Hey, what happened to that chick who was staying with you?" Kelly asked suddenly. "The hot pregnant one whose baby you were adopting."

"She's not here anymore," I said shortly.

"She took off?"

"Sort of. She had the baby and decided to keep it."

Kelly whistled. "Tough," he said.

I gave him the closed-mouth half-smile I'd perfected over the past three weeks for when people offered up their sad eyes and sympathetic grimaces. The smile that said, *Yeah, it's hard, but we're coping. Thanks for the concern, but I'd really rather not talk about it right now.*

Kelly looked thoughtful. "She was really hot," he said.

I slammed the trunk shut and turned to head into the house.

"Later, bro," Kelly called after me.

"Later," I echoed.

When I got inside, I discovered Georgia sitting in the living room with her feet propped on the coffee table, watching television. Otis lounged next to her on the sofa, his head resting on her lap.

"Hi," I said.

"Hello," Georgia replied. "I let myself in. I didn't think you'd mind."

"Who minds having their mother-in-law let herself into the house at will?" I replied.

"Don't be a smart-ass. You've been standing there for a full thirty seconds and haven't yet offered me a drink."

"Why didn't you help yourself?" I asked, turning for the kitchen.

"There weren't any bottles open," Georgia called out. "I thought it would be rude to open one without permission."

I put the perishables away, then grabbed a bottle of wine from the rack and opened it. I poured a glass and brought it back to the living room.

"Thank you," Georgia said, gratefully accepting the glass. "How's India?"

"You haven't seen her?"

"I went up to check on her, but she was asleep," Georgia said.

I wondered if India really was asleep, or if she was just pretending to be. "She's not good. If this keeps up for much longer, I'm going to have to call our doctor. Maybe she needs to be on an antidepressant."

"I think she just needs to process her grief. She shouldn't smother her feelings with pharmaceuticals," Georgia said.

"She's hasn't left the house in three weeks. She barely eats, sleeps, or showers." I looked up at the ceiling, as though I could sense the pain vibes emanating down. "I've let this go on for too long. It's time to get her some help."

"Tosh. We can help her. In fact, I brought something for her,"

Georgia said. She reached into her oversized faux-leather bag and pulled out a spiral-bound notebook. "It's a poem I wrote about the failed adoption. As soon as India wakes up, I'm going to read it to her. I think she'll find it cathartic."

I stared at my mother-in-law. "You can't be serious."

"What do you mean?"

"Georgia. You can't read her that poem."

"Why not?"

"Isn't it obvious? India's not up to hearing something like that."

"What better way to express your sadness, your grief, your desolation than with poetry? As Voltaire said, 'Poetry is the music of the soul, and, above all, of great and feeling souls.'"

Georgia beamed at me, clearly pleased with her quotation.

"I don't care what Voltaire said," I said, trying to keep my voice calm, although the eye twitch had returned. "I'm thinking of India's feelings."

Georgia stood, bristling. "I always respect my daughter's feelings."

"If that was true, you wouldn't be writing poetry about her grief."

"What's going on?" India asked.

Georgia and I both turned, startled at the interruption. India was standing in the doorway to the living room. We'd been so immersed in our argument we hadn't heard her approach. I realized, with a gut-wrenching twist, that India looked awful. She'd lost a lot of weight over the past few weeks, giving her a gaunt, haunted appearance.

"Nothing," I said quickly. "Georgia and I were just talking. I didn't know you were up."

"I was hungry," India said. She wrapped her arms around herself, as though she were cold.

"Good girl," Georgia said approvingly. "Come into the kitchen. I'll make you something to eat."

"You were fighting," India said accusingly.

Georgia and I exchanged guilty looks, like a pair of school-children facing a disapproving teacher. So we did what any kid would do: We lied.

"It wasn't a fight," Georgia said. "We were discussing literature."

India turned pale eyes to me. I nodded vigorously. "That's right. Literature."

"You're lying to me. Both of you." She folded her arms. "Tell me the truth. I want to know what's going on."

"I wrote a poem for you," Georgia said.

"Georgia," I said warningly.

Georgia set her lips in a stubborn line. "Jeremy doesn't want me to give it to you."

"Let me see," India said, holding out her hand.

"No," I said.

"Actually, it's meant to be read aloud," Georgia explained.

"Except that you're not going to read it aloud to her. I won't allow it." I looked at India. "Just trust me. You don't want to hear it."

"I abhor censorship in all forms," Georgia said.

"Let her read it," India said. She gave me a look that I knew all too well: *Just let her do it. It's not worth getting her upset.*

But she was wrong. This was worth fighting for. I hadn't been able to protect India from Lainey. I hadn't been able to prevent her heart from breaking. But by God, I would keep her from listening to an atrocious poem that was written about her pain.

Georgia, delighted at the permission, put the notebook down on the coffee table and turned to fumble about in her insanely oversized handbag for her reading glasses. I took the opportunity to grab the notebook up and ripped out the top page, where the poem was written.

"Jeremy!" Georgia was scandalized. "Give that back to me this instant."

"Sure," I said. I tossed her the notebook, but kept a tight grip on the page with the poem. I glanced down at it, skimming over the words. It was exactly what I'd feared—overwrought prose detailing India's grief over losing the baby. Even the title—"Empty Cradle"—was cringe-worthy.

"Give that to me!" Georgia said again. She stepped forward and tried to tear the poem out of my hands. With lightning-fast ninja reflexes, I whipped it out of her reach and held it up over my head. As I was tall and Georgia very short, she'd never be able to reach it.

"No way," I said as she hopped ineffectively, trying to grab it out of my hand. "I've already told you, you're not reading it to her."

"Jeremy!" India said, staring at me openmouthed. "What are you doing?"

Georgia made another sudden jump for the poem, this time leaping surprisingly high. I backed away and then dashed toward the kitchen. Otis bounded off the couch and followed me, ears pricked up and tongue lolling happily, clearly thinking that this was all a fun new game. Once in the kitchen, I looked around desperately. Where should I put it? If I threw it out, Georgia would just fish it out of the garbage. It was a pity we didn't have a wood-burning oven. Seized by a sudden idea, I leapt toward the garbage disposal. I crumpled up the poem, and was just shoving it into the disposal when Georgia and India reached the kitchen.

"Stop him!" Georgia shrieked. "That's the only copy I have."

I turned on the water and held up the spray nozzle. "Stay back," I warned, with a threatening wave of the nozzle. Georgia hesitated just long enough for me to reach back and flip the switch on. The garbage disposal roared to life, chewing the poem up in its metal jaws.

"My poem!" Georgia cried, covering her mouth with cupped hands.

"I'm sorry it had to come to this," I said. "But I did warn you."

Just then, I heard an odd sound coming from India's direction. Georgia and I turned to look at her. India was laughing. It wasn't just a chuckle, either. She was laughing so hard, she was struggling to breathe. India clutched at her sides as though they were cramping.

"So ridiculous . . . poem . . . garbage disposal . . . ," India gasped. And then she laughed and laughed, while Georgia and I just stood there staring at her. Otis was clearly concerned, too. He went to India's side and licked her hand.

"Oh, my God, she's having a fit," Georgia said worriedly. "Do you think we pushed her over the edge?"

"I'm fine," India bleated, petting Otis to reassure him. But she leaned against the wall, presumably to stay upright, and kept laughing. I started to laugh, too. It was impossible not to. Even Georgia started to giggle, the fury receding from her face.

"It's official: This family is certifiable," India said, when she was finally able to catch her breath.

"You say that like it's a bad thing," I said, looking at India. She needed to shower and wash her hair, to eat a good meal and get out into the sunshine. But to see her laughing—even if it was semi-hysterical—filled me with relief. If we could still laugh, even about something so stupid, well, maybe we would get past this after all. Eventually.

"We're not crazy. We're unique and comfortable with self-expression," Georgia said. She gave me a censorious look. "Although I will never forgive you for destroying my poem."

"I can live with that," I said. "Did you say you were hungry?"

I looked hopefully at India, who was now wiping her eyes with the cuff of her rumpled pajama top.

"Actually, I am sort of hungry," she said, sounding surprised. "I'm craving baked ziti. Do we have the stuff to make it?"

"Let's get takeout," I said. I reached into the drawer where we stored the takeout menus. "Mario's? Or Pasta Pasta?"

"Mario's," Georgia said definitively. "Pasta Pasta always gives me gas."

"Thanks for sharing, Mom," India said, rolling her eyes at me. I just smiled.

Sixteen
INDIA

For a while, everything just unraveled. The smallest tasks—running an errand, doing the dishes, taking Otis for a walk—exhausted me. Work was out of the question. Jeremy called a photographer in town who owed me a favor, and she agreed to cover the two weddings looming on my schedule. Everything else on my calendar was postponed.

But finally, nearly a month after the adoption fell through, I knew it was time to get back to work. As little as I felt like working, I also didn't want my business to go under. It might even be a relief, I thought, to get away from my grief and to focus on something other than my own pain.

Jeremy had already broken down the show of maternity portraits. He'd arranged for the pictures that had sold to be delivered, and stored the rest in the back room, so I wasn't assaulted by a roomful of pregnant bellies and newborn babies as soon as I walked in the front door. But there were all the small reminders that he couldn't possibly have known to remove. The box of instant cocoa and bag of stale marshmallows—one of Lainey's many pregnancy cravings—stashed next to the coffeepot. A set of candid photographs Lainey had taken at a wedding stacked up on my table, ready to be added to the newlyweds' album. A bottle of prenatal vitamins. Feeling numb, I swept everything but the photographs into the garbage.

But even with my newly scrubbed space, I still couldn't escape the constant reminders of what I had lost. On my third day back, I had two studio sessions scheduled—one of a baby girl nearing her first birthday and a second of a pregnant woman who had read about my show in the paper and fallen in love with the idea of having a maternity portrait.

Somehow I got through it. I didn't burst into tears when the little girl held her arms open to her mother and, in a sweet, breathy voice, demanded, "Up," nor when the pregnant woman showed me her stretch marks. I just forced my lips up into a smile and filtered it all through the lens of my camera.

I'd set that afternoon aside to go through the large box of developed film that had come back from the printer. Most of my work—and all of my study portraits—were done with digital cameras these days. But lately—ever since I started teaching the basics of photography to Lainey—I'd been working with film more.

I began to open up every envelope, trying to remember which photographs went to which client. I wasn't prepared for the moment when I slit open a cardboard envelope, dumped out the photographs onto my worktable, and found myself staring down at Liam's exquisite little face, captured forever in black and white. It was one of the rolls I'd taken at the hospital, and it had somehow gotten mixed up with the outgoing film. Only he wasn't Liam anymore, I remembered with a fresh jolt of pain. Lainey had renamed him. Griffin. I stared down at the photo, mesmerized by the soft curves of his rounded face, unaware that I was crying until several teardrops landed on the photograph.

"Shit," I said, wiping my tears off his face.

I scanned every last photo of him into the computer and

then saved them onto my backup drive. I spent the next hour examining the prints on the monitor, blowing them up so I could see every last eyelash, every knuckle, every wisp of hair in detail. I stared and stared, in a trance of sorts. The studio phone rang.

"How's your day going?" Jeremy asked when I answered.

"Not good," I said softly.

"What happened?"

"The photos . . . from the hospital . . ."

"I'll be right there."

"No, don't. I'm leaving anyway. I need to get out of here." I was struggling to breathe, and my skin felt hot and tight.

"I don't think you should be driving," Jeremy said. "Just wait there. I'll pick you up and bring you home."

But I didn't wait. Instead, I climbed into my old truck and drove to the beach. It was a hot, stifling July day, and the beach was crowded. There were the usual packs of surfers—all with long hair and floral board shorts—and sun-baked retirees basking on folding chairs. And, of course, there were the families, complete with small children brandishing plastic shovels and wearing floppy sun hats. I kicked off my shoes at the bottom of the boardwalk and walked past them all across the hot sand to the cooler, wet ground by the water's edge. I stood there for a long time, staring out at the water. Kids bobbed around in the waves like seals, while the adults waded in slowly so they could gradually adjust to the chilly water. Farther out, expensive boats motored by, their drivers red-faced and clutching bottles of beer.

For once, I wasn't thinking about the baby, or Lainey, or my childless future. I wasn't really thinking anything at all. Somehow, between the hot sun and the hypnotic roar of the ocean, my mind had gone mercifully blank. I wished I'd worn my bathing suit—the cool blue of the ocean was irresistible.

"Hi," a familiar voice said from behind me.

I started and spun around. Jeremy was standing there.

"How did you know where I was?"

"Lucky guess," he said. "And I know you like to come here to think."

"That's just it. I'm not thinking. I can't think about any of it anymore."

Jeremy wrapped an arm around me and pulled me close. We'd always fit well together, my curves lining up against the planes of his body. He kissed the top of my head.

"It's going to get better," he said, his voice soft but fierce.

"I'm not so sure. Does anyone ever get over something like this?"

"Maybe that's setting the goal too high. Maybe we should just aim for getting through it first," Jeremy suggested.

There was a catch in his voice. I looked up quickly and saw that his eyes were wet. It occurred to me that I'd been so caught up in my own grief, it had never occurred to me that Jeremy was going through this, too.

"You fell in love with him," I said. It wasn't a question. I suddenly just knew it, the way I knew he had a pale silver birthmark on his lower back and a near-phobic aversion to snakes.

Jeremy didn't say anything, but he tightened his hold on my shoulders.

"I've checked out on you," I said. "I'm sorry. That wasn't fair."

"It isn't a matter of fair or not. We're not like that. When one of us goes through a hard time, the other one is there to pick up the slack."

"But you're going through a hard time, too. And I haven't been there for you."

"We're both doing what we can to get through this."

"Is that enough?"

"It has to be enough," Jeremy said simply. He pulled me close again, one hand softly stroking my hair. After a moment, he said, "You know what really pisses me off?"

"What?"

"There's no word to describe what this is. It's too big to be called disappointing. But it feels wrong to call it grieving. He was healthy and perfect. We just don't get to have him," Jeremy said.

"I know what you mean," I said. And suddenly, there were tears in my eyes, too, and my throat felt tight and knotted. "But it is a kind of grief. We're grieving the future that we won't be able to have."

Jeremy nodded. I looked up at him. His pale skin was already starting to flush pink from being out in the sun, and his hair stood on end, as though he'd been running his fingers through it. A surge of love cracked through then, breaking past the fog of sadness.

"Come on," I said, taking his hand and tugging it gently. "Let's go home."

A few evenings later, Mimi appeared at my front door, brandishing a bagful of chocolate chip cookies, a bottle of vodka, and a net sack full of grapefruits.

"What's all that for?" I asked.

"The cookies are from the kids. They wanted to cheer you up. But don't eat them—they're so hard you'll break a tooth. The vodka is from me. You and I are going to get drunk," Mimi said, sailing past me into the house. I trailed after her back to the kitchen, where she'd put down her wares and begun to rummage through the cupboards. "Where's your juicer?"

"Lower cabinet next to the fridge," I said. "But I'm not really in the mood to drink right now."

"Yeah, well, too bad. We're drinking," Mimi said bossily.

She busied herself slicing the grapefruit, juicing them, and then dumping the vodka, juice, club soda, and ice into a glass pitcher, which she mixed thoroughly with a spatula. She placed the pitcher on a tray, along with two tall glasses and a can of cashews she found in the pantry.

"Now. Where shall we go? Let's sit out by the pool." Mimi decided.

"It's boiling out."

"If we get too hot, we'll just jump in the water."

"Okay," I said, shrugging. In my current state, I was no match for the sheer force of Mimi's will.

It was actually nicer out than I'd thought. The sky was still light, but the sun was low on the horizon and starting to fade to sherbet shades of pink and orange. Mimi poured out two drinks, handed me one, and then clinked her glass against mine.

"Cheers," she said, and tasted her cocktail. "Mmm, that's delicious. I wasn't sure about the grapefruit—they're out of season—but the grocer told me to give them a try. I'll have to report back to him that he was right. Men always love to hear that."

"What's the occasion?" I asked.

"Does there have to be an occasion for vodka?"

I rolled my eyes. "You've obviously come over to give me some sort of a pep talk about getting on with my life."

"No, I haven't."

"Liar."

"No, really. You don't need a pep talk. I think you're holding up extraordinarily well under the circumstances."

"You don't have to humor me. I know I'm a mess."

"You're getting up, showering, eating, even getting back to work. I think that's pretty amazing considering what you've been through. Don't be so hard on yourself."

"You're really not here to give me one of your up-and-at-'em talks?"

"Scout's honor," Mimi said, holding up one hand.

"Like you were ever a Girl Scout," I scoffed.

"You're right, I wasn't," Mimi confessed. "I always thought the uniforms were hideous, and there was no way I'd ever sell cookies door-to-door. How's Jeremy?"

"He's hurting. And he's angry." I sighed and ran a hand through my unruly hair. "I feel badly that I haven't been there for him. He's been holding everything together, while I just unraveled. It isn't fair."

Mimi lifted one shoulder. "Did you ever think that maybe he needs to be the one to hold it all together? That maybe that's how he's coping?"

I shrugged. I wasn't ready to let myself off the hook so easily.

"I should have listened to you," I finally said. "You warned me about Lainey from the beginning."

"Actually, I think I was wrong about her. Don't look so surprised. I think she might not have had the best intentions when you first met her, but I also think something changed along the way. I saw her that last night, when we all drove you to the hospital. I'm convinced she genuinely planned to give the baby to you," Mimi said. She spread her hands, palms facing the sky. "But then she saw him."

"And fell in love," I said. Even now, the waves of longing took me by surprise. It wasn't just that I missed him; that was to be expected. It was that I *pined* for him. It was like a piece of me was missing—a crucial limb, a necessary organ—and I had no way of getting it back. "Maybe it would be easier if I could get angry at her. It's like, she made this incredibly tough decision. Raising a child by herself is going to be so hard. Of course it's not what I wanted, but even so, I don't want her to fail. Just the opposite. I want her to succeed."

"That's because you're his mother, too," Mimi said.

I stared at her, hardly believing that she could say such a thing to me. "I'm not his mother," I said. The words felt raw and sharp in my throat.

"Of course you are," Mimi said gently.

"Spending a few hours with a baby in a hospital doesn't turn you into a mother," I said bitterly. "And even if it did, I don't have him anymore. I didn't get to keep him."

"Once you become a mother, you can't go back and undo it. It doesn't matter if you had him for five minutes, or five hours, or five years before you lost him. That shift that occurs inside of you—the way everything in your life that you thought was a priority just falls away to make room for this new, greater love— that happens instantly. And it doesn't just change back," Mimi said.

Tears started to stream down my face. "Please stop."

Mimi reached out and grabbed my hand, squeezing it gently. "I don't want to make you sad. But I don't think you're ever going to feel better if you just close that part of yourself off forever."

I wiped angrily at my wet cheeks. "I don't know, Mimi. I'm not ready to think about another adoption yet."

Mimi nodded. "I know. But it will hurt less in time," she said. "You won't forget it—you won't ever forget him—but it will become bearable over time."

I shook my head. "I don't know about that."

"Life has a funny way of proving us wrong," Mimi said. She poured us each another drink and handed mine to me. I shook my head, miserable, but she pressed it on me. "Come on, take it. It's medicinal."

I smiled. It sounded like something my mother would say. She'd always sworn by the healing power of two things: swimming in the ocean and the perfect hot toddy. My dad had suffered from chronic bronchitis, and he claimed my mom's hot toddies were the only thing that made him feel better.

My dad. I hadn't thought of him in a while. I remembered the early days after his death, when Mom and I had both walked around in a fog. Mom would get weepy every time she came across an extra pair of his reading glasses stowed in a drawer, or found a book he'd been reading, a corner bent down to mark his page. I tried to remain stoic for her sake, but there were moments when I was alone, where I'd curl up into a ball and weep into my pillow, feeling like everything was forever bleak and hopeless. But then, gradually, over time, the intensity of the pain had faded.

"My dad once told me that the greatest tragedy in life is not when a man is beaten—that happens to everyone sometimes—but when he just gives up on his dreams," I said, turning my sweating glass around in my hands.

"He sounds like a very wise man."

"Well. It's very likely he told me that while he was stoned," I said. I'd finally stopped crying, and gave my cheeks a final wipe with the back of one hand. "But still, he had a point."

Mimi beamed at me. "Good girl," she said.

"I'm not promising anything. I'll just put off making any final decisions about it for now," I said.

"That's enough," Mimi said. She shook her glass, so that the ice cubes tinkled together. "For now, anyway. But don't think I'm even close to giving up. You know me better than that."

"Yes, I do know. You're relentless," I said. "How does Leo put up with you?"

Mimi waved this away. "I bend him to my will," she said. "And I put out."

"Sounds like a winning strategy to me," I said, and we clinked our glasses together.

I heard the bell jingle on the front door, alerting me that someone had come into the studio. I'd thought about hiring a part-timer to replace Lainey, but hadn't gotten around to it yet, so there wasn't anyone manning the reception area.

I stood, but hadn't even walked around my worktable when I heard Jeremy's voice.

"India?"

Oh, crap, I thought, looking at the photos spread out over my table and wondering if there was any way I could clear them before Jeremy walked back. No, there wasn't time. I'd just have to intercept him.

"Hey! What are you doing here?" I said, quickly stepping forward to block Jeremy at the doorway to the back room.

"I was out running errands, and thought I'd stop by to take my best girl to lunch," he said.

"How nice," I said, leaning up to kiss him. "Where are we going?"

"Actually, I brought lunch with me," he said, holding up a canvas sack I hadn't noticed he was holding. "Apple chicken salad sandwiches from the Rip Tide Deli. You said you had a busy day, so I thought you'd probably just want to eat here at the studio."

He started to step around me—when we ate at my studio, we always dined at my worktable—but I held up a hand to stop him. "No, let's go out. It's a beautiful day."

"It's one hundred degrees with ninety-five percent humidity outside," Jeremy said.

"So? We'll go to the beach. It'll be cooler there."

"And get sand blown into our sandwiches? No, thanks."

"A little sand never hurt anyone," I argued.

Jeremy frowned. "What's going on? Why don't you want to eat here?"

"Nothing's going on," I lied. "I've just been inside all day, and I want to get out for a while. Plus I just spread out a bunch of proofs all over the table."

To my relief, Jeremy acquiesced. "Okay. But let's go to that park down the street. They have covered picnic tables there, so at least we'll be in the shade." He turned and started to walk back to the reception area. I grabbed my purse off the hook by the filing cabinet and followed him out. Jeremy had stopped by the reception desk, and was frowning down at his hand.

"Look at this," he said. He held up his left index finger. "I'm bleeding."

I examined it. "It looks like a paper cut. You should put a Band-Aid on it."

"Do you still have a box in your filing cabinet?" Jeremy asked.

"I think so," I said, without thinking.

"Let me go grab one before we go," Jeremy said, moving past me and back into the workroom.

"Wait! I'll get it!"

But it was too late. Jeremy had already disappeared. As he'd have to walk right by my worktable in order to get to the filing cabinet where I kept Band-Aids and other sundry items, I knew there was no way he wouldn't see what I'd been working on. I blew out a deep breath and slowly followed after him.

As I'd expected, Jeremy was standing very still and staring down at the photos spread out on my table. There were copies of the photos I'd taken of Lainey for my show, as well as a few snapshots—one of Lainey sitting on our sofa with a bowl of ice cream resting on her belly bump, another where she was looking up and laughing at me as I snapped the photo. Then there were the black-and-white pictures I'd taken of the baby in the hospital. I'd cropped several of them, showing off all the details of his exquisite face—the nearly translucent eyelids, the tiny snub nose, the full pursed lips.

"What's going on?" Jeremy asked, his voice stiff with pain.

"I'm making an album for Lainey," I said.

"Why?"

"Because I thought she'd like to have these pictures," I said quietly.

"Jesus, India. Even now, even after she screwed us over, you're still bending over backward to please her?"

"No! It's not for her, not really. It's for me. And for him."

Jeremy shook his head. "I don't understand. How does this—" he gestured toward the pile of photographs with a dismissive flick of his hand, "help *you*?"

"Please stop shouting at me," I said quietly.

Jeremy closed his eyes and swallowed. "I apologize for raising my voice," he said. "I'm just trying to understand what you're doing. Because it seems more than a little masochistic."

I rubbed a hand over my brow and tried to think of a way to explain it that would make sense to him.

"I can see why you would think that," I began. "But I'm really not trying to torture myself. And I'm also not doing it to prove anything to Lainey. I just think she should have these photos."

"Why?"

"For him," I said simply. "He should know that from the first moment of his life, he was loved and wanted. Even if he never knows about us, he'll look at these photos and see that the person who took them loved him."

Jeremy stood very still for a long time, staring down at the worktable. I saw his eyes roam over the photographs, barely glancing at the pictures of Lainey, but lingering on the photos of the baby. I watched him, hoping he'd understand what I was doing, that he wouldn't ask me not to. I felt like this was something I had to do before I could move on.

He reached out and touched one of the photos. It was my favorite—I'd stood directly over the baby, when he was sleeping on one side in his bassinet, exhausted from the ordeal of his birth and perfect in profile.

"This one," Jeremy said softly, tapping it. "Make sure you put this one in."

"Okay," I said. I walked up behind Jeremy, wrapped my arms around his waist, and pressed my cheek against the warmth of his back. I could hear his heart beat and the air moving in and out of his body. I closed my eyes and swallowed hard. "I will."

Seventeen

LAINEY

The baby was crying again. Lainey's eyes were open and her feet were on the floor, propelling her up and across the room to the crib, before her brain had even registered that she was awake. Griffin was flailing in his crib, his face screwed up, his tiny fists punching the air while he screamed.

"Shhhh," Lainey said, scooping him up. He began rooting around her neck, smacking his lips hungrily. "Okay, little man. Let's go get your bottle."

Lainey carried Griffin into the kitchen and laid him down in the vibrating sling chair Candace had found at a neighbor's garage sale. She switched it on, before turning to fix his bottle. The vibrations normally soothed Griffin, but the magic wasn't working tonight. Griffin continued to shriek, and the sheer volume of it jangled Lainey's nerves. She attempted to screw the top on the baby bottle, but lost her grip. The bottle clattered to the ground, sending ridiculously expensive formula—Griffin's sensitive stomach didn't tolerate the cut-price brands—splattering all over the cabinets.

"Crap," Lainey said, staring dejectedly at the mess.

It was the last clean bottle. Candace had promised to do the dishes, but she'd started drinking after dinner and never got to them. Plates crusted with ketchup and creamed corn were piled in the sink, along with all of the bottles. Lainey cursed herself for not taking care of them before she fell into bed, too exhausted to brush her teeth. Griffin hadn't slept for more than two hours at a time since he came home from the hospital. The exhaustion was taking its toll on Lainey. It felt like a sandpit, sucking her down while she slowly suffocated.

Griffin sensed that his meal was delayed, and responded by ratcheting up the volume of his screams. Lainey made soothing sounds to him while simultaneously washing the bottle's nipple under the sink faucet and grabbing for more formula.

Candace stumbled into the kitchen, blinking into the fluorescent overhead light. "What in the holy hell is going on in here?"

"What does it look like?" Lainey snapped.

"Oh, Griffin baby, is Mama giving you a hard time?" Candace asked, scooping the baby out of his chair. Lainey noticed that Candace's hands were shaking.

"Here, give him to me," Lainey said quickly. "He's hungry."

Candace handed over the baby without argument and turned to reach into the cupboard over the sink. She withdrew a bottle of Jack Daniel's and poured a slug of it into a smudged glass.

"Haven't you had enough?" Lainey asked, settling down onto a chair, Griffin in her arms. She held the bottle up for him, and he immediately stopped shrieking and latched onto it, greedily gulping down the milk.

"It's to help me sleep," Candace said. "With the racket that kid's making, I need all the help I can get."

"Yeah, me too," Lainey said.

Candace, either missing the sarcasm or choosing to ignore it, offered up the bottle. "You want a drink?" she asked. Candace hated to drink alone. It was, Lainey thought, probably the main reason her mother had put up with one loser boyfriend after another.

"No," Lainey said shortly. She wished Candace would just go back to bed and leave her alone with the baby. It would be different if her mother was actually ever helpful, but when Candace drank, she was no use to anyone. Lainey doubted if her mother had ever really stopped drinking, as she'd claimed. Candace probably thought switching to light beer for two days counted as drying out.

"Suit yourself. Turn off the lights when you're through," Candace said, adding another dollop of whiskey into the glass before shuffling back to her bedroom.

"Why don't you just bring the bottle with you?" Lainey muttered.

"This is how I get my exercise," her mother retorted, her voice floating back down the hall.

Lainey made a face at Griffin. A moment later, Candace's door shut with a soft thud.

"We have got to get out of here," Lainey told Griffin.

She had some money saved in what had once been her Los Angeles fund. It was now her all-purpose survival fund—diapers and formula were not cheap, and despite their promises, neither Candace nor Trav was doing much to help out. She might have enough to put a down payment on an apartment and, if she was very careful, maybe even to live on for a few months. But then what? She'd have to get a job, obviously, but that meant finding day care for Griffin. She refused to put him in some seedy run-down center full of faded plastic toys and grimy kids with perpetually runny noses, but the nicer places all charged a lot of money. Even if she did go to court and get child support from Trav, Lainey was going to have to conserve every last penny to make this work. And that meant living rent-free at Candace's for as long as she could gut it out.

But Lainey had always been a big believer in making plans, and she had one now. She had decided she would go back to doing nails, although this time she wasn't going to take a job with a cheap mall outlet. Instead, she was going to find a position at a spa or a high-end salon. One that would have health insurance and customers who tipped. Flaca had already agreed to babysit Griffin one day next week so Lainey could start applying for jobs.

"And when I get one, baby boy, we will be out of here like *that*," Lainey said, snapping her fingers. He regarded her with serious eyes as he sucked on his bottle. "And I'll just hope to hell that you don't remember anything you might have seen or heard while living in this shithole."

"Ever heard of calling first?" Lainey said when she opened the front door and found Trav standing on the doorstep.

"Hi," Trav said. "Right. Whatever. I was just passing by, so I thought . . ." His voice trailed off.

Lainey supposed she should give him some credit for trying to stay involved, even if it was half-assed. Still, would it kill him to show up with a pack of diapers once in a while?

Trav walked into the house, his hands stuck in the pockets of his nylon workout pants. As he passed by her, Lainey caught a whiff of stale sweat.

"He's back here," Lainey said, leading Trav into the living room. Griffin was there, lying on his stomach on a blanket Lainey had spread out on the floor. Trav stared at the baby.

"He's having tummy time," Lainey explained.

"What's that?"

"It strengthens his muscles, and gets him to start rolling over on his own," Lainey explained. She leaned over and scooped the baby up. "I read about it in the baby book the hospital gave me."

"Oh, right." Trav nodded.

"Do you want to hold him?" she asked.

"Sure. Okay."

She handed the baby to him. Trav always looked uncomfortable when he held Griffin. He seemed to think he had to keep his arms and torso perfectly still, like a robot. Griffin immediately began to squirm, and hiccupped fretfully.

"I don't think he likes it when I hold him," Trav said.

"Just keep him upright, so he can see. He doesn't like being flat on his back like that."

"I don't know. I'm afraid I'm going to break him or something." Trav handed Griffin back to Lainey and stepped back, looking relieved. "Actually, I came by because I have something I have to tell you."

Lainey was too focused on the baby to hear Trav. She held him up, supporting his head with one hand. "See? He's happier now that he can see. Aren't you, baby?"

She gazed down at Griffin, thinking that he must be the most beautiful baby to have ever graced the world. At five weeks old, Griffin had just started smiling—beaming, jolly grins. This was clear evidence of his brilliance, and, Lainey thought, a relief, considering half of his genes came from his idiot father.

"I'm getting married," Trav said.

Lainey looked up at him, blinking with confusion. "Huh?"

"I'm getting married. Me and Jordan."

Trav had started dating Jordan—an enthusiastic bodybuilder he'd met at his gym—after he and Lainey broke up. Lainey had never met her, but supposed she'd have to now. This woman would be a stepmother to Griffin.

Jealousy trickled through Lainey. She didn't care about Jordan's relationship with Trav—Jordan was more than welcome to him. But Lainey didn't want to share her baby with anyone. What if Griffin didn't even like Jordan? Or—and Lainey had to admit this alternative felt even worse—what if he thought of her as a second mother?

"We're moving to Orlando. Jordan's family is there," Trav continued.

"What about Griffin?"

Trav hunched his shoulders up. "I don't know. I mean, I'm not going to be here a lot. And it'd be weird, don't you think? Trying to share him, I mean. Jordan doesn't even know him."

The fear that Jordan would take Lainey's son away from her instantly vanished, replaced by an even greater worry that Griffin was about to lose his father. Lainey held the baby closer to her. She wanted to protect him from this paternal abandonment—she knew what it was like to grow up without a father—but didn't know how to stop it. "Why did you come to the hospital and tell me you wanted to be his father if you're just going to leave now?"

Trav suddenly looked shifty. His eyes darted around the room, and he stuffed his hands back in his pant pockets.

"What?" Lainey demanded.

"Your mom sort of made me."

"Made you? What do you mean she *made you*?"

Trav looked pointedly at Griffin. "I don't think you should yell in front of the B-A-B-Y," he said.

"I'm not yelling. And you don't have to spell out *baby*, especially not in front of a baby, you idiot. Now, what do you mean my mom made you?"

"She said that if I went with her to the hospital and helped talk you into keeping the baby, that she'd . . ." He hesitated.

"Jesus Christ, Trav. Just spit it out."

"She'd give me two hundred dollars."

"She said *what*?" Lainey stared at him. "She gave you money to pretend you wanted to be a daddy? Please tell me you're not serious."

"Actually, she never gave me the money." Trav looked sulky. "And I really needed it. I was going to buy a new iPod. I can't find mine. I think someone at the gym must have stolen it, which sucks. I hate working out without my music."

Lainey shook her head, staring at him in disbelief.

"You're pathetic," Lainey said. "And you're an asshole. Griffin's better off without you."

"Fine, whatever," Trav said. He shrugged and started toward the door. But then he turned back. "You know, I told you back in the beginning that I didn't want to have a baby. I don't know why you thought that was going to change."

"I don't know why I did, either. And don't think this means you're off the hook for child support," Lainey snapped. She clutched Griffin closer to her chest, and didn't look up again until the front door had banged shut.

"It really is just you and me now," Lainey said to her son. The baby shifted and sighed deeply, relaxed and boneless in her arms. And Lainey, realizing that she was really and truly on her own, felt a sudden shudder of fear.

"How is he?" Lainey asked when Flaca opened the front door to her apartment.

"Hello to you, too," Flaca said.

Lainey pushed past her, striding into Flaca's apartment and looking around. "Where is he?"

"Relax. He's in the bedroom, sleeping," Flaca said.

She nodded toward the door, which was cracked open. Lainey hurried in. Griffin was lying in a Pack 'n Play, sleeping peacefully with his arms raised up over his head as though he had been reaching to catch a football a moment before he fell asleep. Lainey leaned over him and rested a hand on his chest. It wasn't until she felt the rhythmic rise and fall of his breath that the knots in her stomach loosened.

"You're okay," she said softly.

"Nice to see you have such faith in my babysitting abilities," Flaca said from the doorway. "Do you want a soda or something?"

"Sure."

They left Griffin to his nap and returned to the living room.

Lainey sat heavily down on a chair while Flaca headed to the kitchen to retrieve two cans of cola. She handed one to Lainey and then sat on the couch, propping her bare feet on the edge of the coffee table.

"How'd the job search go?" Flaca asked, popping her soda can open.

Lainey shook her head. "Not good. I went to, like, twenty different salons. No one was hiring. They all said business was too slow right now."

"It's the summer," Flaca said. "Things will pick up in the winter, when all of the tourists and snowbirds are back in town."

"I can't wait that long. I need a job now. I have to get my own place as soon as possible."

"Candace?" Flaca asked sympathetically.

Lainey looked at her friend with hollow eyes, ringed with dark circles. "She dropped Griffin the other day."

"What?"

"She'd been drinking, and she picked him up before I could stop her. And then she just sort of lost her grip on him." Lainey rubbed a hand tiredly across her face. "Luckily, he fell on the sofa, so he wasn't hurt. But what if she'd dropped him on the kitchen floor?"

"Jesus," Flaca said, shaking her head. "That could have been bad."

"No kidding. I have to get him out of there."

"Have you signed up for the public housing wait list yet?"

Lainey shrugged this off. "No. I don't want to."

"You'd rather live with a drunk?"

"No. But I don't want to live in crack alley, either. I just have to find a job." Lainey said. But almost instantly, her resolve left her. "God, what am I going to do?"

"You'll just keep going. What else can you do?"

A rumble of grunts and moans signaled that Griffin's nap was over. Lainey stood up. "I'll take him home. Thanks for watching him for me."

"No problem. He was a doll. He didn't even poop while he was here."

"Oh, yeah? I think he just made up for that," Lainey said. The odor hit her as soon as she walked into the bedroom, and grew stronger the closer she got to the Pack 'n Play. Lainey closed her eyes, trying to summon her strength. It had been in short supply lately. "Come on, big boy. Let's get you changed."

Trav left town two weeks later. He called the morning of the move and asked if he could stop by to see Griffin before he left. Lainey was going to tell him to go to hell, but then changed her mind. Maybe if Trav saw what he'd be missing out on, he'd realize he couldn't just walk out of Griffin's life. And wasn't a half-ass father better than no father at all?

But Trav never turned up. Lainey waited around for the better part of the day before finally realizing he was a no-show. She gave up and, cursing Trav every step of the way, wheeled Griffin to the park in his stroller. It was late July and ridiculously hot, and Lainey was out of breath by the time they got to the park.

I'm so out of shape, she thought. A year ago, she could run on the treadmill for an hour. Now walking a half mile winded her. The sleep deprivation wasn't helping, either.

Lainey collapsed on a bench and pulled the cover on the stroller down to shade Griffin from the sun. Despite the intense heat, there were a bunch of kids at the playground, red-faced and sweaty as they swung on the swings and slid down the slide. Their mothers sat in the few patches of shade, armed with water bottles and bags of pretzels. A father tossed a football to a little boy. Lainey watched them—the easy arc of the ball, the boy's face lighting with pride as he caught it, his father's encouraging cheers—and felt a fresh surge of fury at Trav for abandoning Griffin, mixed with bitter sadness that her son would never experience this sort of father-son bonding.

To distract herself, Lainey pulled the photo album out of her diaper bag, and paged through it for about the twentieth time since it had arrived by mail the day before. When Lainey first saw the familiar mailing label on the package—*Halloway Photography*—she'd hesitated, not sure she wanted to see what was inside. But finally, curiosity overcame her, and she sliced open the seal with a kitchen knife. Inside, she'd found a photo album, the old thirty-five-millimeter camera she'd used while working at the studio, and a note written in India's scrawling hand:

> *Lainey,*
> *I started this album for him—I thought you'd want*
> *to finish filling it.*
> *India*

Lainey had stared at the note for a long time and then picked up the camera. It had felt familiar and right in her hands. She'd lifted it up and snapped a photo of Griffin, lying on his baby blanket.

Now she paged through the album again, her eyes lingering over the portraits India had taken of her while she was pregnant, and of Griffin in the hospital. There was a photograph of the baby's hand, the extreme close-up showing off every dimpled knuckle, and another of him in utero, a fuzzy outline taken during her sonogram. The photographs in the album were ordered chronologically, showing the story of Griffin's journey into the world.

It was the best present Lainey had ever gotten.

Lainey's cell phone began to trill from the depths of the free diaper bag they'd given her at the hospital. She dug among the spare diapers, burp cloths, spare onesies, and plastic tubs of wipes, all essentials for any foray out into the world, no matter how short, and finally found the phone wedged in the corner of the bag. Lainey didn't recognize the number of the caller, but hoped it might be someone calling her for a job interview. There was one last place she was waiting to hear from—a spa on Palm Beach that had, Lainey heard, recently lost a nail tech. It was her last shot.

"Hello?"

"Hello, is this Lainey Walker?"

"Yes, this is Lainey," Lainey said, trying to sound professional.

"This is Lance Gardam, Streetwise Productions. You attended a casting call back in April for *Looking for Mr. Right*, our new reality show featuring young women looking for love in Miami."

It took Lainey a long moment to digest this. She'd never heard anything back from the casting call and had assumed that was the end of it.

"Yeah, that's right," she said.

"We've had a last-minute cancellation from one of the girls we cast. If you're still available, we'd like to bring you down for a call-back."

Lainey opened her mouth, but no sound came out.

"Hello?" the voice on the phone bleated.

"I'm sorry, but did you just offer me a part on your show?" she asked.

"No, not officially. We'll have to talk to you, make sure you clear the necessary background checks, et cetera, et cetera. But between you and me, if that all goes well, yeah, you're pretty much our first pick. How soon can you get here? Filming starts in a week, so we have to get this moving."

Griffin made a soft mewing sound, distracting Lainey. She glanced into the baby carriage, but he was fast asleep. His long lashes curled against his round pink cheeks, and his rosebud lips were pursed, as though waiting for a kiss.

"I can't," she said. The words came out before she'd really had a chance to process it all—what she was being offered, what she'd be giving up if she took it, what she'd be giving up if she didn't.

"Today's no good? How about tomorrow?"

"No, you don't understand. . . . I can't come at all. I can't be on the show," Lainey said.

There was a pause. "Are you sure?"

Lainey closed her eyes and swallowed hard. All of the fantasies she'd ever had about being on television flooded over her—the money, the clothes, the fame. A life that didn't revolve around dirty diapers and bottles. Nights spent out partying at clubs, followed by blissfully uninterrupted sleep. Feeling young and free again, rather than like an old, wrung-out dishrag.

But then she opened her eyes and looked at her son. He had one tiny fist curled next to his mouth and the other splayed out to one side. He was wearing a onesie with teddy bears on it—a splurge from BabyGap Lainey hadn't been able to resist. Tiny blue-and-white-striped socks covered his feet. He shifted in his sleep, exhaling a low cooing sound that made Lainey's heart feel like it was folding over on itself.

"Yes. I'm sure," Lainey said, and closed her phone.

"You're in a crap mood tonight," Candace complained. "You didn't even thank me for picking up dinner."

The dinner consisted of fast-food fried chicken, whipped mashed potatoes, and congealed macaroni and cheese.

"Thanks," Lainey said without enthusiasm. She was still trying to lose the baby weight, so she passed on the potatoes and macaroni, and instead picked at a chicken breast after first peeling off the greasy fried coating.

"You wouldn't believe the day I had. I had this old woman who came in today to renew her driver's license who was a real piece of work. First she was pissed because she had to wait in line like everyone else, and wouldn't shut up about how long the wait was. Then she failed her vision test and accused me of making the letters on the chart fuzzy just so she'd fail. Can you believe that? I was, like, 'Look, lady, I don't need this shit. Life is too short.'"

"Did you say that?" Lainey asked, knowing full well her mother had not.

"No. What's the point? Leopards don't change their stripes." Candace stood up, went to the fridge, and pulled out a beer. "Want one?"

"Spots," Lainey said.

"What?"

"Leopards have spots," Lainey said. "Not stripes."

"That's what I said," Candace said, rolling her eyes as she popped open the beer can. "Jesus, you're in a mood."

Lainey's head was pounding. It had been ever since the producer had called that afternoon. Whenever she stopped to think about it, a sickening swooping sensation filled her. Was this what the rest of her life would be? Living in a shitty little house, working a crap job, eating greasy drive-thru for dinner? It felt like her future—and Griffin's—was shrinking with each passing day. When she'd gotten home from the park, the day spa Lainey had been waiting to hear back from had called to tell her that they weren't hiring. The nail tech hadn't quit; she'd been laid off.

"Maybe I will have a beer," Lainey said, thinking that if ever there was a day to suspend her no-drinking policy, this was it. She needed to stop the panicked whirring of her mind, even if it was only temporary. Maybe then she'd be able to come up with another plan.

"You'll have to get it yourself now. I'm already sitting down," Candace said, forking rubbery macaroni and cheese into her mouth.

Lainey stood, opened the refrigerator, and stared into it, marveling at how grimy it was. Something smelled vaguely rotten, and a thick, sticky film covered the top glass shelf. Candace had never been much of a housekeeper. Lainey could not remember a time when the floors of the house didn't feel gritty underfoot, or when there weren't blobs of toothpaste cemented in the bathroom sink. She thought of Griffin—who was tucked into his crib—growing up in the sort of dirt and chaos that had marked her own childhood. Despair cut through Lainey. She looked down at her hands and realized they were shaking.

Lainey shut the refrigerator door, without taking out a beer, and instead reached for the cupboard where Candace kept the whiskey.

"Are we breaking out the good stuff already?" Candace asked, perking up. "Well, don't just stand there, girl. Get me a glass, too."

"Waaaaaaah!"

Lainey jolted awake. The first thing her brain registered was that she had to pee. Badly. And then, that there was something uncomfortable and prickly under her cheek. Lainey opened her eyes—a struggle in itself, as her eyelashes felt like they'd been glued together—and she realized she'd fallen asleep on the brown plaid couch in the living room. Why was she out here? Then she remembered the whiskey from the night before, and her stomach gave a queasy lurch.

Lainey and Candace had moved from the kitchen out to the back deck. There, surrounded by the high-pitched whir of mosquitoes, they'd spent the rest of the evening passing the bottle back and forth. Candace grew gregarious when she drank, and was soon reminiscing about old loves and lost opportunities. The whiskey had the opposite effect on Lainey. She'd gone quietly, mercifully numb.

Lainey now pressed a hand to her forehead, desperately wishing her head would stop spinning and pounding. But, no, she had to get up. Griffin was crying. Lainey forced herself to stand up and walk back to the bedroom they shared before her brain registered that standing was not the best idea. Nausea and dizziness struck her like a one-two punch.

I'm going to be sick, she thought, slumped against the wall.

The pitch of Griffin's cries rose steadily, his original complaint now compounded by the lack of immediate response. Candace's room was closer than the baby's, so Lainey propelled herself toward it.

"Mom?" she said, opening the door and staggering in without knocking. Candace had made it to her bed the night before, although she'd fallen asleep fully dressed and lying facedown on the mauve bedspread. She was snoring softly. Lainey tried again. "Mom! Wake up! I need help."

Candace didn't move. Griffin continued to scream. Lainey groaned, and lurched back out of the room and down the hallway. She opened the door to the room she shared with Griffin—it was small, and just barely fit the crib, a small dresser that doubled as a changing table, and the air mattress that Lainey slept on. Griffin was lying on his back in the crib, screaming, his face mottled and his arms thrown out to either side. Lainey started to reach for him, until a wave of nausea hit her anew. This time, she could feel the bile in her stomach rising up, hot and acidic in her stomach.

"Hold on, baby," she groaned.

She turned and rushed for the bathroom, making it to the toilet just in time. Lainey fell to her knees and threw up until her stomach cramped and her throat ached, while Griffin screamed shrilly in the background. When her stomach finally stopped heaving, Lainey slumped forward, more tired than she'd ever been in her life.

I will get through this, she told herself. But at the same time, another thought echoed back: *What if I don't? What if I can't?*

She wiped at her eyes with a wad of toilet paper and then stood on shaky legs. The sound of Griffin's brittle cries broke her heart even while it shattered her throbbing head. She moved woozily toward the sink so she could rinse her mouth out before going back to him, but stopped dead when she saw her reflection in the mirror. Her skin was ashen. Her eyes were bloodshot and swollen. Her hair was flat and greasy. Hot stinging tears suddenly flooded her eyes.

She looked like hell. And, for the first time, when Lainey looked at herself in the mirror, she saw her mother staring back at her.

Eighteen

JEREMY

"What are you doing?" India asked from the doorway of the guesthouse, which was once again serving as my office.

I quickly hit a button so that the Weather Channel's website was displayed prominently on my computer screen, and spun around in my chair. "What? Oh, nothing, just checking the weather. You startled me. I didn't hear you come in."

"I'm making BLTs for lunch," India said. "They'll be ready in fifteen minutes. Actually, they're BLTs with avocado. So what would that be? A BALT?"

"A BLAT, I think. Sounds great. Let me just finish up what I'm doing here, and I'll be in," I said.

"You have to finish checking the weather?"

I glanced at the computer screen. "I was, um, thinking we could go to the beach later. I was checking to see if it was going to storm."

"Come in when you're done." India headed back to the house. I watched her progress across the backyard and around the pool out my office window, and when I saw the door that separated the kitchen from the pool patio safely close behind her, I turned back to the computer.

I closed the weather website and returned to the online article

I had been reading: "International Adoption: A Beginner's Guide." It wasn't that I was hiding my research from India. Not exactly. It was more that I knew she wasn't in a place yet to hear about it. And while I knew that she might not ever get to that place without some gentle encouragement, I wanted to make sure I gathered all of the pertinent information before I broached the subject with her. And this time, I was going to handle the paperwork, and the grunt work, and the endless calls to the various government bureaucracies. This time, India wouldn't have to worry about anything other than packing her suitcase when it was time to go pick up our baby. And this time, we would end up with a baby.

I browsed through the article, then clicked over to a few others I'd pulled up before India had come in. The first decision we had to make—and it was a fairly big one—was which country we would adopt from. Did we have strong feelings about the gender of the child? Did we want to adopt a baby who had spent a significant amount of its life in an orphanage, or was it better to find one who had been cared for by foster parents? How far did we want to travel? And for how many weeks?

I took notes and jotted down the titles of some books that other parents who'd been through the ordeal recommended, and then glanced at the clock. Lunchtime. The BLATs were calling. I headed for the kitchen, where I found India frying bacon. Otis sat at her feet, his ears pricked, all of his attention focused in the direction of the frying pan.

"Mmm, bacon," I said, shutting the back door quickly, before the cold air could escape into the August heat.

"Funny, that's exactly what Otis said," India said.

"Ha-ha," I said.

The phone rang.

"Would you mind getting that?" India said. She waved her spatula at the frying pan, indicating that she didn't want to step away.

"Sure," I said. I headed toward the phone—tripping over Otis—and grabbed the receiver. "Hello."

There was a pause. And then a voice—a familiar voice—said, "Jeremy?"

My body went hot and cold at the same time.

"Are you there? It's Lainey," Lainey said in my ear while at the same time, India said, raising her voice to be heard over the sizzle of bacon, "Who is it?"

"It's nobody," I said, and then I took the phone and hurried into the living room, hoping that India's fear of a grease fire would prevent her from following me. I shut the door behind me and said into the phone, "What do you want?"

There was another pause. And then a sigh. "You're mad at me," Lainey said. It was a statement of fact, not a question.

"That surprises you?" I asked.

"Not really. Is India there? I need to talk to her."

"No," I said.

"No, she's not there?"

"No, you can't talk to her."

"It's important," Lainey persisted.

"I don't care."

Lainey didn't say anything, although I could hear her breathing. Finally, she said, "How is she?"

"That's none of your business."

"You don't understand," Lainey said, and for the first time, a bit of the steel I was used to hearing in her voice had crept back in.

"Yes I do. I understand perfectly. You really want to know how India is? I'll tell you: She's heartbroken," I said bluntly. "And that's because of you. You let her believe that she'd finally be a mother, and then you ripped that away from her. What could you possibly say to her now that would make any of that okay?"

A baby cried out in the background, and I found that the air had suddenly left my lungs. It was him. That was *his* cry. I sat down heavily on the edge of the sofa.

Lainey made shushing sounds. When she returned to the phone, her voice was thin and desperate. "Will you meet me?"

"I don't see what the point would be," I said.

There was a long pause. When Lainey spoke again, her voice was cool and level. "If you don't agree to see me, I'll keep calling until India answers."

As if summoned by name, India opened the door to the living room.

"What are you doing?" she asked. "Who are you talking to?"

I cupped my hand over the phone. "No one. It's, um—" I looked around wildly for inspiration and then spied the dusty air vent. "—the company who services our air conditioner. They're offering a special on vent cleaning."

"Oh." India shrugged. "Sign us up, I guess. Anyway, lunch is ready. Come and get it."

"Okay," I said. Crap. Now I'd have to somehow remember to actually schedule a vent cleaning. But the ruse worked; India re- treated back to the kitchen.

"Are you still there?" I said into the phone.

"Yes," Lainey said. "Will you meet me?"

"Fine," I said, defeated. "Where?"

We arranged to meet at a Starbucks. I arrived early, eager to get it over with. I had no idea what Lainey wanted, but I was deter- mined to keep her away from India.

I ordered an espresso and sat down at one of the small round tables with a chessboard imprinted on it. I wished I'd brought a newspaper, and began to eye one that the woman at the next table seemed to have discarded—was it rude to ask if I could read it?— when a flurry of activity at the door caught my attention. It was Lainey, pushing a stroller in, while a wizened old man made a production of holding the door open for her. She pushed her sunglasses up on her head and looked around. I held up a hand to get her attention. Lainey hesitated for a beat and then, as if summoning her will, headed my way.

"Hi," Lainey said when she reached me.

"Hi," I said.

I wanted very much not to look at the baby, but found it impossible to resist. He was sleeping in one of those car seat carriers, now resting on top of the stroller. It had been two months since I'd last seen him. His cheeks were now rounder, his arms fatter. When he'd been born, he didn't have eyebrows. But they were there now, or at least the beginnings of eyebrows. I had to resist the urge to smooth my finger over them.

I had expected Lainey to bring him. I had not known how painful seeing him would be.

"He's gotten big, hasn't he?" Lainey said, echoing my thoughts. She sat down across from me.

"Yes," I said. I cleared my throat and forced myself to look away from this baby who would have been my son. She was looking at the baby, too, with an odd, almost hungry expression on her face. "What is this about, Lainey?"

"How is India?"

"She's fine," I said. "Or, she will be. Eventually."

"I thought she'd hate me. Then I got that baby album and camera. . . ." Lainey stopped and swallowed.

I knew about the album, of course, but I hadn't known India had also sent Lainey a camera. I wasn't surprised. It was just the sort of thing India would do. She'd have wanted to make sure that Lainey had the ability to record every precious moment of this boy's life, even if that meant being the one to supply the camera to make it happen. I braved one more glance at the baby, then had to look away almost immediately.

"It was such an amazing gift," Lainey finished.

"India's an amazing person," I said.

"I know," Lainey said softly. "I'll never be able to repay her for what she's done for me."

This unexpected admission had the effect of softening my anger. I looked down at my cardboard cup of coffee. "Can I ask you a question?"

"Sure."

I looked back up at her. "Were you planning on keeping him all along?"

Lainey sighed and rolled her shoulders back. "No. I really wasn't. But when I saw him I just . . . fell in love."

I nodded. "Us too," I said softly.

Neither of us spoke for a few minutes. Finally, Lainey said, "Do you remember that reality show I tried out for? Down in Miami? India drove me to the audition."

"Something to do with looking for love, right?"

Lainey nodded. "They called and offered me a place on the show."

"Really? Wow. Are you going to do it?"

"No. I told them I couldn't," Lainey said, looking at the baby again with the same focused intensity.

"Right," I said, understanding. She couldn't bring the baby with her. "Tough break."

"It's probably for the best." Lainey shrugged. "Anyway." She reached into her bag, pulled out some papers, and slid them across the table to me. "These are for you."

I glanced at the papers. They looked vaguely legal to me. "You're not suing me, are you?"

Lainey laughed softly. "Of course not."

I took a closer look at the papers and then, startled, leaned even closer. They were adoption papers. The papers Mike Jankowski had drawn up all those months ago, the ones that we'd approved. I paged through them to the last page . . . where Lainey had scrawled her signature, affirmed by a notary. I looked up at her. "What is this?"

"Adoption papers. I signed them at Mike Jankowski's office this morning. Mike contacted Trav—my ex-boyfriend—and he signed off his parental rights, too. The only thing left to do is for you and India to go in and sign the papers. And then, from what Mike said, in a few months a judge will finalize the adoption. I won't have to be there in court, though. My part is finished."

For the first time, I noticed how pale Lainey was—her skin was paper white and there were dark crescents under each eye. She kept blinking, as though holding back tears that might erupt at any minute.

"Wait. You're giving him *back* to us?" I asked slowly. I was vaguely aware that my hands were shaking.

Lainey nodded. "You still want him, right?"

"I don't understand."

Lainey stared at the sleeping baby, and the look of intense longing returned to her face. "Because I can't do this. Not on my own, and maybe not even if I had help. I can't give him the life he deserves to have. And you can. So I'm giving him back to you."

"Are you sure about this?" I asked.

She nodded once, and tucked her hair behind her ears. "I'm sure." She tilted her head toward the door. "And you don't have to worry about me hanging around and getting in the way. I'm leaving town."

"So you can be on that reality show?"

"No. I turned that down. India was right. That's not what I should be doing with my life."

"So what will you do? Where are you going to go?" I couldn't seem to stop asking her questions. I was still having a hard time believing that this was really happening.

"I'm not sure. I think I'm going to drive north. See how far I get." She smiled. "Maybe New York City. I've always wanted to go there."

"Do you have enough money?" I asked. I reached for my wallet, ready to empty it into her hands, but Lainey shook her head.

"No, I'm fine. Really." She looked at the baby again and then looked away quickly. "I should go."

"Wait," I said. "You're giving him to me *now*? Right here?"

"Mike wanted us to do this in his office, but, well..." Lainey shrugged. "I thought this way was better. You do still want him, right?"

"Yes," I said. "We still want him."

"Then call Mike. He'll deal with the paperwork." Lainey reached out, resting a hand on the baby's leg. Then, just as quickly, she withdrew it, her hand curling into a fist. She stood. "Take care of him."

"We will," I said. I was surprised to find that my throat had gone dry. I stared at the baby, who was still sleeping, completely unaware that his life had just undergone a dramatic, seismic change. He breathed heavily through parted lips, and his eyelashes fluttered against rose-pink skin. "I don't know how to—"

But before I could finish, before I could thank her, I looked up and saw that Lainey was already walking away. Her stride was long, determined, and she didn't look back at us, not even when she passed through the door and out of our sight.

I looked back at the baby—*my* baby, I realized, my *son*—and my heart started to pound, blood rushing to my head. Just then, he opened his eyes, yawned, and blinked at me. *Does he remember me from that first day?* I wondered. *Is that even possible?*

The baby shifted in his seat, his hands opening and closing, his feet flexing, his eyes darting around.

"Hi," I said, reaching out, holding a finger for him to grab onto. His grip was surprisingly strong. His blue-gray eyes met mine, and we stared at each other for a long moment, until I felt something deep within me break. Tears suddenly filled my eyes.

"Do you remember me, sweetheart?" I asked, my voice a croak. "I'm your daddy."

Lainey had left the base of the car seat leaning against the carriage, along with a bag she'd packed with diapers, bottles, formula, and baby clothes. My first job as a father was to figure out how to get the base secured in the back seat of my car, and then lower the baby in his carrier onto it. Lainey had unfortunately not left directions on how to do this.

I rested the baby in his carrier on the ground next to the car, but didn't like how vulnerable he seemed there. I'd placed him between two parked cars, but my thoughts jumped to all of the awful, grisly possibilities. What if someone driving through the parking lot suddenly lost control of his car, or his brakes went out, and he hit one of the parked cars, ramming it into the baby carrier? I shivered with horror and quickly moved him up onto the sidewalk. But then I realized I couldn't keep an eye on him and install the car seat base at the same time. Finally, I gave up. I put the car seat back onto the carriage—this snapped with a satisfactory click—and turned toward home. It was less than a mile walk, and there were sidewalks the entire way. Once I got him safely home, I'd find someone more competent—like a police officer or India—to get the car seat set up.

India. At the thought of her, I stopped suddenly—the baby looked up quizzically at me and then his brow darkened. Walking he seemed to like. Stopping, not so much. He opened his mouth, but before he could give voice to his disapproval, I quickly started moving again.

I knew my wife better than I knew anyone else in the world. But I had no idea what she would say, how she would react, when we arrived. She had been firm that she wasn't ready to start thinking about another adoption yet. But that was because she had already given away her heart to this baby boy, the one who was now looking up at the soft blue sky and blowing bubbles through rosebud lips. His gaze shifted to me, and he smiled suddenly—a wide gummy grin that was so charming I could actually feel my heart growing.

"Your mama is going to be so happy to see you," I told him. "Just you wait and see."

Thirty minutes later, I wheeled the carriage up the driveway and across our flagstone front walk. The front steps took a bit of negotiating—I didn't want to jar the baby by bumping him up them, so I opted to lift the carriage instead—and then it was another awkward moment fitting through the front door.

"India?" I called out.

"Jeremy? I didn't hear you pull in." India's voice floated back from the kitchen, along with the yeasty warm smell of freshly baked bread. She'd been baking a lot lately, working out her frustration by punching at mounds of dough.

"I walked home," I said.

"Why? Did your car break down? You should have called, I would have picked you up."

India appeared, walking out from the kitchen into the hallway. She had a dusting of flour across her shirt and on the tip of her nose. She froze when she saw me standing there. I'd unbuckled the baby from his car seat carrier, and lifted him gingerly up into my arms, careful to support his neck.

Ripples of emotion crossed India's face. Shock. Hope. Happiness. Longing. Joy.

And, finally, love.

I smiled at her. "Surprise," I said.

Epilogue
FIVE YEARS LATER

The white Ford rental slowed and pulled over to the side of the road. The sun was just starting to sink in a hazy sky dotted with a lazy swirl of clouds.

"Are you going to tell me what we're doing here?" the man asked, looking over at his companion. He was in his late twenties, with a lean build and a liberal amount of curly dark hair that sprang from his head in unruly abandon.

"I just need to see something," she said, unrolling the windows. She was also thin, with an angular face and ink dark eyes. A single pearl on a chain hung at her clavicle. Her gaze was trained on a pink cottage across the street.

"Let me guess: You've been lying to me for the past five months. You're not really a photographer, and we didn't really fly down here for a photo shoot. Instead, you're an assassin and you go around wearing a gun in an ankle holster." He grinned at her, his teeth white against newly tanned skin. His eyes, which were the color of whiskey and streaked with gold, were kind.

"That's right," she said, without taking her eyes off the house. "And my hands are deadly weapons."

"And you lured me down here with the promise of a beach vacation—"

"A working beach vacation," she amended.

"A working beach vacation," he agreed. "Where you'd spend all of your nonworking time in a bikini. When in reality, you're about to turn me into your accomplice." He reached over and rubbed the back of her neck. "Is that how it works?"

"You know me so well," she said, flashing him a smile. "Anyway, we've got some time. We're not meeting Flaca and Luis until seven."

"This is kind of a cool neighborhood," he said, looking around. "Very picturesque. Are you scouting it for a shoot or something?"

"No. I used to know someone who lived here."

"Who? An old friend from when you lived here?"

"Sort of. Not a friend, exactly. More like distant relatives," she said carefully. "I don't even know if they still live here."

"Why don't we go knock on the door and ask?"

"No," she said, shaking her head. "I don't want to drop in on them without warning."

"Okay. But if you don't want to talk to them, what are we doing here?" he asked.

She didn't respond. Instead, she watched as a car pulled in to the driveway of the pink cottage. The man who climbed out was tall, with a shock of russet hair. He opened the trunk and pulled out an overnight bag. The front door of the house suddenly opened, and a boy ran out. He was thin with long coltish legs and shiny dark hair. A yellow Lab—an older puppy, with a thick coat and a lolling pink tongue—bounded after the boy across the emerald lawn, a yellow tennis ball clenched in its mouth.

In the car, the woman drew in her breath.

"Dad!" the boy yelled, and hurtled toward the man, who quickly dropped the bag and intercepted the child before he was knocked off his feet. "Mom! Dad's home!"

The front door swung open again, and this time a woman with long, curly blonde hair came out. There was a small Asian girl curled in her arms. The little girl was wearing a floral dress and clutching a stuffed bear to her chest. When she saw the man, she smiled and wriggled to get down.

"Daddy!" she called out.

The woman put her down, and the little girl set off determinedly past a row of hibiscus trees in bloom with extravagant cherry pink flowers to where the man and the boy were. The woman, following behind, smiled warmly at the man above the heads of their children. "Hey, you. How was SciCon?"

"Actually, not so bad. My table was next to the Klingon tent, so I got some overflow traffic from them," he replied.

Inside the car, the woman leaned forward, her body tense as she strained to hear every word.

"Lainey, is everything okay?" her companion asked.

She didn't answer. He lay the flat of his hand on her lower back, then slid it up between her shoulder blades like an arched brace.

The little boy ran down to the end of the driveway, chasing after the tennis ball the dog had dropped. Lainey's hand reached for her camera, which was sitting between the two front seats. She lifted it and snapped a single photo, just as the little boy looked up in the direction of the car and, for the briefest moment, stood perfectly still.

The boy grabbed the ball, pivoted around, and ran back up the drive. The family turned to head inside now, their progress slowed when the Lab careened into the little girl, who fell down in a flood of tears. Her mother and father soothed her, while her brother bounced the tennis ball on the walkway, rolled his eyes, and said, "Honestly, it's not like Elvis meant to do it. It's not his fault Nattie falls over so easily."

"Come on, dinner's almost ready," the woman said.

"What are we having?" her husband asked.

"Chicken tacos," she said. "Griff's favorite."

"You aren't going to try and hide vegetables in my tacos again, are you?" the boy asked suspiciously.

"I would never do that," the woman said solemnly.

"Come on, Elvis," the boy said, and he ran inside the house, the dog barking at his heels.

The father shifted the little girl, still a bit weepy, on one hip and lifted his overnight bag to his other shoulder. She nestled against him, rubbing her cheek on his sleeve.

"Do you want me to take your bag?" the blonde woman asked, turning to look back at him, just before she disappeared inside.

"No, I've got it," he said, following her in. "This way I'm balanced. Take one of them away and I might tip over."

"Noooo, Daddy, no!" the little girl wailed dramatically. "No tipping!"

He laughed and followed his wife inside. The door slammed shut behind them, and the street was quiet and still, save for the distant roar of a lawn mower.

The woman in the car exhaled a long breath and then turned to the man sitting beside her.

"Yes," she said, and when she smiled, the angles of her face softened. "Everything's fine."

"You sure?" He cupped a hand against her cheek, and she leaned against it for a moment.

She nodded. "I'm sure. Are you hungry? Because I'm starving."

"Sure thing. Let's get going." He slung one arm across the back of the seat, the tips of his fingers grazing against her shoulder.

Lainey touched his hand briefly and then turned the key in the ignition. She reversed the car around in a neat three-point turn, and slowly headed back down the street.

About the Author

Whitney Gaskell lives in Stuart, Florida, with her husband and son. *When You Least Expect It* is her seventh novel, all published by Bantam. You can visit Whitney's website and read her blog at www.whitneygaskell.com.